THE CHILDREN OF DANU

THE INNISFAIL CYCLE:
BOOK THREE

The Children of Danu is a work of fiction. Names, places, and incidents in this book are either the product of the author's imagination or are used fictitiously. Any resemblance to actual persons, living or dead, events or locales is entirely coincidental.

Copyright @ 2022 L.M. Riviere
Map Copyright @ L.M. Riviere

All rights reserved.

No part of this book may be reproduced or used in any manner without written permission of the copyright owner except for the use of quotations in a book review.

First Print Edition 2022
Published in the United States by Lights Out Ink, LLC.

ISBN: 978-1-914152-17-7
eBook ISBN: 978-1-914152-18-4

www.lmriviere.com

Cover design by L.M. Riviere

Lights Out Ink is an independent publisher of serialized, digital, and printed fiction. Visit **www.lightsoutink.com** to discover our full library of content and read episodes online.

Chapters

1 - the night path...1
2 - dark horse..15
3 - blood ties..31
4 - tech duinn...45
5 - avowed...63
6 - interlude..75
7 - small mercies...89
8 - the white queen...103
9 - duchfitzdonahugh...115
10 - a king of eire..123
11 - allegiances...139
12 - declaration...153
13 - whence comes the knife..165
14 - in love or vanity...177
15 - surrogates...193
16 - under the white flag..203
17 - scorched earth..215
18 - the skysinger...231
19 - nowhere to run..247
20 - the better man..263
21 - siora's chosen..279
22 - unbearable...93
23 - belladonna...305
24 - the tenth law...323

25 - sacrifice	339
26 - crown of ashes	357
27 - the dawn tide	365
28 - the waning moon	375
29 - bonds	377
30 - a light in the dark	383
glossary	389
dramatis personae	401
author's note	407
about the text	409

Part One

Shadows

PART ONE

WINTER

The Night Path

n.e. 508
dor cromna
oiche ar fad

The light was the worst of it. A hazy sun spun aimlessly through a rose and violet sky, incandescent as backlit crystal and maddening in its course. Its warmth felt surreal as its path, at once warm and chill, neither waxing nor waning. As they walked, Una couldn't decide if she were over or underdressed. The cold sweat dappling the back of her neck made her shiver in the half-summer breeze. For that was the root of the Oiche Ar Fad, no? The contradiction. They strolled through late spring into early summer, billeted by winds, scents, and smells from the opposite horizon. She turned her head rather than stare into that dizzying kaleidoscope in the distance. Brilliant white stars swirled through a sliver of infinite dark as if the nighttime sky shied from the weak sunlight but inched forward anyway: a cold, persistent menace. The barest hint of a full moon crested a nearby hilltop, waiting its turn. In this Otherworld, dawn climbed the sky in the north before it crept south, while twilight traced east-west in equal measure. Thus, it was never whole light nor full dark but a commingling of the two, treading the border between misty morning and evening's chill. Una watched the moon's glacial progress with a wary eye.

She suspected it followed them with interest.

Kaer Yin smirked at her wariness. "Think it can see you?"

She said nothing.

She knew it did.... and that was not all.

The air held alluring scents she could no more classify than the frightening array of colors that assaulted her eyes. Everywhere she looked were greens so lush and multifaceted, the leaves gleamed as emeralds, grasses in violent shades of red-gold, deepest midnight, and dewy sapphires that glowed at the barest touch of moonlight. Merely blinking could alter their façade forever. Each palette seemed to rearrange itself with every gust of wind or shift beneath the queer prismatic light of both celestial bodies.

When the sky couldn't choose between night and day, why should her senses decide upon one or the other?

With each step, her mind feasted upon these strange inconsistencies with wonder and dread. A tinge of honeysuckle and deep loam wafted to her, sunbaked lavender and frost— then the crisp scent of snow-damp pine, night-blooming jasmine... and death. Indeed, amidst so much staggering, confusing beauty lay the omnipresent sense of rot and decay. But there was also life. The fauna she glimpsed through the trees or saw leaping through glimmering meadows as they passed were perhaps even more startlingly lovely than their environs. Great white and gold deer flitted here and there, intransient as wisps of cloud. Slinking cats with haunting yellow eyes hissed from their tree boughs. All manner of birds soared overhead, flashing plumage brighter than any jewel. Sometimes she was so awed by these gorgeous beasts that she forgot that other, less benign things were watching them too. From the shadows of the moon's domain, there were also eyes filled with hunger and very little fear. The allure of sweet mortal flesh was an unspoken reality. She knew if any wandered into that nighttime world alone, they wouldn't return.

Again, she shivered in the almost heat of their morning world.

Kaer Yin's hand found the small of her back. "What is it, *mo grá?*"

She pinched the bridge of her nose. "I feel... things I can't explain."

"What do you mean?" His breath dusted her ear.

She stared into the night with a clenched jaw. A thing she thought she recognized stared back. "Familiar." In that deep dark, she could almost hear the shuffling of many feet. Human feet. "We aren't alone."

His fingers caught hers. "Are you afraid?" She tore her gaze away to find him smiling down at her, a teasing tilt to his brow.

She pursed her lips. "Not at all. I told you, I can't explain it."

He gave her an odd look but didn't reply. Instead, he squeezed her hand and led on, holding his harness with his free hand. Una walked beside him, still fascinated with the creatures winding through the dark on her right. She *should* have been afraid. Rian certainly seemed to be. If Robin felt the same, he didn't show it, nor did any other Greenmaker in their company. She imagined their reticence had more to do with bluster in the face of so many Sidhe warriors rather than any actual emotion. She wished she could mask her expressions so easily. No... she wasn't afraid. She felt something far more concerning, a tremor of elation.

A thrill she couldn't describe tapped its claws lightly up her spine.

They are there, she thought. *They see me too.*

Without meaning to, she shot Rian a glance over her shoulder. Her attention was fixed in the same direction. *Does she feel them, too, maybe?* But she wouldn't ask. Not here. How could she tell anyone that of all the wondrous, terrifying things to see in this place, the dead enthralled her most? The Sluagh were out there, waiting to greet her. This knowledge burrowed deep in her gut, raising goosebumps over her arms. Though, this feeling was not all. Her Spark flared within her blood and had yet to fall silent. Giddy with surgent power, she pressed her free hand to her mouth to halt any uncontrollable laughter.

What was *wrong* with her?

I have sssuch delightsss to ssshow you...

She jumped for the memory.

Kaer Yin stopped, tugging her chin up with his thumb. "Are you all right?"

"Yes," she lied.

He didn't believe her. She could tell. "Shar, why don't we take a break?"

Tam Lin's lieutenant squinted at the sky. "I don't know, *Mo Flaith*. The dawn won't hold for long."

"How long afore we reach yer uncle's digs," asked Robin, pretending he wasn't alarmed by those whispering leaves Una couldn't stop staring at. To his credit, he was a much better actor than she. "Seems we've been on the road a while, and the girls need a rest."

A snort from behind said Tam Lin O'Ruaidh knew better. "If that's fatigue on Lady Donahugh's face, I'll be buggered. She looks a tad inebriated, you ask me."

"No one did," remarked Rian sidelong. She moved forward to press her chin into Una's shoulder. "You don't have to tell me."

Una let out a long breath.

Kaer Yin backed off. "What do you know?" he asked Rian.

"We're close to Tech Duinn now, aren't we?"

He, too, glanced at the sky, concerned. "Yes. Why?"

"He did something to her that night."

Una turned, flushing. "Rian, please. I'm fine."

"What did he do?" His brow darkened.

Rian smoothed a lock of hair from Una's damp cheek. "I don't know, but whatever it was left a mark. Una, let's sit awhile. You should eat something."

Una shook herself, once more tearing her attention back to the road. She gave a sheepish smile. "That's probably a good idea."

"What do you see out there?" Kaer Yin asked.

"Nothing. Everything, maybe. I don't know." She let Rian lead her to her mare, rubbing her eyes. "Robin?"

"Milady?"

"You've any uishge left in that flask?"

Rather than answer, he proffered the vessel with mock fanfare. She took it without further comment.

Tam Lin edged close. "You and Diarmid have met, I take it?"

"For a moment."

His violet eyes cut suspiciously. "And...?"

She refused to look at Kaer Yin, who'd been asking this for quite a while. She took a sip of Robin's uishge and made a face. "He tried to take me... here, I presume. I think he thought he could absorb my erm, gift."

"Is that all?" Tam Lin's brows raised.

"You took his power, instead?" Kaer Yin answered for her, crossing his arms. "That's how you did it? The Sluagh?"

Without seeing her reflection, she knew the shock of white at her temple stood out like a blood-red hand. "I didn't know until it was too late."

"Are you implying she took his power?" Tam Lin prodded, disbelief evident in his expression. "A *Milesian* girl?"

"I'm marching you back in there, thoughtlessly too." Ignoring Tam Lin, Kaer Yin cursed under his breath. "Why didn't you tell me?"

She avoided the tender regret on his face. "I'll be all right."

Tam Lin made a rude sound. "You mean to tell me we're headed to Tir Falias with a woman who stole our uncle's powers, and you are just telling us now? He's going to keep her, surely you realize?"

"Would you *shut* your bloody mouth?" Rian nearly shrieked.

He threw up his hands in response. "What? Do you want me to lie to you?" He pointed at Una. "If she's been marked by *Fiachra Dubh*, she'll never see the mortal world again. You'll have to trade for her, Yin. No bones about it. Whatever he asks for will be dear, indeed."

"I know," Kaer Yin hissed. "That's twice I owe him. Thank you for the reminder."

Una swallowed hard. "I'm sorry. I didn't know how to tell you."

There was foreboding in his expression. "You should have."

He turned and strode into the trees.

She knew better than to follow.

Hours, or perhaps days later— who could tell? — they came to a fork in the leaf-strewn road. The nighttime hemisphere seemed closer than usual, though distant enough that her skin didn't prickle every time the wind blew. Kaer Yin wasn't speaking to her much, which pained her almost as severely as the look in his cousin's eye every time he glanced her way. *Monster*, she read there and wanted to weep. Rian kept close to her side, her presence the only reassurance Una had left. Despite this, she refused to be cowed by an element outside her control. She'd never asked Diarmid Adair to attempt to spirit her and Rian into the Otherworld, had she?

If her Spark hadn't interceded when it did, they might both be dead... or worse. What right did anyone have to judge her? She'd make the same choice again if she must. So, why did she feel so guilty?

Kaer Yin took a turn around the fork, scratching his chin at the various paths. Each trailed beneath grand stone arches etched with Ealig words she couldn't read. In the center of this convergence bubbled a large granite fountain full of sweet water, rimmed by stone maidens bearing deep pots bursting with mature fruit trees. This was a Waycross. Una instinctually understood its importance for the Sidhe magic radiating from its center. Nothing from that ravenous realm on their right could stand within this circle for long. She relaxed a bit in the shadow of the southernmost arch. Her Spark dwindled to a whisper.

Kaer Yin watched her from the opposite side.

"We'll camp here for the night."

"Bad idea. We should keep the night at our backs, Yin," argued Tam Lin, with a firm shake of his head. "Press on."

"We won't outpace the shadows. I'd rather we face them within this circle than out there in the wild."

Tam Lin quirked his mouth to say more but cursed at the sky instead. "You're right."

"What's that mean then?" Robin fidgeted, scowling around.

"Night descends," Shar answered, unloading his pack at the fountain's rim. "We must be ready."

"Ready for what?"

Shar shared a look with his lord. "For what comes after."

"My men, if it pleases the Gods," sighed Tam Lin, hopefully.

"They'll find us," said Kaer Yin. "I pray from the right side."

"What d'ye mean?" Robin heard something in the woods and stepped back into the light. "*Siora*, but I don't like this place, none at all."

"Gerrod and the Tairnganese are with them, so now would not be a grand time to arrive in our midst," replied Kaer Yin. Una looked away when he glanced over. She didn't miss his frown. "Mortal flesh is a powerful lure, Robin. Even our presence can't deter every evil lurking in the nightscape."

"Bloody wonderful."

"Why don't we just leave?" Rian interjected. "They can't hunt what isn't here."

"Not that simple," said Kaer Yin. "I wish it was."

"How so?"

Kaer Yin threw his hands wide to indicate the fountain and arches. "South to Bri Leith—the seat of the High King, then Tir Tairngare— Midhir's gift to your people." He pointed. "East to Croghan and the mountains of the West— to Tir Na Nog. North, to the harbor of Tir Gorias and West, to the halls of Manannan Mac Lir."

"So?"

He exhaled through his nose. "It doesn't matter what the signs read. From any direction, these roads lead only one place."

"Tech Duinn," whispered Una, disheartened.

"Yes," his answer was gentler than before. "We must pay homage to *Fiachra Dubh* for safe passage."

"Mortals must, anyway," said Tam Lin. "If we attempt to steal his due, our uncle will seek vengeance. Family or no, he is lord and master here, not we."

A slight wrinkle etched between Rian's brows. "Wait. This is a puzzle. West is east; North is south, and so on. We can figure that out."

Kaer Yin rubbed his chin. "The Oiche Ar Fad mirrors your world, but that is not all. The only way out is *through*. One must pay homage to the Raven King for that gift or wander here forever."

"Well," laughed Tam Lin. "Until something eats you."

As if the Prince of Connaught bore the burden of prophecy, they swiftly learned the truth of his jest. Una and Rian had scarcely laid down on their shared bedroll by the fire when Una felt that prickling along her skin once more. Her head swiveled round to face the dark. Long shapes slithered out of the trees from the night side, nearly upon them. The drunken, half-risen sun spun away toward the eastern horizon, and the patient moon turned into the center. Only traces of rose gold sky shone overhead.

Twilight loomed.

Kaer Yin wasn't far. He hadn't been since her father had died in Bethany. If possible, she might have loved him the more for the quiet subtlety of his support. That he was still unhappy with her was also readily apparent on his face. All the same, there he was. Kneeling to whisper at her nape, his fingertips brushed hers. "What's wrong?"

She turned back to the woods. "There's something out there."

"There will be until we quit this place for good. Dor Sidhe love mortals, remember? Lu Sidhe too. I expect we'll be stalked the whole way."

She couldn't stave a smile. "And Ban Sidhe?"

He made a face. "Gods, not at all. You'd start talking and ruin our appetite."

"Never heard that fable before."

"Wouldn't want you to guess our weaknesses."

She rolled her eyes. "Oh, that's easy enough."

"That so?"

"*Uishge.*"

Across the fire, Robin burst out laughing.

Exhaling through his nose, he threaded his fingers through hers again. "I was going to say something *far* more romantic, but we've an irritating audience, I'm afraid."

"No need to woo what you've already won, *Ard Tiarne*," she said under her breath, and his pupils dilated. Cheeks filling with blood, she looked away. Rian groaned and pulled her blankets over her head. Embarrassed, Una bit her lip. They'd been here before, hadn't they? "Anyway, I'll stay up for a while. Help keep watch."

"Niall and Bearn have that honor. Sleep, Una. You need it."

The trees ahead shivered in the breeze, and she knew she wouldn't sleep, no matter what she promised. "I'll try." At least it wasn't a lie.

He set two fingers against his heart, then pressed them lightly against her temple. She gathered that he had more to say, but they *did* have an audience. It would have to wait. He stood as she lay down, dragging her blanket with her. "Sleep, *mo grá*. I'll wake you in a few hours."

"What does that mean?"

He tossed her a smirk and strode off without an answer.

She leaned over. "Rian, was that an insult?"

"No," she laughed for a long time.

Una snuggled into her blanket, cursing.

She'd learn the bloody language soon or die trying.

Despite her own opinion, Una did fall asleep after a while. She only knew because she was startled awake soon after. Her eyes snapped open. The disheveled moon hung directly overhead, leering at her like a mad beggar awaiting coin. Then, she heard it. The softest of sighs on her left. Almost afraid to see, she turned her head.

A pair of gleaming opalescent eyes flashed at her from the treeline. No, not one pair... *dozens*. A black shape carefully dragged something heavy toward the forest so as not to alert the Ban Sidhe in her midst. Una drew in a sharp breath. A bevy of eerie, milky orbs flashed her way. They'd heard her. So had Niall. "*Dúisigh*! Dor Sidhe!"

Una scrabbled to her feet, shaking Rian's shoulder on her way up. The other girl had barely blinked when Una's arm was seized from the other side.

"Una!" Rian cried.

All nine hells broke loose at once.

KÆR YIN WAS ON HIS feet with Nemain before Niall finished calling his warning. He had a feeling they'd be attacked tonight. Some Dor Sidhe were bold enough to brave the Ban Sidhe's wrath for such an irresistible feast. As he'd told Una, mortal flesh was a reckless temptation. The first goblin struck him from the front, snapping at his eyes with razor-sharp teeth. Gripping the misshapen little beast by the throat with one hand, he sent Nemain across its middle with the other. Oozing, oily blood scattered over his boots as he flung the creature's hindquarters into the next incoming wraith. He backpedaled as a half-dozen of the snapping; snarling beasts clambered atop him in their attempt to stay his sword arm. This was undoubtedly their plan. While they were no match for Ban Sidhe at the Waycross, the goblins could delay them long enough to spirit their actual targets away. Upon this thought, Rian's shriek tore the clearing in half. "Una!" she screeched. Her screams amplified while Kaer Yin struggled to remain upright.

One of the little bastards took a bite out of his left thumb while he spun about to regain footing. With a roar, he whirled Nemain in a vicious semicircle— hacking many of the Dor Sidhe pests in half at once. Enraged, he stole a glance at the bedroll beside the fire. Una and Rian were surrounded. One goblin had Una by the arm. "Una!"

"Ben!" Rian howled, swinging her little dagger every which way.

"Siora, damn it!" Robin was in similar straits. "A little help, here."

Shar was the first to bound in the right direction. Swords were all but useless in a swarm. He went for his bow. Once the arrows started flying, the Dor Sidhe snarled a retreat. That didn't mean they weren't taking their prey with them. Kaer Yin ran toward the forest, leaping goblins and Sidhe on the way. Una crouched by herself in a sea of hissing goblins, inflicting grievous wounds upon any who dared touch her. In the process, she clung to Rian's hand while slashing wildly with her dagger. They both bled profusely, drawing more and more ravenous assailants every moment. Una lost her footing. She was towed into Rian with a furious cry, who struggled to keep her friend from being pulled into the woods as several Greenmakers had already been.

Horrible sounds rent the air.

Kaer Yin cut deep rivulets in the earth in his haste to dislodge so many grasping claws; Shar and Niall's arrows did the rest. Recovering from the surprise of the assault with their typical, inhuman speed, the Sidhe gathered and fired indiscriminately into any writhing shape. As swiftly as they'd invaded, the goblins departed in a roiling mass. Though a few of their number had perished in the attempt, most of the Greenmakers were alive, if missing hunks of flesh. Una and Rian clung to each other against the fountain rim. The water had gone a pale red. Without thinking, Kaer Yin threw his arms around both. "Are you two all right?"

Una bled from bites on her neck, hands, and fingers. Nothing serious, however. She nodded. Rian was the worse for wear, not having Una's ability to self-heal. She had so many wounds; he couldn't count them all. Her face, arms, and chest bore much of the damage. She, too, would live, as the cuts were shallow and haphazard. She sagged a bit in Una's arms. "I'm all right," she declared, though it sounded more like a question. "Will they come back?"

He swallowed. "Your blood is on the wind."

Rian sobbed. Kaer Yin couldn't blame her.

"We must wash your wounds as best we can and keep moving. Our swords and arrows will deter most."

Una rested her chin over Rian's trembling temple. Her eyes closed. "How long to Tir Falias?"

"Hours if we ride hard."

"Then, what in the hells are we waiting for?"

Not even their burning torches, galloping haste, or steadfast determination to arrive safely in Tir Falias could prevent the next attack, the third, or the fourth. They'd quit the Waycross mere minutes after the horde had struck them at camp, riding at full gallop through the Western Arch. Rian was given to ride with Shar and Una with Kaer Yin, hoping that the Ban Sidhe would mask their scent. Tam Lin's Blood Eagles surrounded Robin and his Greenmakers, bows strung while they scanned the forest on either side. Una could not tell how long they'd been on the road before a giant beast came crashing out of the foliage ahead. Kaer Yin wheeled to a halt just as one of its massive forepaws slammed into the cobbles on their right. Una's heart caught in her throat. A thing like the ghast Kaer Yin had killed in Rian's yard those months before— yet not. This was a bear; if her eyes didn't deceive her… huge and pitch-black, its eyes glowing an unnatural red. She'd never seen a bear in Innisfail but had been told they roamed the wilds of Aes Sidhe by night.

However, she highly doubted *this* particular bear had a thing to do with the world she came from. Its bloodcurdling roar danced along the strands of her nerves, promising glorious pain, snapping bones and muscle hewn from the flesh.

Teeth like long knives, it charged.

Sssuch delightsss to sshow you... Her memory taunted.

Kaer Yin wasted no time. Trusting her to hang on, he kicked his destrier into a canter, pulling Nemain in one hand and a lark in the other. The bear was twice as large as their mount, its vast maw wide and waiting. Kaer Yin slashed as the bear swiped at him from the left, guiding the horse with his knees. Then, he turned his mount to do the same to its other side. A furious, erratic snarl escaped the creature's mouth as it rolled head over hindquarters into an ungainly sprawl. Kaer Yin didn't stop or pause to complete the deed. Instead, Tam Lin severed the bear's head in a single slash while his horse leaped its falling bulk. Like a stone dividing a river's rush, the Sidhe sped past its corpse, sheathing their weapons to gain more speed.

Una buried her face in Kaer Yin's spine, squeezing her eyes shut. She knew the Oiche Ar Fad was a terrible place, but never in her imagination could she fathom the depths of its bloodlust. Every breath, every step a mortal took in this realm— spelled doom. In fables, when men and women were spirited away by the Sidhe, likely none lived happily ever after in the Land of the Undying. They died screaming as soon as the moon's pale light kissed the sky. She shivered to think of it. Still, just beneath the thrum of her pulse, she felt her Spark beat a steady tattoo.

Not you, it seemed to say. *You are no feast.*

Hours later, perhaps, as the light shifted in the west and the nighttime world slunk into the east, they came to a lovely stone bridge. A stream trickled below, cascading down a rocky outcrop bedecked with hawthorn and sweet-smelling berries. Kaer Yin raised a hand to halt their party. While close, it was not yet dawn. He glanced at Tam Lin beside him. "The horses need water. There won't be another source for miles."

Tam Lin looked around, mouth tight. "Swiftly, I think. We shouldn't linger."

"Agreed." Kaer Yin pulled Una down with him. "The water is clear and clean, but don't go near any pools. All right?"

She nodded, feeling Rian limp to her side. Robin's rudimentary bandaging did little to conceal the damage. "I think we'll wait right here, thank you."

"I'll stay with them," Tam Lin assured him, gesturing for Kaer Yin to go on. "Refill my skin with theirs, won't you?"

Kaer Yin caught his skin while juggling the others, mirroring Una's wary expression. "We do this fast. Keep your sword ready, Lin."

Tam Lin saluted as his cousin strode off toward the river, pulling their nervous mounts along by the reins. Robin paused to pat Rian on the head on his way past. Una took a deep breath, watching the foliage glisten in the moonlight. "Don't worry, *ceann beag*. I will look after you." Tam Lin took off his cloak and draped it over Rian's shaking frame. She didn't protest, for once. "*Fiachra Dubh* will heal you both."

Una said, "Before or after he kills me?"

"He won't," he laughed. The sound was dry. "But he will keep you if he can."

"What does that mean?"

He blew air over his lower lip, eyes watchful, hand on his pommel—in case anything thought to spring at them from the leaves. "My uncle is as opportunistic as he is wise. Bit of a cunt, too, you ask me. That you *can* take anything from him means he can't afford to let you go. Not without a price, anyway."

She heard Kaer Yin barking orders down by the river's edge. The sound gave her equal parts comfort and fear. "I won't let him sacrifice anything for me. You have my word."

Tam Lin regarded her in silence for a long while. "If you keep that vow, you and I will square, My Lady."

"I swear it."

His stare turned cold. "We'll see."

A voice peeled from the riverbank in shock and sudden terror. Robin's, if she weren't mistaken. Muttering an oath, Tam Lin drew them both close, sword up. "Yin?" he called. When there was no answer save shouts and the occasional scream, he tilted his head at Shar. "Go." Shar drew his larks and bounded down the bank. The following sounds were unearthly shrieks and the ring of drawn steel. Tam Lin edged near the bridge, keeping the girls at his back, and pressed into the granite wall. A white shape emerged from the far bank, thin and supple as a reed. Its face was almost lovely, womanly. Long black hair poured over its nude body, dragging wet streaks over stone. Its long fingers terminated in claws. Black eyes wide, it crept close.

Hello, sweet ones, it cooed through Una's mind.
Your men are hurting us.
You wouldn't hurt us, would you?

Despite herself, Una felt a pang of concern. Rian covered her ears.

"Get back," Tam Lin warned. The sounds of slaughter reached a crescendo below the bridge. The thing got down on all fours, wailing. Such a voice, Una had never heard. It rent deep wounds in her already knotted guts. Before she knew what she was doing, her fingers gripped Tam Lin's sleeve.

"That's an ondine, isn't it?" Another macabre beast of legend Una had only read about and never knew she'd face. The ondine dwelled in forest pools and seaside coves, luring the unwary with the heartbreaking beauty of its voice. Once a victim fell under its spell, the ondine was sure to seize its prey.

"Yes," growled Tam Lin. "Don't be fooled. She'll suck the marrow from your bones while your heart still beats." He pressed them more firmly into the wall as another siren slunk onto the bridge from the opposite side.

Lies. Males always lie, sister. You know they do.
Come with us, smiled the first with small, pointed fangs. *We will dance among the waves together, fierce and free.*

Una might have been susceptible if her Spark weren't a burning candle at her center. Alas, she held lightning at her core and could not be swayed. "Kill it! Kill them both," she told Tam Lin.

Together, the ondines sprang.

Dark Horse

n.e. 508
06, Dor Enair
Malahide

Castor eyed him quizzically from the mirror, his too-full lips pursed. "You know, *mon cher*, I think it makes you more dashing." He sipped from a silver goblet, watching Damek shave. The bruises and abrasions had all healed, save for a long gash from temple to chin, a gift from the Crown Prince. The wheal was an ugly, red mass of raised flesh and healing scabs. It ruined an otherwise perfect face, as far as Damek was concerned. The razor slipped over his chin with practiced ease. Usually, he'd have a groom to manage this task. They were far from home, the Steel Corps and regular troops of Bethany.

Henry fucking FitzDonahugh had seen to that.

Damek made the last pass, then set his razor down on the larder. Drying his face with a clean rag, he tossed the offensive garment at Castor and poured himself a drink. The lord and lady of Malahide had been loathe to leave their precious silver behind, but what use was finery in one's crypt? They and around three thousand villagers, workers, and farmers had met a rather nasty end—the price for ignoring Damek's generous ultimatum. No city in the South was prepared for the might of Bethany's forces with Lord Marshal Bishop at the helm. He'd warned them not to trifle with him.

Now they were dead, like so many others.

Pity.

"My looks are the least of my concern, or yours. Where are my ships, Castor?" he demanded, working hard not to snarl. When dealing with the Bretagne, he found a direct approach worked more swiftly than a veiled threat. With Castor, most of all. The skinny little shite had had Damek murder his father, after all. "I'm not accustomed to waiting, My Lord."

Castor made an effeminate gesture. "*Non*, I never give my word unless I intend to follow through. You shall have your fleet within the week."

Damek took a long sip of his wine, never breaking eye contact. "You said that nearly a week ago. My patience grows thinner by the hour."

"I've given you six ships already, Lord Bishop. My men tell me you've had them harbored in old Dubh Lin for so long; they'll struggle to navigate the Straits soon. Why ask for more if you're not using those you have already?"

"That is hardly your concern."

"Ah, is that so, *mon ami?* I delivered upon my promise, yet you've given very little explanation for their purpose. With Bethany in your uncle's grip, I'm not sure why you would imagine I'd protest an assault?"

Damek's answering grin was tight. "Shall I repeat myself? Where are the ships you promised me? Do take care to answer with actual dates. I'm weary of asking."

Castor muttered a Bretagn curse under his breath. "Two weeks, no more."

"Your word?"

The Marquis bit the inside of his cheek. "Yes. I swear it, Lord Bishop."

"Good. I'd hate for our relationship to end on the lowest possible note."

Castor bowed from the waist, duly chastened, allowing his long hair to obscure his expression. "As you wish. Still, I am here to advise and aid, *non*?" Damek noted he did not wait for the affirmative. "Were I you, I would not let that mad Kneeler sit your throne long. My spies tell me he assembles an army to march in his God's name. I know you've heard this too."

"I have."

Castor rose, throwing his hands wide. These Gauls were so expressive. "March on them, before 'tis too late! How many Barons have joined his side?"

"Eight."

"Merde! That's half Duch Patrick's bannermen, yes?"

He was sure the Marquis had known the total before he asked.

"Yes," Damek crossed his arms. He was always amused by the effrontery of those who couldn't help but attempt to deceive him. Perhaps it was his bastardy that convinced so many of some intellectual shortcoming? Or maybe… Duch Patrick's death had opened a chasm of ambition among his uncle's inferiors.

Whatever the case, each lord in Damek's retinue, thought to assert influence over him before he became too powerful to control. "The only thing I require of you are ships, Marquis."

Shaking his head, Castor stuck his nose into his wine. "My father, brutal brigand though he was, did know a thing or two. A tower *sans* foundation will fall. You lose face." For a moment, Damek considered killing the anxious little fop today. Castor read the thought as it crossed his eyes. He flushed but did not flinch. Instead, he raised his head. "We are partners in this. If you lose your crown before it is won, I will have wasted millions of *francs* for nothing. If you are no lord of Eire, then I am weakened in Bretagne."

"Is that a threat?"

"Not at all. I am merely curious. What will you do if your uncle succeeds?"

"I'm going to be plain, son of Gaelin," remarked Damek dryly. "Attempting to hedge your bets will kill you, your men, what is left of your family, and wipe your pathetic little kingdom from the face of the earth. My Corpsmen have sacked Bonleith, Gibbons, and Malahide in a fortnight. I'd say they have a real knack for it."

"You threaten *me*, now?"

"No, I promise you."

Castor snorted. "With half the South rising for your uncle and his puny god, no ships to speak of, and the North unwon? I think not. You bluff."

"Ah, but I *do* have ships, my lord."

"In Dubh Lin, where they are useless."

"No, in Portmarnock, being fitted for cannons. Such weapons are hard to come by and even more difficult to conceal. Hence, the necessity for discretion. Lord Devereaux has been most accommodating."

The young Marquis paled by three shades.

"Furthermore," Damek went on. "We've come to terms over two or three vessels. Your lovely, swift clippers, for two massive barges, to break the ice through the Straits. Devereaux seems most eager to please me, Castor, as you might. Did you know whom you were attempting to fleece?"

"*Mon, ami…*"

"We are not friends, kinslayer. We had an arrangement. If you do not have those ships here within the fortnight— and not a day longer, mind— killing you will be the very last thing I do to you. Do you understand?"

The wind rattled the casings outside the chamber window, punctuating the uncomfortable silence. Damek, arms crossed, nodded to his Hisk, who waited just shy of the open door. "See that Lord Gaelin has everything he requires. Well, whatever he can manage from his quarters, that is. I think quill and vellum should be the highest priority."

Hisk, the large fellow that he was, towered over Castor. His gauntleted fist closed over a silk-clothed arm. The Bretagn lord spat, "*Tu! T'es un bâtard!* You betray your only ally?"

"Betray?" Damek shared a long look with Hisk, who guffawed. "I think you'll agree it's wise to protect one's investments. You'll be my honored guest here at Malahide, my lord. You'll want for nothing."

"Save freedom," Castor grumbled.

Damek walked over to clap him on the arm so the Gallic lordling couldn't miss the genuine threat in his eyes. "In future, remember that I have my own spies." He gave Castor's shoulder a squeeze that made the slighter man wince. "Take him," he said to Hisk. Castor sneered as he was led from the room but refrained from further comment.

Damek sank into a chair behind his desk with a groan when they were gone. Though he'd no doubt Castor would eventually attempt to betray him, he hadn't expected it to happen so soon. What he'd said about Henry's moves in Bethany weren't wrong. Damek *did* need to deal with the old bastard— and soon. However, to do so without destroying what he meant to rule, he must have coin… unlimited coin. Where to get it, but from the prosperous Siorai-dominated cities of the North? Malahide was a crucial steppingstone toward a greater goal; Tairngare and the Eirean crown.

His uncle threatened that outcome with every breath. With backing from Kernow, Henry had wed the insipid daughter of the Earl of Penwyth. The girl was no more than a child, barely fifteen years old. Yet, her dowry guaranteed Henry an additional four thousand Kernish troops, a bride price of one hundred thousand fainne, and a yearly stipend of eight thousand from a vineyard she'd inherited in Swansea. She was the granddaughter of the old Lord Rhiannon of Cymru, who had minted the art of cold-growth grapes. Without his genius, the land of Cymru would still be a dry, mountainous backwater. Henry's new wife brought him the money, means, and men required to make himself Duch. All it had cost him were two sons— which, Damek could attest, were no loss. His hoary uncle made much of his righteous zeal, but Damek knew a killer when he saw one. Henry mourned his sons for dashed hopes rather than genuine affection.

In that way, he and Patrick were alike. People held little value if they could not be used. Damek should know. He'd been Patrick's pawn all his life.

Una, too, though she pretended otherwise. At the thought of her, his fists balled of their own accord.

Let me go, she had said, with tears in her eyes.

His fist came down hard on the table.

You will not think of her until you've accomplished what you must. You've no time for self-pity.

Again, he swore himself to his task, and that alone. He would hear nothing, see nothing, nor feel anything until it was done. *Once you are King of Eire, she'll come back, one way or the other. For now, you are a machine built for a single purpose. Machines feel nothing.*

A knock at the chamber door helped purge his mind of that Otherworld dawn and the ignominy of dual defeat. Her sweet face full of sorrow would at once enrage and enthrall him with endless pain if he allowed it to.

He must not. He *would* not.

Clearing his throat, he waited for Martin's salt and pepper head to appear before he relaxed in his chair.

O'Rearden took one look at him and sighed, "Again?"

He coughed. "Report?"

Martin heaved himself into the opposite chair. Damek didn't like to notice how heavy the task seemed to be. Martin O'Rearden was not a young man any longer. All the riding, raiding, and battles had begun to show. He smirked at the concern on Damek's face. "Ah, 'tis nothing, this. Earned a few bumps on our way into the city. Nothing to worry yourself over, lad."

Damek didn't believe him but wouldn't argue. Martin, too, had his pride. "You were right about my ships. They're not coming."

"Of course they aren't. Gaelin is practically impoverished. Why would you ever believe he could produce more warships after taking over a bankrupt kingdom? The Marquis spends what little coin his father left him on silk and jewels. His people will tear Morlaix down around his ears soon enough. That is if you don't kill him first. Be happy we took six, boyo."

Damek's nostrils flared. He sat back. "Four warships are hardly an armada, Martin."

"More than your uncle had, Tairngare has, or Henry could dream of. Devereaux can build more, but it'll be a year or more before they're ready. In the meantime, we need—"

"*Fainne.*"

"Yes."

"I need Tairngare. All else is foreplay."

"Not yet," Martin said, scratching his beard. "I know of at least seven Baronies rife with coin we should turn our attention to first."

"We'll get to them. I'd rather cut Henry's purse strings after accumulating more land and wealth. Every county we march to must be strategic. Why lose men and arrows for lesser prizes?"

"Tairngare is a reach with so few men."

"We have twenty-thousand soldiers," Damek scoffed.

"And they have twice that number in the Cohort alone. The Corsairs make it fifty-five. Not to mention high walls, a self-contained port, and a water supply. They'll outlast anything we throw at them. We'd need an army sixty-thousand strong at least and hope they were fool enough to meet us on open ground."

Damek bit his tongue over the information he was privy to that he could not share— even with Martin. Instead, he cast his eyes to his map and tapped the Red City with a thumbnail. "Nema's new government is weak and fractious. She kills nobles and wealthy Marchers indiscriminately, making enemies of potential allies. You heard what she did to the Cymrian Trade Ambassador— Melba, was it? Nema won't last the year, or I'm buggered."

"I can't speak to her efficacy as a ruler, but the people are behind her. The army, too."

"What army? The Cohort is comprised of boys and beardless men, Martin. All the commanders and their officers fled with the nobles or were executed. The Corsairs haven't been anything but flashy dandies since Dumnain. The time is *now*, Martin. While I have the numbers and the ships."

"You'll still need coin. Malahide was a rich prize, but supplies alone will gobble all that up in a month. Tairngare will take much longer than that to tame."

"I disagree. My spies tell me the old woman is driving herself mad. Last month she even attempted to bend Basa Alvra to her side in hopes the Domina of the Alvra Clan would aid her in her quest to purge Eire of nobles and naysayers. Alvra nearly killed her, did you know that?"

"I did not," said Martin, eyes narrowing.

Damek missed the look. He exhaled a laugh. "She hasn't left the Tenth Floor since, merely issues decrees through her horde of Secundas and uses her honor guard to enforce them. Men, I might add."

"… Fir Bolg, you left out."

Damek had the grace to look away. "Ah, well. They are in the city, yes."

"Please inform your *spy* that I am fully aware of where you're gleaning your details, and I like it not. She, as ever, seeks only one thing, Damek."

Damek was tired of playing two hands close to the chest, but if his mentor knew what was going on in the North, he'd never consent to his plans. "The point is that her meteoric rise precludes a devastating fall. If I strike now, her house will crumble."

Martin sucked his teeth in silence for a while. When he spoke, his voice held a fatherly note. "Be mindful of your own words there, lad. I will do my utmost to propel your vision north if you command me, though I urge you to reconsider."

"Every day we waste in the South costs us men and fainne. Rather than founder them on meaningless trifles, I'd rather expend both to pursue the only goal that truly matters. You know that I'm right. Patrick dared once, but he did so against the full might of a powerful Cloister. In tatters, as it is now, the Citadel's gates will swing wide in no time."

"Or bring us all to ruin."

"… perhaps, but you don't believe so, any more than I do."

"Very well," said Martin, rising. His bones made music along the way. "I need an ale, a bath, a fuck, then a good night's sleep. I'll see to it the men begin drills in the morning."

"Thank you, Martin," Damek said and meant it. Without O'Rearden's support, every plan he'd ever had would have been dust.

Martin paused at the door. "Henry is not going to go away, my lord. He is an experienced soldier and ruthless tactician. He'll fatten like a tick in your absence."

"That is why I must do this now. Tairngare gives me a strength I might otherwise lose in pursuit of Bethany. No other prize compares."

"No matter how they tried, no Donahugh has ever managed to take the Red City. So few men, aside."

Damek felt his lips slide over his gums in a wide grin. "Thank Reason; I'm not a Donahugh."

He stalked through the courtyard sometime later, looking for Aoife. She'd been gone several days already with her bondsmen, doing Reason knew what. Thus far, she hadn't been forthcoming about her plans and tended to come and go like the winter wind. He only knew that she'd somehow managed to break her *geis* and spent most if not all her time on the road. Wreaking havoc, no doubt, and sowing discord in the Mac Nemed name... or, perhaps not? Aoife's motivations were changeable as the tides. Without Liadan's *geis*, there was no way to tell what she would do next. A wild mare without a tether tramples everything in her path. Still, she was his ally, for now.

Whatever designs she spun behind his back were irrelevant until he was in a position of power. At present, allies were a commodity in short supply.

He had no choice but to accept her help.

That didn't mean he had to like it.

He was in a foul mood by the time he arrived at the door she'd mentioned. Knowing he was walking into a trap, however seemingly sweet, did not improve his humor. The structure he equivocated before was a workmen's storehouse or some other facility built into the keep's inner wall. A single candle flickered behind a tattered scrap of burlap in the window. The interior was dark and bland.

He bit his lip. They probably should have brought a guard, at least. His fingers closed over his pommel as he raised a fist to knock. The door swung inward before his knuckles had even brushed the ancient wood. A rush of stale, moldy air blew into his face.

He coughed. "Hello?"

Nothing at first, then a shuffling from within. "Come," Aoife said. "We've been waiting."

He hesitated at the door. "Show yourself."

Aoife made an impatient sound and emerged into the weak candlelight from the hall. Her shorn hair and vibrant eyes made the hollows of her pale cheeks stand out. This was only their second meeting in a month, and he still wasn't prepared for the shock of her appearance. Gone was that burnished beauty he'd known all his life as if the spirit had been roasted out of her. She was thin to the point of waifish. Huge black pools collected beneath her eyes in a face that was more bone than flesh. At the hem of her tunic, her ribs stood pronounced beneath her heavy collarbone. There was a sag and bend to her spine that had never been there before, and what visible skin he could see was covered with pinkish, shiny scars. Damek's jaw tightened. The last time they'd been in each other's company, she'd been tending to him in the shadows of his sickbed, and he had been in such pain that he never really saw her.

"*Reason*, love. What happened to you?"

"Liadan, of course."

He stepped into the room, closing the door behind him and removing his hood. "What did she do to you?"

"What will never be done again," she sniffed, grabbing the candle from the sill and drawing the burlap tight against the window. The light traced strange planes and angles over her features, making her look like a Lu Sidhe sprite. "Were you followed?"

"No, though Martin knows you're here. He's no fool, Aoife."

Laughing, she said, "If he were, he'd be no use to you. Follow me. We should speak where there are no windows."

Inexplicably, Damek felt a chill of fear at the thought. He'd never had cause to be afraid of Aoife before, and she'd gone out of her way to heal him recently— but that didn't mean he trusted her or her two hulking henchmen. Carn and Creahal, he vaguely recalled. Former bodyguards to her father, Sionnavar. He had only seen them once, many summers past, at Beltane in Armagh. He'd been fourteen and meeting his family for the first time. The experience was well remembered. The court at Armagh made Nema's sham theocracy look dull. "I'd prefer to wait here if you don't mind?"

She stopped, framed in the black hall. "What? You don't trust *me* now?"

"I trust no one, Aoife. Say what you must, here."

"I saved your life, you ungrateful wretch."

"You saved my arm and leg."

"Same difference. What do you imagine might have happened if any of your enemies found you so defeated?"

"'Might have' and 'did' are not sisters. Besides, you've given me every reason to mistrust you. Don't pretend you aren't complicit in my response."

She chewed on that in silent condemnation for a while. When next she spoke, her voice held the faintest edge of regret. "If I'd succeeded, you'd have been spared humiliation, cousin. I did it for you."

That was the closest he'd get to an apology, he knew.

"Why am I summoned?" There would be no point in pressing further.

"She brought you here at my request," chimed a familiar voice from deeper within the hall. Aoife half-turned in the jamb, bowing. "I'd prefer to have this conversation where a casual eye might not spy us. Do you mind, Lord Bishop?"

Damek's heart leaped into his throat. Without thinking, he dropped to a knee. "F-forgive me, *Ard Tiarne*. I didn't expect you."

"Obviously," smiled the voice. "Else, what would have been the point? Will you follow me into the parlor?"

"Yes, Your Highness."

Damek rose and trailed behind Aoife as she limped through the hall. His host entered a well-lit room in the back, filled with a hodge-podge of mismatched chairs and dusty tables before a modest fireplace and mantle. There were no adornments or bric-a-brac to be found anywhere in this chamber. The room was peeling paint, bare wooden floors, and charmless furnishings. The prince sat near the fire, gesturing for Damek to sit opposite. His guards eyed Damek from far corners, emotionless and threatening. Damek sat, careful to leave his scabbard unlocked. Just in case. One never knew with the Bolg.

Falan the Younger's teeth were very white against his bronze skin. "It's been an age, hasn't it, My Lord."

Damek dipped his head. "It has, *Ard Tiarne*."

"Still refuse to call me 'father,' eh?"

Damek said nothing.

"Well, perhaps you're wiser than I surmised?"

Being the Prince of Armagh's bastard-born son was not something to bandy about, especially if the prince in question was supposed to be dead.

Damek did not return his smile. "Perhaps."

"Such mistrust I sense in you. You imagine I'd harm my only son?"

"… I have a vivid imagination, *Ard Tiarne*."

The prince's gaze flicked to Aoife for a moment. "As do we all. So," he leaned forward. "One uncle dead, and the lesser claims your throne. How'd this come to pass?"

"Many things happened, not the least of which was a visit from the Crown Prince and his cousin, Tam Lin of Croghan. Patrick collapsed in Court, and Henry had seized the moment. His followers clamor for the old ways, and they are numerous."

"The Adair came for the girl, didn't he?"

A muscle flexed in Damek's jaw. "Yes."

"Interesting," said Falan, rubbing his hands together. "This girl proves a thorn in our *seanmáthair*'s side, it seems. Hard-won power can be easily lost when the right names are involved— as we, ourselves, hope to demonstrate." He leaned back. "I like it not that the Donahugh girl has sided with the Adair Clan. By rights, she should die."

Damek stilled. He knew better than to reveal his irritation. The Prince of Armagh had never been cruel to him, per se, but that hardly implied that he was kind, either. Damek had to be very, very careful here. "I believe the Dannan exile encourages her nonsensical passion for freedom. Una Moura Donahugh will be the queen of Eire if she lives. Escape from that burden is a fantasy and nothing more. She'll see reason. I vow it."

"I've no time for misguided romance, Damek. If she does not sit beside you, she must die. I cannot afford the added boon to Midhir's claim. If he marries her, Kaer Yin will reestablish Eire for the Tuatha De Dannan."

"He won't. The High King would never approve the match. At best, Una would become a concubine or hostage in Bri Leith. Once she sees the truth of this, she'll return home with me."

"Claim Eire by proof of blood and strength of arms, my son. You don't need her."

"If I want the Northers to embrace me as King, then I must have her by my side," Damek paused to clear his throat. He looked down. "No disrespect intended, My Prince, but the opposition to Vanna Nema is proof of my argument. While the peasants in the shade of the Citadel love and fear her, she's alienated most of the nobility in Innisfail with her barbarism. Nearly every Merchers Guild has united against her rule, and the colonies in Alba and Cymru have declared their independence from Tairngare's Charter. What's worse, I've had a report that a force of Dannan Sidhe marching south from Skye, with Drem Moura in their train."

Falan nodded. "I've heard the same, though my informants tell me she is carried in a litter behind the Queen's entourage. Drem is dying, or so I'm told. Surely, Eri Bres means to take the old woman to her father for council."

"With a host five hundred strong?" Damek's brows raised. "Sounds to me like the Dannans are banding together. The second force of nearly the same strength marches toward Rosweal under Fionn Shiel O'More, the High King's Champion. They may not know what we plan here, *Ard Tiarne*, but they muster all the same. Why?"

"Kaer Yin Adair is freed of his *geis*. They come to pay him obeisance."

"So, he gets a force of one thousand peerless Dannan warriors, and this doesn't concern you?"

"He's the Crown Prince of Innisfail, Damek. His return is significant to his people, as mine shall be to the Bolg."

Damek exhaled slowly. As long as he'd been aware that the Prince of Armagh was his father, he'd always believed him to be the canniest man alive. Patient, cunning, and cautious was Falan the Younger. Having fabricated his death, Falan had been free to weave a beautifully subtle plot that spelled ultimate doom for the Dannan High King in Bri Leith. Though… to get there, he must depend upon agents united by their loathing of Dannan rule and sworn to the utmost secrecy. Agents like the power-mad Dowager Queen of Armagh. Did he not see it, Damek wondered? That the fatal flaw in his plans was critical arrogance. "So, while they're gathering to consolidate power, we're— what? Wasting men and resources to spread hysteria in the Midlands and allowing Liadan to destabilize the wealthiest city in the North? Is that all?"

Falan's brow darkened. "I've no need to share my stratagems with you."

"No?" Damek laughed. "Seems I'm the one with an army behind him."

"You threaten me?" The room vibrated a bit at the edges.

Damek wasn't cowed. "Why are you here now?"

"Do I need an excuse to meet with my son?"

"Horseshite. What do you want from me, *Ard Tiarne*?"

Falan's features settled into a calm, observational disdain. For the Bolg, to get straight to the point was the height of ill manners. Damek couldn't give a shite less. In thirty-two years, he'd seen this man who claimed paternity only a handful of times. While it was true that Falan had sent him letters, gifts, and the odd servant (Damek's swordmasters, for example), any feeling or paternal warmth had been lacking.

Damek, as always, was meant to be a useful tool.

Between Patrick Donahugh and Falan the Younger: Damek was unsure which relative he loathed more.

"I wish you to march against the Dannans at the Confluence."

Damek nodded once. "I see. Put Bethany on the hook for Armagh?"

"To defeat the Crown Prince would be a spectacular victory."

"… and while I'm doing your dirty work, what will you be doing?"

"I do not need—"

"Let me stop you there. The answer is 'no.' I've plans of my own."

"You dare defy *me*?"

"I'm talking to a dead man with no army save a smattering of followers from an insignificant city in Aes Sidhe. Your men serve to harass and mystify groups who are far too busy fighting each other to notice."

"I am the rightful *Ard Ri* of Innisfail."

"Perhaps. Suppose I can give you the crown. Isn't that right?"

Falan fell silent. Dark energy radiated from his person like smoke.

Damek was unafraid. He stood. "Whatever you wish for, *I* am the rightful King of Eire, without your blood or blessing. If you wish my help stealing the Dannan crown, you had better start asking yourself what *I* want in exchange."

Falan's voice followed him into the hall. "I will kill the Siorai girl."

Damek shot back, "I dare you to try. Or didn't you ask Aoife what happened the last time she made an attempt?" Aoife's nostrils flared in shame as he passed, but he paid her no mind. Damek opened the door, allowing a blast of chill wind into the tiny house. He knew he'd be heard, even without raising his voice. "Tairngare is my price, *athair*."

"You will never keep it," said Falan, with a sigh.

"You have my terms."

He didn't bother to shut the door on his way outside.

Blood Ties

n.e. 508
09, Dor Enair
Cairngare

Grainne had so little experience with regret; even faced with it as she was now, she was at a loss to fully comprehend the feeling. Her family had made a terrible mistake. Sound traveled quite far in an open market. Once thriving shops were shuttered and bolted, many slathered with red paint that read *'look for us at Tara'* or *'permanently closed'* in the common tongue. In the shadow of the Citadel, nothing moved but the wind and whatever detritus it carried from one empty corner to another. Dirty snow melted from unpatched rooftops in the unseasonably warm sunlight. Avenues lacked cobbles for want of care. Carts and wagons full of broken crates and fraying baskets were scattered over every street as if the people who owned them had fled in extreme haste.

Indeed, Grainne spied only soldiers marching through cross lanes or lurking upon the walls. Despair clung to the city, a heady pall that cast a shadow of fear over the stoutest heart in her midst. Each step they took through the Drough Quarter trumpeted doom. If anyone saw her or her company, none bothered to call out. The Cohort, too, seemed listless and hollow as the streets they guarded. Once they came to the Citadel's high iron gate, Grainne looked up and gasped.

There, dangling from the walls, were the people she'd believed fled.

Dozens of men, women, and even children— rotted to rags and bones in high crow's cages or swung from frayed ropes creaking in the crisp winter breeze. The living wouldn't meet her eyes, as if the hope of rescue had long since faded to rot in their mouths. Their moans and cries sent chills up and down her arms.

The smell hit her next. She gagged, covering her mouth with a shaking hand. Human feces, vomit, and urine assailed her group in a miasmic cloud. The glass-eyed guards who met them didn't appear to notice.

Their captain held his hand out. "What business?"

Bracing herself, Grainne uncovered her face. "We're ambassadors from Armagh. I am Grainne Mac Nemed, daughter of Falan the Elder, King of the Fir Bolg."

The captain didn't blink. He held up a scrap of vellum. "Hm. Says here you were 'sposed to arrive two days ago."

"We were delayed."

"I see," he droned. He waved two more soldiers over. "Search them."

Her guards bristled, stepping in front of her. She spoke around a muscular shoulder. "You have no cause to lay hands upon a visiting dignitary."

Again, he waved his bit of vellum bearing Nema's seal. "Doma's orders."

Grainne stiffened. "Since when?"

"I don't make the rules, highness, just enforce them. Kada?" A lieutenant shuffled over, fingers spread, sporting a broad leer over his blemished face. "Submit or move on," scoffed the gatekeeper with a shrug.

Grainne's retainers drew swords. Her bodyguard, Leal, stepped forward, forcing the young Cohort officer back. "Try it and die, mortal."

Several guards rushed the gate on either side of the wall almost instantly, bowstrings drawing back tight. The Cohort Captain at the entrance dropped his vellum to reach for his shortsword. The Warhammers at Grainne's back drew and aimed their bows. All of this happened so fast that she scarcely had time to suck in a gasp. Just as the moment strained to the breaking point, a high-pitched voice sailed high over the Citadel's wall. Beyond the portcullis, a disheveled, deformed figure slumped into view. The captain's hand halted over his pommel. He turned to see Vanna Nema's servant shamble forward. Hideously scarred cheeks having gone an odd shade of puce, Fawa Gan leaned into the bars, huffing. "Her highness is expected, Captain! Stay your men."

The gatekeeper spat; eyes narrowed. "Bit late. One of these faerie fucks just drew down on my man there. Next one moves will be full of holes."

"The Doma requests the lady Grainne's presence upon arrival, sir. You're ordered to stand down."

The captain snorted, peering around Gan's newly skeletal frame. "Yeah? Who's going to enforce that? I don't see anyone in there but you."

Gan fidgeted. "I ran ahead. Lady MacNemed's train was spied from the Cloister, Captain. Corsairs are on their way."

"Hm," said the captain. "Until I see a warrant, no one gets through this gate. Especially not this ragtag without the sense Siora gave a gnat."

"My men," said Grainne, having found her voice. "Apologize for their weapons. They do so in defense of me. We are not accustomed to such treatment. Men are disallowed from laying hands upon a member of the royal family, Captain."

The odious little man did not flutter an eyelid. "These are dangerous times, mistress. Submit to a search or leave. Many folks hang behind me who thought to argue the justice of our Doma's commands."

Sobered by the warning in his tone, Grainne unbuttoned her cloak and stepped past Leal. "Do as you must, but be quick about it," she said through her teeth. "If that young man approaches me again, many more of you will die at this gate than we."

The captain raised a brow but relinquished his pommel. He stalked over to perform the deed himself. Gan eyed her helplessly from behind the portcullis. She raised her chin while the officious Milesian soldier raked rough hands over her body, none too gently. At least he had the grace to keep his internal opinions from his expression. She might have been a wood block, for all the man appeared to mind. Once done, he waved her past. "Do you have anything to declare?"

"Many things, but none related to your inquiry," she sniffed, shrugging her cloak back on. It was cold in Tairngare now, and the sky promised another light snowfall. Soon, the heavy ice storms of Dor Imba would descend and halt travel altogether. "In the wagon, we've brought supplies for our journey and gifts for your Doma. Every saddlebag contains more of the same."

Having rifled through her belongings, he passed her white leather satchel back, oblivious to the necessary documents inside. He couldn't read Ealig, could he? "Your men will surrender their weapons at once."

Leal's dark brows wound together. "*Lig dom é a mharú.*"

"*Ní anois,*" she answered but nodded to the gatekeeper. "Of course. Most of my retinue will remain and await my return. Those who follow me into the Doma's chambers will do as you ask. Leal?" Leal cursed under his breath but lowered his blade. With the sourest possible expression, he passed it to a waiting Cohort guardsman who couldn't have looked more nervous if he tried. These men had grown reckless in the wake of Nema's ascension. With so many citizens hanging from the walls like discarded meat, Grainne had no doubt the guards would grow bolder by the day. She paused at the gate while the portcullis raised. Gan awaited her on the other side, wringing his hands to ribbons. The captain gave her a mock bow as she passed.

She'd see to it the brute supped on his tongue by nightfall. "Where are your Corsairs?" she asked Gan quietly.

With a glance over her shoulder at the remaining Warhammers and Bolgmen filing through the gate, he lowered his voice to a mere whisper. "What guards, My Lady?"

※

THE SURREAL SILENCE IN THE streets was nothing to the thunderous quiet inside the Citadel. Slack-faced girls in gray robes (Secundas, Grainne recalled) scrubbed already pristine floors and window casings or tiptoed through wide-open spaces usually overflowing with people. As her party passed, no single girl dared to meet her eyes. These nameless Secundas, leftovers from a formerly robust caste system, drifted through empty halls like disappointed ghosts. If Grainne were inclined to such nonsense, she might feel for them. All hope of advancement through the Cloister had faded since Nema had stripped the city of its Libellan and Mercher classes. Who would foster them for the Fifth Ordeal now?

Bound as they were to Nema's edicts, Grainne did not doubt that each was beginning to realize they would likely serve in drudgery for the rest of their lives. Nema had no use for rivals. If a girl did not serve, she would be dispensed with. Grainne hadn't failed to notice that many of the sad creatures begging for death in the cages at the wall bore the infamous grey of the Secundas' robes. Who was there to speak for this faceless multitude of forgotten women? Everyone with any influence had died or fled in the first Cohort purge. Any that lingered soon found themselves in servile grey. Nema was the queen at the heart of an enslaved hive.

Grainne and Leal shared a long look. This was not to plan. None of it was. Whatever was happening here had *never* been on the agenda. Gan led her through several halls and short staircases toward the Grand Arcade and the formal entryway into the Cloister. Here, the cloying stench of burning incense was nearly worse than the sickly-sweet scent of death outside. Though the steps were polished to an impossible sheen, Grainne felt like she was plunging her feet through tainted oil. Another simpering maiden shrank from her advance, making her frown. What in the nine hells was her grandmother doing to these people? Leal clutched her elbow as they climbed the opulent Agate staircase toward Nema's Tenth Floor throne room.

Aside from soldiers and newly indentured servants, was *no one* else left in the Citadel? Had Nema destroyed every one of note within the city... so swiftly?

Macha, Grainne thought, looking around and hearing nothing but the wind tease at the cracks in the walls. *She truly has gone mad.* Nema, drunk with power, had imposed this thorough and terrifying decimation. Every time Grainne had visited this monstrous structure, it had been filled to the brim with stinking, screeching, arguing, laughing, loitering, and otherwise busy mortals. As her footsteps ricocheted from every wall and sparklingly clean surface, even she could not stall a pang for such loss. The cost of Nema's madness was more terrible than she imagined.

It's hush... even worse.

Breathing laboriously, Gan paused at the Ninth Floor landing. The two hunks of odd-shaped flesh where his eyebrows had been knotted together. "My Lady," he leaned in as close as he dared with Leal's burning violet gaze so near. Grainne drew back. If he noticed her revulsion, he didn't let it show.

Quick, this one is.

No wonder he lives where so many have died.

"I must warn you."

"No need. I have eyes."

"Not about this... tomb." He gestured to the massive, gilded doors at the next landing. "About *her*."

Grainne took a breath. "She's run mad. A blind woman would see it."

He fidgeted, his small, piggish eyes roving every crevice and corner. "Lower your voice. I'm trying to help you."

"Who do you believe you're speaking to, little man?" She whispered back mockingly. "I am an emissary from Armagh. She wouldn't dare—"

"You're mistaken, My Lady." His voice took an edge. "She *would*. She has."

Leal towered over Gan. "Speak plain."

"How many of your kind did you leave with her last time? Her guards?"

"Two dozen, no more. Why?"

"You'll find eleven or so in the dungeon beneath the Citadel; the rest seem to share her... malady. They do her bidding, whatever she asks. 'Twas they, who imprisoned the others. Well, those that lived through the exchange."

Grainne sucked in a breath, but Leal asked, "When? How?"

Gan snuck a glance over his shoulder, clearly wary the warriors in question would soon stomp down the stairs looking for them. "There's no time. Her Eminence doesn't like to be kept waiting." He pressed something cold and metallic into her hands. She didn't need to look down to know what it was. "That will open any door in the Cloister, and most in the Citadel, save the Treasury and Archives. Get your men free when you can."

"Why would you aid us? I can feel your hatred from here."

He gave her a dispassionate smile. "Someone has to stop her. Why else would you come to this hell she's crafted after the butchery you witnessed during your last visit? If you're not here to reason with her, why else would you bother?"

"*I* am not here for any such purpose. I've brought gifts from the King of Armagh."

Again, he glanced at the top of the stairs, licking his missing lips. "You're here to read terms from your brother, My Lady." He shook his head at the flash in her eyes. "Yes, we've met, Lord Falan and I. A shame he didn't kill her when he had the chance, for he may never get another one."

"You dare speak so of your mistress?" hissed Grainne. "I should have Leal hang you from the balustrade by your entrails for such disloyalty."

He laughed. "I no longer have much of a nose, but I know fear when I smell it. She's gone too far. She kills on a whim, sometimes a score at once. She won't be satisfied until the entire city is enslaved or dead, and if you believe she means to stop at the Drough Gate, you're sorely mistaken. Her followers, zealots all, speak of marching west and south to press her Reformations deep into Eire. Your 'king' does not factor into her plans at all, and believe me if anyone knows her mind, it's me. I've been her footstool for forty years."

Grainne fell silent for a while, considering his blunt sincerity. She'd told Falan what she'd seen when last she was here, but her brother vowed the old woman had been dealt with and would come to heel. Seeing the city's state and suffering, people only told her she'd been right all along. Liadan Mac Nemed had lost her mind at last. Too many decades spent in the Milesian world had eroded her sanity with her loyalty. "Why are you telling me this? What do you hope to gain?"

"An end, "Gan sighed, shivering. "Before it's too late. For everyone."

Another of Grainne's men scoffed, and Leal said, "You speak as if she were a monster in some tale. She's an old woman."

"I know who she is, sir, and how long she's waited for this chance," Gan said. "If you leave her to this, so many will die. The Transition will pale by comparison."

"You give her too much credit," argued Grainne.

"Do I? Has there ever been a sharper sword than belief? Listen, any moment now, one of her loyal followers— maybe one of your own— will head down here to retrieve us. If you think I'm lying or conflating the issue, share your misgivings about your reception here. I beg you, prove me wrong."

"She isn't all-powerful. She wouldn't dare—"

"Why do you keep saying that? Do you imagine you know her better than Aoife or myself? Do you have the faintest idea what she has done to either one of us or so many others? It goes beyond counting. No. If you march in there and deliver those terms, you'll never leave here, My Lady. I promise you that. She dispenses with those who aren't ready to die by her word in short order. I'm giving you your lives in hopes you'll escape to return in *force*." The jangle of metal and the ring of booted feet trilled down the stairs. Gan went white as death itself. "Decide for yourself when you see her. She's... much changed. I pray you make the right decision."

He made as if to resume his progress upward, but Grainne's fingers caught his sleeve. "If you want to die so badly, why not do the honors yourself?"

His eyes were like two chips of black glass. "Not until she does. Else, how would I ever rest?"

✕

VANNA NEMA DID NOT LOOK like a queen with the world at her feet. She appeared to have lost a great deal of weight she could ill afford to lose and sat the Doma's massive onyx throne like a rumpled, sullen child.

Grainne covered her mouth lest her grandmother see the shock and horror on her face. Nema's hair was unbound and unwashed, trailing over her shoulders in a graying, frizzled rat's nest. Her cheeks were drawn with huge shadows tucked into their hollows. Deep black pools gathered below each of her bright green eyes, making them wider and ever more piercing than usual. Though she wore the Doma's heavy golden robes of state, the reams of fabric did little to hide the hollow bones at her collar, throat, and wrists. When she smiled at Grainne, her teeth were dull and brittle, as if they had not been tended to in months. The glaring evidence of rapid aging aside, the poorly healed scars over her face and neck were most alarming. As if a giant eagle had raked its talons from her scalp to her exposed collarbones, jagged, poorly healing rents tracked diagonally from her right temple to her left shoulder. These cuts may have run further, but Vanna's robes prevented further evidence.

Grainne nearly choked at the sight.

This was the mighty Vanna Nema— the dowager queen, Liadan Mac Nemed of Armagh? *This* was her grandmother, the one woman she had idolized and revered the whole of her long life. At some point, Leal pressed his hand against the small of her back to remind her to breathe.

"Welcome, Lady of Armagh," wheezed Nema, her voice like a broken wind flute. "What news do you bring us of Aes Sidhe?"

It took a while, but Grainne found her tongue. She dug through her white leather satchel for the roll of vellum she sought. From his place behind Nema, she could swear Fawa Gan's eyes flashed in warning. What was she to do? If she came into Nema's presence empty-handed, wouldn't that have been the greater danger? Grainne must as always, keep her wits sharp. "I bring you terms from the King of the Fir Bolg, your Eminence. As requested upon our last meeting, Falan the Elder sends you these gifts," she declared, waving a hand at the chests her men set down. "And his best wishes for a fruitful Imbolg."

"Hm," Nema cackled, nodding to her Cohort guardsman to collect the items and remove them from the throne room. Grainne had never seen so many soldiers around her grandmother before. There had to be a score, at least. Several Secundas stood in tight lines in each corner and archway with their heads bowed, awaiting the slightest command. That chill Grainne felt earlier returned with a vengeance. *An army of dolls*, she thought, her throat constricting. *Puppets have more life in them.* "No need to stand on ceremony, child. How does my son, your father?"

Grainne's head snapped up. "I— I don't... that is—"

Nema's laughter grated like sandpaper. "We keep no secrets in this city, My Lady. Only the loyal may enter the Ancestor's Hall." There was a note here that Grainne readily identified. She dared not look at Gan. "My name is revealed and my purpose clear. Tell me, what is yours, granddaughter?"

Her name 'is revealed'*?*

"I have said, Eminence. I bring tidings from the king."

"To swear fealty, I presume. The Ancestor rules in Tairngare, and soon, all Eire shall bend its knee. Isn't that why you've come?"

Nema's mad gaze burned.

The vellum in Grainne's hand shook. She closed her fist around it so that she wouldn't see. That is *not* what this vellum read. It was a veiled order for Liadan Mac Nemed to return to Armagh and leave the city to Grainne. This was meant to be shared in private, of course. Grainne hadn't expected to be dragged before the throne. "If we may speak in private," Grainne attempted, noting the many sets of eyes that slid her way, none of them friendly. For all he breathed, Gan might have been an ugly statue behind Nema. "There are many items I have been tasked to discuss with you."

The way Nema's thin lips pressed together told Grainne everything she needed to know. She had been right to leave the city when she did two months ago under cover of darkness. She should not have returned, no matter what her idealistic brother proposed. Liadan was insane. Mortality had come for the Dowager Queen, and with it, madness. How long had she dwelled among these Milesians? A hundred years, two? How long had she plotted and schemed to overtake them? Long before she stepped foot outside of the Oiche Ar Fad, that was sure. The mortal realm was lethal for one so old as Liadan, and seeing her now, Grainne knew she had to get word to her brother fast. First, she had to appease the most potent lunatic in the land.

Think, Grainne! Once she reads this scroll, you're doomed. What can you offer? What does a madwoman want? "Fine," she said after several tense moments. "If they know you, *seanmáthair*, then I shall not fear to speak freely. My father, as you know, hasn't the wits the gods gave a toad. Instead, my brother seeks your removal from the Doma's office and a temporary replacement put in place until the Parliament is reinstated."

Those hostile stares grew murderous. A wave of whispers circled the chamber while the Cohort reached for their pommels. From some hidden door came seven fully armed Warhammers— Leal's men— with their black cuirasses shining in the light of Nema's multitude of braziers. Not one of them seemed to recognize Grainne or her party. *Ah. This must be an enchantment. There is no other explanation. What did Liadan trade for the power to bend so many to her will?* But then she thought about the people strung along the walls like hanks of beef and understood.

This is blood magic.

She trades lives for power—no wonder she is rotting from the inside out. Macha, save us all. "However," she was proud of her even tone. She threw the scroll to the shining black floor in disgust. "My brother does not speak for me. I, like you, am my own woman. It is my right to choose whom I serve."

Nema gave a slight smirk. "You would betray the Black Prince so easily? I think not. You've been his faithful dog from the day he was born, Grainne. Where he walks, your adoration follows. You'll have to try much harder to convince me you haven't come to supplant me."

Leal was wise enough not to draw his larks as Nema's guardsmen inched nearer. They might fight free of the throne room, but they'd never pass the city gates alive. There were too many of them.

Falan had miscalculated when he'd sent her here to negotiate on his behalf... or, *had* he? An unpleasant thought crossed Grainne's mind like a cloud flitting over the sun.

He sent you here for an excuse.
You're here to tempt her to violence.

A queasy certainty sank into her blood. Falan, her beloved brother, had sent her here to remove two further obstacles to his scheme. If Grainne lived, he could use her again; if she died— he'd take Tairngare with all of Armagh's blessing. *That… clever, cruel bastard*, she thought. *I vow he'll perish by my hand if I live through this.*

Who'll rule Aes Sidhe then, hm, brother dear?

Keeping her rage in check, Grainne raised her chin high. "Why should Falan rule Innisfail? Why should it always be a man? What has he ever done to deserve the honor? Nothing. He thinks he has the right to take whatever he wishes because he was a male born of an ancient line. I say, why should it be *him*?"

"I hear the truth in your voice, granddaughter. This pleases me. You are the elder child. In Tairngare, primogeniture does not hold sway. A male may only inherit when he is the eldest, and a powerless female is the only alternative. You are not powerless, are you? Armagh is as much your inheritance as his, but only through *my* grace. Do you understand?"

"I do. I will swear absolute fealty to you, *seanmáthair*. If you will have me?"

Nema sat back, weighing Grainne's words. Grainne bowed low, her heart hammering against her ribs. "I don't believe you, child. You're duplicitous as your brother but half as bright. Surely you've realized why he sent you here?" She sucked her teeth. "Must be frustrating to see oneself reduced to a commodity, hm? I know, firsthand."

Leal slipped a dagger into her pocket.

It wouldn't help.

Already, Nema's loyal Warhammers surrounded their small party.

"If you'd intended to offer your allegiance to me as you claim, you wouldn't have fled with Aoife and her lickspittles in the middle of the night. I have a long memory, you see, and forgive very few slights of the sort."

The lights in each approaching Bolg's eyes had long gone out. She wondered how she might have missed that dull, haunted shade. Were the Warhammers in the dungeons immune to influence somehow, or had Nema just not gotten to them yet? Had the Cohort at the Gate been enchanted as well? Likely not. The meanest among the Milesians leftover here worshipped Nema as the Ancestor's second coming. She empowered them: their rivalries, bitterness, and prejudices. Nema gave their hatreds and fears a focus.

The Bolg, however, were a different story.

"My Lady, when I say run, you do it," murmured Leal at her nape.

She opened her mouth to protest, but Nema answered for her. "No need for such theatrics, my young friend. I would not harm my grandchild. I merely wish to… correct her behavior." Nema's mouth was a red knife slash in the distance. "Take her. Kill the others if need be but spare them, if possible. We could use more capable hands around here, no?"

A fellow Grainne remembered as Earc came within a hair's breadth of clasping her wrist. She dropped her satchel and drew Leal's dagger from her pocket. "Leal, get out of here. You are the strongest among us. If anyone can slip through her guards, it's you."

Another reached for her wrist. Her blade nicked out, nearly taking a finger. The assailant recoiled with a grunt. A third guard took his place. She was obliged to slash at this one a few times before he backed away. Aware that she would make it difficult for them, Nema's converts went around her in a circle.

"I won't leave you." Leal insisted, drawing both hammers. His men fanned out before their lady, prepared to do their duty. Grainne retreated within their protective circle if only long enough to spare Leal a frown.

"Only one way to go. From the Seventh, on this side. Falan must hear of this."

Leal exhaled long and slow. He loved her, she knew, and leaving her was never something he'd do willingly. "If you don't, I'm dead anyway… or like them. Go. Now!" She wasted no more energy debating the issue. She dashed toward the closest guard with a small war cry taking a brutal swipe at his cheek with her blade. He staggered backward, giving her the opening she sought. The second set of hands reached out to grab her, but she slipped below them to her knees, gliding effortlessly over the glistening black floor. She'd barely come twelve inches past when she regained her footing. Dagger high, she raced toward Nema on her throne. As every head swiveled in her direction and the guards scrambled to catch her, Leal gutted his cover with one hand and dashed for the open doorway. He didn't get far before the Cohort filed down the stairs after him. Grainne didn't get to see anything else nor hear the distant crack of broken glass, which would signify his successful escape.

An unseen force caught her midleap, slamming her into a far wall.

Nema got up, clutching her side for want of air. The cost of such magic was likely more than one dying Sidhe could handle— and she was, Grainne had no doubt. Nema seemed to shrivel where she stood.

"Stupid girl. You *dare* move against me?"

Grainne cried aloud as she was dragged back to the throne by an invisible hand. She gagged. The force of Nema's power sought to choke the life from her.

"Did you imagine your little ruse would free your man, and he'd run off to tattle to your little brother? How noble, Grainne," Nema said. "I'm quite disappointed in you."

Grainne only had the air to send one last prayer to Macha for deliverance before she sank into that obsidian floor and saw no more.

Tech Duinn

n.e. 508
dor enair
oiche ar fad

At first, Tir Falias was nothing but a glimmer upon a distant hillside, a speck of light in the dark. If one stared too long, its shape would flicker then wink out altogether, like a half-remembered dream. Each step they gained seemed to chase it farther toward the horizon until its turrets crested the foothills of an unfamiliar mountain range. Nearer still, its spires beckoned from the shores of a distant sea. Up, over, under, the road wound— and never did its gates draw close in all the hours they walked, rode, or ran. They trudged through rain, sleet, snow, hail, and even the heat of a summer's day. Hours, days, perhaps weeks passed while they pushed on— ever forward, ever onward.

Still, the hall of the Raven King eluded them.

The wind blew hot and cold at once, and the sights and sounds deceived. When night receded toward the east, and the roseate sun baked the earth beneath their feet, Kaer Yin breathed a sigh of relief. Their worn, bloodied party rounded a rocky outcrop overhanging the path, and suddenly Tir Falias loomed ahead. Ultimately tucked into a high tor surrounded by lush green forest and sweet, rushing water, the hall of Diarmid *Fiachra Dubh* Adair was revealed at last. A sturdy stone castle erupted proudly between two great rivers, encircled by white-capped mountains that crashed into a vast turquoise sea. Hewn from the bedrock beneath the tor itself, the rolling hillside parted from the fortress' high walls like a lady doffing her cloak. A mammoth waterfall crashed from the tallest snowy peak like a gossamer veil, feeding both rivers that diverged around the hillside. A large stone bridge, easily a mile long, spanned the confluence from that bulbous green island.

Robin coughed. "*There's* a sight. Can't say it's what I expected, though."

Kaer Yin passed his old friend his waterskin. The Greenmaker looked like he'd been murdered and resurrected again in the same hour. Perhaps he had? Maybe they *all* had? He glanced at Rian, who glared back from Tam Lin's saddle. Without his cousin's arm supporting her, she would have fallen from her seat ages ago. With his cloak torn to ribbons over Rian's thin shoulders and his tunic in bloodied threads— so might Tam Lin, had he not been occupied with her care. Shar was missing hanks of hair from his nape and bore scratches up and down his arms. Kaer Yin didn't want to think about the cuts, scrapes, bruises, and other wounds he, himself, bore. Robin had lost a tooth and wore a nasty bite wound that would have torn his jugular out had Shar not acted quickly enough. "What?" mused Kaer Yin dryly. "Think it'd be a gloomy black tower in the middle of a swamp?"

"Aye," Robin agreed. "Given what we've seen, I don't think ye could blame me for that." He passed the skin back, his brow heavier than usual.

"No. I couldn't," admitted Kaer Yin, truthfully. Noticing the direction of Robin's stare, he resisted the urge to turn around. "She's fine."

"Is she?"

No, Kaer Yin's jaw clenched.

But I can't bloody well say why, and neither can you.

Robin nodded at the unspoken warning. "This place is no good for anyone, saving maybe ye lot, but it's doing something to her, Ben. Ye see it, plain as me."

"Keep your voice down."

"What are you two jabbering about?" demanded Una. She had the ears of a bat; Kaer Yin was quite sure. On foot, he led his overworked mount by the bit while Una sat high in the saddle, tucked into his cloak. She hadn't had time to prepare for the journey when they'd left Bethany properly, and the night had been cold as it was lethal. Sparing a scowl for Robin, his head swiveled round to face her. The sight of her whisked the air from his lungs all over again. Though she was equally as filthy and unkempt as the rest of their party, she alone did not share in everyone else's general state of shock, pain, and exhaustion. Aside from a few blood smears in places he'd seen her take wounds, she was the picture of glowing, perfect health. Point in fact, he couldn't recall ever seeing her look so lovely— which disturbed him more than the idea that she was healing herself much more swiftly than she ever had before. The question of 'how' lingered in the warming air over his head like a cloud. Her dusky gold cheeks pulled down sharply as she frowned at him. "What?"

Clearing his suddenly dry throat, he glanced away. "Are you all right?"

"Me? I'm bloody grand, thanks. Why?"

"You look… well, you look—"

"Spit it out."

"*Fine*, that's what. If I hadn't seen you take half a dozen wounds last night, I'd never believe it. You're scaring Robin if I'm honest."

Robin threw up his hands. "I didn't bloody say that!"

Una twisted her lip at him. "Right you are."

"— That aside," continued Kaer Yin. "The nearer we come to Tir Falias, the healthier you appear. What's happening?"

Chewing her cheek, she glanced back at Rian, whose lips came together in a tight line. Kaer Yin nearly bristled. What the hells did the girl infer that he didn't? "I don't know," Una answered. "But I can guess."

"Samhain?"

"Yes," she sighed.

"Tell me," he pleaded, leaning close. Even mounted as she was, Kaer Yin's face wasn't far from her eye level. "I don't judge you for something that saved hundreds of lives, Una."

"It's just," she hesitated, scanning the trees in the fading twilight opposite. "I feel… different somehow. Stronger. I don't know how to explain it."

"Maybe Diarmid can?"

She struggled not to flinch. "If he doesn't kill me, yeah."

His hand closed over hers through his mud-stained cloak. "He won't."

"You keep saying that, but we're at his mercy now, aren't we?"

"Some of us are, sure," grumbled Robin.

Kaer Yin pulled away from Una's side, tugging the reins tight around his hand. He led on. There was no telling what his uncle would do when they arrived, but he'd be damned if he allowed anything to happen to her. Diarmid might still be in a snit for the surprise he'd received at Samhain. So be it. Una was family now.

Besides, Kaer Yin knew him better than anyone. Diarmid would never harm a woman, especially one as beautiful and intriguing as Una Moura. His scowl deepened until it might have been carved into his face. That *was* what worried him. They were halfway across the causeway when the sun finally chased the memory of evening into the east. He stole another peek at Una over his shoulder. She had closed her eyes to absorb the sun's hazy rays, her long eyelashes sweeping her cheekbones. His heart squeezed against his ribs. He'd only half-won her and knew, down to his bones, he wasn't done fighting for her.

Diarmid would never harm so unique a prize.

No. Instead, he would try to *keep* Una.

That was much, much worse.

X

BY WHAT AMOUNTED TO MID-MORNING in this strange, hauntingly lovely place— they arrived at the gates of Tir Falias. With the rush of both rivers heavy in her ears, the scent of crisp ozone and fir blowing down the mountains, Una made a slight sound of surprise. Kaer Yin pointed to a more minor, hollowed-out hill about a mile away. It bore a stone edifice with a massive, blackened maw for an entrance.

"Bri Reis," said he. "The Hall of Slumbering Kings."

Huge braziers burned tirelessly from each side of the doorway. Nothing but mist traced the endless dark at its center, yet, she felt watched, all the same. Her skin prickled with gooseflesh. "Who lives there?"

"No one. That's the tomb of Crom Dagda." He and every Sidhe in their midst tapped their temples and bowed to the distant tor. "Bri Reis is the holiest place in the Oiche Ar Fad, where my people are taken when we die. It is a great honor to house one's bones in the Hall of the Dagda."

Una nodded but offered no commentary. She understood the veneration of ancestors more than most. As they filed into the courtyard beneath a wide-open portcullis devoid of soldiers or courtiers, her eye couldn't stray from the Dagda's beckoning monument. Something was *present* about it as if it had thoughts and feelings. Attuned to the undercurrent of energy, she couldn't describe the impression she felt as either warmth or welcome, though neither did it feel expressly hostile.

Curious, she thought. *It sees us too.*

Her Spark flared in greeting.

"Crom Dagda?" Rian wondered aloud, her voice grainy and hoarse from screaming. "I thought he was interred at Tara before the Milesian Invasion?"

"He was," replied Tam Lin, still holding her upright in his saddle. His voice, as usual, held a note of bored disdain. "When Eber Finn was crowned at Tara, he returned Crom's bones to Midhir."

"To placate him?"

"No, 'twas a sign of great respect. By then, the Milesians had roundly defeated us. Their weapons were finer, their numbers too great. When Nuada fell, Crom Dagda gave his life to give us a better one."

"Cromnasa."

"Yes." Again, he saluted Bri Reis. "We were mortal once, or mostly so. The Dagda sacrificed himself to give us dominion over Death and its realm— the land we tread today— Tech Duinn. Its king must be eager for company, don't you think, Yin?"

Kaer Yin grunted as they passed through the portcullis into a second courtyard cloaked in shadows. Una didn't need to read his mind to know how worried he was.

She swallowed the lump in her throat.

"Come, ladies," Tam Lin chimed, dismounting in the courtyard. He reached up to help Rian down. She sagged against him just enough that he was obliged to keep one arm wrapped tightly around her waist. Despite the riot of conflicting fears and emotions raging through Una's heart, she raised a brow at the smug triumph in the Prince of Connaught's expression. Shar noticed too and glared at his boots, jaw clenched.

Una's eyes flashed at Kaer Yin as he helped her dismount.

His compressed lips said it all. *Yeah, I saw.*

"Let's go greet our dreaded old uncle, shall we?" said Tam Lin cheerfully.

Rian allowed herself to be scooped high into his arms without ado. Her acute exhaustion was plain.

Una opened her mouth to protest, but Kaer Yin's hand caught her elbow. "No, love. She can barely walk alone, and he means well, anyway, for Tam Lin. Let it be for now."

Shar Lianor followed the pair through the courtyard.

He seemed far from happy. Had the signs been there all the while?

"How long has this been going on?" she demanded.

"Since Rosweal. She's oblivious, of course." Una socked him lightly in the ribs. He winced. "Ow! What was that for?"

"You're a bloody idiot! That's why," she whisper-screeched. "If he tries *anything*, I will murder him."

Kaer Yin rubbed his offended bruises. "He's hardly a predator, you know?"

She narrowed her eyes. "Consider my warning lodged."

"Well," he cleared his throat, threading his arm through hers. "As threats go, that might do the trick but don't count on it. We have greater concerns, and their affairs are not our business."

"*Our*, nothing. I love that girl, Kaer Yin."

"As do I," he said, realizing he meant it. "No harm that doesn't naturally befall any young heart shall happen to Rian in my care. All right?" On a whim, she stood on her tiptoes to kiss the right side of his mouth. He made a low sound. "What was that for?"

"So you'll keep your promise, no matter what happens in there."

"You're afraid of him, aren't you?"

She looked up at the imposing central keep; rushing water echoed around the courtyard. "I think I'm afraid of myself."

His lips brushed her forehead as he led her up the steps toward the entrance. Robin and the rest of their road-worn band queued up behind them; none seemed overeager. "Let's hope my uncle shares your sentiments."

X

Inside the massive but silent fortress where the servants appeared no more than flitting shades, they walked single file along a grand gallery upheld by intricately carved granite columns. The way forward was lit by gleaming orbs of pearlescent witch light, placed strategically at each darkened corner. There wasn't a shred of gilding to be seen anywhere, nor tapestries or other decoration upon the walls— just stark stone and haunting, cold light. Kaer Yin seemed to know where he was going without glancing up. He worried Damek's Ogham stone between two fingers, frowning while he turned it over repeatedly. Without breaking stride, he hung a right and up a single curving stair, then through a series of stately (if spartan) rooms warmed by blazing hearth fires.

Una had yet to see a single soul, even if she heard their whispers and felt the ever-present tingling sensation between her shoulder blades that told her she was being watched.

"I thought he'd have at least aimed to impress the mortals in our midst by now," observed Tam Lin. Robin pretended to smirk at his jesting tone, but he and the other Greenmakers clutched their weapons, clearly terrified. Down another hall, a large archway led through to a broad chamber that was swallowed up by a floor-to-ceiling slate hearth one could likely roast a bull upon. Beside it stood a frail old man wrapped in a delicate white, woolen cloak. He shivered though he should have been ablaze.

The figure turned as they approached.

Una sucked in a breath. Faris— or Diarmid!

He smiled weakly back at them. Though one could never confuse him with someone else, he was significantly changed, diminished somehow. The light in his skin had faded, and his lustrous green eyes were dull and listless as glass. The ailing King of Tech Duinn coughed. "Welcome, nephews. So good of you to drop by for a visit." His voice, too, held a dusty, hollow quality it hadn't before. Without waiting for a response, he hobbled over to an oversized velvet chair and sank into its cushions with a haggard sigh.

"What in the *nine hells* happened to you, uncle?" Tam Lin whistled as he deposited Rian onto a nearby divan. She reached out, and Una's fingers found hers of their own accord. "You look *lovely*."

Diarmid Adair had not glanced Una's way, but she knew it wouldn't be long. Her heart thundered.

"Yin happened to me, princeling. Bloody Kaer *Yin*." He shot his oldest nephew a glare that should have turned his guts to water.

"I didn't ask you to do it, Diarmid." Kaer Yin dragged a chair away from the inferno in the hearth and flounced down with a petulant scowl. "Why you're being a prat about it now is beyond me."

"Do me a favor and shut your fool mouth," retorted Diarmid, shaking his head. "Given time to think it over first, I might have made a better decision."

Una noted the seeping bandages peeking from beneath his tunic. Their placement was mirrored on Kaer Yin's lanky frame. "You took half," she observed without thinking.

Naturally, Diarmid's head swiveled toward her. "There is much you have to learn, my dear."

She didn't realize the Sidhe had that ability— or could! This was High Manipulation for the Siorai. Only certain Alta Primas in the Cloister bore such skills. She didn't bother to ask him how he'd followed her train of thought. Fascinated, despite her fear, she didn't look away. "Can you heal too?"

"Surely you know I can't, Prima Moura."

"Right. The Sixth Law prevents one from—"

"That's the wrong question, and you've often proven it untrue enough, haven't you?"

She flushed. "No, there is *always* a cost."

His green eyes scanned her from her torn slippers to the crown of her matted hair. "Is that right?"

"I mean…" her tongue felt heavy and sour in her mouth.

"What are you talking about?" Kaer Yin scowled freely now.

"He's a Manipulator."

"Like you?"

"Yes."

"No," Diarmid interjected. "Apparently not."

Tam Lin blew air over his lower lip. "Are either of you capable of speaking the common bloody tongue? What does this have to do with anything?"

Diarmid exhaled long and hard. "You've come here for a purpose, I gather? Aside from safe passage for your mortal companions, that is?" he was addressing Kaer Yin, though he never took his eyes from Una's face. She repressed a quiver, her mind racing with a host of impossibilities. If he was a Manipulator, it stood to reason that he'd be beholden to the Inimitable Laws.

The Sixth Law would prevent him from exerting Spark without exchange— but if he couldn't do it… how could *she*? No trace of his thoughts touched the calm veneer of his face, but something told her he burned with curiosity.

He knows, she reasoned.

He knows what's happening to me.

"Let's get to it, shall we? Mistress Guinness needs attention, so far as I can tell."

Rian said nothing, merely squeezed Una's fingers until she lost feeling.

Kaer Yin got to his feet and handed his uncle Damek's *ogham* stone. "I took that from Una's kinsman after he chased us into the Oiche Ar Fad."

Diarmid squinted at it. "Hm, Armagh?"

"I think so."

"Interesting. Prima Moura?"

Una jumped a little. "Yes?"

"You are aware that your cousin is half Bolg?"

"Ah," she fidgeted. "Everyone in Bethany does. It's no secret."

"You'll have to fill me in; I'm unfamiliar with your family history."

She shrugged. "I don't know much, only that my aunt disappeared at Beltane during a High Council fete in Bri Leith. Months later, she stumbled out of Aes Sidhe alone, half-mad and heavy with child. She died not long after Damek was born. No one ever really talks about it."

"He's a Mac Nemed," added Tam Lin firmly. "I'll wager my best stallion on it. He's practiced in Neithana and Adrac, almost killed our idiot Crown Prince more than once, and pranced through the Veil as if it were merely a flimsy curtain. He's been instructed by someone. Someone with great power."

Kaer Yin twisted his nose at him for the insult but nodded assent. "Agreed. No one wastes so much effort on a bastard child of little import. Only the Mac Nemeds hold any real influence in Armagh. The question is, *which* Mac Nemed sired him?"

"My fainne's on Falan," Tam Lin guessed with conviction. "The old goat might be a useless dandy, but he's never lacked stamina. Half the city is rumored to have sprung from his overused stock." He made a rude sound. "He's as old as you, Diarmid. Gives one hope for the future, eh?"

Una rolled her eyes.

Rian sneered.

Bloody men.

Kaer Yin cleared his throat. "Ah, well, he could be. I've long heard the Bolg King has kept well behind his walls at Tir Macha on the Lough, and in all these years, I've never heard of any of his bastards enjoying the favor Damek must have done."

"Who else could it be, Yin? Aside from Sionnavar and Morcan, the Mac Nemeds are out of living males to extend their line."

"Falan's son was alive then, wasn't he?"

Tam Lin was startled. "Falan the *Younger*? I think not."

"Why? It's hardly a stretch."

"Because I knew him, that's why. He's a cousin on my mother's side. Falan was many things, but a lover of women, never. If you take my meaning?"

"While that may be true, I don't see how it staves my argument. Or do you imagine men who prefer men cannot sire offspring?"

"Oh, I remember the day you two met, well enough. Until that upstart faerie had a go, I've never seen another man put you on your back foot during a duel." He shook his head over a caustic laugh. "Utterly enamored of you, too. Fought hard for your attention that Imbolg. I'll never forget it."

Kaer Yin shrugged a shoulder. "He had good taste. Still, it doesn't negate my argument."

Una pinched the bridge of her nose. "Wait, you're saying Damek's father was the Prince of Armagh?"

"The late prince, yes."

"The one who died at Dumnain?"

Kaer Yin flushed, and Una immediately felt sorry for the reminder. "Yes."

Diarmid exasperated, "Why is any of this important?"

"Because," said Kaer Yin. "Bishop has claimed the Duchy of Bethany, uncle. What do you imagine is next if he is indeed the son of Falan Mac Nemed?"

"He may declare whatever he likes. Henry FitzDonahugh has also lain claim to Bethany. You might remember him, Yin, as the man who near singlehandedly conquered half the bloody Continent for his brother."

"Yeah, five decades ago, when he still had teeth. Bishop boasts twenty thousand men: superior cavalry, infantry, and bottomless archers. These are seasoned knights and yeomen, fully armed and able to wreak havoc in the Midlands. He'll accrue silver and men aplenty the further he's left to his own devices. If I believed that was his purpose. I suspect he'll march on the Red City before long."

Here was Robin's turn to snort. He'd worked his way to the larder, where many wine decanters had mysteriously appeared, and was busy pouring himself a large goblet. "Bollocks and nonsense, that. He's dreamin' if he thinks he can take the Citadel so easily."

With a sharp intake of breath, Una lashed out to knock the vessel from his hand before he could manage a single sip. "What in the bloody hells did ye do that for?" he grumbled petulantly.

"Don't you know where you are, *idiot*?" Rian hissed from behind her.

Diarmid chuckled. "No need for such theatrics, Mistress Guinness. They're hardly poisonous."

Her eyes cut deep. "Forgive me if I don't take your word for it, *Faris*."

"Suit yourself," he said, though his lip bore a slight twitch that spoke volumes.

At the mention of poison, Una stared once more at her shoes, her heart pounding against her ribs like a war drum.

It won't be long now, she thought.

Conversation is foreplay to demand.

How would she answer him when the time came? She snuck a nervous glance at Kaer Yin, who, she knew, played for time. Though he seemed affable enough, she could feel the controlled menace rolling from Diarmid in waves. *He's good at hiding his emotions, but he's angry, perhaps more than that, even?*

She felt a tremor of anticipation.

No doubt aware of her attention, Diarmid craned his neck toward her. "If I'd wanted to harm any of you, I daresay I wouldn't need to be clever about it. You are my guests. You may eat and drink without fear of reprisal or debt. I give you my word."

Robin sauntered back to the larder without ado, sparing Rian an exaggerated brow lift. She wiped her nose. "It's your funeral."

"Now, mistress," laughed Diarmid. "That's hardly fair. I've offered you no violence."

"Perhaps our opinions of abduction, forced starvation, and imprisonment differ, my lord?"

A cold draft crisscrossed the chamber. "Is that right?"

Well, here we go…

Una gritted her teeth and straightened her spine. She had beaten him once. If called to do so again, she'd trust her Spark to answer in kind. "You heard her."

Diarmid sat up a bit straighter, his expression bright as can be given his state. "We come straight to it, then?"

"Might as well."

Kaer Yin drew closer. "Una, *mo grá*. You know I won't allow—"

She held up a hand. "He'll cheat you if he can, and you know it. I'll handle this." She thought she caught the briefest flash of approval on Tam Lin's face but focused on Diarmid. "He's been waiting up here when he could have interceded days ago. Half of us have been cut to ribbons while he twiddled his thumbs. Whatever you ask him, he'll ask for something grand in return."

"Surely, you don't mean to give offense, Prima Moura?" grinned Diarmid.

"Take it however you like."

"Una," Kaer Yin began dubiously.

"No, love. I'm the only one here who's ever bested him. Isn't that right, my lord?"

"I think 'surprised' is a more accurate term," Diarmid pointed out.

"What do you want in exchange for your help?"

"You know what I want."

She crossed her arms. "I refuse."

"What's happening here, Yin?" Tam Lin's wine halted midway to his lip, brow quirking.

"How should I know?" he spat.

"Don't tell me you don't feel the rightness of this place, sighing along your skin, Una. You belong here," Diarmid went on.

Una gave a frustrated sigh. "Look, I can stand here all day and bandy words with you, or we can be done with this?"

"You'll stay with me, willingly."

"No. I'll give you something better than that. In exchange for granting us safe harbor and conduct through your lands, untainted food and drink, supplies, and anything else we might ask of you without hidden agenda or toll— I'll heal you right now."

His mouth opened and closed like a fish. After a while, he croaked, "This is something you can do?"

"I think you know I can. Do we have a deal, or do I challenge you directly?"

"Challenge... *me...?*" He gawped at her like she'd sprouted fangs.

Una clenched her fist, and the chamber seemed to darken around her. Diarmid didn't cringe so much as slam himself back into his chair. Kaer Yin snatched his hand from the small of her back like she'd burned him. Her Spark was a raging river in her blood, limitless and free. "What's it going to be, my lord?"

Diarmid stood with effort, closing the distance between them with exaggerated menace. He stopped a hand's breadth away. She stared up at him (and it was quite a hike) in unblinking confidence. "You," he smiled down at her. "Are a prize I cannot forego. I will heal in time, but you... you will be mine. *My* subject." He raised a hand as if to pat the thickening air around her. "My Lady," he crooned.

"*My Lady*, uncle." Kaer Yin's hand gripped his pommel.

"Does Midhir know whom you're bringing home, boy? He makes much noise about being a humanist, but you and I know he'll never accept a Milesian for your bride. She's better off with me."

Una took a step forward, and Diarmid recoiled. He recovered quickly enough but too late to conceal his reaction. He was afraid of her. Her lips pulled into a leer. "You will heal, sure. In a few weeks, maybe a few months. Yours is not an ordinary wound."

"You promised you'd give me *anything* I asked for in return. Remember? You begged me to save his life. You owe me."

"I refuse," she repeated, though she knew he had a just claim in the back of her mind. "I'd rather fight you and die now. You decide what works best for you."

"You would lose. In the Oiche Ar Fad, one does not simply circumvent fate. I hold your *geis*. Such a vow is forever."

She blew a lock of hair out of her eyes, her fists balling at her sides. "What compromise, then?"

"Una!" screeched Rian.

"Damn you, woman." Kaer Yin rounded on her rather than his uncle. "Have you lost your bloody mind?"

"Answer my question," she continued, ignoring everyone but Diarmid. "What will you take in exchange for all I have asked?"

Diarmid contemplated her in silence for a few moments. "I will set all your friends free, help my nephews with whatever they ask, and come to Kaer Yin's aid when he calls— if you remain here with me."

Kaer Yin drew Nemain. Tam Lin caught his arm. "Cousin, let her manage this, as you admonished me."

"Denied," she argued. "I vow to return all the power I stole from you right now."

"You stole nothing that was not already yours to take. Besides, my powers are not so easily diminished, child."

"What do you mean?"

"Did you steal from me or unlock something within yourself?"

Licking her lips, she shared a nervous glance with Kaer Yin. She hadn't expected such a question and had no idea how to respond. He shrugged off Tam Lin's staying arm. "Enough with this bait and catch. Una is not a mare I'd trade for road access. I am a son of Midhir Adair, and any claim you think to make is moot."

"I am a *king*, boy," laughed Diarmid. "And you are in my realm. You will—"

"No, I won't. I think you'll find this belongs to the High King, my father, and all other realms. I am your liege lord, uncle dear. I do not give you leave to make deals with my future wife."

"The mortals in your midst won't survive your arrogance, princeling."

"You will grant them safe passage because I command you to. You will aid us whenever I deem necessary because I *ask* you to. Are we clear?"

A goblet appeared in Diarmid's hand without fanfare. He took a long sip, and then it vanished again as quickly. He smoothed his tunic. "Only my brother can command me, Kaer Yin. You may outrank me at Court, but not here. In Tir Falias, you are subject to my whims. I prefer to deal with the girl, thank you."

"Should I kill you to prove my point?"

"Again," he smirked. "You're free to try."

Before Una could turn her eye from one to the other, Kaer Yin had shoved his cousin backward and lunged for Diarmid. Though it was hard to track the speed with which the two circled one another, Una saw Nemain score a shallow cut to Diarmid's shoulder, one against his thigh before he clenched his fingers, and Kaer Yin was lifted into the air. With a grunt, Diarmid held him aloft only long enough to slam him into the stone floor with dizzying force. Nemain skittered across the room.

Drink in hand; Robin hopped over it.

Undeterred, Kaer Yin was on his feet and at his uncle again with both larks in hand. Breathing heavily, Diarmid doffed his cloak, eyes fierce. He cracked the knuckles of both hands, a dark shimmer hovering over each digit. She next saw Kaer Yin sailing bodily over the Diarmid's abandoned chair and crashing into the wall. Laughing, Diarmid advanced on him. "Not so confident now, are we, boy?"

Kaer Yin got up, wiping blood from his nose with a filthy sleeve. He winked over his head at Una. "I don't know; it seems I have you right where I want you."

Too late, Diarmid turned to discover Una slipping up behind him. Her fingers dug into the skin at his torn collar. "*Down*," she sang, and down he went—to his knees only— this was the King of Tech Duinn, after all. "*Hold*," she ordered, panting with the effort required to keep him still. Like before, there was so, *so* much power beneath his skin. She struggled to contain her Spark's immense greed at the touch.

She sank with him, whimpering.

To her surprise, he covered her hand with his own. "I'll give you everything you want. Don't be shy."

She struggled with the effort to keep them both still. Her blood surged like molten lava in her veins. She heard the dead whisper from the corner of her conscience and felt their calm presence at the edge of her sanity.

Yes, sister. We feel you too.

She opened her mouth to speak but choked on her words. Her Spark roared, *yes, yes, yes!* — through her cells.

"Una, let go!" cried Rian, one hundred miles away.

But she couldn't. They were locked together, she and the King of Tech Duinn. As she took from him, so did he steal bits from her, an exchange more intimate than anything she'd ever experienced. Her Spark, however, grew so enormous that Tir Falias rumbled beneath her knees. Diarmid moaned with pain and more— pleasure or triumph, she couldn't be sure which, "Enough! Stop, Una, before you destroy yourself."

She could drain him dry now.

She knew it.

He knew it.

Although, he was right. One cannot consume the cosmos and remain corporeal. The flesh could only bear so much. "Compromise, or we both die now."

His spine bowed a bit. His forehead touched hers. He gnashed his teeth. "Agreed. Una, let go."

It took every ounce of strength she'd ever had to pry herself away. They collapsed together on the cold floor, exhausted and breathing hard. Rian limped to her side, though she and Diarmid saw only each other. Kaer Yin caught Rian around the waist, backing her off. Diarmid sat up, once again whole. His hand pressed against his chest, and the wound was no longer there. He exhaled slowly. "I grant you your boon; ask it."

It took a while for her to find her tongue. "My freedom, our freedom, their safety, and Kaer Yin's aid. That is my price."

"For how long?" his tone hinted that he wouldn't wait indefinitely; his eyes gleamed with a desire of a nonsexual nature. He craved the power in her blood. The flesh was irrelevant.

Her nerves thrummed with renewed energy. Whatever had transpired between them, they were bound. She could never deny it. "However long I might live, I will always be mortal. You may have what you ask upon this life's *natural* conclusion."

"Una! Stop it!" Rian whimpered.

Diarmid glowed with health and vigor. "My Lady, we have an accord."

Avowed

n.e. 508
Dor Enair
Oiche ar Fad

"I've come to tell you, you were right. My sources have revealed a large, two-pronged force, moving north as we speak," commented Diarmid from Kaer Yin's doorway many hours later. Kaer Yin kept his back to the door, staring at the waxing moon from his balcony railing and taking long puffs from a witchroot pipe. Seemingly disinterested, he merely grunted in response. Tapping his bowl clear on the stone railing, Robin patted his shoulder on his way out. Diarmid took Robin's place with a heavy sigh. "I did what I must, Yin. You were never meant to keep that girl."

"That is not for you to say."

"Though she may be mortal, she is far from human. You know I'm telling the truth. You've seen her power. She's a Brehon, born and bred." He paused to note the ticking muscle in Kaer Yin's jaw. "In the old days, she'd have been given to me as a child. Unguided power like hers is dangerous."

"Who do you think you're talking to, old man? I know what you want her for, and it has little to do with anything *she* might gain from you."

"I will not deny that she stirs me— her gifts are unlike anything I have ever seen. These many eons, I've never been bested by a mortal. Not once."

"You will be again. I promise you."

Diarmid gave a soft laugh. "She is mortal, nephew. One day you will be parted, no matter how special she is."

Kaer Yin fixed him with an ice-cold glare. "I'll kill you long before then."

"You might be the best fighter among the Tuatha De Dannan, but you're not a god. You can no more defeat me than you could cut the moon in half."

He didn't lie. Many believed the Oiche Ar Fad would wink out of existence without Diarmid's stewardship. Kaer Yin had no idea if that were true but was tempted to toss the old fool from this tower to test the theory anyway. Much good it would do him, Diarmid could fly. "Release her from this vow."

"No."

Kaer Yin took a long, deep breath. "What will you take in exchange for her promise?"

"I've already agreed to wait until her life has *naturally* expired. You will have lost her by that point anyway. I'm being exceptionally generous."

"Generous?" Kaer Yin cringed. "You mean to enslave the woman I love. Whether she is among the living at that point makes no difference."

"She would exist. Isn't that what you want?"

"Do you think I haven't seen the Sluagh here in Tech Duinn? If they've any memories before they were dragged here for one misdeed or other, they cannot share them. You would take her soul, damn her here to this horrible place, all because you're bored or lonely. I'll ask again. What will you take to release her from her vow?"

Diarmid smirked at him. "What if I ask for your throne, Yin? Would you be so willing, then?"

Kaer Yin's rebuttal caught in his throat. Was that even something he *could* give? He didn't think so. Kaer Yin might not have the power to rip Diarmid from Tech Duinn, but Midhir certainly did, and he'd never allow his son to bestow his birthright upon his duplicitous younger brother. "You jest."

"Crom was my father, you realize. The blood that makes you Dannan flows doubly strong within my breast. Midhir rules because his mother was queen while mine was merely a wandering Brehon." He mimicked Kaer Yin's posture at the railing. "I will make her immortal. Isn't that what you want?"

Kaer Yin stretched to his full height. "I care about what *she* wants, you meddling old fool. I will not allow her to bargain away her soul for meaningless platitudes. Name your price, Diarmid."

"Have you considered the damage she might do, the horrors she might sow one day if you forbid my help? You know many things, *Ard Tiarne*, but you are no Brehon. You cannot understand the weight of her burgeoning powers."

"Very well, then train her. Guide her. Be of assistance to her. If you care so much about her future, you can offer her this much without demanding payment in return."

Diarmid laughed through his nose. "You are no god, no Brehon, no king— and I am no Kneeler's saint."

Knowing the argument would further devolve, Kaer Yin tapped his bowl empty against his boot and tucked it back into this belt. "I'm done with this, for now, Diarmid. There will be further violence between us if you don't shut your mouth. You have my offer, and you *will* take it. That's all there is to this. You may believe this place can't exist without you, but I doubt it." Diarmid inhaled to rebut. Kaer Yin cut him off. "I would ask you not to insert yourself into my life and relationships in such a heavy-handed way, uncle. Set your price since you're a selfish turd who can't resist. The next time I broach this topic, you'd better be prepared. Una is not for sale."

"I don't—"

"Tell me more of Bishop's forces," Kaer Yin snarled, shortening his following exhortation. "If you speak her name to me, it had better be with a counteroffer. Now, what of the Southers?"

Diarmid recovered himself, but a deep fire burned behind his irises.

You have no right to take offense, you self-aggrandizing bastard, Kaer Yin thought.

This isn't the dark ages any longer.

He considered that there might be a real contest between them one day very soon. If Diarmid refused Una's freedom, Kaer Yin would have no choice. There was little doubt what Midhir would make of this. The Ard Ri would never support Diarmid's heavy-handed claim to Doma's granddaughter, less the Princess of Bethany. Diarmid was dreaming if he thought he would get away with this.

Unless... another thought tiptoed through Kaer Yin's mind. *She isn't really what he's after.* With no hint of intention, besides mild irritation visible in his uncle's expression, Kaer Yin cautioned himself.

You have only one thing, which Fiachra Dubh could want. His flippant comment from before rang red, despite its seeming sarcasm.

'What if I ask for your throne?'

What if, indeed?

Kaer Yin needed to discuss this with Tam Lin and his uncle Bov. If anyone could help unravel the labyrinth of Diarmid's ambitions, Bov Dearg could.

This is not the first time Diarmid has made a play for my father's crown, and he's one of two men with the power to be a real threat. Be careful here...

"They're amassing on two fronts. I've learned that Bishop marches with a quarter of his cavalry from Tara, which he sacked in one night. They move along the Taran High Road at quite the clip."

"And the second?"

"Infantry, yeomen longbowmen, and short-range artillery, led by some three hundred cavalry. Nearly twenty-thousand men, as you surmised earlier."

"And?"

"Four Bretagn warships follow an ice-breaker through the Straits of Manannan, bearing an additional thousand men."

Kaer Yin swore under his breath. Sometimes, he hated being right. "Then it begins."

"The march to Rosweal must be a feint."

"It's not."

"Why do you say that?"

Kaer Yin shrugged. "He knows I'll be there."

X

U̲n̲a̲ a̲n̲d̲ R̲i̲a̲n̲'s̲ r̲o̲o̲m̲s̲ w̲e̲r̲e̲ the least oppressive she'd seen in the Keep. Despite the impression of its gorgeous setting and backdrop upon arrival, Tir Falias was the coldest, starkest structure she'd ever set foot in. Perhaps Diarmid expelled so much energy managing the vagaries of this terrifying Otherworld realm that he had very little verve left over for himself? What did one do for an eternity locked within a world of death, anyway?

It seems, she thought, ruefully, *you will find out soon enough.*

She paused as she sifted through the clean but straightforward tunics, leggings, and other garments; one of Diarmid's unseen servants had laid out for her. Rian would tell her this was a riddle, wouldn't she? Well, she might, if she were speaking to her. Neither Rian nor Kaer Yin had spoken to her since the fight in Diarmid's parlor.

Una sighed. Perhaps that was for the best, considering she'd have no clue what to say to either. She'd done what only she could do, and rather than try to arm wrestle the most powerful wizard in Innisfail— she'd chosen to trade. Since she had only one thing of value, her friends' safety and a powerful Manipulator's aid were well worth the bargain. Besides, a lot could happen before her 'natural' death. She could be murdered any day now, her deal rendered moot.

There was always an upside, she supposed.

Having availed herself of the giant copper tub before the fireplace and tossed the frayed remnants of Rian's homespun into the flames— Una nearly groaned in ecstasy, pulling a dry, soft linen shirt over her head. One could easily forget such luxuries roaming the wild and dangerous places between realms. Since she'd spent many warm and well-fed weeks at her father's court, she'd nearly forgotten how hard the elements could be on the body. Tucking her tunic into her belt, she glanced at Rian's closed door. She had no doubt one of them suffered more for the latest misadventure. Without thinking, she padded over on bare feet, her fist poised to knock.

"Don't wake her," Kaer Yin said. Her head whipped around. She hadn't heard him come in. "Diarmid's seen to her. She'll be fine."

He leaned against the outer door, eyes glittering with fury, hurt, and more.

She swallowed, lowering her hand to her chest to keep it from shaking. His expression made her nervous. "How long have you been there?"

"Not long." He uncrossed his arms. He'd bathed too and donned the same simple yet elegant linen she now wore. His long silver-blond hair had been combed and plaited along the sides, exposing the nine gold chains in his right ear. He looked beautiful. With a hitch in her breath, she sent her gaze away. Unsure where to go to gain some distance, she went to the window and sat down. Unfortunately, he followed, sparks trailing in his wake. "Anything to say?"

She lifted her chin. "I did what I had to."

"I know you believe that, but you're wrong."

"The two of us together couldn't beat him, Kaer Yin. If I'd held on much longer, we would be dead. I know it." She shivered. "There was so much... *too* much. I'm not omnipotent."

"Neither is he."

"Coulda fooled me."

Exhaling, he sat beside her, moving her legs across his lap. She tried to squirm aside to give him room, but he held on— not tightly enough to be commanding, but enough to send a message. His hand felt very warm through the flimsy fabric of her leggings.

"What's done is done. I know why you did it, even if I know how bloody stupid it was."

She made a face at him. "Fine talk, for a man who has no idea what he's talking about. Diarmid's power is like a sky pregnant with lightning. If you imagine I could absorb all of that on my own, you're mad."

"You've done it before."

"Yeah, in our world. Not here. This place is different. My Spark feels bottomless." She paused, mulling it over. "There was a moment in the parlor where reality felt permeable, like a thread I could pull and unwind the universe. I can't... you wouldn't understand."

He laid his head against the shutters with a soft smile. "I'll never let this go, love. You know that. Your *geis* must be destroyed."

"No argument there." She distracted herself from his nearness by brushing a wrinkle from his sleeve, where it draped over her thigh. "If you've any brilliant ideas, I'm all ears. We must accept what few fortunes this trade has bought us. All right?"

He nodded.

"Good," she breathed a relieved sigh. "When are we leaving?"

"Tomorrow evening, as dawn breaks."

"Is he coming with us?"

"Yes."

She made a face. "He'd better. The bastard."

Kaer Yin's fingers ran back and forth over her knee. If he didn't stop doing that, she'd forget that they had much to discuss. His eyes were mirrors, reflecting the vivid flush of her cheeks. Clearing a small mountain from her throat, she tried to squirm away. He held her legs fast. "That tickles."

"Does it?"

His hand moved higher.

She drew an audible breath. "Yes. Leave off, you. What about Bethany and Tairngare? Shar told me Diarmid had news of the Midlands. What did he say?"

Kaer Yin's pupils darkened.

"I don't want to talk about them right now." Tucking an arm under both knees, he pulled her closer. The fingers exploring her thigh slid up her side to assert the faintest pressure against her breast, summoning a small gasp from her throat. She couldn't recall them ever being so close before. There was always someone nearby, watching. There was no one now but the two of them. Her heart went feral against her ribs, like a trapped hare. "Come here, Una."

"I don't—" she began, but his fingernail brushed her nipple, and she gasped. "What are you doing? We need to—"

"It can wait."

His overlarge hand closed over her breast, soft but demanding. Una's flesh yielded readily, molding to his probing palm like unmolded clay. "I, for one, have waited long enough."

A soft sigh escaped her lips.

Kaer Yin's fingers wound through the hair at the base of her skull, crushing her mouth to his. The next thing she knew, she was entirely astride his lap with his face buried in the 'V' of her tunic. Through the gauze of their linen bottoms, she felt him pressing upward. Her eyes fluttered shut with his tongue tracing a wet line between her breasts and the heat of his length resting against her navel. She moaned despite her nerves. Very lightly, he rocked her hips over his.

When his mouth claimed hers for the second time, she forgot what she meant to say to him. Thoughts leaked from her mind like water from a broken sieve. He unlaced her tunic to her ribs with one hand while the other pressed her bottom against him, establishing a slow but insistent rhythm. After several gasping breaths, Una reached down and unclasped her belt.

Kaer Yin tossed the offensive accessory away with a growl. Her braes and brassiere revealed themselves through the gap in her tunic. She watched his pale hand roam the expanse of the tattooed bronze flesh at her collarbone, gently over each breast through her filmy undergarment… then lower still. She couldn't recall if his eyes had ever been another color besides black.

"May I?"

"You're asking now?" she huffed, working her own hands into his shirt. His skin felt cool at first touch, then heated below her wandering fingers. His upper chest and shoulders muscles were enough to make a sculptor weep. Forcing him back against the shutters, she tore the garment over his head just as his right hand cupped her mound of venus. She cried out into the flesh of his solar plexus, teeth grazing his nipple. He muttered something nonsensical in Ealig, and she sighed, "Don't you dare stop."

Her tunic vanished entirely.

Kaer Yin's fingers pushed below the hem of her braes, working lightly, maddeningly against her sex. Her ears drowned in her heartbeat and the soft but masculine sounds he made as her nails dragged along his shoulders.

She kissed him so hard that his breath puffed into her mouth. A delicious fire built in her low belly, stoked by the unrelenting heat of his hands. As his fingers worked against her, his free hand squeezed and molded her posterior. For several minutes, she lost herself to the ruthless cadence he set.

Una's back bowed.

Her hips moved of their own accord.

At last, when she could take no more, a long slow whimper escaped her throat. Stars swam through her vision, flashing white and red at once. "Kaer Yin!" she cried, feeling herself hefted into his arms.

Though she couldn't begin to tell how it happened, the mattress yielded to her form, now fully nude. Breathing hard, she cracked an eye, finding him leaning over her, his face shining. She doubted she'd ever seen a more lovely sight in her life.

He was winter and summer together, glorious as a moonlit glen and powerful as a sun-soaked mountain. The words to describe him failed her. He leaned over her, all corded sinew and grace. His hair brushed against her naked shoulder. "Are you ready, *mo grá*?"

Her legs wrapped around his waist, drawing him down. "I thought we were done talking?"

X

K*aer* Y*in* *grinned through the* following day (or evening, as all was opposite in the Oiche Ar Fad*)*, unconcerned by the glares and grumbles his comrades sent his way. Tam Lin whistled upon first sight of him. "Someone's awful chipper, considering how buggered we all are."

Kaer Yin poured himself a tankard of mead from the larder, smirking as if it were carved in. "Perhaps a proper bed and a warm meal were just the thing."

"A warm somethin', all right," said Robin with a squint. "Thought ye were peeved enough to boil her yesterday?"

"Looks to me like someone boiled his brains, instead," commented Tam Lin, absently chewing on an apple while Shar loaded his horse. He turned out rather smart, considering the long ride they were about to undertake. The distance might be covered much more swiftly here than in the corporeal world above, but it would be an arduous journey. All that fine white linen would be smattered in mud— or worse— in no time.

Still, Tam Lin managed to appear resolute. He wore his long red-gold curls in a complex braid clipped with a silver club. If Kaer Yin cared enough to ask, he might wonder aloud why his cousin had made such an effort. Then, he saw the girls come down the outer stairs, each clean and dressed in crisp white linen and fur. Rian's hair was unbound and silver-white in the queer Otherworld light. Diarmid's magic had done its work well. She appeared healthier than he'd ever seen her.

Sparing Tam Lin a long side-eye, Kaer Yin quipped, "Whose brains are boilt?"

"Nonsense. Lacking cuisine, one must make do with *hors d'oeuvres*, no?"

"Hey now," Robin spat from around his pipe stem. "Say that again, and it'll be me that ruins yer fancy duds. That girl's a good'un, she is. Mind yer manners."

Tam Lin raised his hands. "No harm. Just a mild fascination with a pretty face. Ask Yin; he'll tell you all about it."

Kaer Yin's fist cracked out faster than Tam Lin could account. He staggered backward, clasping his hand over his streaming nose. "Ow! Why'd you do that?"

Stubbornly smiling, Kaer Yin shrugged. "If I didn't know she'll tell you to go to the hells herself, I'd warn you to watch your mouth."

Shar tossed a handkerchief at his lord but otherwise made no further move to help him. Tam Lin scowled. "You too, Lianor?"

Shar didn't answer. Instead, he beamed at both girls as they arrived on the scene, confused at Tam Lin's bloodied nose and Kaer Yin's stupid grin. He bowed. "May I help you with your bags, ladies?"

Rian accepted, but Una waved them off. She sidled around Kaer Yin and Rian to her mare. "Made a disparaging comment, I take it?"

Kaer Yin held her bridle while she looped her bag around her saddle horn. She flushed a gorgeous shade of dusky rose at his nearness. That he could affect her so powerfully, so quickly… made him smile the wider. Her skin against his, fists balled in her hair, the cradle of her hips rocking above him, tracked through his thoughts nonstop. He was the luckiest man in Innisfail. "Nothing of import, I swear."

"Humph," she said, turning toward him. "You're as bad a liar as ever." Standing on her tiptoes, she kissed the center of his chin before swinging herself into the saddle. Once seated, Kaer Yin handed up her reins. His pulse pounded in his neck. "Stop looking at me like that. We have places to be."

"I think Rosweal can rot."

"Now, now," chided Robin from his saddle. "That's not very nice, is it?"

"Later," she promised, with a wink that turned his guts to jelly.

"For Maeve's sake," groaned Diarmid from the stairway. "Can we *please* proceed without the ridiculous mating rituals?" He didn't look overly happy to be leaving the comfort of his home, either. He was the only one appropriately dressed for the occasion, head to toe in black. The depth of his scowl only deepened the singularity of his appearance. He leaped onto his destrier's back in a single motion— a move so graceful that Kaer Yin was reminded his people were once horse lords of a distant tundra. "It's not even spring, is it?"

"No," remarked Kaer Yin dryly. "It's not. Though Beltane will be here soon enough."

"Don't hold your breath, princeling. I know your father better than you."

Kaer Yin knew something too. His epiphany at Samhain sang through his blood. "I don't think you do, old man. Anyway," he sighed, swinging himself (far less elegantly, mind) into his saddle. "How long before we reach Gerry and the others? All of them had better be hale, or you and I will revisit yesterday's conversation."

"They're fine," Diarmid enunciated through his teeth. Well, wasn't his uncle in a black humor today? Kaer Yin grinned wider. He couldn't help himself. "They never made it to Tech Duinn. We'll find them sheltering at the Crossroads."

Tam Lin had managed to clean his face up enough to look sullen. "Lucky for them. You let us be hacked halfway to the Kneeler's Hell. Why's that, by the by?"

Diarmid rolled a shoulder. "I wasn't feeling well."

Una twitched beside him. "All better now, aren't you?"

"Immeasurably." He bowed.

"Excellent. Renege, and you forfeit. Remember that."

"As My Lady commands."

Kaer Yin thought he'd be bloodying another nose in moments, but Robin broke the spell. "Ah, for fuck's sake! Can we get to the bloody war already? This is boring the shite outta me."

"Indeed," smirked Kaer Yin. "I hope Barb's brought all the uishge up from the river by now. I think we deserve a few drams."

Interlude

n.e. 508
05, dor enair
Rosweal

Barb was, for once, at a total loss. She crumpled the third message in as many days and tossed it over the balustrade. This newest message had been brought by post rider from Pormark— the very same village Damek's expeditionary force had marched from the *last* time they'd attacked Roroweal. At least the little bastard was consistent. Dumnain, then Vale would be next; she didn't need to be told. Though, on this occasion, it seemed that his cousin wasn't Bishop's primary objective.

'Bend the knee, or suffer my wrath,' it read.

'*Any resistance to the one true lord of Eire will be met with swift, lethal force.* She'd just bet. *'Divest yourselves from Tairngare's corrupt influence. Submit, and be rewarded.* At swordpoint, no doubt. *'You have one week to comply,'* it went on, then finished with a bit of bollocks. Barb laughed out loud to recall. *'I await your favorable reply. Signed, Damek Bishop Mac Nemed, son of Falan the Younger of Armagh— the true Crown Prince of Innisfail'*.

Well. One could never accuse Lord Bishop of cowardice, could one? His balls swung lower than any man she'd yet encountered. In Barb's case, that was quite a number. Pormark had surrendered without a fuss. Dumnain knew better than to try, given their history of defying Souther lords on the march. When his army reached Vale, Rosweal would receive no such warning. She'd already made friends with the Lord of Clare once before, hadn't she? A sound somewhere between a snort and a growl issued from her throat. Beside her, Dabs slunk away. "Don't fash yerself, Dabs. I haven't killed anyone yet for bad news. I don't aim to start with ye."

Dabney, all three hundred pounds of him, visibly relaxed. Sighing, she crossed her arms over the railing, looking down on her rebuilt taproom. It had only been a few weeks since the last assault, and she had no desire to repeat the process a third time. Alas, she knew life wouldn't trade a tinker's fart for her wishes. No stranger to adversity was Barb Dormer. Unlike many wealthy cousins, she hadn't spent her life in the Red City. She'd started there, but life in the Cloister hadn't been in her cards.

Watching the workers dart around, she thought about all she had lost and gained. *The Hart* had never quite been the soul of comfort or refinement, though it bore a certain rustic charm as most things in Rosweal tended to.

There were no fine oil lamps, plush carpeting, or velveteen curtains to add that touch of class. Instead, the walls and floors were simply grooved pine. Large timber beams raced along the ceiling to meet at the crux of the primary support, which had once been the keel of her father's last merchant vessel. From this, a vast chandelier crafted from iron and antlers squatted over the tap's center, a macabre centerpiece, she reckoned. Still, with two massive stone hearths, clean tables and chairs, and a brand-new oak bar— what need did she have for finery?

The Hart was handsome enough, her girls were clean and attractive enough, and her pride of ownership was more than bloody enough.

The Hart was hers.

It was *hers*.

Her father had left her a windowless, dirt-floored taproom stuffed with dive barrels, broken stools, and semi-conscious inebriates. In just fifteen years, she'd built this place into an institution, carved its stellar reputation from literal muck and gloom. Barb's mother's family had been something in Tairngare long ago. They'd been right sorts, with plenty of wealth and position. But fortune, as ever, had been a cruel bitch of a mistress. After her mother's death, her father made many bad investments, eventually costing Barb her place in the Cloister. She lacked the Spark to attain a rank higher than Nova and was summarily dismissed for non-payment. Without her mother's family's support, she and her father were left to scratch a living out of this most inhospitable corner of Innisfail. Her father drank himself to death in this very room.

And she… well, she'd ventured to Ten Bells for a span, then to *The Butterfly* in Bethany. She soon made a name for herself among the lower Bethonair nobility for a time. When her beauty began to fade— as often happens in this, the oldest of professions— she came home.

Now here she stood, fifty years old, owner of the best if the least presumptuous establishment in the Borderlands. Barb Dormer was the undisputed queen of the Greenmakers' Guild, the most influential gang of ruffians, thieves, courtesans, and smugglers this side of the Straits of Mannanan. She'd be Siora-damned if she were going to hand any of that over to the Duch's calculating prick of a nephew.

Dabney, sloe-eyed and quiet, waited while she struck a match. Her eyes met his as she took a long pull from the fancy brass pipe Robin had brought her from Ten Bells. "How many barrels of oil did we find in Matt's cellar, Dabs?"

He shook his meaty head. "Dunno, missus. Lots."

She sucked her teeth at him, poor lamb. It wasn't his fault Siora had neglected his brains for his girth. "Do they fill at least half the cellar?"

He thought it over for a while. "'Spose so."

She took another drag, mind racing. Georgie, Pad, and Mac stared up at her, afraid. They'd worked night and day to fortify the town walls for weeks. Most houses on the Hilltop had already donated garden fences, carriage houses, and even rear walls in their quest for more stone. She could almost hear a collective groan from their overworked minds. "An' how much of that black powder did we find in Solomon's warehouse? Someone other than Dabney, if ye please?"

Mac cleared his pimply throat. "'Round fifty crates, missus. However, half was soaked through after the attack. All that rain and no roof left."

She nodded. "That should be plenty. Mac, I want ye to take Dabs down the docks to Brewer's Quarter and bring me every brewer, tanner, and doper left in Rosweal."

"What for?"

She gave them all an earnest grin. "We're gonna show this faerie bastard why no one in all of Innisfail has the bollocks to fuck with Rosweal twice."

※

Five days later, Barb got the news she'd been expecting. Dumnain had thrown the gates wide for the Lord of Clare's advance army. Though this was far from a surprise, there were two other tidbits her messenger included, which she hadn't expected to hear. Damek Bishop wasn't with his men; he encircled Tairngare with the bulk of his forces, including his vanguard. Twenty-thousand men, or so her messenger told her with wide, bloodshot eyes.

The two thousand camped at Dumnain were an expeditionary force meant to accrue coin and secure the roads between each small town and hamlet, while Bishop and his allies went for the grand prize. It didn't make Rosweal any less fucked; it just gave them a bit more time to prepare for the most epic suicide one could muster. Cursing, she made her way over the planks her boys had lain over one of her fancy new moats to ogle their progress on the inner wall. Mac Looked up, sweaty and half-starved. He was a shit digger, being all knees and bony elbows, but his side of the trench between his and the outer wall fared better than those across the field.

With naught but women and skinny lads between the ages of thirteen and sixty, Barb couldn't afford to be particular.

"Mac, make sure they're savin' that dirt. We'll need it for mortar." Without waiting for a response, she took a turn around the eight-foot by a four-foot-wide chasm that she'd ordered dug through the center of what had been the Slums three days prior. As was the case before Robin had left with Ben on his fool's errand, anyone inexperienced with masonry or woodcutting, or too young or too small for stone-cutting or hauling— had been sent outside to dig.

All the massive conifers to the south had been cleared, revealing a killing field some one-hundred and fifty yards deep along the Taran High Road. The timber had been used to erect her two beautiful guard towers at either end. With nearly three hundred and sixty degrees range, standing fifteen feet high, and constructed of sturdy oak and ash, her Greenmakers could pick off Damek's cavalry from hundreds of paces away. Two more were being erected on the east and west ends, respectively.

She stepped back to admire her new trench.

It was one of three.

She'd gotten the idea from a book her father had given her many years ago, some yarn about a city defended on three sides by six concentric rings of a deep, complex moat. She couldn't manage all six with her limited resources, but she *could* and *would* make sure these three were done right. When finished, their newest defense mechanism would boast hundreds of sharp, merciless skewers below the waterline.

Instant impalement would deter any fool that dreamed of attempting to leap in, and with an eight-foot-wide mouth— impossible to wheel siege towers up to any of Rosweal's lovely new walls. Her towers stood sentinel above a settlement of some might; thanks to her fainne, quick thinking, and ornery nature, she didn't mind boasting. Their little backwater had been the sad, crumbling relic of a bygone era a few months before.

Now, it was a fortress.

She hoped they lasted long enough for Robin to see it. Tugging her furs high around her thinning throat, she paced the edge of her soon-to-be moat. "I want another row here," she shouted to Kira Boma, another Tairnganese reject of former middling importance. He was at least twelve years her senior but had studied law and engineering at the Libellum in his youth. If it could be built or argued, Kira knew his way around it. "They should jut out— like so." She gestured.

"At a seventy-five-degree angle, you mean?" he sounded bored, though he had worked as many hours each day as the rest.

Barb made a face at him. "Whatever the bloody hell ye need to do, Kira. I want whole and half trees sticking out here, ready to unhorse or impale any man brave enough to get this close. Am I clear?"

"As glass."

"How many days we have left, missus?" Mac had crept up behind her. She scowled down the Taran Road. Instead, they might have marched along the Navan High Road, but the terrain was much less agreeable for large machines and far too marrow to avoid raids from the trees. The Taran High Road was a much broader and more meandering affair, with far less cover for Greenmakers and other bandits to get ambitious about. "It takes a long while to march that many men and horses up a hilly road, miles, and miles from where they started. I expect they'll take longer than last time, lad. Soldiers need to eat, fuck, and pillage, ye know? I should think, as long as his lordship keeps busy at Tairngare, we have a few weeks yet."

Mac's face went a ghastly shade of grey. "Will we be ready?"

She didn't have an answer that would appease the boy reasonably, so she spun him about by the shoulders to get back to the dig. Kira followed her at a sedate pace.

He knew better than to ask.

X

On the twenty-ninth day of Dor Enair, a pale sun climbed into a snow-bright sky. The southern wall had grown by another six feet, and her spike-filled ditches were ready to take on water. The wall was rudimentary, lacking functional elegance of formative appeal. Large stones were haphazardly stacked on top of the other, mortared with black clay, stone dust, and sap. Kira's invention, as it turned out, and while perhaps not impregnable, it certainly was sturdy. No attempts to dislodge the stones housed in the center proved fruitful. This was hardly proof positive of its intrinsic value, but Barb would take what she could get.

Many timbers were cut into wide planks atop this wall section, piled in soaring rows some ten feet high. Plenty of height to deflect the average arrow and spear, but low enough for her towers to peer over the side at the killing field. Kira's woodworkers had done a beautiful job fitting and forming these planks into rows so tight she couldn't slip a finger between them. Beside herself with pride, she strutted across Rosweal's fresh ramparts with a sloppy smile. Though she was fully aware, with an army over two-thousand strong marching up the Taran High Road— their efforts might not be much more than window-dressing. Still, the Southers would take it as an ominous message of the ingenuity of Rosweal's stalwart residents.

Lord Bishop would get no free meal here, by Siora.

Her jaws aching from all the smiling, she caught a strange sound on the wind to the north. Her head whipped around. The mists of Aes Sidhe, as ever, occluded the distant shore. It sounded again, and her watchmen at the north wall answered belatedly. They would have to work on that bit, wouldn't they? She hefted her skirts high and bolted along the ramparts toward the horns. She'd never been much of a runner, but she dashed off as if Siora's flames licked at her ankles. It took a great deal longer than was flattering, but soon she made it to the ancient northern wall facing the river. Huffing, she saw some of her boys skip into the street. Dabs and two of Lily's brats had been busy loading barrels of gunpowder onto a wagon. They froze when they saw her, red-faced and wheezing, atop the wall. "Which way did that horn come from?"

Dabs scratched at his balding pate— the nonce.

One of the other lads pointed behind her at the river.

What? She thought.

It can't be?

Before she could crane her neck toward the border, the horn came again.

That horn *was* from Aes Sidhe!

Faster than she imagined, she skidded down two ladders to the muddy ground and out the rickety iron gate (which would also need fixing). At the docks, she stopped cold, heaving and clutching her side. The others had followed her, each wide-eyed and whispering.

From the misty shore opposite, there came the gleam of white and silver armor, the flash of pure, sylvan steel by the hundreds. They materialized from the trees— fair hair shining in the weak sunlight, brilliant eyes flashing, white stag banners snapping overhead— the Sidhe walked their mounts into the Boyne. Barb's heart flew straight into her nose.

An Fiach Fian…

The Wild Hunt.

The personal guard of the High King himself had come to Rosweal.

X

In the Oiche Ar Fad, the realm above was reflected in every body of water they passed. The stench of smoke and blood drifted toward them on a gentle morning breeze. Kaer Yin watched Una's face fall when she glimpsed the distant spires of the fortress at Tara in flames as they moved west through Tech Duinn, so the world above spun east. They would head south for two days, then swing east to reach Rosweal. Kaer Yin remained silent beside her but knew what she was thinking, regardless.

He opened his mouth to speak, but Diarmid beat him to it. "It's not your fault, Prima Moura."

"Whose fault is it, then?" she scoffed, her amber eyes full of flames. "Is this happening now?"

"No. This was some weeks past. Your cousin took Tara and Malahide by surprise, but this wasn't the first time they were attacked."

"What do you mean?"

"Groups of Sidhe raiders dressed in the High King's colors ransacked towns and villages for almost two moons before Bishop chased you from Bethany."

"One of Gilcannon's boys said something about that," Kaer Yin added. "I wouldn't put it past Bishop to attempt to turn the poor against the Ard Ri in such a low way."

"It wasn't Bishop," Diarmid argued. "A girl named Aoife Sona led the raids at the behest of her grandmother, the new Doma."

"*NO!*" Una hissed. "That *cannot* be!"

Diarmid shrugged. "I assure you it is. Liadan Mac Nemed is your Nema's true name. I always wondered how a name like 'Nema,' as in 'no one,' managed to escape the learned women in Tairngare for so long?"

Una tugged her horse to a halt. She'd gone a milky sort of green. "You know this for sure?"

"I know many things you don't, Una. You have but to ask."

Kaer Yin wanted to knock his uncle's teeth out daily.

"Yin," Tam Lin cut in. "That solves your conundrum. He is a Mac Nemed."

"I knew that already."

"Liadan Mac Nemed is the matriarch of the whole Clan, which includes him if we're right. They took Tairngare for him."

Kaer Yin shook his head. "No, they wouldn't. However highborn he is, he's still illegitimate at best. Why would Armagh plot to put a faerie by-blow on the Eirean throne? It doesn't make sense."

"He's not just *any* bastard, is he? He's Patrick Donahugh's nephew. I assume they engineered this from the beginning," Tam Lin reasoned. "Alis Donahugh disappeared from a feast at your father's table, Yin. The Duch declared war on Aes Sidhe for the slight when she returned. Wouldn't it have been convenient if the Crown Prince *had* died after Dumnain instead of Falan the Younger?"

All the warmth leeched from Kaer Yin's head at once. He struggled to hear anything but the rush of blood in his ears for a moment.

"All this time," breathed Una. "Nema was my grandmother's nemesis for forty years. That's quite an interlude to plan a rebellion."

"The subtle knife plunges deep," agreed Tam Lin.

"Took her time, didn't she?" asked Robin.

"I'm a bloody *fool*," Kaer Yin whispered. His hands shook.

"What was that?" inquired Tam Lin.

"I said, I'm a bloody fool!"

"How so?"

"'Wouldn't it have been convenient if the Crown Prince had died instead of Falan the Younger?'"

Tam Lin laughed, "I said it two seconds ago—"

"I was *supposed* to die, Lin! Only the Sidhe knew I hadn't. Falan... it was Falan all along!"

"Slow down, love," Una said, laying her hand on his. "Falan did what, exactly?"

Kaer Yin sucked in a deep breath to cool his ringing ears. "Falan was in my vanguard that day before Dumnain. He was my *aide-de-camp*. After the first day's skirmishes, he came upon me in the tent as I was preparing to break camp. Patrick was planning to withdraw and march east. I meant to follow and stamp his bones into the earth, once and for all." He winced. "Forgive me, Una."

She waved his comment away. "Go on."

"Anyway, our plans were laid and agreed upon by every officer. Falan had been the sole dissenter. He posited that the citizens of Dumnain had plotted to betray the High King from day one, which is why they eagerly joined Donahugh's rebellion. He argued in Council that we should raze the city as a lesson for the next town that would foolishly throw their coin to Patrick's banners. I remember he and Fionn arguing over the matter for nearly an hour before my uncle Bov silenced them. I might never have thought of it had you not said anything, Tam Lin."

"I still don't have the first bloody clue what you're on—" Tam Lin started.

"Don't you see? Falan Mac Nemed tried to lure me into a pointless conflict, which would have placed me in a precarious position in Eire. If I'd accepted his advice and chosen to attack, I'd have broken Dannan law at the very least. Otherwise, he could have had me killed somewhere in those narrow, twisting lanes."

"Yeah, but he got himself killed in an early morning raid on Donahugh's baggage train, and you... well, you know."

Kaer Yin stared up at the sky, laughing coldly to himself. "Who do you think ordered him to raid that train after I was informed of the execution of our prisoners in the town square? He seemed so eager to chase the perpetrators down."

"Are you saying that the townspeople didn't murder your men?" Una's voice was very soft.

"Not at all. A dozen or so *were* guilty. Many more fled when they heard Patrick had abandoned them. That was why I sent Falan to round them up, but then I saw what had been done to our men— and I— anyway, Falan and Sionnavar's agents were responsible for bringing the information to me. Patrick had given orders upon his exit, and the townsfolk had gotten carried away. The horror on Falan's face when he told me."

He pinched the bridge of his nose. "We'd cut our men down, punished the few guilty parties, and were about to leave, when the situation changed. The townsfolk grew aggressive. Someone tried to shoot me from my horse twice. The next time I looked up, I'd… everyone was gone."

Una's fingers melded with his.

"So, you're saying Falan led you into a trap? Bollocks. He took a spear to the throat an hour later," sneered Tam Lin. "If he was a criminal mastermind, he died an idiot."

"Unless," Diarmid broke in. "He didn't die."

Kaer Yin's eyes darted toward him. "You know, don't you?"

"I am not omniscient, Yin. Recognizing a face and voice from my past is hardly mysticism."

"How long have you known about Nema?"

He pursed his lips. "Years. It doesn't matter."

Una squeezed Kaer Yin's fingers so hard he thought he might lose one. "Ah, leave the skin, if you please?"

She ignored him. "If you knew who she was, why didn't you ask yourself why she was there in the first place?"

"Why would I? Do you know how many human lives *I* have chosen to live, My Lady? Eternity is quite a long time. Many of us choose to live among mortals for a span. Break up the monotony. Liadan is older than I."

Una struggled to absorb that statement. Instead, Rian asked, "So you thought a Fir Bolg queen in a position of contentious power within the greatest city in mortal Eire wasn't nefarious in the least?"

"I assumed she sought to live for a time among mortals. After all, what are seventy years in five thousand?"

"Still—"

"Nothing!" he snapped. "I might have investigated beforehand if I thought there was the cause. Until her coup, I never had reason to bother. Have we all been duped? Yes. Am I evil for failing to see it? No. Try focusing on things you *can* change rather than things you failed to."

"That comment means nothing if Falan is alive." Kaer Yin wound his reins around his right fist. "If he is, he'll take Eire through his bastard, and Bri Leith is undoubtedly next."

Tam Lin scrubbed a hand over his face. "Diarmid. If Yin is right, Tairngare will surrender without much fuss. What possible purpose would her reformation have served if not to help her family to power? On that note— how fast can you get to my father?"

"Quick enough," he answered, his pupils shifting with unnatural light like a nighttime predator.

"Do it," Kaer Yin urged. "Once we meet up with the rest of our party. Go ahead of us. Please, Diarmid. This isn't about Una and me anymore."

Diarmid's expression held sarcasm, sadness, and malice. "I doubt it ever has been or will be, princeling."

※

ANOTHER ODD, HALF-FORMED DAY passed in the Otherworld before they came across their lost party members. Having spied them first, Gerrod flew out of the Waycross on bare feet. His hair had grown long and shaggy, and his chin bore a fair bit of stubble. Beaming, Rian dismounted and threw herself into his arms. Robin grabbed them around the waist to crush them against his chest in a great bear-hug. Eva poked her head out the door next, squealing for joy when she set eyes upon her niece. Una was crying openly when her arms encircled her. Kaer Yin couldn't help the grin that split his face from ear to ear at the sight. In tears, Eva whispered something into Una's ear that had the girl nodding into her shoulder.

Robin tousled Gerrod's hair. "Ye've grown a bloody mile since last I saw ye."

"Well, it's been almost four months, hasn't it?"

"Wait, what?" laughed Rian. "It's been a few days, silly."

"Not for them, it hasn't," said Diarmid, brushing a stray snowflake from his nose. "This close to the Veil, time runs nearly parallel with Innisfail."

Rian gaped at him like he's just told her the sea was full of jelly. "*Four months?*"

"At least."

Gerrod gave her a bashful smile that looked odd on his new adult-like face. "I'm older than ye now, I gather?"

"Are you daft, other than this codger," Tam Lin jerked a thumb at his uncle. "Rian's the oldest thing here."

Gerrod and Rian ignored him simultaneously. Instead, they made room so Rian could hug Mel Carra, Small Dan, Finster, then Tall Dan. A few others made the rounds. She'd half-killed herself, once upon a time, to tend to every one of them, and was well-loved by all. Even Carra's tiny cadre of Tairnganeah took their turns. The only person who seemed more enthusiastic to great everyone was Una. The pair couldn't have been happier to see so many friendly faces if they'd tried.

Tam Lin crossed his arms. "Bloody women."

Kaer Yin dismounted in one leap without comment and caught Gerrod in a bear hug that almost cracked the lad in two.

Diarmid examined his nails next. "Indeed."

"Right," said Robin, wiping a stray tear from the corner of his eye. "Let's go home, shall we?"

Small Mercies

n.e. 509
20 Dor Imba
Cairngare

Dor Imba descended upon the hills at Drogheda with snow flurries and famine. A fortnight later, an army of Southers followed. By the dawn of the fifteenth day, they'd surrounded the massive outer wall in neat rows, dozens deep. By mid-morning of the sixteenth day, bare-chested men by their hundreds painstakingly hacked shallow trenches into the frozen ground. By noon of the next, they'd already begun constructing a timber wall on the opposite side of their growing ditch. Back-breaking work, to be sure, but they neither stopped nor slowed. The Southers' speed and strength of arms were astounding to witness.

Gan observed all from the Citadel's topmost tower. Nema had tasked him to keep watch and send regular reports to the Tenth Floor. One of her newest guardsmen had kicked him from bed two hours before first light, dragged him up to the roof by his collar, and left him with two Secundas to stammer messages to the Cloister. By mid-afternoon, Gan had watched Damek Bishop's army gather for about twelve hours in the frigid cold. Gan had had enough by evening, knowing that Nema did not need him on the watch to understand what was happening. When the tents started popping up in the distance, Gan handed a milk-faced Secunda his spyglass and took his leave without ado.

It wouldn't be long now, anyway.

He might as well greet death warm and well-fed. Heading downstairs, he encountered the same Fir Bolgman who'd forced him upward. The fellow's dark violet eyes narrowed as Gan attempted to squirm past him. He must have come up to see the encampment for himself.

Gan wished him the joy of his discovery. "Let me pass," he sighed.

The Bolgman's dark hair spilled over his collar when he leaned down to sneer back. "You've been ordered to remain aloft."

"I decline," giggled Gan. "If you'd prefer to beat me rather than feed me, I should warn you; I no longer have the nerve endings required to register physical blows. My lungs and eyes, however, do feel the cold. I need food and a warm drink. Unless you'd like to kill me now and save Bishop's men the trouble?"

The Bolgman glanced out the latticed window where thousands of fires flickered to life outside the city. "They'll never breach the Gates."

"Oh, I doubt they'll need to. You see, Bishop has studied his Classics. In ancient times, Caesar had perfected this strategy at the battle of Alesia. A mighty king named Vercingetorix thought his superior numbers and high walls would save him, too. He was wrong, and so will you be."

"You're barking, old fool. We have twenty thousand Cohort and Tairnganeah behind these walls."

"… and half a million mouths to feed. Half a million disease vectors. Half a million corpses to clog the streets and cloud the air with flies."

The Bolgman cringed a bit. Perhaps whatever Nema had done to him might wear off in the face of bald logic? Gan certainly was no expert. Nema's powers grew more horrifying the madder she became… and she was now mad as a rabid mare. Whatever malady which leeched the color from her skin and eyes, added that sag to her once sharp cheeks, and thinned her glorious hair— had set to work in her mind. The last time Gan had snuck into the dungeons to visit Grainne (who looked as well as one should expect while starving in prison), she'd said Nema was finally afflicted with true mortality.

She'd grow madder still before the end. It seemed the Sidhe were only immortal so long as they never strayed far from their Otherworld home. Nema had been plaguing the city of Tairngare for half a decade. For one as old as Nema, the mortal realm was a slow poison.

Grainne had posited the only way Nema could maintain herself now was through blood magic, but the more she used, the worse the rot became. Finally, understanding that their chosen hero was a beast in disguise, the people had turned from her en masse. They kept to their homes; doors locked, and windows shuttered. The silence in the streets was a deafening harbinger of impending doom. While Bolg goons kicked down doors to drag unwitting citizens from their hearths to supply their mistress with fodder for her dark sorcery, many escaped to the townships, bringing news of Nema's misdeeds to greater Eire, at last. In the Midlands, Gan had learned, a petition to reinstate the Libella and reelect a new Doma made rounds. So far, it bore twelve-thousand signatures, or so he'd been told. The Reformation's brutality was no longer a secret. The Union of Commons was disbanded. Several of its ranking officers had already committed suicide or fled.

Vanna Nema existed on borrowed time.

Elated at the prospect of imminent freedom, Gan couldn't care less which happened first. Nothing would deflate his mood now, not even the threat of violence or death. It would happen whether he feared it or not, so why worry? "Now, if you don't mind, I'd like to eat before we're starving."

The Bolgman stepped aside with an elegant gesture. "To your demise then, stooge."

"And yours, barbarian." Gan bowed as he passed.

The Bolgman snorted but made no further effort to stall him.

X

Inside the Citadel, chaos reigned. Secundas raced hither and thither, carrying grain sacks or other perishable items from the kitchens to the cellars or moving already sparse furnishings against the windows as rudimentary blinds. As for the Cohort, officers and archers crowded the windows and rooftops, fumbling for position. Most of these soldiers were newly minted, children of suddenly elevated commoners or impoverished recruits with family members imprisoned or swinging from the outside walls. These Secundas were the first orphans of the Reformation. They had no idea which threat they should fear most, and their confusion was palpable.

Gan sympathized. He strolled through the halls toward the Grand Arcade, munching on a moldy piece of bread and humming to himself. A veritable concert of noise, frenetic activity, and dread enveloped him.

He couldn't help but smile. How many times a day did he shuffle up and down the Grand Stair, praying for a falling star or another cosmic catastrophe to crash through the ceiling? Hundreds. Now that calamity had finally arrived, Gan couldn't be more at ease. Soon, Nema would meet her end; her ruthless, absurdist regime would topple. Her bootlickers and apologists were fodder for the flames. The stain of her rule would be scrubbed away like so much muck.

Gan was finally free to die.

He was ready.

He'd *been* ready for so long; he couldn't contain his joy. No more suffering, waking each morning with the blinding pain in his joints, his head— worst, his soul. While his outer flesh might be numb, he writhed in torment internally. Every step he took was agony. For the incessant tremors plaguing his damaged nervous system or the insufferable spasms that intermittently ripped through his muscles, he hadn't achieved a whole night's sleep in ages.

To make matters worse, with his tear ducts now only moderately functional, he'd been forced to carry a tincture of saline on his person. Now the apothecary who procured it for him was dead, having become a member of Nema's Wall of Fame. Gan's headaches had become unbearable in the weeks since, and both eyes were puffy and inflamed. He carried boiled water to help mitigate the struggle, but to little avail. If the infection persisted, he would very likely go blind. Well, he need no longer fear fumbling through these stairwells on swollen feet, blind, and insensate with pain.

It would all be over soon, thank Siora.

If he had the ability, he might skip up the stairs to Nema's throne room and dance a jig for her bemusement.

In the end, he did not.

When he stumbled into the Obsidian Hall, a contingent of Southers had taken up residence before the dais, in full armor and mail. What bright uniforms they had! All done up in cobalt and silver, with splashes of crimson. Beside them, the youngish Tairnganeah crowding Her Eminence's throne looked drab, under formed, and untested. The second tallest man in the group stepped from the center of that handsome mass of knights. He had long, raven black hair curling over each shoulder, bright hazel eyes with flecks of green and violet around the iris, and wide, broad shoulders. If Gan weren't mistaken, the lad bore an uncanny resemblance to someone he'd seen recently. He glanced at Nema, swaddled upon her throne in her garish yellow robes.

He looks a lot like her Falan, doesn't he?

The height, the eyes, and the hair... even Grainne bore these similarities. Neither looked much like Nema, save for the size and hair, maybe?

They're related, surely?

Has this always been her plan? He wondered.

Though he second-guessed himself at her reaction, Nema was furious. He knew her well enough to know when she wore her mask and when she didn't bother. "Lord Bishop," her voice slithered from the throne without welcome. "We're quite amazed to see you here today, in such company."

The Duch's nephew smiled. Even Gan's heart fluttered. *Definitely related.* "Not at all, your Eminence. I think you'll find that I am answering a summons."

"From whom?" She raised an imperious brow. "To what purpose have you marched an army of invaders onto our lands and encircled our city?"

"Liberation," he smirked, accepting a stack of rolled vellum from his superbly tall and scarred attendant. A colonel, or somewhat more, perhaps? Bishop held one roll up. "Each of these begs the Duch for aid. A tyrant has taken over the Red City and systematically executes its citizens without crime or trial." He tossed the messages onto the polished floor. They rolled to a stop at the dais stair.

She coughed disdainfully. "Who are *you* to accuse us, Lordling? The Duch is dead, or so I hear, and his brother has taken his place. Another son is on the way already. You? You're no one, boy. A bastard whose lands have been seized, backed by an army of brigands and lawless thieves. I ask again... *who do you think you are?*"

"The bastard son of a king, madam. That's who I am." He turned to give the audience the full effect of his posture. "I am the son of Falan Mac Nemed and the rightful Duch of Bethany. My father—"

"You *lie*—" Nema attempted to shriek.

"— the true Crown Prince of Innisfail has ordained me the rightful Lord of Eire. Though I am eager to grind my murderous uncle to dust in Bethany, I am here at Falan of Armagh's request. Anyone who seeks to flee the city now will be granted safe passage through our ranks. No harm will come to a single man, woman, or child who braves the gates until dawn tomorrow. If you do not or cannot flee, we urge you to take cover and surrender to my commanders once the walls have been breached. Any that take up arms in this viper's defense will be granted no quarter."

"Are you mad?" screeched Nema, rising. "*My grandson* would never acknowledge—"

"Ah." Damek waved her comment off. "But he has, grandmother. Martin?"

The tall oak tree beside the Duch's nephew stepped forward, drawing a warrant from within his tunic. "'*I*,'" he boomed. "*Falan the Younger Mac Nemed of the noble Fir Bolg, Lord Marshal of Armagh, and rightful Crown Prince of all Innisfail— do decree—*"

Nema covered her ears with shaking, liver-spotted hands. "Stop him, stop him, STOP HIM!" She screamed, though no one made a move to do any such thing, including her loyal Fir Bolg honor guard. They watched Damek Bishop pace the room like men possessed. The Cohort, however, clutched their weapons, indignant but wary.

"*— that my son and sole heir, Damek Bishop Mac Nemed, is tasked to remove the heretical threat from the Tairnganese throne and set the city to rights. To the usurper who now occupies the Doma's robes, I admonish you to surrender your miter and crown, along with the prisoners you've detained in your dungeons. My commander Leal, who escaped your clutches only weeks past, will join Armagh's elite forces with Lord Mac Nemed's, their every intention to remove you from your unlawful occupation of Tairngare. My sister Grainne is to be released, unharmed, into Lord Mac Nemed's keeping. Defiance demands death, seanmáthair. Signed, Falan Mac Falan Mac Nemed, of Armagh.*'"

When finished orating, the large fellow dropped the page and used his boot to slide it across with the others. The wink he spared Nema gave Gan's pulse a pinch.

Apoplectic with rage, Nema struggled down the first step. She pointed. "We do not recognize Falan's authority here, *bastard*! A man who falsified his death has no moral authority over the Red City. We abjure his demands, claims, and anything else you would have of us. *Get you gone* from our halls!"

At the intensity of her tone, the Cohort found a bit of their brass. Around twenty drew swords to surround Nema's dais. Damek was undeterred. He moved closer, tucking his hand into his belt, and bowed deeply. Through a range of leveled spears, his eyes met hers squarely. "If your people survive tomorrow's bombardment, and perhaps the next— they will starve within weeks. No supplies will reach you here in your high tower, *seanmáthair*. How loyal will these boys be when they are dead or wasting away?"

She made a snide sound. "What fear have I of a ground assault, boy? In three hundred years, no one has ever breached these walls. The Citadel is impenetrable."

He cocked his head and stood up. From his cloak, he retrieved a spyglass. "You, there?" He nodded at a nearby Cohort officer. "Tell your Doma what waits outside in the harbor." The boy gaped at him for an uncomfortable amount of time. "Hurry up now. We don't have all day."

The boy took the glass and rushed to the rear, eastern window past the golden doors and above the Grand Stair. Everyone in the room heard his gasp before he raced back, huffing. "Ships, your Eminence!"

"How many?"

"Four, but…"

"Out with it!"

He cleared his throat, his puny adam's apple bobbing. "Our fleet, m'lady. It's already burning."

With a furious squeal that should have cracked the onyx beneath the lad's feet, Nema reached out with one gnarled hand and clenched her fist. The boy convulsed, went purple, then collapsed on the spot. While a collective gasp spread through her audience, Nema staggered to her knees, wheezing. Damek looked on in horror. After a silence so deep one could hear an eyelash fall, he glanced up to find her clawing herself back atop her throne. "You *have* gone mad, haven't you? Look at yourself, Liadan. It's not too late to see what you've become."

At last, after regaining a bit of her composure, she glared down her long nose at him. "We will hear no more. You shall have your answer at first light tomorrow, Lord Bishop. You will vacate our city within the hour."

Knowing that was as good as he would likely get, Damek relented. His beautiful eyes rested a moment on Gan, who flushed with shame at the revulsion writ there, but there was more too— sympathy, if he weren't mistaken. That was enough for Gan. Not many powerful men possessed such emotions to display them. He would help the young lord before the end if he were able. "My offer for clemency stands. Any brave souls who dare shall fear no reprisal. We have hot bread and ale for the hungry and warm tents prepared for families. I bid you all Godspeed."

When he turned on his heel to stalk through the doors, it was as if the light had been sucked from the hall.

X

T is no simple matter, to abandon one's *geis*. As he made his way from the kirkyard along the western wall toward the Southers' timber and shield wall, Gan thought he finally understood why it had taken Aoife so long. His lungs, one of the few organs he had left that didn't pain him as much, felt like they might burst the further away he went from the city. A few stragglers crept beside him, hoping the darkness would protect them. That soon proved false when the Cohort lit the night sky with flaming arrows. Many temporarily bathed in their light were immediately impaled from above, their twitching bodies illuminated in the fog. Gan rushed as fast as anyone would, despite his malady.

When he'd made it a good fifty yards, halfway to the enemy line, his heart was seized as if by a cold hand. He collapsed just as a flare went off overhead. An arrow whizzed out of the dark, but someone had rolled him over. "Watch yourself, Master Gan," whispered a boy with a familiar voice. The sparse light available through the haze of smoke and torchlight afforded him a glimpse of cherubic cheeks and lovely copper skin.

"Lon?" Gan asked, mystified. Once upon a time, he'd been one of Gan's 'boys.' Through the pain and discomfort, Gan burned with shame. He remembered Lon had had a beautiful voice. His clients paid top fainne to hear him sing... before.

Gan swallowed hard, though his throat was as dry as his eyes.

Lon gave him a cautious smile. "The same." His voice was deeper. "Can you make it over the ditch on your own?"

A white flash of pain tore through Gan's mind at the thought. "I... I don't know."

Lon was quiet for a moment as if weighing his options. The flares above them resulted in further cries from those attempting to escape. The next thing Gan knew, Lon had a grip on his collar, dragging him along.

"What—why are you helping *me*?" Gan asked the night sky since Lon was engaged out of eyesight.

"You were less cruel to me than my parents. I won't forget that."

Gan wept without tears. "I sold you. You should leave me to die."

"I didn't say I forgive you, old man, only that I won't leave anyone to die out here like a dog. Besides," Lon's shadow sniffed. "I'd say you've been punished plenty."

The fourth round of flares went up, and a screaming woman was summarily silenced.

Lon recovered quickly, his teeth glowing white in the dark. Gan was dragged through bramble and thorn. He knew he had to be bleeding though he couldn't feel it. Aside from this small blessing, the claws piercing his heart relaxed the further away he was led.

He took a tremulous breath. Lon ducked over him as a fifth flare exploded over their heads. This time, the arrows came down in a torrent. Several voices cried out at once as the missiles fell. Lon slumped over his knees with a grunt, then teetered sideways; an arrow had taken him through the throat. Straining with every ounce of energy he could muster, Gan crawled over to him on his elbows. Dead. A boy with every cause to hate him had traded his life for his. Making dry hacking sounds, Gan shoved himself up to his knees. The ditch was just ahead. Lon had dragged him almost fifty yards and a thousand miles through his *geis*.

Gan must not waste this chance.

Nema had to be stopped.

An officer stared down at him from their shield wall, ten yards away. "Better hurry," he said, tugging his chin at the sky. A sixth flare went up. The men and women in Gan's company scrambled for the trench. Gan threw himself forward on all fours with a guttural scream and fumbled like a wounded dog for the ditch. He had only one thing left to live for.

Gan would be damned if he'd forget his purpose now. When the arrows thudded into the earth beside and behind him, he tumbled arse over heels to the bottom. With a stranger's foot in his face and a tangle of limbs around his torso, Gan looked up to note the Souther winking at him.

"Welcome to Bethany, folks. It looks like you're just in time."

X

At dawn, Damek strode up the rampart with Martin and his officers. Two shieldmen stepped aside so that he could view the killing field below. The sun had yet to rise, but the city was backlit against the horizon by her glow. In the quickening light, last night's degradation was revealed. The plain was littered with bodies, many of them children. So many that even Damek's stomach turned. The crows had been at work for hours already. For a moment, he turned away to collect himself. "How many?"

"Around four hundred, my lord. Give or take," answered Hisk.

Damek cursed under his breath. "That bloody woman is a demon."

"No argument there."

"Any chance she'll surrender, you think?" Martin's frown was leaden as he handed Damek his spyglass. "She didn't strike me as the surrendering sort."

Damek held the glass to his eye and shrugged. "Who knows, Martin. You ask me; she's no fool. She must know they're doomed without the harbor or their fleet."

So far, he could spy no activity at either visible gate nor along the ramparts save for Cohort and archers. The bodies swinging along the walls made his stomach oily. He removed the eyepiece for a moment to scrub his face with the back of his hand. Damned if he wasn't tired. He'd been marching for weeks, sacking one town after another. Now that he was here and his goal was within reach, he wanted it over with as soon as possible. All those people… Damek had never seen so many casually discarded humans. The hardened soldier that he was found it unsettling. "She's gone insane. Leal, forgive me for doubting you."

Down the line of officers, Leal pressed a fist to his chest. "No offense taken, *Mo Flaith*. Who could believe a woman would incarcerate and starve her people to such a degree?"

"I've never seen so many corpses outside of a battlefield. Those are simple townsfolk dangling from those ropes. Here, the same." Martin covered his mouth. Despite the cold and the wind, the dead still reeked of rotting flesh and shit. "Forgive me, but she deserves to die for this."

Damek made a face. "I agree, but that wasn't part of the bargain with Falan." Martin flinched a bit at the name. He didn't care for the reminder that Damek had been keeping secrets for thirty years. He'd always had his suspicions; of course, O'Reardan was a wise man. But Damek had never actually told him who his father was until now. Martin had learned when the men had, which was most unfair of Damek, given their relationship. Damek vowed to remedy the rift as soon as possible, but he was starved for time with the long marches, changing tactics, and preparations.

"We're meant to take the city, liberate whoever's left alive down there, and hold her until he comes to claim her. Apparently, there's a punishment reserved only for those of her advanced age. I don't much care, as long as that old bitch is gone by week's end."

"That's a trifle ambitious, lad," chuckled Martin. "It takes a city that size, with those high walls, *months* to give in. Hells, this could drag on for a year if we're not careful."

Damek shook his head. "No. She doesn't have a year. You saw her, Martin. What do you think all those people are doing on the wall?"

"I don't take your meaning."

"Blood magic," Leal answered for Damek, his violet eyes very bright in the rising light. "Forbidden to our kind. She sustains herself with death. Whoever can't be bent to her will, she kills." He gestured to the south wall. "If she stops, she dies. She'll grow madder and madder the more lives she claims."

"Wonderful," Martin grumbled. "After this, we have the bloody Northers to look forward to. Again."

"Which Northers," Leal asked.

Martin cut an exasperated glare at Damek. "I imagine you'll find out if we survive this siege."

Finally, lights flickered on the Citadel's southern parapet. Torchlight. A line of men and women followed the lead torch. Brows drawn, Damek set the glass to his eye once more. There walked Nema, with her bright vermillion robes, tiny and frail against the might of those red granite walls. She held the lead torch. In her wake trailed dozens of Tairnganese citizens— women and children all. Each had their hands bound behind their backs and nooses tied around their throats. Screaming, they wept into the void.

"*Reason*, Martin!"

Hisk handed his Commander a glass.

Martin stiffened beside him. "She wouldn't."

Damek jerked back when the prisoners were shoved over the wall, one by one. The youngest of these was barely out of swaddling. The toddler's tiny legs kicked out for nothing when she went over. "Oh, gods!"

"What, what's happening?" Leal demanded.

Rather than answer, Martin handed him his glass.

The Bolgman made harsh choking sounds at the back of his throat for the barbarism he spied there. Damek himself felt like throwing the offensive item into the mud and spilling his guts over a nearby fern. He did not, however. He counted the lives being snuffed out for his benefit. Fifty, by the end; most, just bairns.

They died to defy him.

He owed them his full attention.

Despite the distance, Damek caught a flash of Nema's coy grin like a knife in the dark. Wait, or was the knife in her hand? A final prisoner was dragged up the line by a rope at her throat. This one was tall and lovely, with long dark hair, wearing the dregs of formerly delicate garments. He'd never met his aunt Grainne, but she looked so much like Falan that it would've been difficult to mistake her for anyone else. A guard wrestled Grainne to her knees. Even with the rope, she put up a good fight.

Leal ground his teeth together so hard that everyone heard it. His shoulders shook. "Grainne!" he shouted, though she'd never have heard him.

"Reason damn it!" barked Damek. Don't we have a ballista with the range?"

"Not that won't hit the lady too. I'm sorry, my lord." Douglas answered.

Leal whimpered like a wounded animal. Damek distantly realized that he probably loved her. He wondered how he would feel if it were Una up there, waiting to die.

His chest seized with the thought.

Grainne's head was jerked back by the soldier with the rope. Another held a silver bowl just beneath her collarbone. Nema drew the blade across her granddaughter's slender throat with a vicious leer.

Leal's anguish was nothing to the pounding in Damek's ears.

The rearguard held Grainne's body upright while the second milked her open throat over the bowl. One final convulsion, and the pair kicked her twitching body over the wall. Throat cut from ear to ear and dangling at an awkward angle, Grainne lived but a few moments more.

Nema lifted the bowl to her lips when she went still and drank deep.

Damek couldn't be sure, but he might swear he watched the years fade from the Doma of Tairngare like an unwound clock. Victorious, she raised both hands to the sky. *Tairngare is mine*, her smirk seemed to say.

Not for long, you old bitch, Damek thought.

"Martin," he said.

"My lord?"

"I changed my mind."

"How so?"

"We will not march within the hour."

"What order, then?"

"Fire their markets, docks, fields, and granaries outside the city, and I want every rooftop within range aflame by mid-morning."

"Aye, and what else?"

Damek let out a long breath. He gripped the spyglass so hard that his palm bled. "Bring up the trebuchets. This ends now."

The White Queen

n.e. 509
26 dor imba
dalriadan pass

Drem woke to discover the Queen of Scotia staring down at her. Long white-blonde hair coiled over her shoulders in a complex braid that brushed Drem's knuckles when she moved. The wind howled outside their carriage, attacking the shutters with a vengeance. Eri Ap Midhir Bres' beautiful cheeks were tinted pink from the frosty Innish air.

"Good morning, Eminence. Did you sleep well?"

Her famous silver eyes tilted upward at the corners when she smiled.

Drem understood the look as kindness, though it also held a note of condescension. She tolerated it as she'd learned to tolerate so much of late. "Well enough," Drem lied. Her bones felt hollow as a reed flute and brittle as aged vellum. It had been quite some time since she could recall a day without extreme discomfort or pain. She struggled up to her elbows, wiping her eyes. "How long did I sleep?"

The High King's daughter pursed her lips. "A half-day, no more."

Drem winced.

That was far too long. The sudden illness that had kept her abed in Bres for weeks might have abated enough for travel to Dale, but she knew every mile cost her more than time. Just then, a deep, rasping cough overtook her. When she'd finished, and her ribs felt shredded from the inside by unseen talons, Eri Bres passed her a clean handkerchief. "I beg you; please allow me to arrange rooms for you at the *Windbreaker*. We'll be there in less than two days. I'd prefer to carry your tidings to my father without further risk to your health, Eminence," she pleaded.

They'd been having this debate for many weeks now.

As usual, Drem shook her head, folding the handkerchief into her fist so the blood might escape the queen's notice. A certain tilt to her chin told Drem their argument would soon reach a climax, and there was minimal guarantee that Drem would win. Each day that passed, she grew weaker, her lungs more volatile. *Pneumonia*, her studies whispered at the back of her mind—a product of her weakened immune system.

Too far gone.

Without the Spark to purge her lungs of bacteria and viruses, she was fully aware that she didn't have long. Something worse crept through her body like a sneak thief, robbing her Spark of fortitude and cellular renewal. This rapacious entity had a name.

Cancer, her Practicum of fifty years before, assured her.

To ascend to the Fifth and Sixth Floors in the Cloister, one must achieve merits in natural law. Cellular Disease was just one of the many subjects she had excelled in. *Ironic*, she thought, *that I should perish of the very same sickness that had intrigued me so much in my youth.*

She might have laughed if she could spare the breath. "No," she replied firmly. "I must speak to your father personally. Even if it is the last thing I do."

"It shall be," Eri sighed without malice. Cold she was, but never cruel. She simply refused to mince words. Drem liked that about her most. "You're dying, Eminence. I see the black thing nibbling at your lungs quite clearly. If you were to rest and remain well out of the cold, you might live a few months more. At this rate..." she trailed off, shaking her head. "I doubt you'll make it to Bri Leith, Doma Moura."

"Perhaps if we took ship from—"

"We've been over this. The roads are impassable whence we came, and the marshes are treacherous in the best weather. It would take weeks to sail around Dingle and negotiate sleds and barges for the Straits, which are nearly frozen solid. You'll be dead long before then, I'm afraid."

Drem swallowed a fresh surge of despair at that. She didn't feel her years as many her age might and longed for life as a drowning man pines for shore. There were many things she had yet to see and do, so many plans gone awry that she could set to rights if only she had time. Though, in her heart, the queen's words rang true. Drem had just enough Spark left in her to be certain.

"What would you have me do? My city is overrun with lunatics in service of a tyrant. My people are scourged or swinging from the Citadel's high walls. My granddaughter has been kidnapped twice, chased through Eire by a power-mad warlord, and has only just lost her father *and* her inheritance to a zealous uncle. I do not have the luxury to fade into the wilderness while Eire burns. I must speak with your father, garner assurances—" she meant to elaborate, but another coughing fit took over. This one left her breathless and trembling for a long span afterward. She lay back against her cushions with the queen's hand wiping the sweat and blood from her mouth. Moments like these almost convinced Drem that perhaps death would be a relief after all. Deep in her marrow, she knew she couldn't go on this way.

The pain had become a relentless, daily trial.

The indignity of such an end was infinitely more taxing.

"You don't have a choice, Drem," said Eri, meeting her eyes. "I refuse to let you die in the back of a wagon for an uncertain outcome. I'm afraid Dale will have to do."

Drem bit her quivering lower lip, feeling hot and cold at once. From what she had gleaned of the High King's daughter over these many weeks, she recognized regal finality when she heard it. She would simply have to seek alternative methods when they reached the famed Scotian trading hub and keep her own counsel till then. Though Drem was fully aware the queen had her best interests at heart— Drem Moura was not one to be told when she was done with anything. She would get her way, whatever the cost. *In her Spine*, she chanted to herself.

Siora would see her through. She must.

"Tell me, what news of Bethany?"

Eri reclined against her cushions with a scowl. "Henry FitzDonahugh has a new child on the way, I'm told. He's wed some Kernian woman's girl and declares the South independent from my father's rule. My source tells me that citizens must attend mass at Court nearly three times daily. Those who don't are fed to the stocks, their lands confiscated by the crown."

Drem made a noise. "He and Nema are two sides of the same coin."

"Yes. Though one at least believes the drivel he espouses. Liadan Mac Nemed has only ever solicited for one deity; herself."

Over the decades, Drem might have suspected that the mysterious Vanna Nema was more than she claimed to be but never in her life would she have imagined the viper to be the ancient dowager of Armagh. In hindsight, she supposed there had been legions of hints and warnings she should have examined. At this late stage, torturing herself with the past seemed redundant. Nema had eons to enact her fatal plans. Drem only had weeks, at best, to reverse them. "Perhaps, I should linger at Dale for a while?"

The queen laughed softly. "My brother is the gullible one, Eminence. You'd make other arrangements as soon as my back turned."

Drem thought about lying, but what would be the point? The hourglass ran thin. "I am not your subject, Highness. You have no right to dictate the terms of my death to me. This is a thing that must be done for my granddaughter's sake."

Eri Bres was silent for a time, mulling over the sincerity of Drem's proclamation. If the woman had any sense of justice, she could not refute her logic. Death was a highly personal issue, of the sort the queen of Scotia might never experience. Who was *she* to order the ruler (albeit former) of a sovereign city-state to meet hers in any other way aside from that she chose? "Drem, what good do you think you'll do?"

Drem was too tired and sore to bristle. "I have allies. If I won't live long enough to reach your father, there are others to whom I might apply."

"There are not. Your allies are defeated or fled. Tairngare is at Liadan's mercy until my father intervenes, which he will, but in his own good time. Your desperation to achieve nothing is admirable but misguided. I remain your best and most logical course."

Siora damn her eyes, thought Drem.

She is right, as usual.

She swallowed her retort.

"Una," Eri went on. "Is safest with my brother. I suppose he will look after her since he refuses to be parted from her."

The last made Drem quirk a brow. "Their alliance bothers you?"

"Mystifies me, more like. You only met my brother once, I recall."

Drem bobbed her chin. "At the High Council meeting. My daughter was there. That was the first time Patrick spied her."

Cursed be his name.

"Intriguing that so many chance occurrences during one occasion would affect us these many years later."

"If you prefer to look at it that way. I view that Gathering as a curse."

"Yes, I understand why you might. However, you've a legacy *because* of these events, however distasteful. Is that not right?"

Drem mused over the past once more, as one was wont to do when their future bore a certain finality. At the High King's fête, Alis Donahugh had been kidnapped by an unnamed Sidhe lord, an event that instigated a vicious civil war and ripped Drem's daughter away from her.

She still remembered the moderately handsome young Duch in his smart blue cloak and scarlet tunic, kneeling to request her Arrin's hand. The look on his face when Drem summarily dismissed him. She might have known he was not the sort to accept the rebuff of a mere woman— however powerful she might be. When his sister was taken, he and his men disappeared overnight from Bri Leith's keep. Drem would always rue the day she allowed Arrin to travel to Ten Bells for her Law Practicum. Ahead of his declaration of war against the High King, Patrick had snatched Arrin from the High Road in bald daylight.

The rest, as they say, was history.

She'd never seen her beautiful, brilliant daughter again. "Loving my exceptional granddaughter is no chore, Highness. Nevertheless, the circumstances of her birth still wound me deeply."

"I understand. I've lost children too."

Drem winced. She realized; she was a very selfish creature.

The Queen of Scotia had lost two sons in that same war. One to a Souther arrow and one to a festering wound some months later. Even the Sidhe, however long-lived, could be slain.

"I'm sorry," Drem said. "I forget myself in my grief."

Eri Bres peeked through the shutters at the white, whirling sky. "I have a daughter still. She is young yet, but I wish to keep her safe. I empathize with you, Eminence."

To be a mother and a ruler requires a strength few men could dream of.

"Then you understand why I must carry on?"

"Your courage is admirable. What is that phrase you Siorai use?"

"*In her blood, in her heart, in her spine*," answered Drem.

"That's the one. Well," Eri exhaled long and hard. "If you choose to live out your final days on a snowy road within a dispassionate Sidhe entourage, then you have my permission, if not my approval. If this is what you wish, I will honor your choice."

"It is." Drem's eyes welled with tears. She blinked them back. Mourning or acceptance, she couldn't be sure which, untied the knot of tension at her core. "I remember your father fondly, Highness. He will not turn me away, and my plea will be best served personally."

"I am sure he's already been apprised of the situations in Tairngare and Bethany. Though I do agree, he will respect and honor your efforts."

"Thank you, Highness."

"You are most welcome, Doma Moura." She pressed three fingers to her temple, then broke into a smile. "I must admit, I am anxious to see my father again. It's been—" she broke off, head jerking toward some sound outside that Drem could not hear.

Their carriage ground to a halt.

"What is it?" she asked, alarmed.

Eri leaned forward. "Men... *many* men, ahead."

Before Drem could reply, Eri leaned over and grabbed a beautiful black longbow from the center wall. Its shaft was inlaid with carvings of trouping nightmare beasts Drem had no names for. *Dorchadas*, the famed bow, was named; literally, 'Darkness.' Eri paused at the wide oak partition long enough to grab her quiver and sling it over her fur-cloaked shoulders. "I think you should stay here," said she before throwing the door open and allowing a blast of winter air inside.

Beyond the Queen of Scotia's elegant frame, Drem spied riders in black whipping their mounts directly into the Scotian line, their long, dark hair billowing behind them. Their eyes blazed violet or green, furious and bloodthirsty.

Fir Bolg?

Drem had but a moment to marvel before the first arrows were loosed.

✕

Two shafts pierced the door, inches from Eri's right cheek. Without thought, she ducked and returned fire. The Bolg horseman tumbled from his horse into a snowbank, dead. Her *garda* whipped themselves into a frenzy in retaliation. Hers was an advance party. The bulk of her forces yet negotiated the Dalriadan Pass, some ten miles behind them. Others lay ahead, stationed at the Skenian Outpost, before Dale. Only twenty Dannan warriors stood between the Queen of Skye and this incoming troupe of Bolg lunatics. She leaped from the wagon, kicking the door shut as far as possible.

Drem Moura's blanched face stared back at her from the remaining crack. "What's happening?"

"An attack, apparently."

She heard Drem heave a rattling sigh. "I am ready."

"No," argued Eri. "Stay where you are. We'll handle this."

Another arrow whizzed past Eri's flank, and she hissed as it grazed flesh. Again, she drew and returned fire, and again, her assailant slid into the snow. Indiscriminate shouts and the ring of steel on steel accompanied by the sweet tang of Sidhe blood filled the air.

Thankfully, Skenian warriors were the finest in Innisfail, or so they proved. Their white and amber cuirasses winked like gems against the leaden sky.

Eri drew and slew two more before a sudden crash on her right alerted her of a new presence. He came at her fast, silver hammer poised to bash her brains into the snow. Eri spun on her heel, bringing *Dorchadas* up by her butt to smash her shaft into the fellow's windpipe. The force of the blow painfully reverberated through her elbow. Hands stinging, she couldn't regain her grip in time to halt the next Bolgman from slamming her back into the wagon. She had not thought to wear larks and daggers in her lands, thus had nothing left to fight him with but claws and fists.

He raised her to his eye level by her throat, teeth clenched. Choking, Eri kicked out with everything she had, and he merely grunted when the toe of her boot glanced at his testicles. He smiled down at her as if he might enjoy watching her eyes dim. Just as her eyelashes began to flutter closed, his nose and mouth erupted in a steaming geyser of blood. Twitching, he fell backward. She slipped into the snow to retch and claw at her bruised flesh.

Another fellow attempted to take his place, but Drem stepped between them, wielding only a shaking bare hand.

The Warhammer leered. "What's this? Milesian bravery?"

"Milesian *sorcery*, you gobshite."

Brandishing his hammer, he rushed her.

Without a shred of fear, Drem closed her fist and whispered, "*Break.*"

The Bolgman crumpled like a wet cloak.

Blood welled from his mouth as his eyes took one last glimpse of the sky. Two of his comrades raced toward Drem with their weapons high. With her spine as straight as it could go, her iron-gray braids blowing in the breeze, she looked like a vengeful deity, risen to exact retribution. Eri's heart clenched, for she was educated enough to understand what it cost her.

Unmoved by the Warhammers' theatrics, Drem swiftly twisted her fist once to the right, then to the left. Both men fell in a tangle of limbs, their necks bent at unnatural angles. Drem dropped to her knees, coughing.

Eri saw the blood dripping from her chin.

The skirmish was nearly over, with Eri's Skenian forces emerging victorious. Though, a few stragglers remained to cover their general retreat. Having as yet failed at their goal— the assassination of the Queen of Skye— a trio of braves made a last-ditch rush to get the job done. Eri managed to drag *Dorchadas* and her quiver over by the straps, but she didn't have time to nock before a hammer glanced the wagon door over her head. She drew a short dirk from the bodice of her gown and slammed it to the hilt into the Bolgman's boot. He'd barely had time to cry out when she withdrew the blade again, only to ram it into his kidney. Climbing his falling body, she nocked. Her next arrow caught another assailant in the back of the neck as he fled the scene.

Amriel, one of her stoutest *garda*, made it to her side with both larks drawn. He was splashed head to toe in blood. "*Mo Bhanríon*," he huffed. "*Bhulaileamar ar ais iad.*"

"Not yet," she rasped, pointing.

The last pair dashed toward them. Amriel whirled into the first, sylvan steel flashing. The second ducked one of Eri's arrows, smacking it into the reddened snow at his feet. She had two arrows left in her quiver aside from her dirk, but she'd never have time to nock before he was upon her. They stared each other down. While Amriel was engaged, the rest of her *garda* chased the bulk of the Bolgish raiders from the road.

"Who sent you?" she demanded.

"The Ard Ri," the Warhammer laughed proudly.

She must have blinked. "Are you daft?"

"Not at all, *isasaeligh*."

Without further ado, he ran for her. Eri braced herself to accept his impact, confident that if she could displace his weight far enough, she could ram her dirk into him before he could strike. However, he anticipated the move, cracking his hammer into the ball of her right knee instead. Brilliant stars burst behind her eyes. Brutal fingers gripped her hair. He prepared to run his dagger over her throat. She backed into him, bringing her undamaged heel into his groin. He grunted and let go long enough for her to drag herself partially away. She held her dagger up. "Come on then. Whatever happens, you'll leave full of holes."

"Don't you know when you're bested, Dannan bitch?"

"She might," said Drem from behind him. "But I sure as hells don't."

Then, a horrifying sight that would haunt Eri for the rest of her days greeted her wide-open eyes. Drem Moura displayed a feat of power no Sidhe could ever hope to match. Lips trailing blood, she held out her palm, fingers up. The Warhammer was lifted into the air by an unseen source. He made a strange mewling sound as if he guessed the fight was over already. Drem gave him a cruel, dry smile. "*One, two,*" she sang, tucking her pinky and thumb down. His right arm and left leg snapped 90 degrees the wrong way. His frantic cries were drowned out by the power throbbing from Drem's rich, singsong voice.

"*Buckle his shoe. Three, four*", she chanted, and he inverted in the air. "*Lock the door. Five, six, pick up sticks.*" His left arm and right leg snapped forward until he resembled a half-broken scarecrow.

Eri didn't know how she got to her feet, unable to look away. She could only hope to face her death with such courage and pride.

"*Seven, eight,*" Drem grunted, balling her fingers into a fist. The Bolg Warhammer's spine cracked in the center, folding the fellow neatly in half, the wrong way. "*Lay them straight.*"

When his body struck the ground, he might have been a pallet of stained clothes; he lay in such a tidy stack. He gurgled a bit as he died.

Drem shot Eri a triumphant grin before tumbling face-first into the snow. With a cry, Eri skittered to her side, rolling her over. "No, no! Why would you do that, you silly mortal? Why?"

Drem smiled despite the blood bubbling freely from her mouth. The Doma of Tairngare had proven herself mighty, indeed. "You will speak for my Una."

"Yes," agreed Eri, as her battered *garda* gathered around, mystified.

"She is... the rightful Queen of Eire. Swear to me."

"You have saved my life today, Drem Moura. *Twice.*"

Bloodied fingers clasped the ruin of Eri's bodice. "Every... thing I have... all of Tairngare... all hers. Take nothing... from her. She is better than me."

Eri set a hand over her heart. "I will see Una Moura Donahugh claims her birthright. I vow it."

Seemingly satisfied, Drem let out a long sigh that rattled in her hollow chest. Her mission was accomplished to the best of her abilities.

She died smiling.

※

Eva's eyes snapped open from deep within the curling folds of steam licking their way along her face and shoulders. Instantly, her heart clenched. A jagged, guttural cry escaped her lips, and she jerked forward in her bath, splashing piping water over the floor tiles. In a flash, Mel was by her side, nude but armed, nonetheless. He took his paths seriously, no matter the occasion. Between rasping gasps and wails, she stammered a disjointed explanation.

Drem Moura was dead.

Not one for tears, Mel Carra, could not help but respond as any human beloved of another might. Great salty tears poured down his cheeks to mingle with the dampness of Eva's hair. She shuddered against him, teeth grazing his collarbone in her wide-mouthed anguish.

"Gone, all *gone*," she moaned.

His guts twisted to knots. "I am sorry, love."

After a while, her wracking sobs calmed, though she remained pressed against him, small and trembling. He would have done anything to take the pain for her, as that was the duty of the Bonded. Though, some pains could never be assumed... only observed. He slipped into the bath beside her, tucking her into his lap. She shrank into him, frail and childlike, as she would never appear to anyone else. Not Eva Alvra, the most feared of Drem's enforcers.

She shuddered, and he knew without asking what came next. Her prescience tended to follow emotional triggers. A shock such as this was bound to summon at least one. Her spine jerked backward, and he instinctively clasped the base of her skull to keep her head above water. She convulsed a few times, eyes going glassy and dark at once. Her breath stilled while she stared through the ceiling to the universe beyond. The sight always made the hair on his neck stand at end.

"*The black knight,*" spoke the cosmos through her. "*Burns, high and low.*"

Yes. He recalled that bit. They were to face the man himself soon enough, were they not?

"*Child of dark, child of light… the price of peace.*"

He hadn't heard that bit yet.

Cocking his head at her, he asked, "What child?"

"*Siora's chosen.*"

He closed his eyes. "Will Una survive?"

The glassy black of her pupils seemed fathomless. "*All that is born must perish. Look to the tide.*"

His throat squeezed at that, but before he could ask her to elaborate, she sat bolt upright, eyes clearing gold. She blinked up at him.

"What did I say?"

"Una."

She swallowed. "No."

"Do you feel the truth?"

Her face fell, and he mourned for her anew.

"How soon?"

"I can't see, but not long now," she whispered.

They sat in mutual grief, clutching at one another for strength.

"Can it be averted?" he asked, hopefully.

"I don't know."

He sighed heavily into the crown of her head. "The last Moura."

"Yes," she wept.

"Regardless, we will try, won't we?"

She gripped his hand hard. "We will."

Duch
FitzDonahugh

n.e. 508
10 dor marta
bethany

Henry shoved his fat little piglet of a wife to the opposite end of their marital bed. She was heavy with his child. That thought alone should have made him hard as the crags at Dingle, as there was something quite stirring about the visible evidence of one's potency. On that score, Henry had never failed to congratulate himself. Even well into his fifties, as he was now, he could still fill a woman's belly with legacy. Despite this, he had never cared for round girls like this, never mind her plump rump, and swollen teats.

When he took her, he had to work very hard to achieve the threat of a broken bone or a bleeding vulva. Henry preferred his girls bony and fragile. What could be more pleasing than seeing one's handprint over a tiny white backside or the spine-tingling crunch one could elicit by pounding a less sturdy cavity? His member throbbed at the thought. God did say a woman's purpose was to be put to 'use,' did he not? Upon second glance at his young wife and her mash of bruised flesh, he went limp again.

Useless witch.

He'd find better fare elsewhere tonight, as usual.

Henry tugged on his robe while the Kernian girl wept into her pillow. He didn't see what she had to cry about. She would soon be a queen, wouldn't she? All she must do was spread her meaty thighs and bear a few grunts and blows to manage it. The ungrateful sow. "Stop your grousing, or I'll fuck your skull. You didn't like that much last time, did you?"

Immediately, the girl shoved a fist into her mouth to still her sobs. Disgusted, Henry shrugged his robe over his head. This one was much finer than the rags he'd be relegated to while his criminal brother had yet lived. Now, he wore black Bretagn silk rather than coarse wool, and his body no longer ached from pretending to hobble for Patrick's benefit. He stood, finding himself in the mirror beside their bed. The Duchy had done wonders for Henry FitzDonahugh. Languishing for a decade in the blackness of a damp cell had robbed him of his hair and most of his teeth. The wooden dentures his brother had crafted for him had been replaced by good porcelain, and the muscle mass he'd lost shivering in the dark was mostly regained. He would never be the handsome rogue he'd been in his youth; years of deprivation and malnutrition would do that, but he *did* cut a fairer figure than the last Duch.

He smirked at himself in the glass.

Yes, God cared for his faithful servants, didn't he?

Almost sad to abandon his reflection, he turned to tug on his breeches and boots. "You may keep to your quarters this eve, my dear." He sighed into his collar while he fastened his belt. "I've had enough of your sniveling at supper."

"...but My Lady mother will—"

"Never utter a word about you if she's wise, and I believe she is."

She sat up, her face purple and ugly. "I hope I bear you a daughter, you filthy old beast."

Henry paused to shrug at the door. "A former maid bore me a son this past week. God will forgive you if you prove worthless, but I will not. Be a shame to elevate a common woman's child over my own duchess' get, but needs be, I suppose."

"You wouldn't dare!"

"Wouldn't I?"

He didn't bother to bandy further insults with her. She had a brain as soft as her face and the mettle of a pile of feathers. Her mother was no fool. Lady Penwyth had engaged the runt of her brood for a reason. The girl was expendable. If she proved fertile and obedient, she would live to serve as a forgettable queen. If not, she'd merely be forgotten—her fault for stuffing herself with pie rather than improving her feeble mind with scripture and sense.

Whichever way God laid her fate, Henry couldn't care less. There could be no replacement for the truly excellent sons he'd lost to his brother's perfidious slut of a daughter, but he'd be damned if he'd allow another woman to stand in the way of his God-given destiny. Soon as he found his vicious Tairnganese witch of a niece, he'd finally have everything he could hope for to avenge himself upon her and his brother's failed line. Henry FitzDonahugh had a calling, after all: a sacred undertaking.

He would be the first Christian king of Eire in nearly two thousand years.

With his head high, he strode into the hall, where two of his vassals waited. Taylor and Corrick bowed, then dogged his heels as he stalked toward the Great Hall. Upon entry, his courtiers silently ducked their heads. The women dipped curtsies from the gallery above, where they belonged. He never understood why his brother thought God's lesser creatures deserved a place among the men at Court. Feeling jaunty, he threw himself into his throne, tossing a leather-clad leg over one arm. Above him, a half-finished stained-glass relief celebrated Saint Brendan the Navigator, whom Henry had taken for the patron of his house. As Henry was tasked with leading the people back to God, he felt Brendan a kindred spirit. Besides, determined as he was to erase all evidence of the Sidhe from this land, if the previous relief of Kaer Yin Adair slaying his grandfather hadn't been shattered in the revolt— he'd have had it removed, regardless. Already, the pagan symbols etched into his grandfather's chapel were being scratched away, as were all semblances of Sidhe influence from the city and townships beyond.

Henry would stamp them out in every possible way.

Sparing a newly charming grin for his Court, he waved Shanley forward with his scrolls. "What news of the North?"

Patrick's former toady bowed low, unraveling his first vellum. "The new Doma of the Cloister of the Eternal Flame has been revealed for a Sidhe convert from the House Mac Nemed."

"Yes, yes," Henry groaned. "That was last week's news."

"Forgive me, Your Grace." The steward bowed double but didn't relinquish the floor. "She has also taken her grandchild captive, Grainne Mac Nemed."

"That's interesting. Why?"

"Our sources say the girl decried the old woman's tyranny in Court and attempted to maim or kill the Doma when such failed."

Henry chuckled. "A shame she failed. And Shanley? Grainne Mac Nemed is nearly one thousand years old, last I checked. Nothing 'young' about her. Well, what happened?"

The steward flushed. He wasn't a brave man. Henry despised him on principle, but there was no man better suited to the job at hand for now. "Our source does not say, though another assures us she was executed before the Traitor's army a week ago. To what purpose, we do not know."

"That's easy enough," growled Henry. "They're related, my mutant nephew and this atrocious Sidhe witch. What might she do to one such as him if she'd be happy to slay a favored grandchild? Very good. Mayhew? Have you anything more?"

The black-cloaked baron stepped forward to bow. "Yes, Your Grace. The rebel Southers have been encamped now for a fortnight. I feel certain the siege will break before the month is out."

"Sooner than that. It's winter, and Nema has not prepared the city for a protracted engagement. Their defenses will fade with the food, and if I know my nephew as I had my brother— Damek will figure a way to shorten it further by trickery or whatever else he can manage. The boy is a bit of a martial genius, I must admit. If sources are to be believed, he seeks to march on the Western settlements against the Sidhe. One can only pray he is so arrogant."

"Yes, Your Grace."

"Excellent. Let them hack each other to bits before we march. Either victor is our weakened enemy. Lord Pough, what news of our proposal to Ten Bells?"

Pough shuffled forward with a nervous cough. "Rejected, Your Grace."

That wiped the smirk from Henry's mouth. "What reason do they give?"

Pough trembled a bit at his tone. Another coward. Unfortunately, Henry's court was full of such men. How Patrick stomached them all, he'd never know. "Well, Your Grace, they, ah… do not recognize the ascendancy of your house."

The Court went so quiet; Henry could hear the clock ticking on the wall in the next room. "Is that right?"

"It is, I'm afraid. My source was quite appalled."

As they fucking should be, thought Henry.

"To whom do they grant their recognition?"

Pough looked eager to tunnel through the floor. "Lord Bishop, Your Grace, in consort to Lady Donahugh."

"*Lady* Donahugh rests upstairs, heavy with my babe."

"So my source argued. The Libellan Council confiscated his house and tavern, Your Grace. He was turned from the gates as a rabble-rouser."

Henry sat up straight, grinding his teeth. "They would dare denounce *me* in favor of my brother's murderer?"

"The Alderman claimed they have no right to reject the ancient claim of House Donahugh, on scant evidence from a…" he swallowed. "From a…"

"Spit it out!"

"'From a debauched zealot, likely guilty of fratricide.'"

Henry went silent for quite a while, willing the blood to course through his veins unabated by ice.

Those heretical cunts have tried you before.
Why shouldn't they now?

He took a few deep breaths before he spoke. "And our funds, what of them?"

Pough went very pale. "The same, Your Grace. They refuse you in the most colorful language."

Again, Henry kept silent for several moments. At last, he said, "Lady Penwyth?"

"Your Grace?" she answered from the gallery.

"Will you stake a hundred-thousand fainne to make your daughter Queen of Eire?"

She snorted, "Of course."

"And you, Lord Mayhew, will you match her to wed your first grandchild to a child of mine?"

"Gladly, Your Grace." Answered he.

"Well then," said Henry. "Seems we're off to reclaim Bethany's inheritance and eliminate the idolaters who preside over the city. All in favor, say '*aye*.'"

Only a few voices went unheard.

Thus, it was decided.

Henry would have his holy war.

X

Later that week, while the munitions, horses, arrows, and swords were accounted for, a messenger was dragged into Henry's study, sopping wet from head to toe. He'd been caught in a snowstorm in the Midlands and suffered frostbite at the end of his bulbous nose and swollen left hand. Henry knew the fellow would lose both when he was done delivering his message. He poured the brave Christian soldier a drink with his own hand. The messenger needed help to hold it to his mouth but bowed deeply in awed gratitude. "Your Grace, I bring the direst news from the North."

"He's broken through?"

"Yes, milord. Bretagn ships blocked the harbor at Drogheda from the start and have been bombarding the city daily. Five days ago, an agent fouled the city's wells and the river mouth. The Citadel surrendered at dawn yesterday. Only the Cloister resists now. Lord Bishop's men have taken the Red City."

"I suppose his men will loot and burn to their wicked content?"

"Lord Bishop has expressly forbidden it. Instead, he brings aid— food, medicine, oil, and peat, to the people. Most have already sworn fealty."

In less than one month, his nephew had managed to do what neither Henry nor his brilliant brother ever could. The lad undisputed King of Eire… for now. Henry would just see about that, wouldn't he?

"How many men does that give him if the Cohort kneels?"

Shanley replied, "Another twenty thousand, Your Grace, give or take."

Twenty thousand? "Giving him *seventy* thousand, in total." Henry cursed. "We stand no chance if we do not make an example of Ten Bells, my lords."

"Your Grace," Mayhew interrupted. "Perhaps we should start with Patrick's Barons? Many have opted to sit on the sidelines rather than choose a banner in this contest. They have two thousand men or more who can be pressed into service or face the gallows."

"You're right," muttered Henry, looking at a map. "Lords Wender, Morley, Dorr will give us an additional 6 thousand troops and piles of fainne. I like the way you think, old boy. Where else might we improve our average?"

Mayhew pointed at a dot on the map.

Henry smiled. "That would be rather crass, don't you think, as they've only just been sacked by the traitor's army?"

Alistair Mayhew rolled a shoulder. His family had scores aplenty to settle in the South. Henry was as amused by the man's many hatreds as he was impressed by his devious mind. "They make up his supply train, do they not? Hamstring him there and purge the heathens while we're at it. Besides, our men could use the practice before Ten Bells; I'll wager."

"We'll send the Cyrmians to deal with old Wender, then march through Malahide on our way to Ten Bells."

"Perfect, Your Grace."

Henry said to the poor, frostbitten messenger, "And you, my loyal friend, will receive a Corpsman's salary for such timely news at such personal loss."

"T-thank you, Your Grace." The messenger looked like he might topple over any moment.

Smiling, Henry rubbed his hands together over their modified map. "The Christian Kingdom of Eire. I rather like the sound of that, Alistair. I think Our Lord does too."

A King of Eire

n.e. 508
27 Dor Marta
Tairngare

The sack of Tairngare took far longer than Damek had hoped in the end. After the trenches had been dug out and the Tairnganese fleet had been fired, all the Southers had to do was wait. Thirty or so days might seem a miracle to any other commander (not the least of whom had been his deceased uncle, who'd spent years in the failed attempt)— but Damek had three times the men, Bretagn ships loaded with newly minted cannons, and a lifetime's example to learn from. He had won the greatest city in Eire in a handful of weeks... and it still felt too long. Despite his momentous victory, he itched to move on.

Damek would be crowned today.

That did not mean he felt he deserved the honor.

Not yet.

He might walk through the Citadel to accept the obeisance of twenty thousand Tairngaenah and reams of half-starved, grateful citizens, but the crown would feel weightless upon his head, his achievement hollow. He crumbled the hastily scribbled note in his left hand and tossed it through the open window to the icy street below. In the frame, the Cloister rose like a red phoenix from the ashes of its surrounding structures, impervious and aloof. In her high tower, his ruthless, bloodthirsty great-grandmother ignored her defeat.

Having lost the Citadel, which Damek and his men now occupied, Nema and her remaining zealots had locked themselves inside the Cloister and barricaded every entrance. Since the enormous inner fortress was comprised of one seemingly smooth piece of red granite, it was impervious to cannon fire. While her city smoldered around her, the best Liadan could manage was to hide in plain sight.

His sigh cut bone-deep.

Men and women were tossed daily from a high window to the cobbles beneath the Cloister.

Blood magic, Leal had once said, and Damek had no reason to doubt him. It seemed Liadan could go on indefinitely, so long as she had willing victims to tap for life.

Coming up behind him, Martin matched his sigh. "Staring at it won't help, lad."

"There are innocents in there with her. Dying for her."

"Some have chosen to. Some are beyond our aid. Torturing yourself over it won't change their fate."

"I helped put her there, Martin."

"Well," said he, failing to mask a sharp note of disappointment. "I daresay neither you nor your noble father expected she would change course mid-plan. You cannot account for everything, in any case. These events were in motion long before your birth."

Damek flinched. "I'm sorry I did not tell you, old friend."

"I'm merely a soldier, highness. You owe me nothing."

"That is far from true."

Martin disarmed him with a warm grin. "The river rolls on, lad. We swim, or we drown, no?"

"Yes," answered Damek, though he was not mollified. He let the subject drop. Martin wouldn't appreciate further meaningless apologies.

"What does he say?" asked Martin, jerking a thumb at the window.

"'*Tairngare is yours, make Eire mine.*'"

"To Rosweal, again?"

"Of course," Damek laughed dryly. "The High King's army gathers as we speak."

"How many?"

"Two-thousand, maybe three."

Martin coughed. "That's a rather large number for an insignificant hamlet full of thieves and beggars."

"The Dannans place importance upon it for the same reason Falan does. That is where Kaer Yin Adair will take my cousin on his way to Bri Leith. The Prince of Armagh would fain see his rival reinstated as Crown Prince."

"Yes, and you bear a rather strong grudge there yourself, Highness."

Damek discovered he didn't care for the title as much as he thought. Although he might have won Tairngare's people, soldiers, and fainne, Nema defied him. His success was far from total. Then, there was Rosweal and the coming clash with the Sidhe to think of too. Could he genuinely call himself a king when both outcomes remained undecided?

Sensing Damek's train of thought, Martin clapped a hand over his shoulder. "You aren't claiming the crown for yourself alone, lad. You're doing it for all of us. A king of Eire, even one afflicted with enemies, has more power than a simple warlord. You've won the grandest city in the North and bear the support of most of the Souther lords, merchers, and townships. Your uncle may twist this way and that, but you managed to do what neither he nor his brother ever could. Even the Sidhe would fail to see the merit of your claim, and in the end, 'tis better to bargain from a seat of power."

"Unless we lose, Martin." Damek looked away. "Kaer Yin Adair is a general of no mean skill. We have set two thousand men down the Taran High Road, who might be swamped by the Sidhe any day. Once he arrives, if he hasn't already, it will begin in earnest."

"You'll be there."

"Will I?" Damek doubted aloud. "Nema must be seen to. She cannot linger in that tower unchecked. There is also the matter of my uncle marching toward Malahide with his Kneeler's army and the prisoner I can't bear to lose."

"Castor will cut his deal. What of it? Even together, neither can hope to match the combined might of Tairngare and the majority of the South."

"Even if we lose at Rosweal?"

"Aye, highness," replied Martin. "Even if. Supposing one hand is slapped away from Rosweal, the other bears a force fifty thousand strong. The Northers are behind you, as Nema has done her job well. The High King may have superior forces, but they are not all gathered, and Rosweal is a terrible place to defend a kingdom. Whatever happens in this contest, you will remain the undisputed King of Eire."

Damek heaved a heavy breath and squared his shoulders. A king who suffered no doubts was a fool or madman. Damek was neither. "So be it. Let's get this farce out of the way, shall we?"

Taking the golden fillet that had belonged to his uncle in one hand and clutching his sabre hilt in the other, Damek sighed. Martin dipped a curt bow and kicked the door open. The Grand Arcade, which had previously housed the courts of Parliament before Nema's ascendancy, erupted into cheers. A thousand people, soldiers, and citizens alike, leaped to their feet in roaring approval. Despite himself, Damek smiled.

See uncle? He thought.

This is what it's like to be loved by those you mean to rule.

From Nema's obsidian terrace, he held the fillet above his head; arms stretched taut. The crowd in the Arcade below hushed. "You have suffered," he said, his voice clean and clear. "You have waited." He turned, holding the fillet to the light that filtered through the massive holes in the once beautifully arched ceiling. "You have longed for justice."

He turned to bask a bit under his foster father's misty eyes. He set the crown upon his head. "Your king hears you."

X

LATER, AT THE FEAST, AOIFE came to him with the Warhammers that filtered into the West Hall, the sole room of any size in the Citadel that still bore a roof. Damek sat in the center of the room upon a hastily constructed dais in a simple wooden chair. He drank but, so far, had yet to feel any joy. He had yet to earn the crown he wore, and it chafed at him—the itch to leave and prove his worth burned beneath his skin.

Aoife saw it soon as she saw him. Her knowing grin irked him. "Majesty," she mocked a bow and took a seat without waiting for permission. "The warriors of Armagh have come to swear fealty to their Crown Prince."

Leal led them before the dais, decked out in the red and black cuirass and greaves of House Mac Nemed, and wearing the kohl stripe over the eyes, which signified mourning. All two hundred of them bore the same black line. An homage to the slain Princess of Armagh, whose body Leal himself had washed and burned. Leal's mighty left fist struck the metal over his heart: the black bull of Ulster. "Armagh comes to swear allegiance to their mighty Prince and serve him as King of all Eire. Will you accept us, *Ard Tiarne*?"

"I do," said Damek, hand over his heart. "I choose you as my honor guard, Leal MacDenron, you and twenty of your chosen warriors. Do you grant me leave to claim you?"

Leal beamed. "I am honored, Your Grace."

"Excellent." Damek snapped his fingers. Ridley and twenty Corpsmen rushed over with new benches. "Be seated among my officers and hold yourselves high in my regard."

Though leery of their newfound Fir Bolg comrades, the Steel Corps cheered them as they took their place beneath Damek's eye. Aoife snorted from beside him. He spared her a dry glare. "No one invited you here, Aoife."

She snatched a bite from his plate. "Here I am all the same. So, how does it feel to have what you've always wanted?"

He resumed his seat while the feast reached a raucous volume. "Aren't there two mindless servants somewhere you should be fucking?"

Her hair was finally growing in. It gave her sharp cheekbones a pixyish set when she laughed. "What's the matter, dear cousin? Bed grown a bit cold, has it?"

"Is there a reason you've come?"

"I longed to see my handsome cousin take his place among the kings of old, of course." She sat back, popping a dried grape into her mouth. "Most impressive feat, my love. I congratulate you."

"Thank you," he minced. "Now, what do you want?"

She took a deep sip from his wine. Damek waved Hisk away, whose hand had already pulled two inches of steel from his scabbard. Seemingly oblivious to the threat, Aoife smacked her full red lips. "I'm not here for you."

"Good, because you'd be bound to be disappointed. I leave by week's end."

That did wipe a bit of the smirk from her face. "She will be the death of you, you know?"

"I go for Falan, not Una."

She laughed with just her throat, still possessing his wine. "Do I look like a fool?"

"Think what you like." He shrugged, wrenching his wine away. "I want her back, of course, but this isn't my primary focus. Not at the moment."

"If she falls into your hands, you can pretend it was an accident. Do you think you have the stones to rape her, I wonder? I don't imagine your men will support you for long without a string of heirs to solidify your House."

Damek's molars ground together, though he didn't let the urge to throttle her show on his face. "I've no need. Once the Dannan prince is dead, she'll choose me. She chose me before he came for her." He willed his heart still. "But if she does not, no matter. I am king, in my own right."

Aoife, for once, did not cut her eyes at him sideways. She gave him a long look full of something he'd never seen on her face before: *pity*. "She never deserved you, my love, whatever happens."

Damek opened his mouth to retort, but that horridly burned creature limped into his line of vision, escorted by none other than Martin himself. Aoife stiffened at the sight of him. The disfigured fellow shook against Martin's staying arm. "Your Grace," Martin asserted. "This is Fawa Gan. He has something to say to you, privately."

Aoife got to her feet, staring at the shrinking mass of ruined flesh.

"Gan," she whispered, half-menace, half-promise.

"You're here for him?" Damek asked her aside.

She shook her head. "For Nema. Though, I owe him too."

Then, Damek saw it— the trembling was anticipatory, not fearful. *He wants to die.* Damek frowned to himself. *So might you, if you'd suffered what he has.*

The King of Eire got to his feet. "Follow me."

✕

Some hours later, Damek, Martin, Leal, Douglas, Hisk, and a dozen more of his men and honor guard crept through a tunnel toward a hidden door. Gan and Aoife followed at a sedate pace. One breathed so hard Damek feared they'd pull the Cloister down around their ears. In a small, dank room, the large black door loomed in the light of Martin's torch. Damek nodded to Hisk, who pulled a chisel from his belt and applied himself to the door. With so many of them crowded into that musty chamber, Damek was surprised to catch the faintest glint of white in the deepest corner. He trained his torch toward the object.

A small bundle of bones dressed in the remnants of a Nova's brown rags lay crumpled in a dried puddle of effluence. Damek covered his mouth and nose. The burned man squeaked, then fell to his knees before it. Aoife stood behind him. "Another of your victims, Gan?"

He turned away, nodding. The child couldn't have been much older than five or six.

The Tairnganese call us barbarians, thought Damek.

"Shall I do it here?" she asked softly, squeezing his shoulder.

Gan seemed to gather himself. "I would see her brought low, first."

"As would I," she said, helping him to his feet.

Damek wasn't sure what they meant but heard the lock spring free under Hisk's clever fingers. When the door swung open, a blast of chill, fetid air rushed into their faces, sputtering the torches. He turned to Gan. "After you."

Gan wiped his nose and stepped into the dark.

✕

GAN LED THEM THROUGH HALLS and stairs once bustling with people: servants, students, and craftsmen of all stripes and stations. Now, the halls were frigid, hollow, and empty. Their footprints left shallow impressions upon dusty floors, their tremulous breath the only sound. Gan seemed to stand taller the farther they delved into the interior.

Huge tapestries bearing the Golden Dragon ascending over an ink-black field hung tattered or partially torn in the Grand Arcade. An open roof spilled fresh snow into the courtyard, and ice dangled from Nema's newly constructed balcony. They didn't spy a single soul on their way up the granite stairs.

Damek felt like a fly in a web. "Where is everyone?"

Aoife didn't appear to share his trepidation. "Dead, I expect."

"*Blood magic.*" Leal covered his nose, looking around. "I can smell its foul taint from here."

Aoife nodded. "She'll be waiting for us."

"Wonderful," said Martin, gripping his sabre.

Gan paused at the top of the stair. He reached for Aoife's arm. She didn't pull away. Damek couldn't help but be surprised. She even patted his hand. "I know. I vow you'll live long enough to see."

The relief in his eyes commingled with something else; courage, Damek would swear, though he had little experience of the man. Fawa Gan didn't seem the sort, whatever his truth was. Aoife trailed the fellow up the stairs, her mouth a firm line. Damek had no idea what was between them but suspected a lifetime of shared indenture to a madwoman formed certain bonds.

At the mouth of the Grand Stair, Aoife took the lead, drawing her dagger. The look on her face was almost giddy with anticipation.

"Martin," Damek whispered. "Whatever happens, see she doesn't kill the old woman."

"Why *not?*"

"What do you think is a worse fate for someone like Liadan Mac Nemed? A swift death or long internment?"

"Neither sounds ideal."

"She'll fight us if only to encourage the first outcome."

By the Fifth-Floor landing, the truth of Damek's statement rang clear. There was no railing in the Grand Stair. Nothing but a long, twisting column of vivid roseate stone curled upward, with intervals at each level. Without torches to light their way, the first few screams seemed to come from nowhere.

A body barreled into Aoife first, knocking her into Gan, who yelped. The next caught Martin with a grunt. When a fetid-smelling missile caught him around the legs, Damek barely had time to draw his sabre. Instinctively, he slashed at his attacker, who slumped forward at his feet, dead. He scarcely realized the assailant was a child before three more were upon him, snarling like dogs. One went over the stair face first, taking a while to strike the bottom with a sickening crunch.

Another tried to sink stinking teeth into his throat while its companion struggled to jerk the sabre from his hand. "Martin!" Damek shouted though it would do no good. Bethany's Commander at Arms found himself similarly inundated. Cursing, Damek grabbed the tallest of the group and flung them bodily into the stairwell. He bashed the smaller ones together like bookends, and they crumpled, alive but unconscious. "Stun them if you can. They're insensate."

"Witchcraft," agreed Leal, tossing two down the steps to the next landing. Damek thought he heard one neck break, but the other might live.

Aoife didn't share Damek's optimism. Beneath her breath, she spoke, and the stairway filled with an uncomfortable electric pulse. All the hair on Damek's neck stood on end as a bright violet light whipped through each tiny chest, felling five children in one go. The smell of burnt hair and scorched flesh assailed his nostrils. The remaining children stopped their ravening assault to watch the others tumble into the void. A whimper or two was all they managed before skittering down the stairs while hugging the walls. Whatever she had done, Aoife had stripped Nema's spell from them. Undeterred, she lifted her chin and continued upward.

"Warm one, isn't she?" quipped Douglas.

Martin, who loathed her, said nothing— but Gan replied, "It costs her more than you will ever know, soldier."

"Gan," she said over her shoulder. "That's enough."

He obeyed, resuming his place behind her.

Damek had some idea of what he meant. The cost of such magic would grind a lesser practitioner to nothing. Even Una, whose power was fearsome indeed, had her limits. He could only guess how hard Aoife struggled to conceal the effects.

When they arrived at the Ninth Floor landing, it wasn't feral children they encountered but armed Warhammers. Gan pressed himself into the wall to avoid a crushing blow to his temple that would have killed him on the spot while Aoife rammed her dagger into a Bolgman's neck. As for Damek and Martin, they were too busy defending themselves against the vicious hammer falls and short-sword thrusts to be much help. Leal dispatched one of his countrymen, then was quickly engaged by another.

"*A bhráithre, nach bhfuil aithne agat ormsa?*" he pleaded. They did not seem to hear him. Worse, they did not slow.

Damek was sweating two minutes into this skirmish and knew if he didn't take every opportunity he could muster, one of Nema's Bolgmen would cut him in half. "Aoife, if you've got more of that in you, now would be the right moment!"

But Aoife was too busy fighting for hers and Gan's lives to heed him. A Warhammer thrice her size had them both pinioned against the wall. Aoife's teeth flashed as she fended him off. Redoubling his efforts, Damek managed to slay one of his two attackers and then hurl himself her way.

His sabre slammed into the back of the fellow's head, nearly skewering her through the eye. She gave a little gasp but scrabbled from beneath the falling body with a hiss. Already back to business with his third dangerous opponent, Damek only had the air to bellow, "Aoife, now!"

He couldn't tell what motion she made, only caught the barest suggestion that her hands had come up. She huffed something he could not hear.

His opponent dropped his blade, blinking.

Unfortunately, Damek had already thrust forward before Aoife's counter-spell could do its work, and his sabre plunged through the fellow's guts into the wall. With an apologetic glance, Damek withdrew his blade. The Bolgman slipped to the floor, burbling. The rest, blinking at their raised weapons, backed away, mystified. Leal said something to them. Damek couldn't hear over his racing heartbeat. He knelt beside Aoife.

Gan had taken a severe gash to his ribs. He grew paler if that were possible. Aoife's nostrils streamed blood. "Are you all right?"

She ignored Damek's outstretched hand, instead helping Gan to his feet as if he were the most important person in the world to her. The ugly lump leaned against her. "I'll make it."

"Yes, you will."

They brushed past Damek and resumed the path upward.

Damek understood then, seeing their shapes huddled together in the shadows.

They *both* meant to die.

Something sharp gripped Damek's heart. "Aoife?"

She didn't turn, but her voice carried down to him without effort. "Leave it alone, my love."

X

THE GREAT VANNA NEMA, OR LADY Liadan Mac Nemed, appeared neither great nor a lady as she wheezed at the base of her onyx throne. Instead, some slithering, boneless monster with sagging brown jowls and huge hollow eyes quivered upon the steps in a heap of yellow and saffron fabric. Her miter was smashed to an unrecognizable mess near the windows. The throne room reeked of stale breath, unwashed flesh, heady magic, and rot. There was no one in the chamber save Nema... and a dozen or more corpses, abandoned where they had fallen. The floor was stained with blood, a hard reddish crust that marred the perfection of that glossy midnight floor.

"Aoife." The thing tried to smile.

"Yes, *seanmáthair*. I have come for you. Look, Gan's with me."

Nema gurgled at him as if cooing to an infant. She reached out with one desiccated hand. Gan sank to his knees before her.

"Don't touch her," Aoife warned. "She'll do the same to you just to cheat us."

"Aoife let us—" Damek began.

"Stay out of this," she snapped. "This has nothing to do with you."

"I think you'll find," he said as Martin and Leal approached her, bleeding and deadly serious. "That it does. Come away, Aoife. There's been enough death on her account."

Aoife's skin bleached a pale gold. "What did you say?"

"You heard me. Let Falan choose what to do with her. Leave her, both of you."

Martin got closer than Leal, but his usual loathing did not reach his eyes this time. There was, however, a noticeable dose of sympathy there. Aoife lashed out. Martin backed off, only slightly. "You wouldn't *dare* do this to me, Damek. Not me. Not now."

"Self-sacrifice is not your style, Aoife."

"How would you know, you arrogant, self-absorbed fool? Do you know how long I've waited for this day? Slaved for this day? Bled for this day? Do you have the faintest idea how old I am, how many decades this horrid beast commanded my every waking thought? You see Gan here and shake with pity and contempt. She did the very same to me, Damek. Only my blood has the power to reverse the external wounds. Inside, Gan and I are the same!" She reached out and clasped Gan's hand in her own. "How *dare* you attempt to interfere."

Gan leaned close to Nema's twitching face. Her eyes were wild though her throat could not form the words she sought. "We're ready to go, all three of us together. That sounds nice, doesn't it?"

He made as if to smooth her hair. Aoife drew in a sharp breath too late. Nema's hand closed over Gan's, where it lightly connected with her brow.

"*Fuil san, Fhuil amach,*" she croaked.

Aoife shrieked a warning, but Gan shriveled where he knelt. His body hit the stone floor with a sigh, bloodless and shucked of all vitality.

Nema pushed herself upright like a wounded boar.

"Gan!" Aoife wailed, kicking against Martin's shins.

Swelling now with the life she stole, Liadan Mac Nemed's eyes found hers. She opened her cracked lips to speak, but Leal jammed his sword straight down her gullet. With a growl, he drove the point in until the tip struck sparked against stone. "No more spells for you, *cailleach*."

When he withdrew the blade again, Nema was long gone.

Aoife's shrieks rent the stone above. "No, no, NO!"

"Martin, let go of her!" warned Damek.

The speed by which O'Rearden obeyed suggested he'd done so seconds before Damek said anything. Aoife slipped to her knees and then scrambled forward. The air around her crackled with energy. Over Gan's husk, she wept the first real tears Damek had ever seen from her. When she turned to him, her eyes flashed with unholy light. "You *betrayed* me!"

"Damek, get back!" bellowed Martin.

Hisk threw himself before his king, but he needn't have bothered. Leal got there first. He struck Aoife once, hard, in the temple. She slumped forward over Gan's corpse, whose fingers lay scant inches from his former mistress'.

Damek couldn't tell for sure, but the strange little fellow seemed to be smiling.

※

By the first of Ban Apesa, Damek MacNemed, King of Eire, boasted an army nearly seventy thousand strong. He controlled most of the North, the Midlands, Bretagne, the Reaches of Bethany, and much of Kernow. He was the undisputed master of the wealthiest city in Innisfail. He boasted of a fleet of twelve ships. Those who survived the Bretagn assault now bore his colors above every mast. Come spring, he expected to have twice that number.

Damek had the support of the Merchanta Charter in Tairngare, who were now returning to the battered and bruised city with their families. The citizens who'd fled during Nema's brief but tyrannical regime came home to discover Damek's soldiers already working to repair their roofs, clear their streets of debris, and rebuild houses smashed in the onslaught.

His men did not rape, pillage, or otherwise maim his subjects, taking his cue from the Sidhe they would soon meet on the field. Instead, they were rewarded with fine housing in the city or the countryside and funds to set aside for their families and future businesses.

There wasn't a single soul in Tairngare who did not love their new king... save one.

With the bulk of his army preparing to march west, Damek climbed the Grand Stair to the Tenth Floor. Nema's devices had been ripped from the walls. The filth and taint of death had been scrubbed from the floors. People began to return to Cloister for work and duty. Secundas poured through the halls, paving the way for the arriving Primas and a return to their devotions.

The Citadel's renovations were already underway, as Damek claimed the fortress for himself. The Southern Wing had become his royal residence, with its gorgeous floor-to-ceiling windows, high iron doors, gold wainscoting, and gleaming mahogany floors. The Siorai were welcome to maintain their religious pursuits in the Citadel, but he vowed to return the city to secular rule. The renovations he'd ordered would ensure the Citadel would become the hub of law and order while encircling and protecting the pastoral pursuits of the Siorai faith. Tairngare was to be his northern stronghold and his seat of power in greater Innisfail.

It would never again rise a theocratic empire.

The days of absolute religious autonomy were over.

Whether Damek died on the battlefield in a month or a year... the Siorai would fail to reclaim power in Eire. It may have taken a thousand years for Tairngare to build such fabulous wealth, learning, and prestige— but it had taken less than a year to produce a tyrant responsible for the deaths of thousands of innocents.

Damek's first promise to the people was, 'never again.'

He appointed Seamus Wender— the Lord of Kerry's heir apparent and a shrewd commander— First Minister of Eire. Wender's purpose would be to entrench the new, secular, Eirean government and reinstate Parliament under the crown. A return to law and order being his sole task. In Damek's absence, he would manage the city coffers and

Parliamentary proceedings as well as the stewardship of the Eirean war machine. Thirty thousand troops would remain at Tairngare to defend the city. Another five thousand marched to Tara with its new Governor and workers.

Five thousand were sent to Damek's holdings at Clare to guard the West against Henry's advance… and five thousand to Killarney with Lord Bellin to defend the Coast and make his uncle nervous. Damek was marching west with his loyal Steel Corps and nearly twenty thousand men in the vanguard. The Sidhe might have three times that number in the north, but he gambled that the High King was unaware of the danger Damek posed.

He would, soon enough.

For now, Damek looked up at the ornate golden doors ahead, wishing this task might fall to someone else. He would rather be anywhere else in the world but here. His guards shoved the doors open for him. The Doma's throne room was empty, but he felt he knew where Aoife had hidden herself. With a narrow eye, he strode past the onyx throne. Before he left today, he'd be sure to leave orders to have this monstrous misapplication of wealth stripped-down, panel by panel and stone by stone. He'd never seen such hubris in his life. Actual gemstones greeted his eyes from each chamber. Soaring walls in every variety of precious metal, chandeliers dripping diamonds and rubies or worse, accosted his sensibilities.

No bloody wonder Drem Moura believed herself divine.
Just look at all this rubbish.

In a room decked with silver and garnets, he found her. In a plain white shift, Aoife hugged her knees to herself on the windowsill, staring down at the forces that gathered in the streets, cheering their new king. She didn't look up. "They're hailing you as the Star King," she said.

He leaned against the doorframe. "For Reason, of course. The Southernmost Star. Lord Wender made a lovely speech about the importance of secularism and Reason in the newly formed Parliament. It charmed some, as it was meant to."

She made a rude sound. "Secularism? Wait till they see what their new High King has planned for them."

"He can plan as he likes. I will fulfill my vow to engage his enemies, but the people here answer to only one king."

Her head finally swiveled his way. "You can't be serious? He'll destroy you."

He pursed his lips and crossed his arms. "The soldiers here will never bow to him, and he doesn't boast a tenth of the men to hold them all. Whether he takes Bri Leith or not, I am King of Eire. If I am killed, Tairngare will be run by Parliament and Ministers, as it should be."

She watched him in silence for a moment. "You expect to be killed?"

"I accept that it's possible."

"Perhaps you *would* make a great king, my love." Then, he felt it, that tiny crackle of malice. "You cannot hold me here forever, you know?"

Such was life, was it not?

One long series of accounts marked 'to be paid.'

According to Aoife, this is one debt he could never clear.

"Forgive me," was all he said.

"Never," she vowed in return.

Allegiances

n.e. 508
07 ban apesa
Rosweal

"Obviously, Mistress Dormer," sneered Fionn Shiel O'More, the High King's Champion, from Barb's favorite chair. "We are in command of this outpost. Consider yourselves fortunate that the High King has seen fit to honor your rabble with his advance guard. I fail to see how a brothel-keeper should hold delegatory powers in a martial matter?" The Marshal of Bri Leith's Wild Hunt and Commander of the Dannan Legion stared down his long, patrician nose at Barb. This man was Midhir's right hand, closer to the Ard Ri than his brothers. Aside from Ben, Fionn O'More was the most decorated soldier in all Innisfail. Such ego demanded utmost respect.

Well, Barb was used to arrogant males attempting to diminish her.

Calmly and with all the pride she could muster, she leaned over her pilfered desk (the Lord Marshal had ruthlessly appropriated her *entire* office). Wordlessly, she poured a handful of black powder onto the outdated and frankly useless map he and his fellows had been examining. It took her nearly two damned months to get this far, and the fury of being in limbo for so long rankled.

This was her bloody joint! Her office, her desk, and *her* Siora-damned chair! She might be glad to have a thousand extra archers on the walls—but that didn't give these big, blond bastards leave to order her about in her own home.

The two guards beside him reached for their sword hilts. Fionn halted them with a gesture.

Barb resisted the urge to leer at them.

One wore his long hair in a complicated series of braids doffed at the ends with silver clubs in the shape of maple leaves. Like most Dannan Sidhe, he had the cornsilk and cream coloring only found in the Ban Sidhe of Nuada's kin. Almost all were taller and broader through the shoulder than your average mortal man: their features were sharper, finer, their eyes brighter, keener.

As for Fionn himself, he wore his hair short, trimmed neatly around his chin. Dangling from his right lobe, six gold chains caught the light from her open shutters. His pale jade green eyes narrowed at her in disapproval. His white cuirass, decorated with a silver stag crowned by three stars, creaked when he steepled his long fingers. His armor must not have seen much action of late—too much wax.

"What is this?" he asked, more tired than annoyed. He had the mien of a man who'd rather be reading at his hearth than marching off to war.

"I think yer lordship knows very well what this is," answered Barb, crossing her arms over her shrinking bosom. Her dress, which once hugged every curve like a stretched canvas, now had to be pinned beneath her arms to keep it in place. She tried not to dwell on it.

Fionn's lip curled. "Gunpowder is illegal in Innisfail, Mistress. I'm sure you're aware?"

Dragging a free chair under her rump, she waved at a glass of amber liquid near his elbow. "So is uishge, now ye mention it, Lord. Does that mean I should stop havin' it hauled up the stairs for ye and yer men?" She gave him her best, gap-toothed grin.

She watched his pretty eyes slide from the glass to his braided comrade, then to Barb with an accompanying frown. "Fair point, Mistress Dormer."

"It's just 'Barb' if ye please?"

"Fine," he relented. "I'm listening."

She pointed. "I have fifteen casks to work with and over sixty barrels of unfiltered lamp oil. I'd like your leave to use them as *I* see fit. Your men have commandeered the oil. I'm telling you, that's a mistake."

He regarded her carefully, his expression dubious. "Jan Fir?"

"*Mo Flaith?*" answered the tallest Sidhe on his right. This one had sea-green eyes, purest emerald at the iris, ringed in a startling storm-blue. He wore his hair long and loose, save for two strands tied back at the temples with a silver pin. His cuirass was as white as the others, but the device was a roaring bear in copper. Barb found him slightly more inviting than his companions. There was something nearly human about the sardonic tilt of his chin.

"Do we have sixty barrels of lamp oil at our disposal?"

"*Stolen* barrels," added Barb.

Jan Fir's lip twitched at the corner. Yes, she decided she liked this one much better than his friends. "We might."

Fionn exhaled through his nose as her grandfather used to when he was vexed. How *old* was the Lord Marshal? She could only guess. Most Sidhe were obscenely long-lived, true, but only the Daoine Sidhe, like the High King and his kin, were genuinely immortal. "If— and I use that term very loosely," his tone was dry as sawdust. "I allow you to take these items, what purpose do you intend for them?"

"The bloody defense o'this town, of course," she hissed. "I'll remind ye that yer even now, sitting in me own Da's chair, in me own establishment, in me own fecking city!" She leaned forward again, so he couldn't miss her point. "I'll thank ye for yer help mannin' these walls we've just built— but don't ye get on makin' yerself free to take whatever ye like! That oil is mine. I'll have that and me feckin' tavern back, *right bleedin' now!*"

The only perturbation her speech seemed to inspire in Fionn O'More, was the barest elevation of a single golden brow. "I beg your pardon, madam, or you'll do *what*, exactly?"

Sure, that took a fair bit of wind out of her lungs, but her temper burned on. "Why go out o'yer way to make enemies of allies? By necessity or otherwise, our end goal is the same, is it not?"

"No," he answered without pause. "I think you'll find we are *not* here to help you, Mistress, any more than your many poachers and brigands have attempted to aid us. You raid our lands, take our sacred creatures, rob the unwary, and break the Ard Ri's laws with every breath we've allowed you to take for the last hundred years. Our presence here is tactical. To halt an assault upon our border and return Innisfail to lawful rule. Perhaps in your short-sighted arrogance, you assume we intend to allow you and your ilk to retain your autonomy? If so, I assure you, you're mistaken."

He stood, taking a pinch of powder between his fingers and dropping it onto his open palm. "What I find most disconcerting about you is the pride you exhibit by barging in here with something many have been sentenced to death for possessing and then demanding I return these ill-gotten gains to you." He shook his head at her. "Yours is a most perplexing species."

Barb swallowed her fear. She was an old woman now, no getting around it. An old whore, thief, and criminal profiteer. She'd neither deny it nor bother to explain herself. Her ilk was nothing to these grand Sidhe lords, never had been, never would be, but she had something they didn't: *knowledge.* "That's all very well, yer lordship, but I ask ye, how many men do'ye imagine gather down the Taran High Road? How many spears would that be against yer handful of capable warriors?"

"My scouts tell me some two thousand. A rabble, largely comprised of foot soldiers."

"'Fraid not. They've some two thousand in this expeditionary force, yes. Twenty thousand are on their way from Tairngare as we speak. Yer not just outnumbered ten-to-one, yer outfoxed too."

At last, he flushed. "Damek Bishop is entrenched at Tairngare. If he leaves the city, he loses his advantage in the Midlands. His zealous uncle will receive the brunt of his next assault, or the man is a fool."

She'd been trying to tell him for *weeks.*

"Not true. He's comin' here, first."

"Madam, the Ard Ri has sent us to guard the border and hold for reinforcements. It is not our duty to march on Tairngare… yet."

"Yer not gonna have to. He'll come here first, as I've said many times."

He shared a long look with his braided lieutenant. "Rosweal serves no tactical purpose. The Ard Ri agrees that there is a need for a strong Sidhe presence here, but aside from this, has given no orders to prepare for the assault."

She raked a hand through her thinning hair. "Look. Ben hisself knew that Lord Bishop would be back. Even now, his men are marchin' this way, and ye still won't listen."

Fionn gave her a tight smile. "You've a fertile imagination, Mistress Dormer."

"Do I?" She reached into her cloak and brought out a wad of crumpled missives, which she tossed onto her desk for him to gape at. "That's the thing about us 'criminal' types, milord. We're well connected and informed. You'll find the latest news there if ye sort through to the bottom. Not only has Damek Bishop begun his march west, but he's also been hailed the King of feckin' Eire! How is it the grand lot o'ye lack the spies to tell ye where yer arses are?"

Furiously, Fionn rifled through the various scraps until he came to the one she'd indicated. He growled down at the crumpled vellum like it had bitten him. Disgusted, he passed the message to Jan Fir. Jan Fir tossed it back onto the desk with a snort. The braided fellow, she hadn't caught his name, asked, "Bretagn ships broke the siege? But why? Aes Sidhe has many bonds of fellowship with Bretagne."

"Ain't it funny how that works?" she asked. "When was the last time any o'yer folk sat down with the Colonials in Council? People tend to change with the times they live in, ye know? Life may be grand yer high towers in Aes Sidhe, but here, where real folk live, die, and scrabble in the muck to survive — *autonomy*, I think he said? — sounds pretty feckin' good to men and women who've never seen their lofty masters from some faraway land they're forbidden to enter."

"Madam," attempted Fionn evenly. "While I will admit the most recent news is surprising and concerning to us, the Ard Ri's orders stand. We are to—"

"Sit here with yer cocks in yer hand with an army headed yer way? Don't ye get it? He can't *be* King of Eire if towns like Rosweal are loyal to Ben. He'll stamp us into the dirt to solidify that claim and outnumbered as ye are, yer just askin' for what's comin'!"

While the trio of Commanders mulled over her words, a slight commotion kicked up in the hall. Barb refused to be distracted from her purpose here. It was probably just another scuffle about rations again. She'd sort that once these fancy fools gave her bloody gunpowder back. "Now, I know yer all smart enough to see that this were no accident. I'll bet the late Duch and Nema had something worked out between 'em. The boy finished it. Either way, yer about to have yer bollocks handed to ye by a King of Eire, and I, for one, would rather die than kneel to him."

Fionn opened his mouth to respond, but the commotion outside escalated to an intrusive level. Suddenly the door blew inward on its hinges, slamming into the plastered wall with a clacking bang. In walked a ragged but no less proud Dannan retinue, with one particularly tall silver-haired male in the lead. The newcomer sported a white yew longbow over one shoulder, a frown that could cut through steel, and nine gold chains chiming from his right ear.

Barb had never been so relieved to see anyone in her bloody life! "Ben!"

Ben Maeden… rather Kaer Yin Adair spared her a wink that nearly melted her heart in her chest. Behind him stood the arrogant redheaded prince of Connaught, eight chains chiming in his left ear. Barb watched him tuck his hair behind that ear, so none could mistake which two men bore the most adornment. That slight motion hammered home the stark reality of the company she had been keeping all these years.

Ben Maeden *was* the Crown Prince of Innisfail.

She swallowed.

As if on cue, the two lieutenants at Fionn's side, with only ten gold chains between them (Jan Fir bearing six), sank to their knees. "*Ard Tiarne*," they breathed in surprise. Fionn, however, did not deign to show homage.

He stilled.

The little Tairnganese noblewoman that had started this whole mess in the first place slipped into the room behind Ben. Barb knew none of the events were her fault but couldn't halt the curl Una's presence added to her upper lip. If the girl noticed, she didn't respond.

"Fionn Shiel O'More," said Ben dryly. "Nice haircut."

Ah, Barb thought.

Ben don't care for this prig neither, I see.

"Kaer Yin Adair," Fionn saluted as he might to a subordinate.

A third tall Dannan behind the redhead growled, his blade halfway drawn. The Prince of Connaught caught his elbow, shaking his head. "What's this, Lord O'More? Since you mean to disrespect the son of your Ard Ri, do you intend to give insult to Connaught as well?"

"If you stand behind this vagabond... this traitor, you have your answer."

This time, three more Dannans stepped forward, weapons already bare. The two on the floor made no further movements. Just then, Barb felt the room was suddenly overcrowded with aggressive Sidhe in a pique.

Her chair made quite a racket as she scooted out of the way.

Ben burst into laughter for quite a while. When he stopped, he swiped a tear from the corner of his eye. "Ah, Fionn. It's good to see that at least some things haven't changed. I won't force the issue if you don't care to genuflect. Shar, Niall, Conor? Put your blades away. We didn't come here for this."

"What *did* you come for?" asked Fionn, noting the speed at which the two Blood Eagles obeyed. Barb saw it too. "I see you've taken command of your cousin's warband? How sad for you, Prince Tam Lin, to blindly relinquish your blood guard to this—" he snarled "— relic of failed ambition."

Tam Lin's smile held all the warmth of a cairn. "Jan Fir Brés?"

Jan Fir stood, looking mightily uncomfortable. "*Mo Flaith?*"

Tam Lin jerked a thumb at Ben. "You're his sister's consort, are you not? That makes you the Crown Prince's bannerman."

Jan Fir bowed. "Yes, my prince." He turned to Fionn with apologetic candor. "My Lord O'More, please relinquish your weapons."

Barb let her hand slide over her heart.

That's the King of Scotia? she thought, then remembered her studies. There were only three kings in the Dannan lineage, with the High King at their center. All else were lords or consorts to queens. Ben's sister was the Queen of Scotia in her own right. Therefore, this Jan Fir was a great lord indeed to be wed to the High King's daughter.

"That won't be necessary, Jan." Ben smiled. "We came here to help, not pick a fight."

Barb released the breath she'd been holding. "Where's me man, then?"

"He's in the tap, drinking a gallon of uishge and telling the tale," Ben chuckled. "He said he'd come up when he was sure none of us were about to kill each other."

"Ah well, that remains to be seen."

Ben shrugged. "What else is new?"

"Help?" Fionn repeated. "What possible need have I for *your* help, traitor?"

Una bristled. "I would watch your mouth were I you, My Lord."

"Una, must you?" Tam Lin glared.

She held up her hands, then crossed her arms.

"Yes, Fionn, *help*. You have an army twenty thousand strong marching this way. Damek Bishop means to hammer you into the Eirean border and any Sidhe that might imagine themselves his overlords. My uncle tells me he's been crowned king."

"The Red King is not here."

"Not him," Tam Lin interrupted. "The other one."

Despite his bravado, Fionn paled. "*Fiachra Dubh* is here?"

"Was," corrected Ben. "He will return with reinforcements, gods willing."

"From Connaught?"

Ben nodded. "And Bri Leith."

"Then," sighed Fionn. "I don't see where we should worry overmuch."

"Even traversing the Shadow Path, it will take two weeks to muster their forces and arrive here, at the fastest," argued Tam Lin. "We don't have two weeks. We have half that, if not less. We saw the echoes of Bishop's handiwork in the *Oiche Ar Fad*. We may need to evacuate the city."

"Oh no!" Barb broke in. "Not a-bloody-gain! I'm ready for that fancy fecker. You best believe that. He won't take nothin' more from us."

"We saw the palisades and towers on the way in," Una broke in. "I believe you might be brilliant, Mistress Dormer."

Barb tried and failed to conceal her blush.

"Anyway, whatever happens, we have one week to get ready and a prayer to stall them for another." Ben paused to allow Fionn a long look at his face. "Fionn Shiel O'More, I am taking command of my father's forces here at Rosweal. I ask you to relinquish your men as the Ard Ri's bannerman and, therefore, mine. Will you do so willingly?"

Fionn's perfectly composed features immediately lost their luster. He sputtered. "Over my corpse, you arrogant—"

"Your objection is noted," Ben cut him off. "Mordu?" He turned to the braided fellow, who leaped to his feet in salute.

"*Ard Tiarne?*"

"Tell the troops to assemble at the docks in a quarter-hour. I would address them directly. I come to them, Kaer Yin Adair, Crown Prince of Innisfail and Lord Marshal of the Wild Hunt."

Mordu grinned from ear to ear. His fist slammed against his heart with such force that Barb felt sure he'd broken a rib. "It is my honor, *Ard Tiarne!*"

"As for you, Fionn, I'd have you at my right hand if you'll take it."

Fionn sputtered, he went for his scabbard, but Jan Fir gripped his arm. "I will NOT! You cannot do this! You've no right!"

"I think you'll find," ice wouldn't melt in Ben's mouth. "I bear the *only* right, by birth and blood. Shar? See, Lord O'More has a good long time in private chambers to clear his head."

Shar saluted. Between Jan Fir and Niall, they managed to lead him from the room without much fuss. Ben sat on Barb's desk and heaved a heavy sigh. "Well then, Barb, love?"

"Yes, Yer Arseness?"

"What were you trying to tell the most stubborn fool in Aes Sidhe before wiser fools arrived?"

✕

"He's challenged you to single combat, Yin," japed Tam Lin. "As if we'd time for theatrics just now. Bethany's scouts were spotted down the road only this morning."

Kaer Yin, shirtless and covered in mud and filth, set his spade down to glare at his cousin, who was spotlessly clean and impeccably dressed from head to toe. "What else is new?" He went back to digging. Despite the rudimentary ramparts and hastily hacked trenchwork, Kaer Yin was impressed by what Barb had managed in their absence. With all hands bent on last-minute tasks preparing for the oncoming assault, Barb's bloody moats were the most important thing to finish now.

At dawn, Kaer Yin, Mel Carra, Shar, Niall, and any available men not assigned to various labors, had volunteered to see the thing done.

They'd received further news from Tairngare in the night.

Vanna Nema was dead.

The North had bent the knee to Damek Bishop.

The Duch of Bethany's nephew, who was also Falan Mac Nemed's bastard son, had claimed the crown of Eire. That his crazed uncle now sat on Patrick's former throne and marched against cities that had declared for Bishop and that he now must contend with the Sidhe to prove himself worthy of the claim— seemed to make no never mind to the people. After months of Nema's insane rule, the people of Eire were desperate for the stability he might provide. Already, he'd taken pains to reinstate Parliament and set up a secular Court.

This was a wise move that Kaer Yin couldn't help but be surprised by. The fellow hadn't appeared so clever when they'd met, but he supposed a man in love might be forgiven the odd act of hubris. Bishop's standing order that his troops refrain from raping and pillaging was even more interesting. Any man caught disobeying that edict found himself twisting from the end of a rope in short order.

Again, this showed tactical brilliance.

The Lord of Clare came to the people a savior, which meant, even when the Sidhe eventually put him and his audacious rebellion down... they wouldn't be loved for it. The longer Kaer Yin was subjected to the man, the more he was obliged to appreciate his intellect. Bishop might be a rash, headstrong bastard, but a fool he was not. The self-styled King of Eire now marched toward them with nearly twenty thousand men out of a standing force of almost triple that number. Damek would not send the entire force to Rosweal. No, that would be overkill, Kaer Yin reckoned. Instead, he'd split his forces and send half south and west to secure a safe route to Ten Bells. Regardless, Rosweal faced an incoming force boasting ten-to-one odds.

Kaer Yin was immensely proud of the martial skill, endurance, and cunning each of his warriors possessed— the Greenmakers included— but such would not save them.

He knew it.

Bishop surely counted on it.

The only hope they had to halt a force of such size was to delay for as long as it might take for Bov Dearg to march from Connaught. Once the fighting began, even if the new walls and ramparts managed to keep Bishop's army out, Rosweal would last days, a week at best. If they couldn't hold the walls long enough for reinforcements to arrive, they'd have no choice but to concede the border. If Bov did not arrive in time, Kaer Yin's father would have lost his grip on Eire. Something that had not happened in a thousand years.

These events foretold a crisis and no mistake. That tiny, insignificant Rosweal should bear the brunt was a failing on the Sidhe's part that Kaer Yin would be hard-pressed to repair. Thankfully, Barb had an uncanny sixth sense about the ambitions of ruthless men. She'd prepared as well as anyone could have hoped. Now it fell to him to ensure none of her work was wasted.

He sighed, leaning against his spade.

About six feet ahead of him, Niall dug at a furious pace that should have made all present men quake with shame. Beyond his immediate band, Kaer Yin caught a glimpse of a golden head bobbing along the walls. He hadn't seen much of her outside of the occasional midnight visit when no one was meant to notice him creeping to and from her chamber in his old tenement. He'd been busy with the men and fortifications, and she'd been… well, he had no idea. As always, she was a mystery to him. He wondered what it might be like to wake with her hair spilling over his chest in the light of the morning sun, to watch her golden eyes flash from beneath her dark lashes as he pressed himself into her. It would be wonderful not to have to sneak around.

Not that they fooled anyone, of course.

Shar had the dubious honor of guarding his chambers on the second floor every night, keeping his eyes trained tactfully on the ceiling whenever Kaer Yin crept past. Though he knew he was the luckiest man in Innisfail to have that warm, infuriating, sinuous creature to himself, Kaer Yin starved for the sight of her during his waking hours. At the thought, someone hoisted her up onto the rampart. Dangling there, she ran her hands over the wood, chanting with closed eyes.

When he could tame the absurd rush of his pulse, he asked, "What's she doing up there now?"

Two of Barb's burlies held her steady while she was lowered to the masonry layer by rope. Her aunt Eva leaned over the wall to grab one of her arms. She kept her eyes closed. Kaer Yin guessed she was either lending her niece strength or praying she didn't fall and crack her head open. Maybe a bit of both? He caught that sound of rushing insect wings, which usually hinted that Una used her powers.

He shivered at the sound.

Tam Lin made a rude noise. "Something more or less useless, I suppose."

Kaer Yin speared him with a level glance. "You would prove the expert in that quarter, wouldn't you? Have you lifted a finger to do anything but gossip all day?"

Tam Lin raised his chin. "That's for peasants and people with hope, *Ard Tiarne*. I am neither."

Before Kaer Yin could give him the earful he was itching for, another round of horns went off at the docks. Fionn's *garda*— well, Kaer Yin's *garda*, now reclaimed— announcing newcomers. Without waiting for a second blast, Kaer Yin clambered up the trench to shove his cousin aside and stomp toward the river. When he got to the docks, a wide grin split his face. Without fanfare, a host of riders swept over the river from Aes Sidhe. This one was easily five-hundred strong, most bearing the Ard Ri's device upon their breasts. Some, he marveled, wore the red eagle of the *Eiloar Bas*. Hundreds of cavalrymen, pikemen, and bowmen bearing the leaping silver stag arrayed before them. At their front rode Diarmid, wearing his plain black cuirass, his midnight cloak billowing behind him.

Fiachra Dubh needed no sigil to mark him out.

As he dismounted, his nephews pushed toward him. Kaer Yin's smile flickered when he saw the look on his uncle's face. "Herne. What now?"

Diarmid pulled them both close by the shoulder. "We need to talk."

Declaration

n.e. 508
13 ban apesa
Rosweal

This far north, the air chilled dramatically as night approached. Though Sidhe did not feel the cold as powerfully as a Milesian might, tonight, Kaer Yin couldn't seem to get warm, even squatting before a roaring fireplace. Perhaps he owed his thinned blood to the relatively balmy temperatures of the *Oiche Ar Fad* or the long hours he'd spent outside helping bolster the city's defenses. Now wearing only a thin tunic over mud-soaked woolen trousers, he realized how weary he was. His limbs were leaden, and his back was sore in several places. He half wished Damek's army would show up already and put him out of his misery. Una took the seat beside him and tucked a tankard of spiced ale into his frozen palm.

If possible, he fell in love with her all over again.

Kneeler's bloody angel, this one.

He thanked her profusely with a glance, his free hand around hers.

They were in the tap at *The Hart*, one of the few solidly built structures left in Rosweal. Some months ago, most homes and buildings had been razed in the last Bethonair attack, including Kaer Yin's Hilltop abode. Whatever remained of that neighborhood housed the bulk of Rosweal's citizens or had been deconstructed to build Barb's impressive triple wall. As for the complex moat she'd imagined, they would open the floodgates tomorrow and see if her mad plan held merit. Kaer Yin thought it might, although even that wouldn't halt such a large force of hardened pikemen and cavalry. Besides, he knew Damek and his men had cannons and trebuchets. If that weren't dire enough, he had a feeling his uncle Diarmid was about to deliver worse news. Or would, whenever the Greenmakers finished fumbling around to make the old bastard comfortable, of course.

Having so many Sidhe strutting up and down their streets, bartering freely in the enfeebled markets, and drinking in their jukes and taverns was one thing... hosting the Lord of Tech Duinn was quite another.

Fiachra Dubh was afforded the finest seat in the house, upstaging Kaer Yin as if he were merely an errand boy. Diarmid was a king. Kaer Yin supposed he needn't begrudge his arsehole of an uncle a better chair.

Everyone seemed to be gathered according to their political importance, which was Barb's doing, no doubt. He and Una sat together at the banquette near the fire, with Tam Lin and Eva opposite. Barb and the others gathered at tables surrounding the bar. Diarmid shifted awkwardly in his seat. If not for the stares the gathered townsfolk gave him, perhaps for Eva's, because the Siorai unnerved him, Kaer Yin was pleased to note. Diarmid ogled the ale in his hand and leaned closer to Kaer Yin. "Is this... palatable?"

"Try it and find out," Kaer Yin said, tapping his tankard against it and draining his pint in one go. With a small cheer, Robin and the others toasted and tipped back their own, even Gerrod, who let out a rather large belch which made him flush red to the roots of his dark hair.

Rian didn't seem to notice, so he needn't have bothered. She was far away, at the opposite end of the tap with Shar Lianor.

"Uh oh," said Una, sipping her cider. "There's another broken heart, I fear."

Kaer Yin winced, trying not to see how Rian smiled at Shar. "Might have to bloody well wall her up at this point." Tam Lin, who was not meant to hear that exchange, followed Kaer Yin's darting eyes. His scowl cut deep lines into his otherwise effeminate face.

"See?" Kaer Yin added to Una, aside.

"Shar is merely being friendly to the girl. He wouldn't pursue such a lowly quarry," Tam Lin sniffed, pretending boredom. Kaer Yin saw the tick in his jaw, regardless.

Una set her mug down to glare over at the Prince of Connaught. "Listen here, you. If I even *dream* you attempt anything with that girl, I'll melt the hair from your head. Do you hear me?"

"Una, love. Be nice." Kaer Yin warned half-heartedly.

Tam Lin pressed a hand to his chest. "I do not starve for partners, thank you."

Una's smile rattled. "Consider yourself duly warned."

"If she chooses to come to me of her own accord, what business would it be of yours, *My Lady*?" Tam Lin grinned back. "The girl is an adult, by all accounts."

Well, fuck.

Kaer Yin leaned back in his seat, crossing his arms. Diarmid seemed too intrigued by his ale to notice this tiny pre-meeting storm. Across from them at another table, Eva sat up a bit straighter, ready to defend her niece at the first provocation. That would be terrible news for Tam Lin. Kaer Yin opened his mouth to interrupt, but Una beat him to the punch.

"I'm adopting her. I will never give you consent, and that, my dear princeling, is that." Una retorted.

"You can't adopt a fully-grown person."

"Males get such ideas," quipped Eva dryly from the rear.

"I'm technically the Duchess of Bethany and the Domina of the Moura Clan. I'm quite a wealthy woman, and I vowed to give that girl every advantage she might have. While you two have been digging, drinking, or playing cards, I've been busy. By the time my signature reaches Ten Bells next week, Rian will be the Countess of Ardgillan— a property of no mean size. Balbriggan and the fishing port at Skerries will make her an heiress of spectacular means. So, from now on, you may call her 'Lady Ardgillan' rather than 'unworthy quarry'... you abominable twat." She took another long sip, then sliced her eyes away from him with a dismissive sniff.

Tam Lin blinked rapidly for several moments. "I didn't mean to give the impression—"

"Too late," she snapped.

Speechless for a moment, Tam Lin spared Kaer Yin a confused shrug, then buggered off to glare at Una and Rian from a far corner. Kaer Yin could see his cousin couldn't decide which woman was more vexing by the look on his face.

"I didn't know you'd been making wills, love," Kaer Yin said, trying and failing to catch her eye.

"It's not a will. The properties and monthly rents are hers as soon as she wants them. I presume my signature will hit the Libellan Bank sometime in the next few days. It's done. Furthermore, I've granted her an additional two-hundred thousand fainne and set aside funds for Gerrod and his sisters. The people of Rosweal have also been granted enough funds to purchase their charter from Tairngare. Provided we win, I've seen to it all."

Kaer Yin was dumbfounded. "You don't think we're going to live through this?"

She rolled a shoulder. "Whether we do or not, we will have left something behind for those who didn't deserve what we brought upon them. That's the very least I could do."

His fingers threaded through hers, overwhelmed by a feeling he couldn't explain or quantify. "Does she know?"

"Not yet. She'd argue, and I can't bear it."

"Una... I love you."

She gave him a sideways smirk. "You'd better."

Diarmid was close enough that Kaer Yin caught his raised brow. "What?"

His uncle shrugged. "Just musing over the charms of youth."

Kaer Yin opened his mouth to retort, but Barb got up on the nearby table to bang a wooden spoon against a pot. "Shut yer gobs now! The fancy folk have things to say!"

A swift hush swept the gathered, and Diarmid took his cue. He set his empty tankard beside Kaer Yin's and stood. The room instantly felt smaller for the command of his presence. Kaer Yin couldn't help a smirk. He hoped to bear one-tenth of his uncle's gravity one day. "I am come to tell you, good people of Rosweal, that Bov Dearg is delayed in the west." His green eyes were soft as a collective gasp and murmur followed. "It seems Lord Bishop sent a contingent of Armagh's Warhammers over the border some weeks before he sacked Tairngare. These Bolg fighters belong to his honor guard, I'm told, special forces. As a result, the bulk of Croghan's forces are engaged in the hills of Sligo, thus will never make it here in time to halt Bishop's advance." Here his attention shifted to Una, who reddened under his scrutiny.

"The Ard Ri has been made aware of the peril here and has sent what soldiers could be mustered in so short a timeframe."

Leaning against the bar, Barb pinched the bridge of her nose. "Ye mean to tell me, the High King sent the pittance what came with ye?"

Diarmid spread his hands in answer.

"*Feckin hells*," she spat and drained her tankard, wiping her mouth with her sleeve. For the first time, Kaer Yin thought her very small indeed. "Well, that's that then, innit? By the time Ben's da manages to rouse the whole of Aes Sidhe's forces, or the Red Boar can rout Lord Bishop's advance forces... we'll be properly buggered already."

Diarmid spared her a sad smile. "I'm sorry, Mistress. None in Aes Sidhe could know the depth of Patrick Donahugh's conspiracies. A plan this audacious and far-reaching can have no other author. That man was cunning as a badger."

Una shifted beside Kaer Yin. In his heart, he burned with rage for the injustice of her blood. Barb, however, felt no such loyalty. Her nose twisted deep. "Ye there, missy. I believe I told ye once, Rosweal will not bear the brunt for ye, didn't I?"

"Yes," said Una. "You did."

"Here we are anyway, huh?"

"Seems so."

Kaer Yin bristled. "Now, just wait a minute—"

"Shut up," they both hissed at once.

He did.

Una stood, glaring back at Barb. "I am committed to stopping my cousin cold."

"Is that right?"

"Yes."

"How?"

Una squeezed Ben's fingers, which was all the warning she gave him. "I have offered myself and my titles in exchange for Rosweal's neutrality. If Damek accepts, I will reside in Bethany as Duchess once it is liberated from my uncle."

Kaer Yin shot to his feet, blood rising, but Barb held up a hand to halt his comments. She bustled over to press her knuckles against the tabletop between her and Una. They stared at one another in silence for several heartbeats. "Aye," said Barb, finally. "I know ye did."

Una crossed her arms. "It's rude to read others' mail, you know."

"Do I look like I care?"

"I damned well do!" hissed Kaer Yin through his teeth.

They ignored him. Una crossed her arms. "Well, then you know I'm telling the truth. My terms should arrive any day now."

Barb laughed. "Ye've some bollocks on ye girl. I'll give ye that. Who gave ye the right to barter for Rosweal, anyway?"

"What bothers you more, Barb? That I'm the reason you got caught up in this mess or that I'm the solution to the problem?"

"If either were true, I might." Barb sucked her teeth. "Too bad ye don't get to make those decisions, Princess."

Una opened and closed her mouth, looking to the crowd as if they held an answer for Barb's cryptic comment. "What is that supposed to mean? I'm trying to—"

"I bloody know what yer trying to do, but I'm tellin' ye, it's not yer place to do it. Yer comin' got lots of Greenmakers killed." Una flushed, but Barb went on. "That means ye owe us. Ye think ye'd be buyin' our freedom by surrenderin' yerself to that kin o'yers, but we're not foolish enough to believe any o'that's why he's makin' his way here. Did ye not hear that he's the son of Armagh's heir yer own self? A man that wants to be king doesn't march on a foreign prince for a bloody woman. He's comin' for Ben, not ye… and don't ye fool yerself none about that."

"I agree with Mistress Dormer," offered Diarmid, though no one asked.

Internally, Kaer Yin seethed. Bloody women and their stubborn, foolhardy, arrogant, devious minds! "Una, I think you and I need to discuss this privately."

Again, she ignored him. "Perhaps you're right, Barb, but I am within my rights to try, nonetheless."

"Nah, yer not. Ben's made some claims that many a loyal ear has heard. Ye mean to marry him or not?"

Now it was Kaer Yin's turn to flush to the roots of his hair. Tam Lin ogled him sidelong.

Una cleared her throat. "Well, I mean, if I had the luxury to—"

"Oh, fer feck's sake, girl! Yes or no will do."

Una wouldn't meet his thunderous expression, which was as well because he might throttle her before the whole of Rosweal. "If I were free to choose for myself, I would never choose another."

Now, with that spear tip to the heart, he couldn't decide if he'd kiss her before throttling her or not.

Barb stood up and returned to the bar where a fresh pint waited. "That settles that, then. Whether I like it or not, if yer the Crown Princess o'Innisfail, yer *not* free to barter yerself for anyone. As our lady, ye'll do no such thing."

"But I've already sent—" but Barb pointed to a thin face sitting at the opposite end of the bar. Colm, whom Dabney's bulk had partially obscured, shrugged back. Una flashed her teeth at him, and he shrank into his tankard, looking guilty. "Bloody Greenmakers."

"Now that's settled, yer majesty, please tell us how buggered we are."

Una resumed her seat with a sulk. It took a moment of staring daggers into the top of her head before she snarled up at him, "He never took my message, obviously," and said no more.

Mollified, Kaer Yin tried not to gloat.

He decided Barb should have her patent of nobility soon.

Diarmid cleared his throat. "Yes, well, you gather the gist, I'm sure. With no further reinforcements and a force of Bishop's size on the way, my advice is to evacuate all civilians from Rosweal, posthaste."

"Appreciated, but denied," disagreed Barb, sipping her pint.

Diarmid started. "Madam, many thousands of men will be here within the week. More to arrive. The only hope we have to retain the Ard Ri's grip on Eire rests with the time we might delay Bishop's army long enough to be reinforced."

"Ah, but we have somethin' better than men, yer majesty."

Diarmid quirked a brow at Kaer Yin. "Bravado is not a boon in warfare, Madam."

Barb held up a finger while Robin handed her a little pouch. She took a tiny pinch of the black powder and tossed it into her emptied tankard, which she then set on the floor a foot away. Every Greenmaker scrambled to get clear. A long, slow smile spread over Kaer Yin's face as Barb struck a match and threw it into the pewter tankard. A loud BOOM sent the mug upward, pinging from the ceiling to the bar, where it ended its trajectory after bouncing off Dabney's broad forehead. The big lug could only blink and mumble, "Ow, Barb!"

Fully grinning now, Una said, "That's bloody brilliant."

Diarmid scratched his chin with interest. "And how much of this do you have?"

Barb's gold tooth winked at him in the firelight. "*Loads.*"

⚔

THREE HOURS LATER, KAER YIN, Barb, and Diarmid stood on the docks while Robin, Dabney, and four Greenmakers hefted the winch on Barb's floodgate. Stripped to the waist in the cold current, each man gave a grand cheer when the gate slammed upward, diverting the second river of tea-colored water into their meticulously hewn trench. In moments, Rosweal suddenly boasted a fully serviceable moat, eight feet wide and easily as deep. Robin roared in victory and allowed himself to be tugged from the river before his lips turned a dangerous shade of violet. He pulled Barb into a playful waltz at the far end of the dock while Gerrod and Dabney shared a pint of warmed cider.

Diarmid was the only one who seemed unaffected by the general mood. He kept his attention trained on the western gate. Kaer Yin followed his eye to witness Tam Lin and Shar escorting Fionn to the water's edge. Fionn's mood didn't seem to have improved during his brief internment. Kaer Yin met them at the end of the dock. "What's this then?"

Fionn wouldn't look at him.

Diarmid grasped Kaer Yin by the collar without ado, shoving him to a knee. "*Ack*," Kaer Yin managed to get out before Tam Lin nodded to Fionn.

With all the dignity he could summon, Fionn sank to his knees. His face could carve wood. Diarmid retrieved a small vellum scroll from within the folds of his cloak. "Fionn Sheal O'More."

"*Fiachra Dubh,*" he droned tonelessly.

Diarmid unraveled the scroll.

Kaer Yin's heart thundered to life at the seal he spied at the bottom.

A stag crowned by three stars.

His father's seal.

"'I, Midhir Mac Nuada Adair, Ard Ri of all Innisfail and lord of the Tuatha De Dannan, declare the *geis* of my son and heir Kaer Yin Mac Midhir Adair, satisfied. To wit, all titles, real and honorary alike, are remitted to their former owner once more. Kaer Yin Adair is reinvested as Crown Prince of Innisfail. The combined forces of Bri Leith, Croghan, and Scotia are his to command as Grand Marshal of the Wild Hunt and Commander of Aes Sidhe. All those who bear the blessings of the Oiche Ar Fad owe him fealty as the future Ard Ri. In Crom Dagda's name, and with our love and blessing, we beseech our son to defend the Continent in this time of need'," read Diarmid aloud in the Common Tongue for the human audience gathered around. "It lists Kaer Yin's necessary titles and those who owe him allegiance." He handed the scroll to Fionn, who regarded it as if it were a pot of piss. "Your name is at the top there, O'More. He expects your signature, next to mine and Tam Lin's."

He pointed.

Tam Lin held out a quill while Shar passed him a pot of ink before presenting his back as a makeshift writing desk.

It took several moments of audible molar grinding, but Fionn eventually dipped his nib and signed away his leadership. His loathing and derision couldn't be plainer, but none could or would refute the word of *Fiachra Dubh* nor the signature of the Ard Ri. In moments, Kaer Yin Adair went from vagabond usurper to lord and master once again.

Fionn bowed his head, though curtly. "My prince, I am yours to command."

The Sidhe as one, knelt.

Diarmid jerked Kaer Yin upward and jabbed a thumb stained with ash and blood between his eyes. Mystified by the speed of Diarmid's hands, Kaer Yin hadn't seen his uncle cut open his hand. The next thing he knew, Diarmid drew his dagger across Kaer Yin's palm. He winced as Nemain's pommel was then thrust into that bleeding hand. "*Ard Tiarne*, will you defend the people of Innisfail with your last drop of blood?"

"I will," Kaer Yin coughed.

"Will you honor the Gods of your homeland and revere the memory of your ancestors till the day you are carried to Bri Reis in Tech Duinn."

"I will."

"Speak your oath to the Undying and take your place in the Innisfail Cycle."

Kaer Yin took the dagger from Diarmid's outstretched fingers, then drew two thin lines down either cheek. Warm blood dribbled over his jaw and neck, staining his recently cleaned tunic red. "I am the sword at the fountainhead. I am the stone that cleaves the waters of the world. I am the storm that hides the evening star. I am Kaer Yin Mac Nuada Adair, and I swear blood, bone, and spirit to the house of *Dagda Ri*."

The Sidhe chanted in return, but Kaer Yin could not hear them. Marked by ash and blood, he sheathed his sword. Turning from Diarmid, he looked over the gathered.

Diarmid called out in a voice that shook the treetops, "Let those who would be counted come and swear fealty to their future King!"

Robin, of course, elbowed his way to the front of the line. He took a knee. With a snort, Kaer Yin dabbed a dot of blood in the same place Diarmid had him. "Blood binds, and spirit cleaves. I take thee, Robin Gramble as my captain. Do you accept?"

"Course I do, arseness."

Kaer Yin gave him a sideways smile. "Rise a member of my household guard and a knight in the Ard Ri's service. Robin Gramble, Lord of Navan."

Robin paled to a dull ochre and stumbled to his feet. "What's that?"

Kaer Yin gently pushed him aside for the next man in line but winked at his old friend. "Well, I promised Barb I'd make a lady of her, didn't I? I suppose you'd better make an honest woman of her before she has you murdered and takes the title anyway."

By nightfall, every man, woman, and child in Rosweal had sworn fealty to the Crown Prince... and only the night air seemed to fear the coming dawn.

Whence Comes
the Knife

n.e. 508
18 ban apesa
the greensward

The nightly raids began to take their toll on his men. Superior numbers or no, a large army was a fat snake swallowing roads and villages on its slow course to destruction. Were it not fed; it would starve. Were it to gorge itself; it would implode ... and were it to pause too long; it would wither. Their progress was glacial, racing toward Rosweal at a spectacular clip of nearly three miles a day. Moving troops, artillery, beasts, and supplies required more space than a single road could accommodate and more food, drink, women, and blood than the sparsely populated north could provide.

Already this week, Damek had ordered three dozen men hung for desertion or rape and an additional thirty or so branded and scourged for theft and dereliction of duty. Whether to the cold, disease, or mischief, his army dwindled. But this was not all. Every night, the raiders came. Each morning, Damek ordered the corpses of a score or more men burned. His second march through the North cost him a hundred men a day.

Since leaving Tairngare, he'd lost nearly three thousand soldiers. At this rate, they'd lose another fifteen hundred before they made it to

Vale, where he intended to set camp for his campaign against Aes Sidhe. Marching at the tail of winter was never a simple prospect. Still, with so many men in such cramped quarters, in such hostile territory— they might have been sending out invitations to every thief, criminal, and rebel for a hundred miles in every direction. Yet, what choice did he have? Falan the Elder had set this *geis* upon Damek in exchange for his crown… besides which Damek knew he'd never truly be king so long as Kaer Yin Adair drew breath.

So, they pressed on.

Thoughtlessly, relentlessly, ruthlessly.

He burned the weak and punished the treasonous, gritting his teeth against the cold, the death, the tedium, and the raids. By the time they neared Navan, Damek was immune to all but his purpose. He saw nothing but the road ahead, swirling with snow, ice, and inevitability. He heard nothing but the thrum of his heartbeat and the steady trudging of many thousands of feet. Nothing would stop him now, not even the Gods, however much he expected they cared.

Even Martin's jaw set in a determined line. His steel-grey eyes had taken a hard cast, unwaveringly resolute. When Damek commanded men to be slain or punished, Martin attacked each task with an emotionless efficiency that might have shocked Damek once. With so much riding on the outcome of this endeavor, even stolid O'Rearden had pinned his every hope upon this march.

The die, as great Caesar had once boasted, was cast.

After another grueling day amidst the frozen waste of trees, sleeting snows, and frigid mud… the raiders came again. No matter how prepared they were by sundown each night, the attacks could never be halted. Desperate men believed they had nothing left to lose and would risk anything for the mountain of supplies Damek's army dragged behind them. Others might imagine themselves as freedom fighters and wish to exact their vengeance upon the new King of Eire. Whichever the case, Damek's men took the brunt of these attacks every night, trailing a gory line of human waste back to the gates of Tairngare.

Damek's officers carried on.

The men greeted nightfall with the same tired, irascible sense of purpose. They were all of them, working toward a single goal— *glory*. Then, the raids grew more vicious. The attacks costlier. Damek no longer faced a rabble of ragged bandits or displaced villagers. They were in Greenmaker territory now, and these men knew their business.

In a single night, Damek had lost four wagons loaded with costly arrows and spears, two sleds full of dried rations and tea, and four dozen horses. Damek's vision doubled over the report, leaning over the desk in his tent by midafternoon's accounting. Opposite, Ridley and Douglas fidgeted. None wanted to be the bearer of bad news, especially when their new king was in the mood he'd been in since the Tairngare. Damek leaned forward on his knuckles, his expression flat. "How long before we're ready to march again?"

Douglas blanched. His damp hair hung in greasy tendrils over a breastplate stained with days-old blood. He, nor any of Damek's officers, had been afforded much time to bathe or rest. "Two days at the earliest, My King. The men are—"

"Unacceptable," snapped Damek. "I want to be back on the road within the hour."

"But My King, there's simply no way we can manage that with our supplies in such disarray! We've men to burn, supplies to replenish or recover, and must somehow account for the horses our cavalry has lost."

"I don't want to hear excuses, Sergeant. By week's end, I want to be twenty miles down the road."

Douglas looked to Ridley as if he could answer for the absurdity of Damek's request, but he merely averted his gaze. "It's not possible, My King. Forgive me, but—"

Damek brought his fist into the tabletop, turning over his tankard, which spilled sweet-smelling ale all over his report. "Do you know how many men we will have lost by the time we make it a score of miles down that road? Nearly *five thousand*, Douglas. Can your small mind grasp what a blow that is for any commander, least of all a newly consecrated king?"

Douglas swallowed. "We marched North with much fewer and succeeded."

"In autumn, yes, when the roads were passable and a night without a fire wouldn't cost a man his legs. When every cutpurse and rogue for a hundred miles didn't know exactly where we were.

"When a thousand men weren't burning up with fever or shitting themselves bloody in their bedrolls. When a horde of practiced bandits and a few hundred extremely lethal Sidhe weren't picking us off from the sidelines. No, Douglas. A winter march with this many men is a far different animal altogether."

Douglas chewed his cheek. Once, before his lord had become a king, he might have had the bollocks to laugh in Damek's face… but not now. If Damek wished to, he could have him hung or burned alongside the rest of the traitors. He cleared his throat. "Forgive my insolence, My King, but perhaps we should split our forces or return to Tairngare until spring?"

Damek inhaled slowly, his mouth cracking into a dangerous smirk. "With twenty miles to go, you'd have me make it easier for the Roswellians to pick our bones dry?"

"My men can close that gap in less than a day, my king. Give me the men, and I'll serve Rosweal to you on a platter."

"And give Kaer Yin and his crony Robin Gramble— a man that has made a career out of forest ambush, I might add— the means to crush my Steel Corps before I even arrive? Absolutely bloody not."

Frustrated, Douglas sent Martin a pleading glare. With a heavy sigh, O'Rearden stepped out of the corner he'd been standing in. The light from Damek's boiling braziers cast heavy shadows over his grizzled features. "A word, My King. In private."

Damek's nostrils flared. He stood his flagon back up and poured himself another. "So you can plead the same case with a fatherly tone? Save yourself the trouble."

Martin coughed. "Fine. I agree that we should pause the march until the thaw. This Reason-damned weather, the raids, and the bloody flux are costing us more men than you account for, my king. Five thousand men are more than the standing army of a reasonably large city."

Damek knew. Oh, he knew.

Yet...

"I've no choice, Martin."

Martin pulled a face. "My king, I beg to speak about this privately."

"I said I have no choice, Martin!" Damek's voice nearly cracked. He threw a hand at the open tent flap as if it encompassed the whole of his camp. "Either way we march, we lose men. If we hunker down in Navan, the Sidhe will harry us every night before you suggest that. If we retreat, we lose yet more... only to attempt this when the Sidhe have gathered their full strength. That is a battle we likely lose, Martin, twenty-thousand men against thrice that number under the most celebrated commander in Innish history. We must strike them *now* and strike hard, or we'll lose the whole of the Greensward to the Sidhe by Beltane, then Tairngare and Ten Bells by Samhain. Let's not forget, my uncle gathers his Kneelers in the south whilst we're up here wanking off in the trees. The only move I have is forward, Martin. You are wise enough to know this."

Several long minutes passed while Martin processed Damek's point. After a while, he turned to Douglas and Ridley. "Leave us."

They looked to Damek askance.

He waved them away. "You heard your Commander."

Martin poured himself a flagon and took a long draught. When he was finished, Damek was surprised to discover his old mentor was angrier than he'd ever seen him. Without realizing it, Damek took a step back. "Look here, boyo. I warned you not to meddle with the bloody Sidhe, and make no mistake— I give no shites who your bloody father might be. I bleedin' *begged* you not to swear any oaths to those duplicitous whores in Armagh.

"When you stood upon the dais at Tairngare, that was the proudest day of my life. My foster son, my squire, become King of Eire on his own. He was under no obligation to anyone that day, save the people he'd come to free." He took another drink, then sneered, "Now look at you! Had the whole bloody Continent quivering in their boots, replete with a *justifiable* claim upon the greatest cities in Eire, for which you might have negotiated fairly with the High King. Now? You're not a liberator or a king.

"You're a warlord in open defiance of the High King's throne. You're the puppet of a lesser prince and a traitor to boot. You're no hero now, boy. You've made yourself a villain.... *and I helped you do it!*"

Damek flinched as if he'd been struck.

Martin threw his cup onto the carpeted floor. "All this potential, so bright, so shiny and new. Just look at us. You've gone and made us the black hats, Damek. I hope you're pleased with yourself?"

"I—Martin, how can you say this to me? I am no villain. Every action, every decision I've made, has been to give us the opportunity for liberty. To free the South, to give our people autonomy, power, and purpose."

Martin snorted. "No, every action and decision has been orchestrated to get you what you wanted and nothing more. You wanted to be king. I presume if you win this fight for your dear ole Da, you'll be out to cross him next to climb higher still... and I wonder if you even recognize these facts, or if you're so far gone that you're even lying to yourself now."

Damek went quiet. His hands shook. In all his life, no one had ever held power to wound him more than Martin, not even Una.

"Martin, be careful—"

"Or what?" Martin laughed. "You'll string me up with the rapists and deserters? The ashes of thousands follow us down the road to Rosweal, Damek! You lost *five thousand bloody men* in less than a month, and still, you would spend more to chase your obsession to Tech Duinn! Why can't you see it? What happened to that bright, beautiful lad I raised?"

Damek's guards rustled shy of the door, and Martin, unfortunately, watched the possibility of violence cross Damek's eyes. "Oh, fuck you, boy. You might be a king, but there's one order I dare you to make."

Seething, hurt, and confused, Damek shook his head at his guards, and they let the flap fall back over the exit. "Stop calling me 'boy,' damn you. I am your king."

Martin made a rude sound. "Then bloody well act like one. Your men, your good loyal men who love you and saw you crowned with tears in their eyes, are out there dying for your ambition. I hope you make the right decision." He spun on a heel and made to stalk out of the tent, but Damek's voice caught him shy.

"Where are you going?"

Martin half-turned to ask over his shoulder, "Do we press on or no?"

Damek gulped air like a goldfish. What did he expect him to say? He had come this far. They had *all* come this far. Tucking tail now would finish him faster than the Sidhe ever could. Who would follow a half-legitimate king who couldn't even take a little town at the edge of nowhere, defended by a smattering of criminals and browbeaten Sidhe? No one! He couldn't turn back now… he *would not*. "You knew the answer before you asked, Martin. We're committed. We must be."

"Then I'll be with the men, My Lord, where I belong. Inform Douglas of any strategy you might think will cost us least after the next massacre."

He didn't wait for Damek's rebuttal.

The tent flap swung into place behind him.

That night's raid was something special. They came out of the setting sun; faces painted white and black with ash and soot, silent as the spirit of winter itself. Long white hair streamed behind this set, short swords with white-boned handles dealing death in every direction. Naked to the waist save for whorls of white and black paint over their chest and shoulders, they attacked in a swath, a single, swift wave.

The men weren't prepared for the Sidhe, not *these* Sidhe.

Damek emerged from his tent when the first shouts went up to spy several tall men racing through his forward line, targeting officers, specifically. With deadly accurate archers providing cover from the seemingly barren Greensward, these elite warriors— and it would be pointless to argue otherwise— cut through men and beast like a knife through hot cream. They dashed through their line like the wind, never pausing, never wavering.

An Fiach Fian, Damek recognized them immediately.

The Wild Hunt.

For a few moments, all Damek could do was stare at the speed and precision of these inhuman beasts. No mortal man could move so quickly nor kill with such accuracy that they need not stop to guarantee their blows were true. Knowing that his sword would be useless in such a shock attack, he grabbed his bow and quiver from their place near the entrance of his tent. He'd never been the finest archer, as he preferred the sword, but at least two of his arrows found their mark. Two blond creatures sank to the frozen earth between the ranks thanks to his meager efforts. When he drew back for a third shot, a flash of red dragged his eye to the right. Roaring with fury, Hisk threw himself at a Sidhe nearly twice his size, with flaming red-blond hair and a rudimentary eagle painted on his chest in dark woad. The redhead sidestepped Hisk's clumsy thrust, grasped his face with one massive hand, and snapped his neck like kindling. As he tossed Hisk's body away, he must have heard Damek's growl.

He turned with an unperturbed grin.

The Prince of Connaught, Damek thought, fumbling to draw. *I will kill you, you jolly bastard.*

But his arrow went wide, pinging from a tree and harmlessly into the snow. The redhead smiled the wider, waggled his fingers at Damek, then took off after his fellows. By the time Damek had a moment to drop his bow, the Sidhe were gone. In their wake, a blanket of bodies littered the ground surrounding his tent. All the officers in steel armor wore cobalt and scarlet tunics bearing the Southernmost Star.

A painted target might have been more subtle.

Cursing, Damek rolled Hisk over just as Martin and Douglas jogged up with their swords out. Damek noted that neither blade bore a drop of Sidhe blood. The darkening sky overhead reflected from Hisk's glassy brown eyes. A creeping rage kindled in Damek's gut, then tracked upward into his throat. Douglas, who'd been Hisk's mate from swaddling, wept openly. Damek looked up into Martin's deepening scowl. "Thirty men. Officers, all."

"I know."

Martin spat. A thin trickle of blood raced down his chin. "They'll be back."

"I'm sure we can expect them daily between here and Rosweal."

Martin's expression bordered outright mutiny. "Your orders, *My King*?"

Damek stood. He clapped Douglas on the back and sighed. "We must move faster. That is our only option now. The longer we delay, the more it will cost us."

A single angry nod was all Martin could give him. "If that is your decision."

"It is," hissed Damek. "Order an inventory of all nonessential supplies and personnel. These can be redirected to Navan, which will be simpler to garrison than this icy hellscape. I want them stripping timber for walls by midday tomorrow."

"Very good, my king," his tone implied this was a forced concession. "And the rest?"

Damek's head swiveled to glare westward along the road. "We ride for Vale, posthaste. I want a speeding train of steel and horseflesh barreling into town at dawn."

Here was Martin's turn to sigh. "We'll kill our horses in the process."

"Would you rather we lose another thirty officers in the night? Thirty more the following, and the next? We're a juicy pie waiting for the knife out here. I'd rather cram this steel engine down their gullets, thank you."

"Point taken, My King. Some wagons have been damaged beyond repair, and loading the others will slow us down."

"Leave them."

Martin scoffed, "These are essential supplies."

"They'll likely burn or be stolen while we dawdle here with our cocks in our hands. The moment The Wild Hunt entered the fray, this became a matter of speed. We're too slow, and that is to their advantage."

Douglas wiped his face with the back of a gloved hand. "I'm tired of waiting for them to pick us off. My sword is thirsty."

"Go, prepare the Corps. We leave within the hour. Ranks tight, steel ready, and eyes sharp... do you hear?"

Douglas slammed a fist against his breastplate. "As you command, my king."

When he took his leave, Martin sent Damek a wordless warning. Damek exhaled and shook his head. "I can count, Martin. I know what you would say, and I hear you… but to retreat now would finish us faster than defeat."

Martin went silent for a time, staring down at Hisk's mangled body. "You're going to lose, Damek. Whether you win or not makes no difference."

Damek tried not to flinch. "I know."

"I hope it was worth it." He stalked off for the second time that day without waiting to hear his king's reply.

X

Henry supposed he had his nephew to thank for the ease of Malahide's capitulation. His scouts had barely made it a quarter-mile past the gates when their new mayor and several of the city's Merchers rode out to welcome him. Not a single drop of blood was shed, more's the pity, and the entire town seemed eager and happy to fête and feast him. Indeed, he'd spent two pleasant days in the mayor's house, enjoying his ale and fucking his boniest servants.

On the third day, and thoroughly bored with the events of the previous two, Henry decided to line the townsfolk up to determine their level of heresy. He couldn't, after all, be a genuinely Christian king if he suffered idolaters the run of his kingdom, could he?

At first, the mayor and his councilors balked at his 'regressionist' policy. In response, Henry had each man nailed to a cross just outside the city walls, lining either side of the old Innish road to Tairngare. Their Bretagn silk robes flapped in the frigid, early spring breeze, ill protection against the elements. Most died in a matter of hours, frozen stiff. One or two lingered a bit, their moans useless, ignored. Afterward, the next mayor had fewer qualms about converting to the true religion. Similarly, the townsfolk suddenly discovered a newfound zeal for Henry and his faith.

Pleased with himself, Henry watched the townsfolk gather to toss their Siorai trinkets onto the bonfire his men had erected from the guts of the previous mayor's home. One by one, the people ushered past, dumping books, pendants, artwork, or other sacrilegious materials into the roaring flames. If any felt the situation amiss, none dared to voice those concerns. Instead, they filed past, glassy eyes reflecting only the fire and the armed men standing by.

Henry had received word that the other half of his forces had already visited similar judgments on the towns of Killing and Morn, round Kerry, Mayhew's territory. Served the fool right for backing Henry's mutant nephew over God's chosen in Innisfail. Still, the people must be shown. They must learn that Innisfail was God's territory, and no man-hating she-cults or star-worshippers would be tolerated.

When the flames died down and the people retreated to their homes, Henry, delighted with himself, winked at his Lord Tendrick. "Ten Bells next, d'you think?"

Tendrick shared Henry's faith, though he was the more cautious man by far. "Should we not consider smaller fare first? Perhaps Tara, or—"

"Why waste resources? Ten Bells is the prize we need to upend my nephew's claim to the North. Without the banks, he's buggered, and he knows that."

Tendrick appeared uncertain. "My Lord, while I agree that we should make ingresses into Ten Bells, perhaps we might take a lesson from your grandfather and avoid stalling commerce in the city?"

Henry exhaled through his nostrils. "I aim to stop all currency exchanges, Tendrick, until ours is the only standard on the field."

The young lord bit his lip lest he say more.

Henry liked that about him. He knew his place.

Clapping the fellow on the shoulder, Henry strolled back indoors, gnawing on a tea cake. His mood lightened by the hour. "Let's be ready to leave by mid-morning tomorrow. I think it's time for a real test, don't you agree?"

In Love or Vanity

n.e. 509
19 ban apesa
Rosweal

"Invitation accepted," sang Tam Lin jovially as he stalked into Kaer Yin's war room. Barb, whose office it had once been, was not around to frown at its misuse. When Tam Lin made his entrance, Kaer Yin himself had been in conversation with Colm and couldn't help but smile at his cousin's bravado. "You're sure?"

Tam Lin blew air over his lower lip while he helped himself to a dollop of Kaer Yin's uishge. Nearly the first thing Kaer Yin did when he assumed his title and honors once more was to claim a hefty share of the uishge in Barb's cellars. She couldn't say 'no' to the future king… though she did try. "We watched from a distance. He split his forces as you said he would, cutting his supplies into thirds and dividing the bulk of his cavalry from his infantry. The latter was on its way to Navan when we left, and our friend is even now riding hells for leather to Vale with his Corpsmen."

Kaer Yin clapped his hands together. "Bloody well done, Lin!"

Tam Lin shrugged and took a seat on Kaer Yin's desk. He was filthy and covered in blood, running with ash and woad. He smelled fantastic too. On his opposite side, Mordu covered his nose. Tam Lin ignored him. "I thought this fellow was meant to be a military genius or some such?"

"He managed to sack Tairngare in a handful of weeks. At the very least, he's not stupid."

Robin looked up from the map he'd been studying. "I'd say he knew very well that he might be forced to split his forces. Don't mean he wanted to, just that he knew it might happen. Why else would he bring such a large number o'lads with him? Marchin' in winter would mean an obvious loss to a goat."

"He's in a hurry," agreed Kaer Yin. "I gather Falan didn't grant his support without a price. Thank the gods, because he has twenty-thousand men headed here, let's not forget."

"Fourteen now," interjected Robin. "Or at least by week's end."

"Which means we're still outnumbered five to one."

"I'm likin' the odds better every day, meself."

"Me too, but that won't stop them from razing this town." Kaer Yin shoved Tam Lin's leg from his desk so he could have a look at Barb's map. He traced the distance between Navan and Rosweal first. "He wants us to attack Navan for the supplies he's setting out as bait."

"Which we need," remarked Robin.

"Which he *knows* we need. Meanwhile, he'll dig into Vale like a mole while we split our defenses to attack his leavings. No. We stick to the plan," argued Kaer Yin, moving his finger to Vale. "If this drags on, Navan will be there, waiting."

"Aye, all defenses up and waitin' for us. We won't get a better shot at 'em."

"No plan is perfect until it succeeds."

"Ben, I love ye, but ye know that's puttin' us in the middle of two large armies. We'll be bloody surrounded, and no one and nothin' will be able to get supplies in or out if it comes to a long siege."

"If he lacks officers to carry out his orders and manage the rabble, he won't last more than a week. I assume he knows *that* too," said Tam Lin dryly. "Tonight, we took at least twenty. If we take the same tomorrow, he'll be forced to throw everything he has at us before hunger, desertion, and disease do the rest. His men are already suffering the flux, piles, and trench foot. Hells, half the men marching on Navan are similarly plagued."

Kaer Yin scratched his eyebrow while staring down at his map like it would answer a riddle. "We share that opinion, Lin. We have one shot at this."

"Do we want him to throw all he's got at us?" asked Robin. "Not for nothin' he's draggin' bloody cannons behind them warhorses. My girl did a grand job shorin' us up, but them walls won't stand cannon shot."

"They will," said Una from the doorway. Rian, as usual, took up space behind her. Her amber eyes slid to Kaer Yin's. "At least for a while."

"So that's what you were doing up there?"

She nodded. "They can never be solid as the Cloister, but they'll stand up like stone. Buys us time, anyway."

"That's brilliant, love."

Una flushed. "Well, Rian and I came to say the bathhouse is ready and set up for patients if anyone needs stitching."

Tam Lin raised his brows. "None of my men were injured, ladies, but I appreciate it."

Rian folded her hands in front of her. "I assume that will change soon enough." She didn't wait for his following comment. She pivoted and bowed to Kaer Yin, which sent his hackles up. She only deferred to him when she was about to bust his bollocks in front of everyone. His chin sagged in a scowl. "My Prince, I intend to make that my ward for the duration. Do I have your blessing?"

He blinked back at her like a cow.

Una chewed her lower lip.

No help there.

"Ah, I intended you'd take up residence in the tunnels below the north wall with the others."

Rian straightened. Her lovely face seemed a bit drawn at the edges. "I'm the only physician we have, Ben. People are going to need me."

Kaer Yin waited for Una to say something, but she crossed her arms in unhappy solidarity. *They've already hashed this out, and Una lost. Fuck.*

Robin, too, looked away. The blasted girl had come here to ambush him in full view of his council. *Fine.* "No."

Rian took a deep breath. Her eyes were cold. "Respectfully, Your Highness, you can't deny me the right to save lives… lives that will surely be lost for my absence."

"Actually, I can. Una Moura Donahugh is my prospective bride."

Una tensed, realizing too late the card he was about to play.

Don't blame me.

You should have handled this, he told her with his eyes.

"What does that have to do with me running a clinic?" demanded Rian.

The glow of murder settled around Una like a halo, but Kaer Yin ignored her.

"You're Una's heir." He rummaged through a bundle of vellum until he came to the one with the bright blue seal, the official seal of the Libellan Bank. "Lady Rian Guinness of Ardgillan, to be precise. You're, therefore, a member of my extended family."

Rian's head rolled toward Una as if tugged by strings. "*What?*"

Una was the most petite woman he'd ever met, but her ire seemed to gain her ten feet in stature. "You bastard."

Kaer Yin made a face. "Don't make me the villain, love."

"*What?*" Rian repeated, louder.

"Would everyone excuse us for a bit, please?"

"Not on your life," said Tam Lin, slapping his knee. Robin and the rest of Kaer Yin's council quietly exited, shutting the door behind them.

Rian's face blazed red. "When were you planning to tell me?"

Feeling cornered, Una raised her chin. "This is the first I'm hearing their answer. I didn't take you for the sort to read through one's mail."

"Jan Fir is in charge of all communication coming in and out of Rosweal. It got tossed onto this mess," Kaer Yin gestured to the mountain of papers wadded at one side of his desk. "Obviously, you should assume Barb read it first."

Una rolled her eyes and sniffed. "Crooks, the lot of you."

"I don't give a shite about any of that," cried Rian. "What gives you the right to decide my future for me, Una?"

The look on Una's face spelled danger for Kaer Yin later. So be it. He'd been itching to hash this out with her, himself. He might as well take care of both issues in one go. "You should answer, love," he prodded gently.

"Because I can, and bloody well should." Una stood her ground. "Whether I want to or not, I technically own half of Eire, Rian. I owe you my life. Kaer Yin owes you his life. At least a hundred people in Rosweal owe you their lives. What I have done is guarantee you'll live well; however this plays out. I love you and want you to be happy."

Though her face could set a brushfire, Rian burst into tears. Both males in attendance flinched away, unsure where to stand. Una wrapped her arms around Rian, who attempted to swat her off. "Why are you writing wills, Una? I don't want anything if you're not here."

"Hush," Una said into her hair. "This is not a will. From this point, the title and income are yours whenever you want them. I cannot go on without assuring you're cared for. All right?"

"I don't want it."

"It's done, Rian. You can pick it up or lay it down, as you please."

Rian backed up, wiping her eyes.

Kaer Yin took the opportunity to press his case. "Now, as a seventeen-year-old girl of my household, I can't in good conscience allow you to—"

"You shut your stupid mouth, Ben," sniffled Rian. "First of all, I'm eighteen as of last Friday and legally an adult."

"Wait, what? Why didn't you tell me?" gasped Una.

Rian tugged a shoulder at her. "It wasn't important with all this happening."

Kaer Yin exhaled. "Doesn't matter. I still have—"

"No, you don't. I'm an adult, apparently of means, and have skills the people in this town desperately need. You may order me not to, but you won't win the love of the people that way."

Now it was Kaer Yin's turn to sweat. Una quirked a lip at his discomfiture. "Rian, it's too dangerous. When the Southers breach the walls, they'll look for anyone they can find to sate themselves upon—women first. I can't allow you to do this."

She clasped her shaking hands together. "We all know what happens during a siege. I'm just as scared as everyone else. *I* don't have a choice. Don't you understand?"

"You do not know what happens during a siege, girl." This was from Tam Lin, who hadn't been invited to remain. Kaer Yin shot him a dark look. "If caught, the old men and young boys will be slain on sight. The women, whether whores, old women, or young girls… might escape with a rape or two. But you—" here, he let his eyes roam every inch of her to make her squirm. "A sweetmeat like yourself will be passed around for a long while. The Southers aren't like the Sidhe. Many sign up for the promise of a treat like you."

"Bishop ordered his men not to rape in Tairngare."

"If you think that'll work here in this backwater no one gives a shite about, you're mistaken."

Rian swallowed though she put a brave face on it. "Then give us guards."

"Can't spare the men," Kaer Yin said.

"So what? You'll leave the bloodied and cleaved to their own devices?"

"Rian," sighed Kaer Yin. "There won't be time to evacuate you when the horns blow. You know that. You might save one or two, but surely you realize those that can't walk will be left behind? We are not omnipotent, and we're vastly outnumbered."

"I know that!" she snapped. "I'm not asking, gods, damn you! 'One or two lives' are no meager thing to me. Nor should they be to the prince they're dying for!"

Kaer Yin leaned over his desk to snarl, "I said *no*. That is final."

"You can't do that!"

"For Siora's sake, you two," attempted Una.

"What are you going to do about it? Tie me to a uishge barrel in the tunnels?"

"Keep giving me ideas."

"I am not a child, nor are you my brother, husband, or bloody father!"

"I'm the Crown Prince of Innisfail, and my word is law."

"Ha! We'll just see what Barb says about that."

In a moment, he would leap over his desk and choke her to death; he was pretty sure. As he opened his mouth to issue the threat, Tam Lin raised his hand with a self-satisfied smirk. "I will give you the guards."

Kaer Yin growled, "Stay out of this."

Tam Lin pursed his lips. "The girl isn't wrong, Yin. She's proven herself before, hasn't she? Who else could manage the task better?"

Una's eyes lowered to slits.

Undeterred, Tam Lin's teeth were very white. "What say you, Mistress Guinness… or should I say, Lady Ardgillan?"

"I need your men on the walls, Tam Lin," warned Kaer Yin. "I don't know what you're playing at, but—"

"What do you want in exchange for your help?" Rian interrupted, her mouth drawn in a dubious line.

"Nothing," he answered. "You are right to ask for them, and I can offer them. Yin may be my liege lord, but my father is a king in his own right. I don't owe my position to the Ard Ri. The men are yours because I will it so."

The tilt of his cousin's jaw began to give Kaer Yin indigestion. "Tam Lin…"

"You know," his cousin cleared his throat. "I can ensure that you never have to ask this ingrate's permission for anything, should that be your wish?"

"*Tú mac soith*," hissed Kaer Yin.

Una's fingers closed over her belt knife. Kaer Yin caught her arm before she could launch herself at his cousin.

Rian asked, "How do you mean?"

Tam Lin affected nonchalance. "You could become a member of my household, instead."

Una ground her heel over Kaer Yin's big toe. The next thing he knew, Una's right fist glanced almost comically from Tam Lin's bemused face. It took Rian and Kaer Yin pulling at full strength to pry her from him. Inverted and huffing, she pointed a finger at him. "Next time, you won't be laughing."

Tam Lin patted his swelling cheek. "You would threaten to murder one of the peers of the realm? Rude."

"I *warned* you. How dare you insult her like this."

"Insult her? I'm offering my hand, woman, not a life of shame."

Everyone stopped at once. A single whistle could have dropped Kaer Yin on the spot. "What?"

Una, too, said, "What?"

Abashed, Rian said nothing.

Tam Lin went on, "My father won't love her heritage, but my mother was hardly a princess when he claimed her either, so he won't have much room to gainsay me. *You* made her a wealthy countess, which makes this appropriate." He rubbed his chin. "We will have to do something about her apparel, though."

Kaer Yin paled. *"Nach bhfuil sé seo greannmhar."*

Tam Lin's smile widened. *"An bhfuil mé ag gáire?"*

Rian rubbed her face with both hands, then stared down at her own feet like they might explain this to her. "Since when?"

"I believe my interest has been marked, girl."

"Don't call me 'girl.' I mean, since when did you decide this?"

"My father's been pestering me to choose a bride for eons. Why shouldn't it be a girl I respect, my cousin the Crown Prince, and my own men respect?"

She pondered that in silence for a moment. Kaer Yin thought that might have been the first compliment Tam Lin had given her. "Without any conversation with me, any idea what I might want, any clue if I would even consider such an offer?"

"We've had several conversations. I am second in line to the throne. Any woman would consider such an offer seriously unless she were mad."

Rian closed her eyes and mumbled beneath her breath as if she were praying. "Ben?"

"Yes?" his voice came out a squeak.

"Will you give me the men now?"

Una glared up at him with a genuine threat burning from her irises.

He cursed under his breath. "Those I can spare."

Tam Lin's brow creased, but Rian gave him no further chance to wax moronic. She gave him a serviceable curtsy. "I decline, your highness."

Before he could say anything else, she stalked out of Barb's office with her back straight as an arrow. Una was not far behind.

Kaer Yin held out the remnants of his flask.

Tam Lin took it with a curled upper lip. "Traitor."

"What in the hells did you mean by that? You've spent months complaining of her in every possible way, decrying any interest in her above the illicit and generally being a prat."

"Seemed like a good idea a moment ago."

Flabbergasted, Kaer Yin could only stare at him.

"Shar asked me for her hand."

"Is that what prompted this? Competition?"

Tam Lin was quiet for a time. He drained the dregs and tossed the flask onto Kaer Yin's desk. "Who knows?"

He was gone before Kaer Yin could gather an appropriate response.

X

LATER, AFTER RIAN HAD GONE to sleep, Una snuck out of their quarters and into Kaer Yin's. Shar was nowhere near the door, which was unusual. It wasn't like the men to leave their *Ard Tiarne* unguarded. But she found Kaer Yin huddled over his maps and sipping uishge from a tankard beside a dying fire. He scarcely looked up when her arms came around him. "Can't sleep, love?"

He grunted into her hair. "I managed an hour, maybe."

She pulled away to rifle through his maps. The fire cast her hair in molten gold—"Same. Rian finally drifted off. It took some doing, I can tell you."

He chuckled. "There's no way she hasn't gleaned that Barb's been dosing her."

"I think they've agreed to a détente on that score. One can pretend they're doing a good deed, and the other can accept a good night's sleep without guile."

"You bloody women."

Her lip quirked at him. "Still, she did have much on her mind tonight."

"Yes," he said, shifting uncomfortably in his seat. "Una, what's worse is I think he means it."

"I don't care if he does."

He pulled her into his lap and toyed with her fingertips. "That is not for us to say. She's rejected him as he deserved, but her choices are hers from here on. He wasn't overstating his worth. She might change her mind."

"He's a womanizer at the very best."

"To be fair, I haven't seen him with any women since we've been back. I think he means this, and no one is more shocked than me, save maybe Tam Lin."

She chewed at her cheek. "She said 'no.' That's that."

"Maybe." He clasped her hand to his chest so she couldn't miss the sincerity in his eyes. "I don't think it's fully one-sided."

Una snorted. "Bollocks. She's rejected every advance he's ever made. Has rebuked him in front of everyone, slapped his arrogant face, and—oh." Her brow crinkled. "*Oh no.*"

"Right. I don't think she's aware of it either."

She stared off into the distance. "What a mess! Did you know even poor Gerry has been asking Barb for a better position in order to earn enough to marry?"

"Yes," he said. "And Shar Lianor himself asked Tam Lin for her hand only yesterday. The girl is a headache."

"She's beautiful, brave, intelligent, and kind, Kaer Yin. Of course, this would happen."

"Annoying, pinched of face, rude, lanky, and bossy."

"Well then. I must seem a beast by comparison?"

"Oh, the very worst. I don't know how I can bear to look at you sometimes."

She gave him a long kiss that turned his brains to jam. When she finally laid her head against his shoulder, he said, "I suppose Tam Lin and I might have similar tastes."

"Rian's not ready to marry anyone. I don't know that she's even aware of men for their own sake. She was quite sheltered, as you recall. What if she prefers women, like my aunt Eva?"

"She doesn't."

"You don't know that."

"Yes, I do. I've seen how Rian looks at Shar, and so have you."

Una paused for a moment. "Well, I guess so."

"… and Tam Lin."

She wrinkled her nose.

"Nothing to be done about it. We'll just have to wait and see."

"Tam Lin will be bored of this by tomorrow."

"I doubt it. I've never seen Tam Lin behave this way. He's got the time, as he sees it."

"And Shar?"

"Even then."

Una sat up to stare down at him incredulously. "You can't be serious? He's his liege lord."

"Shar could ask to enter my household, and I would be obliged to accept. Tam Lin will never approve of the match, but if Rian wants it, he can't stop his lieutenant from taking his bride to a new court. Even so, Tam Lin may issue a challenge for her. It will get bloody complicated if Tam Lin wants it to be."

"I'll talk some sense into him."

"You?" Kaer Yin coughed. "You just punched the Prince of Connaught in the face, love. You're the last person I expect he means to be scolded by."

"Fine. I'll talk some sense into her."

"How's that worked out for you so far?"

The sour look on her face was his answer.

"Thankfully, Rian is a smart girl with more stones than my best fighters. I doubt she'll choose any of them. At least, not for a long while."

"If Siora is kind," prayed Una. "But I worry."

"Why's that?"

"Young men don't hold a monopoly on callous behavior."

"You think she'll do something stupid?"

Una shrugged and settled against him. "She is wise beyond her years. More than I ever was. I hope you're right."

The following morning when Una reentered their apartment, Rian was gone. Her bedside had been neatly made, and her homespun hung from the mantle to dry. The remnants of her breakfast were perched on the larder, covered with a handkerchief. Rian must have gotten up long before the sun broke, as its light only dusted the horizon a dull pink when Una entered their chamber. Una bathed and dressed without much concern to seek her out in the bathhouse. When she arrived, the girl was again nowhere in sight. Cots and carts they'd cobbled together and scrubbed for use lined each dry wall in tidy rows of eight. Many more were stacked in the hall outside. The floors and walls were spotlessly clean, and the baths themselves had been covered with wooden planks to keep them free of effluence. Una spied Violet and Zania coming to prep the workstations they'd been assigned to, yawning and carting piping hot cups of tea—but still, no Rian. Perplexed, Una tugged on the rabbit fur cloak Mel Carra had brought for her and went in search of her friend.

After nearly an hour of strolling the length and breadth of the Quarter, she returned to *The Hart* nonplussed. Barb hadn't seen her, Colm, Dabney, or Kaer Yin's lieutenants Mordu and Jan Fir. It wasn't until she returned to the tenements to wake Kaer Yin did she spy the girl in the causeway, wound tightly in Shar Lianor's arms. Eyes wide, Una stopped dead in her tracks. Visibly embarrassed, Rian broke from their embrace, her cheeks livid. A lovely smile stretched her bruised lips wide. "Ah, good morning, Una."

"My Lady." Shar bowed, not removing his fingers from Rian's, Una noted.

"Oh no," Una muttered.

Fidgeting, Rian held out her left hand. "Ah, well, we wanted to wait to tell everyone, but," she wiggled her ring finger, which bore a silver band it never had before. "I'm glad you were the first."

Una needed a stiff drink... maybe five.

She stared at a scrap of metal like it were a snake that might bite her friend at any moment. Rian didn't seem to notice her discomfiture. Her face was rosy with youth and infatuation. Shar, however, was not so naïve. He gave Una a sheepish smile. "I apologize, *Ard Bhean*. We meant no offense."

"Whether you meant it or not, you have to know you're giving some," said Una. Rian bit her lip and shifted her eyes away. "You have a liege lord, which complicates things for the Crown Prince. Rian? I need to speak with you *now*."

But Shar dropped to a knee before her. "I am at liberty to choose whom I serve as a free member of my tribe. My father is *Tuaithe* of his rath, and my mother was descended from Bov Dearg's line. It is my right to choose a bride and offer my services to you, *Ard Bhean*, should you deem me worthy."

Ah, thought Una. *He's clever, this one. Damn.*

He pressed a hand against his heart. "I will serve you faithfully unto death if you allow me."

Kaer Yin, always with impeccable timing, rounded the opposite end of the causeway just then. His silver eyes were wide as saucers. "Oh, Fuck," was all he said.

Unsure what to say or do, Una tried to look anywhere but at Lianor. Rian caught her eye instead. Her expression was earnest, frightened, and the least of which, a bit desperate. "Please, Una."

What could she say?

Rian is no fool, however innocent she may be.

If this is her choice, you owe her your support.

"Is this what you want?" she asked Shar, though her eyes never left Rian's face. "Once you make this decision, I think it'll be fairly final."

"Shar…" Kaer Yin said softly. "If you do this, he'll never forgive you. Enter my service, and I'll let you two marry when an appropriate amount of time has passed."

"Una, *please,*" begged Rian.

"I am sure, *Ard Bhean,*" said Shar. "I would not be the stone that parts the waters."

"You'd ask it of me, instead." Una tapped her foot.

He dipped his head. "Forgive me, but you are an outsider, not a party to our politics. This is the most elegant solution we could devise."

Una supposed it *was* elegant, even if it put her at odds with the Prince of Connaught. She let out a long breath, appropriately hoodwinked. She splayed both hands at Kaer Yin, who shook his head vehemently. "Rian, I would advise you not to ask this of me. Let us get through this siege first, if we even make it. Don't put me in this position."

"This is my choice," said Rian, and only when her cheeks flamed a brilliant scarlet did Una realize Tam Lin, Robin, and Barb were behind her. Una heard Tam Lin's gasp. Rian squared her shoulders, regardless. "We are already handfasted and only require your blessing, Una. Will you give it?"

"Are you giving me a choice?"

Rian fidgeted. "I'm sorry."

Fully aware of the anger boiling over her shoulder, Una accepted Shar's dagger and jabbed it into her waistband. "Shar Lianor, I accept your service. Go now and celebrate with your bride."

Tam Lin's hiss of fury was barely audible over Kaer Yin's cursing and Rian's girlish squeal. Shar clasped Rian's hand and stood without fear or shame, leading her past Una and a growing collection of surprised onlookers along the way. Shar gave Tam Lin only the briefest salute.

After they'd gone, Barb fanned her face. "Bloody me. Who needs a dram?"

Una raised her hand, but Tam Lin caught it and swung her around to face him. "How could you?"

The emotions in that voice dented even Una's less than warm heart. "I'm sorry, your highness. I daresay this was a brilliant trap."

"You took them both."

"Neither was yours to barter." He squeezed her hand so tight she heard her bones grind together. Still, she did not flinch. "If I had my way, Rian would remain free of connubial strings her whole life. It seems I am overruled."

"I won't forgive you for this, *Ard Bhean*." He made the last sound as derisive and mocking as possible.

"Tam Lin," growled Kaer Yin. "This is not her fault. Go and drink it off somewhere."

"It's done," Una sighed. "I'm sorry for you."

Tam Lin let her go and stalked away, nearly flattening Barb in his haste.

Robin held her upright.

Kaer Yin glared at Una for several pregnant moments before he followed his cousin out.

"Siora," cooed Barb. "Our girlie seems to have stirred it up this morn. Who knew she even thought o'the boys that way?"

"That's what I said," agreed Una darkly. "Not the first time I've been wrong."

"Nor the last, I suspect," laughed Barb. "Well, no point to long facin' it through the day. Might as well get good and soused afore the Southers come to kill us all for our brass."

Una nodded eagerly. "For once, Mistress Dormer, we are in perfect agreement."

Surrogates

n.e. 509
20 ban apesa
Rosweal

By noon, Una was fully inebriated. With her head resting on Colm's bar, and her hand woven through her aunt's, she sat groaning into the small puddle of ale accumulating beneath her tankard. Beside them, Barb, who didn't seem drunk despite the dozen ales she'd already downed, winked at Eva.

"Lost in the woods, this one," she said, patting Una's shoulder.

Eva sighed. "It's been a trying day."

Una made a rude sound. Colm tossed a folded cloth at her, which she ignored. Instead, she sagged into her seat and sighed at the ceiling like it might hold the answers she sought. "I'm a terrible mother."

Barb choked out a laugh. "Well, yer not her mother, ye know."

"I know."

"But I agree, ye'd do a shite job."

"Thanks so much, Barb."

Barb saluted her with her tankard. "Anytime, love."

Ignoring that comment, Eva tucked a lock of Una's hair behind her ear, as she had when she was still a girl. "You were a brilliant mother, Una. Rian is not Zeah, and the circumstances are not the same."

Barb's elbow froze mid-sip. Her eyebrows shot up. "So that rumor was true then?"

"Yes," answered Una, atonally.

Barb set her ale down, sharing a long uncomfortable look with Colm, who threw up his hands and sauntered off. "Ah... well, fuck me then. What happened to the lass?"

Una teared up and buried her face in her hands.

"Ah hell, girl. Pay me no mind."

Eva rubbed small circles into Una's back until she was sensate enough to hiccup into her tankard. "Zeah died young. A fever."

"I thought ye Mouras were illness-proof?"

Eva looked down. "So did we."

"I'm sorry."

Una nodded blithely, staring at nothing. "I don't confuse her and Rian, so you know."

"Of course not," Eva swiftly assured her.

"I just want a better life for her... than *this*."

"Well, ye don't get to decide that fer anyone, bairns included."

Eva sent a sharp eye over Una's head. "What were their names?"

Barb laughed mirthlessly, "Ye'd have to ask Robin. I couldn't bear to give 'em any."

Una stopped and looked up. "You?"

"Oh, aye. Four or five o'me own. Only two drew breath more'n a week, poor mites."

"*Siora*, Barb. Forgive me..."

She waved her comment away. "Oh, hush. We're three decades on now. Done me grievin'." She paused to make sure no one was paying too close attention. "Does Ben know?"

"Yes."

"That why yer cousin can't let ye go?"

"Partly, I believe. For the other half, Damek's been obsessive since I was young enough to understand what that meant. When he fixates, it's forever. I'm certain that's why he's such a good swordsman and soldier. He threw himself into that part of his life with a razor focus."

"And ye?"

"I think I represent a normal life. He always wanted to be my father's son and the people to respect and love him. I think he believes I'm the way he can have all that and more."

"Love is a strange mistress, I'd say."

"To Damek, there is 'useful,' 'significant,' and 'detrimental.' I oscillate between the latter two."

"You don't believe that's love?"

Una grimaced. "Do *you*?"

She pursed her thinning lips. "As I see it, that's one way to, yeah. Men ain't like us, ye know. They don't burn with emotion the way women can. Rather it's boilt down; ye know what I mean? Cut away the introspective parts, the keen eye for detail, and yer left with the core thing. That's love to men. That thing they can't describe or quantify."

"That's rather apt," added Eva. "I believe I agree."

Una scratched her nose. "Kaer Yin can quantify. That's what I like about him. He isn't afraid to feel things."

Barb threw her head back and laughed until Una's face was red as a winter beet. "Oh love, ye have no bloody idea how *dull* that lad is, do ye?"

"Well," Una sniffed. "My experience with him might differ from yours… or anyone else's."

"That's as may be, but I promise ye, he's as lost as the rest of 'em. They know they want. They know they need. Maybe even know they'd die for ye. Just don't ask 'em to explain why. Bloody lost, the whole lot."

"And Shar Lianor," asked Eva pointedly. "What do you think he feels?"

"Lust. Bit o'competition. Maybe an ideal or two to scratch?"

"He loves her," said Eva confidently. "As men do. It's the girl I fear hasn't the same notion."

"I bloody *knew* that." Una cracked her fist against the bar, splashing herself with dark red ale. "I said as much to Yin."

"A young girl's head is filled with wax and her gut with fire. She's acting out, though she hardly realizes it."

"I should talk some sense into her. Who gets married to prove a bloody point?"

"I'll talk to her," vowed Eva, turning to her pint. "You finesse matters between the menfolk if you can."

"Ach," Barb winced. "'Fraid that'll make it worse. No offense intended, Princess, but yer the worst diplomat I've ever met. *I'll* talk to the men."

"You'd do that?" Una hiccupped.

"Who better? I, unlike ye, speak 'male.'"

That was a fair point.

Una nodded. "All right then. What should I be doing in the meantime?"

"I 'spect ye'll be asleep fer the better part o'the morrow."

"Nonsense," hiccupped Una again. "Liver of a god."

"Robin'll be tickled ye stole his line."

"It's a good one," she giggled before laying her head back on the bar. "I hope I don't fall through this time."

"Believe ye me," Barb inhaled. "So do I."

X

At the opposite end of town, Kaer Yin and Robin were busy shoring up the defenses along the Navan Gate and working very hard to stop themselves from throwing Tam Lin over. He was, for once, avidly ignoring everyone who spoke to him, including Kaer Yin. Miffed that he should be caught up in such a meaningless debacle, Kaer Yin grew more irascible as the day progressed. Robin, too, was at a loss about how to proceed.

He pulled Kaer Yin aside for the second time that afternoon. "Ye sure ye can't just brain him like ye did last time?"

"It wouldn't solve anything," frowned Kaer Yin. "Besides, it isn't me he wants to fight."

Robin squinted over at Tam Lin and spat. "This is a bad business all the way 'round."

"I won't argue."

"Lovelorn fools fight like piss."

Kaer Yin scowled. Is that what this was? He had no idea. Tam Lin never gave a half-hearted fart for any woman before; he couldn't be sure he did, even now. Was this for show? Grandstanding for the sport of it? Tam Lin caught his eye, sneered, and turned his back. That did it.

"Hey! I bleedin' saw that ye blighter," huffed Robin. "Why doncha get over here and explain yerself before we each take a turn bashin' yer bloody brains in."

Tam Lin drew himself to his full height, nearly a head and a half taller than the wiry Greenmaker. "Try it, Milesian. I won't go easy on you just because my cousin enjoys the shape of your arse."

Robin turned to Kaer Yin, bemused. "That true?"

"Tis a fine arse, Robin, all told."

Robin pursed his lips and shrugged. "Well, when yer right, yer right."

"Why do either of *you* care about my business?" demanded Tam Lin over his shoulder, crossing his arms. "I don't see how it's of concern to anyone, and we're busy, aren't we? Find something else to titter about with the rest of the women."

Kaer Yin threw his trowel at Tam Lin, where it pinged from his chest, eliciting a dull grunt. "You're being a twat. Again."

Tam Lin faced him, fist clenched. "Say that once more."

"Of fer feck's sake," muttered Barb on her way up the stairs. She smelled more strongly of uishge than she had in years, though it did little to stall her gait. "Don't ye wee bairns have any other way to manage yer troubles?"

"None as fun," answered Kaer Yin dryly.

She rolled her eyes at his jest and wagged a finger at Tam Lin. "Now ye know ye've stuck yer foot in, so I won't waste me time tellin' ye what a prat *I* think ye are, but I got one gal down there drinkin' herself twirly for guilt and another determined to wed the first prick that passed fancy at her to avoid ye. Mind tellin' me why yer makin' me climb these stairs to ask what in the hells is yer problem?"

Tam Lin blinked slowly. He still wasn't used to the sheer volume of insults lobbed his way since he took up residence with the citizens of Rosweal. "I beg your pardon?"

She made a rude sound. "I don't give a tinker's shite for your title, so save yer indignance. Ye need to get down there and make it right with yer man and apologize to that sweet girl before I lose my temper."

Tam Lin coughed, "I was *trying* to marry the bloody girl, thank you. I still fail to see why this is such a godsdamned insult to everyone within fifty miles of Rosweal."

"Yeah, right," argued Barb. "Ye might be tellin' yerself that now because it makes ye feel better about challengin' yer man for a prize, but ye must realize I've known yer sort me whole life, and not one o'ye *ever* means it when they make a promise. None o'this is about her. It's about ye bein' bored. It's about yer man darin' to leave yer service to claim somethin' ye don't value. It's about winnin'. 'Marry' the girl my bleedin' foot."

Tam Lin said nothing.

Kaer Yin cleared his throat. "If she's wrong, Lin, say so now."

He still didn't answer.

Robin scratched at his scar. "Mate, if ye did that to me when I was a younger man, I'd have yer ears by nightfall. Shar's a bleedin' Kneeler's saint, ye ask me."

"Tam Lin?" Kaer Yin repeated.

Cursing, Tam Lin threw his tools down and stomped down the rampart in the opposite direction. Men and Sidhe scrambled out of his way, lest the look on his face was meant for any of them.

Barb threw up her hands. "Ye shoulda beat him senseless, love."

Kaer Yin wasn't sure how to respond to that. "I don't think it would help," he repeated for her benefit.

"Think it's gonna be a long week," Robin sighed.

⚔

N<small>IALL CAME TO TELL</small> R<small>IAN</small> that Kaer Yin had agreed to give her three men, so long as she decided to move her patients beneath *The Hart*. While she was less than pleased by the prospect, she figured it was best not to add to the trouble she'd caused the night before.

Everyone was furious with her.

Niall was curt as ever, but before he took his leave, the look in his river-green eyes told her what he thought of her at that moment. When she came up to the tap to ask the girls for help setting up the cellar,

Gerrod cut his jaw so hard that she felt like her stomach had been sliced clean open.

He took his leave with nary a word to spare for her.

Indeed, even Rose winced at her coming up the stairs. "Ach, love," she said. "Yer in for a shite day, ain't ye?"

Rian would have loved to argue, but Rose's words proved prophetic. Most of the Greenmakers in the Quarter found a reason to visit *The Hart* that day, and every one of them seemed excited to ogle her over their tankards whenever she came into the tap… which she had to do rather often since she was busy preparing the rude, ungrateful clods a clinic, the while.

At first, she was angry, but then she empathized.

Rian was also mad at Rian, so there was that.

She was busy cramming clean linens into an abandoned dresser drawer in the cellar and cursing at the fresh splinter she'd given herself when Eva swept downstairs with a small dagger already to hand. Rian cursed anew when she clasped her hand and dragged the offensive finger beneath her blade. "I'm not sure I like your abilities, Eva."

With a smirk, she deftly swept the half-inch splinter from Rian's finger, who immediately wrapped the stinging appendage in a rag soaked with witch hazel. "So the Crown Prince has repeatedly remarked."

At the word 'prince,' Rian gave the barest flinch.

Of course, Eva noticed. Her smile deepened.

"That's irritating too," grumbled Rian.

Eva crossed her arms to lean against the stone doorjamb. She wore a simple red dress that, on any other woman, would manage to look gauche. On Eva, it might have been spun from the finest silk, such a figure she cut. She wore her long black braids loose this evening, and the bells woven into the tips chimed slightly where they brushed her hips. Her impressive golden eyes, Una's very own, stared down at Rian with a warm, motherly sort of humor. "Got yourself into it today, haven't you?"

Rian huffed, her cheeks burning. She scooted away to pretend to work on something else across the room. "I don't know why everyone is making a big deal about this."

"Yes, you do."

"It's not anyone's bloody business, is it?"

"It's Una's business now, isn't it?"

Rian felt a deep pang of guilt. She set down the scissors she wasn't going to use anyway and swallowed hard. "I didn't mean to take advantage of her adopting me."

"But you were angry with her for her presumption."

"I mean…"

"And knew she would defend you."

"That's true, but—"

"And also knew the Crown Prince would not gainsay her in front of his men."

Now, Rian fidgeted. "I don't… I mean, I didn't want to…".

"You understand that the Sidhe marry forever, right? Shar, even if you grow apart or die before he does, he'll never take another wife. If you take him this way, you'd be doing him and yourself a disservice."

Rian went quiet for a moment, her thoughts racing. She had to wipe tears from her face when she spoke again, but Eva didn't move to comfort her. Her eyes were hard as amber. "I didn't mean to. I was angry, and I thought it would make everyone happy."

"Rian Guinness," Eva sucked her teeth. "Do you suppose I can't hear that bald lie?"

Rian threw up her hands in defeat. "How do I fix it?"

Eva sighed and shrugged. She entered the cellar, lingering over the humble collection of medicinals she had bought for Rian in Ten Bells. "You're a smart girl. Probably smarter than I am, and I have been an Alta Prima, Domina of a great Tairnganese Clan, sometime spy, and counselor to a Doma of the Cloister. You know what you have done and must do, though neither sits well on your conscience."

"I don't want to hurt him."

"Which one do you mean?"

Rian's head snapped around at that. "You *know* it wouldn't be him!"

"Hmm," hummed Eva. "Not yet, you mean."

Rian quickly cleared her throat. "If you came down here to judge me…."

"Oh stop, silly girl. You'd hardly be the first foolish woman of some relation I've ever had to council against an unwise match."

"Which relation?"

Eva smiled. "You instantly recalled a name that your lips did not utter. See? Smart, as I said."

Rian scrunched up her brows. "With *Patrick?*"

"He was quite dashing in his youth. I recall that he made Arrin laugh something awful during the High King's Council. Such affairs last weeks, and they got to know one another quite well. Drove Auntie Drem completely mad."

"Oh, *Siora,*" Rian's hand went to her mouth. "But everyone said he kidnapped her on the High Road in broad daylight."

"Well," Eva sniffed. "Your brain conjured her name because you already had doubts about the whole sordid tale. Are you shocked to hear confirmation?"

"They... *eloped?*"

"They did. Against my urging and Drem's command, of course."

Rian's head raced through a thousand conversations at once. "Does Una know?"

"I intended to tell her when the grief and anger over her father's death subsided, but perhaps I should do so sooner, given our approaching doom."

Rian took a seat. Well, *that* certainly changed things. "Una told me she suspected her father had her mother killed."

"My aunt commanded me never to speak of Arrin to her daughter upon pain of disinheritance, and I, too, blamed Patrick for my cousin's death. So, I obeyed, and that silence has complicated Una's life." She folded her hands tight. "I often wonder if all of this might have been avoided if only Una knew how much her parents loved her and each other."

Stunned to total silence, all Rian could do was blink back at her.

Eva toyed with a stray braid. "What are *you* going to do, little bird?"

Sucked back to her reality, Rian immediately shut her mouth with a snap. "I have no idea. Everyone hates me now."

"Everyone does not hate you, but you did overplay your only hand. Honestly, I would ask you what you were thinking, but I believe it's fairly obvious."

"I thought marrying Shar would make me powerful enough to tell them all to go to the hells. I thought I liked him a lot and enjoyed his company... and erm, the things we do together." She flushed. "I thought I would make Ben treat me as an equal and not a burden, and I thought it would twist that redhaired bastard's nose to no end."

"Well, some of that turned out to be true, at least."

"I hurt Una, instead."

"Yes, but yourself, first."

Rian chewed her lower lip hard enough to make it bleed. "What do I do, Eva?"

"You tell Shar the truth."

"It'll hurt him."

"The fiction will hurt him more."

She squirmed under that imperious gaze. "Tam Lin, won't he try to take revenge, somehow?"

"Do you believe Una would ever allow that?"

"After what I have done, maybe she'd consider it."

Eva let out a long, patient breath. "Do you love Shar Lianor?"

"I have no idea," Rian answered truthfully. "I know I love Una and Ben, but it's different."

"They're surrogate family."

"Yes."

"Do you want to marry Shar Lianor?"

"No... I don't know."

"And Tam Lin O'Ruiadh?"

Rian colored as she ground her molars. "*Never.*"

"Hmm," Eva repeated. "Then, after this battle is over, you need to tell him."

"Which one?"

"You decide."

Under the White Flag

n.e. 509
23 ban apesa
Rosweal

Damek strode through the oppressive canopy of trees, old snow crunching underfoot. A limpid sun hung from a light blue sky, and the air was so dry it whisked the moisture from his lungs. Leaving the warmth of the headwoman's bed before dawn and up the Taran High Road, over hills, through dales, and past several frozen villages on his way, he set about the day's parlance. From this elevated vantage, he could see down the crested hillside where the two rivers wedded in the crux of the flatlands— and following the thinner of the snaking brown lines, he saw the little walled town he expected to see.

Only, all was not as he remembered it.

A newly fortified hillfort sat beneath a thick white cloak upon a corrugated plain, bisected into two broad sections between an eight-foot moat and an earthen bulwark another ten feet from vastly heightened walls. Massive chunks of masonry topped with upended timber rose almost a dozen feet from the ground. The walls ran in a uniform semicircle around the southern approach, marred only by rectangular arrow slits and the occasional murder hole. Behind the wall on either side of the reinforced gate stood two siege towers built into the framework, each featuring half a dozen archers and flying the silver and white standard of House Adair.

Damek smiled mirthlessly.

Rosweal had been busy.

He passed his spyglass to Martin with a laugh he didn't feel. "They've divested me of my trebuchets."

"*Reason*," Martin breathed, pressing the glass to his eye. "How in the hells did they accomplish all that in less than six months?"

Damek shrugged, settling his chin into his ermine collar. "Desperation is a master motivator."

This was disappointing. He had been expecting more challenge from the ruffians in Rosweal— but he wasn't expecting *this*. With the night raids and the snows deepening around them, this siege could become quite troublesome for him in no time. Men would continue to desert, and the colder it got, the less he'd be able to mitigate his losses.

"They're waving the High King's standard," observed Martin.

"I saw."

"And that moat must be what— nine feet wide, give or take? That negates cavalry too." Martin jerked the spyglass down, gnashing his teeth. "Ripped down over five hundred trees to build up that wall."

"More."

Martin turned to him, incredulous. "Noticed maybe a handful of rooftops still visible in town. Tore their own houses down too." He exhaled through his nose. "In this weather? There's a message in there for you."

"Of course. Some blather about freedom meaning more than comfort, but we'll see how long that bravado lasts when they're starving, and the late winter snows are piling around their ears."

"That'll be a fine kettle of rotted fish for us all, I expect." Martin's temper had yet to cool from their argument a few days before. These were the most words they'd exchanged in several days. "I bet they're better supplied than we are."

"But not better armed. Wooden walls are still made of wood, no matter how high."

"They're forcing a protracted siege."

"I can see that, Martin."

"Puts a damper on many of your plans."

"So it does."

"That's all you have to say?"

Damek passed the spyglass to Ridley. "My cannons have range."

"True," acknowledged Martin. "But if I'm not mistaken, those are oak trees lining the walls. Oak doesn't burn easily. What's worse, from the look of things, they've managed to move all habitable dwellings closer to the river and far from the walls. Whoever planned this... I'd like to shake his hand before I gut him because he's bloody brilliant."

Ridley winced as the glass came away from his eye. "When it snows again, there'll be nothing to catch fire at the southern gate, and with soaking wet thousand-pound tree trunks lining a reinforced rampart—we're gonna be here a while."

Damek refused to be cowed. "We'll have to draw them out, bring them in reach of our cavalry. How many mounts do the Wild Hunt hold within their vanguard?"

Ridley took another look in the glass; his face scrunched up. "Can't tell, but with less than three thousand soldiers and civilians, it can't be more than two hundred."

"Not enough to challenge us in an open field," mused Damek. "But enough to give us a headache or two if they catch us from the sides—which I expect they're aiming to. Notice the trees on the east and western flanks? They mean to funnel us right up to the walls."

"No," disagreed Martin. They'll use footsoldiers and archers on either flank. They'll save the cavalry for anyone we get over the walls. I've seen Sidhe lords use this tactic at Dumnain. When Fionn O'More and his four hundred horse evaporated from the field, Patrick's men found them again once they'd breached the walls. Numbers count for nothing in narrow streets and alleys, doubly so when mounted combatants are barreling down every one."

"Wonderful," grumbled Ridley. "We'll have to starve or draw them out, no matter what. This could mean weeks of fucking around in the freezing mud with the flux, the pox, and all with nearly sixteen thousand mouths to feed. Bloody Tairngare is proving less a challenge." He drew his cloak tight and stamped his feet. Ridley was a brave bear of a man, but the cold was one of his least favorite things, and it would only worsen.

The mercury in Damek's brass barometer had already swept well below zero. The longer they mired here playing the waiting game, it would dip lower still.

"No," he said. "Impressive as these new defenses are and irritating as they were meant to be— I am not going to waste men and time on them."

"What orders then, My King?"

Damek eyed the slow, ice-infested Boinne as she made her way east to the Sea of Mannanan. The trees had been stripped naked by months of merciless, frigid wind. The air itself felt static and charged. It hadn't snowed in several days. The season's usual blanket of thick, iron-gray clouds had given way to a weak low-slung sun and nights illuminated by starlight. He felt himself smile. "Take two hundred of our best yeomen and send them five miles upstream toward the confluence. Send a second, ten miles west. I want them gone before the sun sinks over the mountains."

"They will have expected us to foul the river."

Damek continued, "Each man must carry ten liters of pitch and lamp oil in his travel pack."

Martin couldn't help but laugh. "It *is* dry as Siora's cunny out here."

"Ridley said it himself, when the snows come back, we'll be at their mercy. I'd rather not wait to give the Sidhe that advantage."

"You sure it'll work?"

Damek took off his glove and spat into his palm. In seconds, the little wad iced up, then crumbled. "Yes. In these conditions, a forest fire can quickly get out of hand. Let's hope so. Ridley, you have my orders."

Ridley saluted. "Yes, My King."

Damek considered the little hamlet in silence for a moment. "They mean to funnel us into one approach and let the weather do the rest. Well, I must refuse their invitation. Once the forest is aflame, I'll have that eastern gate down. Keep our men back, and don't risk anyone unnecessarily. I want them too busy putting out internal fires to stop the Greensward burning on either side of the river." He'd be damned if he'd be foolish enough to march his men into such an obvious trap. His eyes drifted north over the Boinne.

He knew exactly where he would strike next.

"At dawn, I expect to see the valley scorched black. In the meantime, let's go down and say hello." He couldn't wait to show these people how ruthless he was prepared to be.

✕

AFTER THE HORNS, KAER YIN flew up the watchtower to glimpse the approaching horde for himself. A cadre of mounted men waving Bethany's cobalt and scarlet colors stood in the killing field below the southern wall. Damek Bishop at the center, waiting patiently, stared straight at Una, whom Kaer Yin hadn't even realized was standing just at his elbow. Her conflicted frown irked him a great deal. "I didn't mean for him to see you," he said, incensed by the self-assured smirk on the bastard's face at the sight of her.

"It doesn't matter. Even if I weren't here, he'd treat you no differently. It's the premise that got him this far. The reality is merely a footnote."

Kaer Yin studied her. She was so small. The crown of her head barely crested his ribcage, yet she swallowed so much space in his mind's eye that he could scarcely breathe. He felt a little overwhelmed by the thought. "It will galvanize his troops, regardless. For a while anyway. When the cold gets to work, maybe that will change." While he spoke, Damek raised a hand to wave at them. It would be a simple task to put an arrow right between his eyes. The distance might be too great for most, some five hundred yards or more, but not for Kaer Yin's. Sinnair was the most famous bow on the continent. Kaer Yin gripped her topmost pinnacle, leaning into her impressive height, and watched the mirth drain from Bishop's face.

Sinnair meant 'king killer' in the old tongue.

Sometimes, irony had its perks.

"I will go down with you," Una stated, chewing her lower lip earnestly. She was afraid, he knew. Not for herself. She feared for the others, Rian, and the people of Rosweal. She blamed herself for all of this and would doubtless take matters into her own tiny hands if he let her. He'd never met a woman more endearingly reckless in his life.

"No."

"Are you telling me what to do?"

"I'm not telling you— I'm asking you to stay up here where I won't be goaded into a scuffle in the first three seconds of this parley."

"Fine, but he's only doing this to pick your ribs. He wants to draw you out."

"He'll try."

Una threw up her hands. "Well, what do I know? I just grew up with him. Why are you looking at me like that?"

"Like what?"

"Like that." She squinted up at him. "Don't."

"I'm not doing anything."

But he lied. Before she could stop him, he pulled Una in for a brief but very public kiss that was sure to pick the fight Kaer Yin was after far more efficiently than words would ever manage. On the stairs below, Robin groaned.

"Ben, can ye knock that off afore it comes to battle *today*? The lads ain't ready yet."

Kaer Yin broke away as noisily as possible.

"You might be overplaying that leer, my love," remarked Una coolly, though her cheeks were red as an apple. "Now, get out of here before you get in your own way."

"Later?" he asked, lowering his voice for her ears only.

"Not until you stop embarrassing me in front of all of Rosweal."

With a grin that said he knew better, he took the stairs two at a time on his way to threaten the newly minted King of Eire.

X

Damek's jaw ached from grinding his teeth together. That lecherous inhuman dog! How *dare* he treat the Duchess of Bethany like some common dockside trollop? Damek would see the man's guts served to his hounds in tidbits. He would drink ale from a goblet shaped from Adair's skull. He would nail the man's teeth to his spurs. The insolence! The sheer, bloody arrogance.

Sitting beside Damek, Martin moved his brindle destrier closer. "Easy now. Surely you know that was for your benefit?"

"I will eat that creature's heart, I swear it."

"And that's what he wants you to feel. Angry men are not prudent men."

Damek took several stilling breaths as he watched his enemy and two other riders approach from the southern gate.

"Smile, My King. Give them no advantage of you."

Damek couldn't smile, but he managed to smooth his face into the pleasant mask he'd perfected in his uncle's tutelage. The riders neared. The leader's silver hair gleamed nearly white in the weak winter sunlight. Beside him, the Prince of Connaught and another Sidhe noble in a plain black cuirass and obsidian cloak took Damek's measure. Damek had never seen the fellow before and had trouble placing him. Meanwhile, Una watched from the rampart. It took every ounce of effort not to look up.

"There's a lamb," Martin coughed into his fist. "Don't give 'em the satisfaction."

Without answer, Damek kicked his roan into a canter to meet the prince's entourage. Each group halted five paces from the other.

"Well met, friends," called the rider in black. His silver-blond hair was very similar in cast and color to the Crown Prince's. Though where there was a solid, almost brutish angle to Kaer Yin Adair's bones— by Sidhe standards anyway— this one's held a nearly feminine beauty and grace. The figure's sheer, unfair elegance tugged a sneer from Damek's mouth.

On the newcomer's opposite side, the Prince of Connaught had a go at him. "I don't think he cares for your face, old man."

Martin cleared his throat before the mysterious fellow could respond. "If it please you gentlemen, we are come to discuss terms with the townsfolk of Rosweal," he said. "We've had the pleasure of meeting the Prince of Connaught and briefly encountered his highness, the Crown Prince. You, sir, we do not recognize."

The man in black gave the ghost of a nod. "Mortals rarely do, Martin."

Something in his tone made Martin stiffen.

Damek crooked a brow. The dark rider's green eyes burned into him, and he could admit to the slight tinge of unease his attention inspired. "I'll have your name."

"You have the very *great* honor," interrupted O'Ruaidh dryly. "Of meeting *Fiachra Dubh*. Diarmid Mac Nuada Adair, Lord of Tech Duinn, and of the *Oiche Ar Fad*, king."

Damek's men twitched and whispered amongst themselves; several backed away. Damek himself raised a dark brow. *This* was the infamous Raven King? This too pretty, effeminate creature was the Lord of the Sluagh?

Bollocks.

Why would the High King's brother bother to meddle in Milesian Eire?

"That's easy enough to answer, My LordBishop, if you'd repeat that question aloud?"

Martin shifted in his saddle. Damek willed his nerves still. It would take more than parlor tricks to intimidate the blood of Patrick Donahugh and Eochaid Mac Nemed. "Very well. What business have you here, My LordAdair? This is a regional matter and none of your affair."

The Raven King smiled enigmatically, but he did not answer right away. The wind turned colder, slithering into the crevices between Damek's armor and flesh. He repressed a shiver. "You lay claims to lands that don't belong to you, Lord Bishop. In this, I am my brother's right hand."

Damek knew better than to quibble over the title. One did not rebuke the king of the underworld lightly. Damek chose his following words carefully. "We are not here to quarrel with the High King, nor you, Your Grace."

"Your presence here, in such force, begs to differ."

"Forgive me, but while I do not seek to insult you or the High King, the land of Eire has unified under my banner. We are here for our queen, which your nephew has stolen. Should we come to terms today, you and all your people may leave in peace with our blessing."

Diarmid Adair's mouth quirked at that. "Is that all?"

After a few tense moments, Kaer Yin found his voice. "What I wish to know is why you make war upon innocent, loyal citizens of Eire. You burn their villages, rape their women, and plunder their resources. You realize, the Ard Ri has not given you license to claim land and titles that are his— and only his— to grant or take?"

"Forgive me, My LordPrince," interrupted Martin. "But we do not condone rape and slaughter. Either is punishable by death."

"Hm," beamed Tam Lin. "How noble we've become, all of a sudden."

Damek finally met Kaer Yin's eyes, inwardly seething. "You've stolen my wife, the Princess of Bethany, Domina of the Moura Clan, and Queen of Eire." He paused to make sure she was watching. "I want her back."

"No," Kaer Yin denied him. "Una will not be your excuse. She does not subscribe to Bethonair laws, whichever way they are twisted to suit your cause. You're here for me. Well, on that score, I won't disappoint you. I promise."

Damek absorbed this statement and shared a look with Martin. "Nevertheless, here are my terms. One, you will surrender the Queen of Eire to my company, alive and unharmed. Two, you will immediately march your occupying force back into your cursed lands. Once there, you are free to rule your people and decide the fates of your women as you see fit. Three, you will renounce your claim to Eire and divest yourself permanently from matters here. Four— and this is non-negotiable— you will cross that border and never return. Those are the terms I offer you as a courtesy. Accept them or die."

To Damek's eternal irritation, Kaer Yin laughed through an open mouth. "And here are *my* terms, boy. One, your union with Una Moura Donahugh was annulled in your youth, making your presence here is illegal as it is laughable. Two, she rejects your claim... I reject your claim, and the whole of the Tuatha De Dannan rejects your claim to the crown of Eire. Three, if you linger here, you will never leave the Greensward alive, and all the men who followed you on this foolish quest will be hunted down and slain for this insult to the Ard Ri's family name."

Tam Lin tugged his chin at the men behind Damek. "I wonder how many men will fight for you when they're starving. Through the wet and cold, hounded and terrorized by ruthless cutthroats, poachers, and bloodthirsty creatures of the Otherworld— all so you can steal another man's bride?"

Something bright flared behind Damek's eyelids. "We'll see how many of you live to make good those threats. Presently, you are alone. None of your allies have made it in time to save you. How many women and children are you holding hostage in there? You talk a good game, Adair— but I have the numbers, and you will feel them soon enough. Tomorrow it begins." He jerked his reins to turn his horse around, but Kaer Yin's voice caught him short.

"Do you know how I met her, Lord Bishop? The mercenaries you hired to kidnap her from Tairngare spirited her away in burlap and kept her bound and starved for three days. It was I who freed her. When I saw her next, she was hunted down and nearly beaten to death right in front of me. Ever since, she's been chased from one end of Eire to the other, captured and held prisoner, then nearly raped and murdered by her own kin. All this, and the only thing you can whine about, is yourself. *Your* right to her. *Your* claim to her father's lands and titles. Everything, *yours*."

Kaer Yin paused, the derision on his face plain.

"I could have killed you once, remember, but Una stayed my hand. Despite all, she thought your worthless life held value. You think about that the next time we meet. I will."

Damek thought about the bloodied linens he'd found in that ramshackle farmstead in autumn. The rage, knowing whom they belonged to. The fear and uncertainty of searching for her for weeks on end. The relief he experienced when he found her at last… and the burning jealousy he felt now, knowing this man had been there for every moment he'd lost. "I'll look for you on the field, Highness," promised Damek with every ounce of loathing he could summon from the deepest recesses of his gut. Spine rigid, he kicked his mount away without another word.

Only when Rosweal shrank in the distance did the fear settle in. It wasn't the presence of the Raven King that unnerved him, the bitter justice he read in Kaer Yin Adair's frank expression, nor the unspoken but genuine threat either represented. This was something else. Something deeper, darker.

For the whole of his life, he'd never felt such an inexplicable, insidious emotion— and it ate at him, even as he slumped in his command tent, surrounded by thousands of capable Bethonair troops who believed in him.

The feeling was doubt.

Martin was right.

He didn't like it one bit.

Scorched Earth

n.e. 509
24 ban apesa
Rosweal

Dawn had just begun to creep over the tops of the tallest trees in the east when the first noxious clouds of smoke descended upon Rosweal. The air had been dry enough to irritate the end of every nose in town during the night, which was just the sort of feast that a forest fire would require to consume an entire region. Kaer Yin, who got up well before sunrise to install the windlass on the southern rampart and oversee the return of last night's raiding party, had been one of the first to spy the orange haze on the horizon. His throat seized at the sight long before he smelt smoke.

They'd been expecting Bishop to burn the trees to the west of the city— counting on it, actually— but the scale… the way the sky also lit up red in the west said they had been far from prepared.

Kaer Yin raced along the rampart to the Ward Gate without wasting a moment in shocked silence. Already, the heat was staggering. Flames raged over the western hills, nearly twenty feet high. When he skidded to a stop facing the north wall, eyes watering, he covered his mouth with the back of his hand. Tam Lin and Robin were already there, pouring buckets of melting snow over the wooden walls. Barb, who was never up at such an ungodly hour, directed more up the stone steps at the north end. A raucous shout went around the city from the Quarter to the vacant hilltop. People poured out of homes and rundown buildings, hauling whatever vessels they could carry to keep the walls from catching. With a nod to Tam Lin, who busied himself with managing the traffic along the ramparts, Kaer Yin leaped to work, shouting commands to heave water from the river and moats to keep the supply steady.

Oak and ash did not burn quickly, but under such blazing temperatures— even ten yards away, the walls would get so dry that the slightest spark could catch. No matter how strong the wood, it would still burn. Barb's brilliant moat system might keep that risk at bay for a while. He could only pray that whatever Una had done would help.

"Keep these walls as wet as possible!" He heard Tam Lin roar against the quickening blaze. "Set up lines here and there," he pointed to Robin and Dabs, who'd just dashed up the steps as fast as his bulky frame could carry him. "I want a constant chain of water streaming over these walls until that fire molders out."

Una, too, raced up the steps at the far end. She came around Tam Lin, her face already smudged with soot. Dark ash fell from the sky like snow. "What can I do?"

Tam Lin turned. "Can you put out a forest fire?"

She blinked back. "I don't think so."

"Then nothing." He wiped his nose and spat, eyes shifting to the Navan Gate on the east side of town. Muttering a colorful curse in Ealig, he noted, "On second thought, I want every available yeoman and pikeman along that wall and double the men on the southern rampart." He gesticulated so Robin and Barb would hear him. Robin nodded and dashed off, hollering for more men.

Una followed his gaze. "You think he'll attack from the east?"

The rising sun gave them a better glimpse of the distant inferno. Though the fire raged right beside them in the west and east, the worst of it was yet miles off; encroaching but slowly. Tam Lin gave Kaer Yin a stern look. "He won't come from the south. Too many traps. He'll want to pull his trebuchets in as close as possible, and the Navan Gate is weakest."

He was right. Kaer Yin could glean the logic as clearly as his cousin. He snatched Jan Fir by the collar as he passed with an empty bucket.

"No one is to drink the water they take from the river, nor use it to treat any burns."

"You think they fouled it?" he asked, hair black with ash and eyes smudged.

"Count on it." Kaer Yin nodded to Una. "Make sure Barb and Rian know and spread the word, fast."

She took off at a run.

Robin, huffing, and coughing, came past her. "What now?"

"It's time," Kaer Yin replied. "The Navan Gate."

Despite the severity of the situation, Robin's teeth flashed whitely in the haze. Kaer Yin grabbed him by the sleeve before he sped off to do his duty. "Make it hurt, Rob."

"Oh, Ben," said he. "It'll be my pleasure."

Kaer Tin looked around when he'd gone, searching for the one figure he needed to see most. "Where's Diarmid, Tam Lin?"

Tam Lin threw up his hands, then accepted another bucket. "Fuck if I know! I'm a bit busy here."

Niall jerked a thumb behind him. "I've seen him, *Ard Tiarne*."

Kaer Yin gestured for him to lead the way. "Good, Niall and Conor, with me!"

⚔

After nearly an hour of searching, barking orders, and lending a spare pair of hands wherever needed, the fire had mostly burned itself out at the western approach. Far afield, however, the hills were red with roaring, furious flames that sent massive billows of smoke downwind into Rosweal. The ash came down in deep drifts that were often deep enough to sink into.

Untold thousands of acres burned. The Great Greensward was swiftly reduced to a smoking scar upon the Riverlands. In the west, the devastation appeared total. Charred sticks and blackened earth buffeted by cinders and grey ash swallowed the eye for as far as one could see. To the east, there was no telling how far the fires reached. Possibly even to the walls of Navan or beyond.

Bishop hadn't merely intended to remove any additional cover the Roswellian forces meant to preserve— he intended to utterly destroy the land itself: the forest, river, and valley that could revive the city, should they manage to survive the assault. Through the rage and despair that clenched his heart at the knowledge, Kaer Yin resolved to focus on the task at hand. Bishop had studied his classics, it seemed. Scorched earth served to crush an enemy's resolve and, in this case, make clear there was no escaping Bishop's wrath.

Well, Kaer Yin thought.

Let's see how you enjoy my *strategy, young lordling.*

Finally, he spotted Diarmid at the Northern rampart, leaning into the wind. Diarmid's cloak and hair were entirely coated in soot, but he didn't appear to notice.

"Uncle!" Kaer Yin asked, breathless. "Have you been here the whole time?"

Diarmid absorbed his question without reply, nor did he turn to acknowledge him. Instead, he stared intently over the river and into the mists shrouding Aes Sidhe, a heavy furrow between his brows.

Kaer Yin drew up short. "What is it?"

He knew the look on his couldn't be good news.

"A threat. One I cannot do much about and remain here."

"What do you mean?"

Diarmid met his eyes, his expression solemn. "Your father has charged me with your support, Yin. The outcome of this battle will decide much."

"I don't know what you mean." Kaer Yin tried to crane his neck around Diarmid to see what he was staring at when his uncle's arm snaked out and brought their heads together.

"Don't look, Yin."

Kaer Yin broke the uncharacteristic fatherly embrace with a nervous laugh. "Diarmid, I don't know what you're on about...." But then Diarmid moved, and he saw for himself. A glimmer of light— a glowing made unearthly and soft by the near-impenetrable mists over the border. Just a hint, but every moment he stood there gaping, it grew broader.

Aes Sidhe.

The fire had spread over the river into sacred lands—their home, their gods... burning. Rooted to the spot in horror, Kaer Yin watched the glowing snake further northward through the mist, like some mythic wyrm writhing beneath a cloud. Within his dawning shock and outrage coiled a kernel of fury so bright that it threatened to shove his bones through his skin.

"Yin, stay the course," Diarmid warned, though, for the blood pounding in his ears, Kaer Yin scarcely heard him. "If you give him the satisfaction, you will forfeit every advantage we've gained. Use your head now, not your heart," he went on, trying to set himself between Kaer Yin and the view.

It didn't work.

Whatever Diarmid said, Kaer Yin could no longer hear him. All he could see were the flames rolling casually north, hear the cries and bleats of beasts and birds attempting to flee the blaze, and taste the char at the back of his throat. The Greensward north of the Boinne was virgin forest.

Sacrosanct.

Many of those trees were well over a thousand years old, some *far* older. Their roots reached far underground, while their towering limbs soared to heights sometimes exceeding a hundred or more feet.

This was a heresy akin to genocide.

His uncle was right. Damek Bishop had no intention of suing for peace, ever. He was declaring war on *all* of Kaer Yin's people.

You're going to get what you're asking for, isasaeligh.

Kaer Yin slid Nemain from his back, his hand shaking on her pommel.

Diarmid's hand shot out to stall him. "It's what he wants you to do."

"I don't care. That boy dies today, I vow it."

"If you go out there now, everything you planned will fail. The people here will be slaughtered or enslaved, and Una will become his pawn. Is that what you want?"

He didn't answer. A general outcry circled the walls. The Dannans, having finally seen what was happening across the river, rushed to gape and moan at the north wall. Their horror and grief were palpable. This fire, easily double the height and twice the ferocity, choked the air with so much ash and smoke that the sun was entirely blotted. Everyone and everything in Rosweal stopped as if time itself held no meaning. Many hardened Sidhe warriors wept openly, Kaer Yin included. He heard a woman wail somewhere below him and knew true despair.

He made to brush past his uncle, but Diarmid pushed back, physically placing himself between Kaer Yin and the ladder he aimed for. The keening grew to a terrible pitch. "I am as angry as you are, but don't hand this usurper the advantage."

"Get out of my way!" Kaer Yin attempted to shove him aside again, but the old Brehon might have been made of iron.

"Listen to *Fiachra Dubh*, *Ard Tiarne*," said Fionn, who materialized from the smoke behind him. His long face was grave, though Kaer Yin could see the flames reflected in his eyes. "We must hold our defenses."

Fionn's mouth pulled into a knife-slash line. He had never used Kaer Yin's title before, which gave him pause enough for Diarmid to turn him around. "Swallow it down. Save it for the appropriate moment," he urged.

Kaer Yin's blood ran cold as the ice in Donn Bay. "The appropriate moment?"

He watched Diramid's jaw clench and unclench. There wasn't a Dannan among them who didn't feel this sacrilege to their marrow. "Can you stop the fire, Uncle?"

Diarmid shook his head. "The cost would be tremendous, and you need me now, Yin. More than ever. I promised my brother."

Kaer Yin closed his eyes, counting to ten, twenty, a hundred. When he opened them again, his hands had stopped shaking. "Fionn. You'll take the South Wall?"

"*Mo Flaith*," he saluted, fist to his chest— for the first time since Kaer Yin had been placed in his service as an adolescent so many eons ago.

Fionn disappeared through the smoke whence he came, and Una was suddenly there, brushing his fingers with hers. "I can help." Only the whites of her eyes and teeth were visible.

"Can you?"

She sent Diarmid a pointed glance. "You said before what happens here echoes in the Otherworld, right? Like a reflection?"

He shifted. "Yes, but time is not always relative."

"You can change that, though, can't you?"

"The cost, Una, as you know, would be—"

"Let *me* worry about that. Is it possible or not?"

Something calculative slid behind Diarmid's façade, and were Kaer Yin paying more attention, he would have been furious to have spied it. Just then, he was having a hard time keeping himself from launching over the wall with naught but Nemain in one hand and a song in his heart. "It is, Princess."

"Then, let's go." She pulled Kaer Yin's face down for a brief kiss. "Stick to your strategy, love."

Kaer Yin held her tight for a moment, then clung to her shoulders so she couldn't miss his nod. "I will. Una, are you sure?"

"I am. I'm useless here, and Eva says Damek's men will attack next. Let me try."

"All right. Please… just don't—"

"I won't." She squeezed him again, then stepped away to take Diarmid's outstretched hand. Without further commentary, the two snapped out of existence with that horrible ear-popping sound that all Sidhe understood as the key to the Oiche Ar Fad.

Kaer Yin stared into the space they'd vacated, feeling a surge of anxiety that he didn't have the luxury to fret over. *Be safe, my love*, he thought but knew he had his own trials cut out for him today. He turned to find Gerrod and Shar Lianor waiting by the steps.

Kaer Yin's sigh was bone-deep. "Boys, let's get to work."

X

As the fire raged over the Boinne, dark shapes flitted through the wasteland that was now the eastern approach to the city. They waited for the sun to sink over the smoldering hills in the west to strike. First, two catapults were wheeled up the Navan High Road, guarded by a host of some four hundred pikemen and troopers with long iron shields. They moved in a phalanx that would prove troublesome for any ground defenders. Behind them, yeomen with longbows prepared to fire volley after volley over the wall. The defenders braced themselves for assault. Sidhe archers returned introductory fire from the ramparts with far less efficacy given their vastly inferior numbers. Many men that had been busy fighting fires on the western edge of town were late arriving at the eastern wall. All was as Damek had planned. From the rear of the attacking horde, he raised a mailed fist.

Issuing a guttural cry, five hundred uniformed infantry raced through the forward line toward the wall— axes, cudgels, and swords held high. Every tenth man dragged yards of rope from vicious grappling hooks that dangled over their armored shoulders. Many didn't make it past the smoking treeline before they were shot down, but dozens did. Soon, these howling soldiers were pouring up the wall by the hundreds. Meanwhile, the phalanx of pikes and shieldmen directed their attention to the gate. In under twenty minutes, an overwhelming number of screaming, bloodthirsty Southers, who'd been told the only way home to their warm hearths was through Rosweal, ran for the walls as if they intended to chew through them. They had more to gain than lose, given the confidence in their numbers.

Damek watched his men scramble over the wall, largely unchecked.

Hand still high; he closed his fist.

The catapults and their protective phalanx of shields moved into position.

He brought his fist down.

Douglas shouted a command. Seven-foot balls of hawthorn and bramble dipped in pitch and oil were set ablaze.

Damek swept his arm forward.

"At will!" Boomed Douglas.

A trio of steaming, white-hot missiles streaked toward the Navan Gate, swiftly followed by another round and another— until they were launched regularly at five-minute intervals. Cries of alarm rang throughout Rosweal as the newly built wall bore the assault. The defenders hasted to solidify their positions upon the ramparts. Damek waited another twenty minutes, surprised but undaunted by how long it took the Gate to fall.

He had more yet to throw at them and plenty of time to wait.

"My King, the walls!" Second Lieutenant Ridley gestured from his right. "They've been shored up somehow, and I'm not sure we have the ammunition to—"

"No matter," said Damek, knowing only one person who could manage witchery of that kind. He refused to pay it any mind. "Bring up the battering ram."

The Navan Gate was the only part of the newly heightened wall that was not surrounded by the defenders' hastily constructed trio of moats. The water system curved around the outer walls in a crescent, bisected by large, sharpened stakes and wooden arrow blinds. The lack of its continuance wasn't a failure of ingenuity but rather a nod to basic geography, which Damek had no doubt the Sidhe intended to exploit. The old stone road here snaked along a high escarpment, shored up by loose earth and soft sand. They didn't need to extend their moat around this side to keep his larger siege toys at bay. The road was too narrow and uneven here for his twenty-foot, top-heavy siege towers to be wheeled up to the walls or for the massive and cumbersome wagons required to haul up bulky cannon or trebuchets. The south end would have once been the ideal place to use his trebuchets, but that moat and all its new decorations completely prevented that. He might not be able to drag heavy ballistics up to the walls, but he could hammer the hells out of them with his lighter, ten-foot slings and a focused assault on the weakest spot they bore.

Today was not about showing off.

Today was about speed and efficiency.

Damek gambled that they'd spend so much time putting out fires on the west end that the east wall would be distracted long enough for his men to get that gate down. However, he was no fool. He understood that Kaer Yin had always planned to draw them to the east gate, but with the Sidhe busy putting out fires and their nerve unsettled by the blaze over the river— Damek hoped to be in the city well before the Dannans could marshal the defense they'd prepared for. No matter what surprises Rosweal had in store, the Navan Gate was still their greatest weakness. A fatal flaw, he hoped.

Just in case, he had plans aplenty.

"Ridley," he said. "Redirect one sling at the southern approach. I want every arrow blind and bit of moat furniture in ashes by midday, whether this gate is down or not."

"Yes, My King."

Ridley barked his orders, and the sling was reloaded and aimed at the wooden defenses along the southern wall. Many were aflame in minutes.

A killing field worked both ways; he was sure to remind Rosweal if the siege stretched on. If the Dannans could hold those walls for one more day, Damek didn't want a single obstacle to mar the perfect scorched ring of earth around the city. He held the bulk of his forces in reserve for today's adventure. Still, by the following day, those same men would encircle the town from the opposite end and erect their blockade— trapping the Roswellians in a circle of death and barren land without food or untainted water. But that plan would only be necessary if he failed to knock the wall down today... and on that score, he had a seventy-percent chance of success.

He would take those odds.

Rosweal could tuck in and ration out supplies for a week or so, but without fresh water, they wouldn't last more than ten days. Given the sad state of his own supplies, he needed to make this quick as possible. Knowing the averages, however, did not negate the need for caution.

Kaer Yin Adair, Fionn O'More, and Diarmid Mac Nuada Adair all together at once... Damek knew speed was his sole ally. There was a trap here; he was well aware. These Dannans were all celebrated commanders.

Not one would leave an open door for him. His eyes roamed the wall from the south end to the river.

Where is it?

"Douglas. I want at least five guards per every officer in our midst. Double that on each of our slings."

"Already done, My King," Douglas assured him from the Corpsmen's line. "I've ten more pikemen in check for your guard as well."

"Good." His officers were on the same page, as always. They could smell a snare as well as he. "When it begins, you know what to do next."

"Yes, My King." Douglas pounded his heart.

Damek inclined his head at Ridley again while watching the gate shudder under a succession of blows. One section of the timber wall had finally caught flame. Whatever wards Una and that Dannan devil had set upon them worked far better than he liked. "Send in another hundred infantry. Archers to the forward line."

Ridley called the order, but Kinney, his foremost legionnaire, stuck his neck out. "Won't we hit our troops?"

Damek shot him a blank, dispassionate glare. "Are you insinuating that our men lack aim, Captain?"

"No, Milord," Kinney paled. "Just figure it stands to reason they'd take some friendly fire."

"It's possible, Captain. But, which man here would rather starve than fight?"

Damek watched his adam's apple bob. "None, My King."

"Then do as I command."

Kinney bowed and gave his men the signal to advance. With hair-raising war cries, the foot soldiers threw themselves at the walls. On the way, many trod over fallen members of the first wave, who'd taken arrows or had been cut in half by a Dannan blade. If they minded, the legionaries didn't show it. They leaped onto the ropes and hauled themselves upward, dodging arrows and stones the whole way. Some did not make it, but a handful did. For several minutes, Damek watched them square off with the defenders on the ramparts, blade to blade. At least half of those who made it up were thrown back down in a trice. In the meantime, the gate groaned beneath its bombardment but did not topple.

"Doubles," he ordered next.

Douglas repeated his command, and the slings were refitted with their backup loads of heavier shot. When the catapults were fired, the iron ball at the center of each burning knot of oil and bracken struck the gate with a resounding thud. The earth beneath their feet shook for each strike. By the third round, the stone lintel cracked under strain. Damek didn't allow himself to smile, though that was his first instinct. The Roswellians had obviously been preparing for that gate to come down for months. Thus he wouldn't write them off to failure just yet.

"Proceed to phase two," he said.

Kinney jerked forward to advance with his men, his squire following with a raised flag depicting a black longbow on a red field. "Yeomen!" he bellowed, his voice louder than a man of his short stature should expect to own. "Forward march!"

From the river's edge, just east of Damek's middle flank, Robin, Gerrod, Skinny Colm, and a smattering of capable Greenmakers watched the Bethonair mass wind up the Navan Road toward the gate. Behind them, over the river, much of Aes Sidhe burned or smoldered beneath the enchanted mist that had ever obscured its details from Eirean eyes. But that was not their concern now. The Sidhe soldiers Fionn O'More had led further east had more reason to care than the Greenmakers did— and they went about their duty, as had been carefully laid out by their Crown Prince. As for Robin and his lot, their livelihood had already been consumed beyond recognition. The lives of their families, of every man, woman, and child in Rosweal, were on the line.

"We should go now," Gerrod whispered, eager to wet his shiny new axe with Souther blood.

"Not yet." Robin spat a wad of witchroot into the duff, his scarred jaw hard against the flickering backlight. "We wait for the Champion's signal, as agreed."

Gerrod pulled a face. "I don't like it, boss. That Bishop cunt is a lot cannier than we thought. He's got to be expectin' us to make a move. He'd know we left the road clear for a reason."

"So we did, Gerry," griped Robin. We're here to give him what he expects, remember?"

"I know, but—"

"Are you questionin' my orders, boyo?"

Gerrod paled. "No."

"Then shut yer gob and get ready."

Without another word, Gerrod shuffled back into position.

They waited for an eternity, watching the gate take a third critical hit that bent the top planks inward. Then, they heard an unmistakable horn blowing from the southeast, where the bulk of Bishop's forces waited in reserve.

Robin's smile was gruesome in the half-light. "Let's go, lads!"

Like phantoms, they slid up the riverbank and into the trees.

⚔

Damek heard the horn, same as every one of his men, but he barely had time to register surprise at its direction before a screeching mass of soot-blackened men came streaking into his lines from the river. Men with axes, cudgels, daggers, and pikes scattered through his right, rear flank— hacking down light-armored infantry with haphazard ferocity. In the vanguard, the Corpsmens' chargers shied as the road filled with wet, sickly sounds: shouts and the occasional scream. Murphy, another captain from the Dingle Peninsula, darted forward to place himself between the raiders and his lord, but Damek's hand shot out to halt him.

"Be still. We must give them something to aim at." His composed smile was a flash of white against the firelit sky. He turned back to

Ridley, who sat his mount with practiced ease. He returned his lord's lazy, unconcerned grin. "Ridley, you're up."

"My king," Ridley saluted and dismounted with a flourish. He drew his sword, not the typically thin, folded sabres Southers were known to favor. This was a proper two-handed broadsword, a brutal weapon meant to cleave bone and sinew. He stalked to the curve in the road, the southern edge of the remaining forest at his back. When he was about ten paces away from Command, the Roswellians came straight at him with hellish determination for Damek's standard— Ridley cupped a hand over his bearded cheek. "All right, you lazy cunts! Time to quit lyin' down on the job. Second battalion, to *me*!"

From the tangle of remaining trees over his shoulder, well over fifty men emerged from the ground as if they'd sprung from the earth itself.

Damek spared a laugh at the expense of the raiders who'd sped straight into the jaws of a well-laid trap. Experienced, well-blooded swordsmen had been lying under cover for hours, waiting for this moment. He watched as a half-dozen Greenmakers died in the first rush, eyes round with shock. Amused, he turned to nod at the standard-bearer on his left. The lad hoisted a red flag emblazoned with three swords. The call went up, and a path opened for Damek and his cavalry officers. Ridley and his unit closed ranks behind Damek and his chosen knights as they cut sharply south along the treeline. They headed for the horn they hadn't expected to hear so soon.

Damek's honor guard raised their shields high, protecting their king from sharpshooters along the walls. The gate that protected them wouldn't long survive the iron-tipped battering ram his infantry were dragging up the road. But just as Damek and his guards rounded the south-eastern curve of the city wall, an ear-splitting boom shook the ground they'd vacated. The blast bore such strength that it nearly unhorsed him. Correcting course as quickly as they could, his officers locked shields around him again, leading him back to cover at the far end of the southern line. They had almost made it when yet *another* explosion followed the first.

For several moments, all was chaos.

Damek couldn't tell where the sky started nor the earth ended. He tasted blood and soil. His ears throbbed with heat and pain. When the dust cleared, and his equilibrium returned, he could hear the defenders cheering atop the wall... over the screams. Damek rolled upright. He'd barely missed being crushed by his bisected horse.

Holding himself aloft in the blood-soaked mud, he took stock of the situation. Huge, smoking pits had opened a chasm between the damaged but still intact gate and the bulk of his forces racing away from his fallen standard. Those who bore all of their limbs, anyway. His battering ram, catapults, and at least two hundred infantry and their captains lay scattered around the Navan approach in various pieces.

He felt the blood drain from his face.

The raiders had been a feint!

They were meant to discharge explosives buried well before his troops had surrounded the city. *That* was why they had left the gate wide open.

He'd been sucked into his own godsdamned strategy!

Arrows struck the ground near his broken mount, and he scrabbled for cover. Not having a bloody clue who was left alive among his officers, he cried, "Sound the retreat!"

Someone dragged him to his feet, only to take an arrow through the throat and topple forward into the mud. Damek lost his footing again. Another lethal missile sailed past his cheek, taking half his left ear. A junior Corpsman, Forsey, flung a shield over Damek's head and half-ran, half-slithered with him to cover, taking arrows the whole way. They trod over the pieces of so many men and horses that Damek couldn't begin to guess how many of his Corps and infantry had just been blown to bits in the killing field.

"Orders, milord?" Mouthed Kinney as if from a great distance.

Damek was glad to see him alive.

"To O'Reardan! To the rear!" he rasped, waiting only to hear his command being reissued before he let himself be shoved into a waiting saddle.

X

Having made it to the safety of his rear lines— the majority of which straddled either side of the Taran High Road for ten miles— he was just in time to watch another explosion rip through his reserve infantry: some three hundred men-at-arms, two of his trebuchets, and several of his supply weapons. Men and material launched into the air only to return to the earth in misshapen pieces. Another line of archers on standby and the lead cavalry in Martin's rearguard took the brunt of the falling debris. The soldiers who weren't flattened by flaming hunks of metal or showered with human gore scattered. Those few infantrymen who weren't blasted to the Hells with their comrades wandered about bloodied and dazed or fled for cover in the southern treeline. The scene was utter chaos. With an angry, frustrated growl, Damek spurred his mount for the remnants of Martin's center.

Be alive, godsdammit!

About ten paces from the smashed phalanx of officers at the center, Damek caught sight of a flurry of silver and white cuirasses, dealing death in every direction. He didn't need to issue an order; someone in his surviving honor guard had blown the cavalry horn, drawing every knight left in his vanguard to heel. Groaning in pain, Damek kicked his charger harder this time, drawing his sabre.

The Dannans were nothing if not efficient, disciplined, and calm in the face of his advancing cavalry. He was so intent on getting to Martin's side that he didn't see the next danger until it was too late. Several pale shapes gathered at the edges of his vision. Too slowly, he turned to watch in useless alarm as these newcomers queued up, knelt, and drew their arms back over their massive longbows.

Oh, fuck!

A volley of arrows sailed directly into his flanks.

In the lead and moving fastest, Damek was the first to come down.

The Skysinger

n.e. 509
ban apesa
oiche ar fad

Una's Spark surged the moment she stepped through the Veil. Its violence sucked the air from her lungs, dropping her to her knees. This was something new. Her first breath in the Otherworld drew white-hot lightning to her core. The blood in her veins seemed to freeze, thaw, then reorder its flow. Her ears popped, and her eyes cleared. Even in the unending rose-hued gloaming, her vision came into sharpest focus, as if she'd been wandering blind and hampered through the fog for her entire life. She felt a current track through her cells, overwhelming and so painful it was almost pleasurable. For a moment that spanned an eternity, she trembled in the soft, blue-bladed grass, trying to will her lungs back to working order. Goose flesh tracked up her arms. A cold sweat trickled down her spine.

... *come home, Lady,* the Sluagh whispered in her mind. She shivered so hard that her teeth clacked together. She rolled over onto her back, huffing at the dizzy sky.

What is happening to me?

"Una?" Diarmid asked from somewhere nearby. The world spun around the edges. The next thing she knew, she was on all fours, retching into the soft loam. When her stomach was finally empty of all but bile, she bit her lip and turned her face away in shame.

Will you piss yourself next?

Diarmid's hair spilled over her collarbone as he leaned over her, cool fingers tracing her brow. "Tell me."

She opened her mouth but had to wait for her tongue and throat to recall how to form words. His nearness made her bones quake with queasy fear. Confused and terrified, she reached for him. Without a word, he pulled her to him, stroking giant circles into her back like a patient grandfather. Her helpless tears soaked his collar. "What haven't you told me?" he asked.

"I feel... different," her voice sounded alien to her ears.

"Your Siorai markings are gone."

"What?" She struggled upright to stare at her naked palms. But for the barest hint of an intangible sheen, her skin was as bare as a newborn. Mystified, she tore at the lacings of her tunic, searching for the blue dragons winding over her breastbone. They, too, were conspicuously absent, as were the wards etched over her shoulders, forearms, and legs. When she finished her fruitless examination, her frantic sobs rent the peace of their small clearing like a series of alarm bells. Diarmid folded her against him once more, as one might a startled pet. She had never been more frightened in her life.

... sssucch sights to show you...

"Hush now," he crooned. "You're all right."

The molten current at her core leaped at his voice.

Jumping, she buried her face in her hands. "I d-don't know."

"Every time you come here, it gets stronger, doesn't it? The pull."

Elation and fear braided through her taut nerves. She bit her lip until it bled and bobbed a response.

He pulled away to smooth the tears from her cheeks.

"I can feel it," he said softly. "The Oiche Ar Fad quakes within you."

"Feel what?"

He smiled that sad, enigmatic smile. "Whatever you took from me on Samhain... it is growing inside you like a seed. When it fully blooms, I wonder what you will be?"

"What is that supposed to mean?"

"You're changing, Una. *Becoming*."

A frigid spear of dread caught her in the throat. "Becoming what?"

The wind teased at the curls at her nape and then over her cheeks like a kiss. She brushed a stray lock away, only to realize that her hand hadn't moved an inch until after she'd done it. Shock replaced fear, and she stumbled to her feet, bombarded by surging vitality and quickening perception. A riot of color and sound accosted her senses, imparting jubilation, comfort, and terror. Her heart hammered against ribs that warmed from the inside, like stones around a hearth. Her scalp tingled, and her teeth ached. She again examined her glowing, unmarked skin, feeling a pang for the loss.

Her tattoos had been earned, as her aunt Eva's had been. They *meant* something. For every floor she had climbed in the Cloister, for every Ordeal, her skin had kept the record. Now they were gone. The Siorai, too, were all but gone. Her life as it had once been. All of it… *gone*. Tairngare was irreparably changed. Her family shattered. Her father was dead.

She was being erased.

"Remade," Diarmid corrected.

"Stay out of my head."

"Apologies."

Wrapping her arms around herself, she shot him a look. "That almost sounded sincere."

A flicker of a smile. "That is how it shall be between us."

"There is nothing between us."

He gave a subtle shrug. "There is." He gestured at the swirling clouds above.

Swallowing, she looked away. "I don't know what's happening, but I feel…" the words eluded her.

"Take your time."

Every moment she stood in that clearing, gathering her thoughts, she felt more and more at one with everything around her. The rush of the river beside them, pure and impossibly clear as it could never be in her realm— glittered in the half-light, making music she could never describe.

The air tasted sweet but smelt of wet slate, blooming wildflowers, and damp pine— and many more sensations far outside her experience. Even the grass beneath her booted feet thrummed with charge.

That rhythm seemed to say *home, home, home.*

Her eyes drifted closed, and she reached out with her Spark. The answering current nearly doubled her over again. There was so much, too much, to take in… yet flood through her every fiber, it did. Could she hear her pulse echo from the trees and her breath on the wind? The power building inside her was too massive for one body to contain, yet hers did.

"It feels like… I can do anything."

Diarmid walked in a slow circle around her while she stood there, hugging herself in rapturous fear. "Show me."

Of a sudden, they knelt at the river's edge together. Una took one of her hands in his and pushed it below the crisp, bubbling surface. The water was deliciously cool. "What do you see?"

She opened her eyes, expecting to find her reflection staring back at her. Instead, an afterimage of the world above flickered beneath her gaze, as the cities had when they passed them on their way to Rosweal. In the reflection, the Greensward behind her burned— a blaze so bright and fierce that it hurt to look. She could feel the flares, smell the smoke, hear the snapping limbs and cracking timber. Tears welling, she glanced over at him. "I don't know what to do."

"Can you feel the heat?"

Her cheek felt like it might blister sitting so near that reflection. "Yes."

"Smell the charred wood, taste the ashes?"

"Yes. Can't you?"

"Of course, but you shouldn't." He leaned his chin against his knuckles, a shrewd calculation behind his impassive features. "When you called me, what was it? A 'manipulator' at Tech Duinn— that was no insult, was it?"

She flinched inwardly. "Ah, no. It's how we describe our gifts in the Cloister. A girl born with the Spark, or the ability to 'manipulate' particles at will. Not every girl is born with Spark enough to change the basic composition of an object. Still, some, usually girls from the oldest families, can rearrange those particles to alter that object entirely. We call these girls 'Manipulators'. Only..." she wasn't sure if she should share so much of this with an outsider, especially the King of the Underworld.

"'Only' what? You may speak to me about anything, Una."

"Males are never born with that much Spark, and none I have ever heard of achieved the status of a true Manipulator."

"Ah," he said, reclining away from her. "'Never' is an odd word that rarely holds any meaning. For instance, my instinct tells me you— a female of Milesian heritage and a mortal to boot— hold gifts only Skysingers like myself should possess. Isn't that funny?"

Her brows drew close. "I don't know what you mean... what's a Skysinger? Is that also a sort of Manipulator?"

He laughed. "Well, if I'm forced to answer in simplistic terms, yes. In a way. A Skysinger is a born Brehon— a person who can channel the gods' power or command elemental spirits. In the Old World, Brehons would commune with whichever spirits they were attuned to. Some held an affinity for earth and wood spirits, some water, some the flames that kindle or consume all life. A select few held sway over the spirits of the air, rain, wind, ice, and more. Skysingers are stormbringers." He paused, his lip quirking sardonically. "I was born a Skysinger, was venerated by my tribe long before the birth of the *Oiche Ar Fad*, many thousands of years before the Transition."

She knew the Sidhe were very long-lived, but this man... Kaer Yin's vindictive, flirtatious, mendacious uncle was *ancient*. Before she knew her mouth had opened, she asked, "How do you stand it?"

The briefest flash of a bottomless sadness crossed his face, and she felt something akin to empathy for him for the first time. How could anyone stand to live so long? She would never know, thank Siora. As swiftly as the emotion crossed his expression, it was gone. "All boring tales are best told over mead, my dear. As we have none, I think it prudent for you to tell me how you knew you could help me quench the Greensward."

She considered him in silence for a time. She had volunteered, and if they didn't try something soon, Aes Sidhe would burn to cinders while everyone she cared for risked their lives. They didn't have time for mistrust and prevarication. Rosweal needed them— him, more than anyone.

"The cost."

He stilled. "What's that?"

"All magic— Manipulation— bears a cost. We've briefly discussed this before in your keep. For Siorai, it's the Spark-drag; that's our First Law. Once massive energy has been expunged, it must be replenished."

"And?"

"And I don't know how or why I know— but I can feel it. There's this void... perhaps that's the wrong word? This *well* of energy at my core. Like my Spark is replenishing itself from the air around me in this place. The farther I reach inside myself, the deeper that pool gets."

He stared at her as if what she was telling him was as absurd as it was to her. "You mean to say that's how you healed me before by giving me some of this Spark?"

"Exactly. That's the Ninth Law and forbidden... but I knew I could do it."

"How?"

She shrugged. "Because I've done it many times, in reverse, in Eire. If I can take energy when my Spark is limited, I could surely give some back when it's boundless."

"*Boundless.*" He made a sort of half snort, half-strangled whimper. He scrubbed his face with the fingers of his right hand. "Una, do you know who I am?"

"The King of Tech Duinn."

"No. I *am* Tech Duinn. My father's blood was the price paid to create this realm for his kin, and that same blood ensures its stability. Do you understand?"

"No."

He gestured at the clearing around them. "I am what remains of his blood, my brothers and I. We keep the realms together but separate;

without us, both would either fade to nothing or be ripped apart by eternity. Innisfail is kept warm and hale despite the ice threatening to swallow her whole. Even now, the blood in our veins heats the currents surrounding this continent, fills the earth with black, rich soil, and blankets her reaches with game and vegetation. If even one of us were somehow eliminated from this precarious equation, the entire system would collapse. This magic, the Dagda's sacrifice, is the engine that powers the world as you know it. Without the Tuatha De Dannan, Innisfail would be a barren tundra choked with ghosts and human scars."

"Why are you telling me this?" In her mind's eye, she could almost see the white hellscape he spoke of. Nothing alive for hundreds and hundreds of miles in any direction— just sparkling white death blown about by a merciless northern wind.

Ice age, her education whispered. *The earth as it was before man took over—an empire of ice and death.*

"Yes," Diarmid said. "As it will be again if the Sidhe should leave these shores."

She struggled to piece that together. "That can't be true."

"It *is* true. Your ancestors destroyed what they stole from us those many eons ago at Magh Tuiradh—raped every corner of this world too, from the deepest ocean floors to the highest peaks, until there was nothing left in the soil to sustain them. Rivers ran dry. Every creature, great and small, save those kept for livestock, dead or dying. Seas near to boiling in the southern reaches and clogged with refuse. Cities choked with toxic fumes and pestilence, born aloft by teeming hordes of mortals without function or purpose, all clamoring to subsist on chemicals and technology— none aware that they had died long before the Transition. They didn't understand that men can't multiply in a poisoned mire, though try they did. For hundreds of years, your people existed this way, taking, scraping, consuming everything in sight.

"Eventually, their world collapsed as it was always going to. Millions perished in the first few seasons. The seas slowed, became toxic, and rose so high they gulped your cities down like sweet succor. Men used to believe their world would end in fire, the whip-crack tongue of some celestial serpent. Instead, it ended slowly, painfully with the unceasing wash of stinking, venomous water." He shook his head. "My brother couldn't ignore the suffering, though I wish he had. When Midhir returned to Innisfail, the land bloomed anew. Trees sprouted in long-barren lands. Rivers were purged of their foulness, and animals returned to these shores. He took the Milesians in... all who came to beg sanctuary. All of them. How was he repaid for his blessed kindness?"

Una dipped her head, ashamed of a culture she had no control over. "They tried to take it from him."

"Yes," he smiled. "Again. They tried to take what they did not understand, nor deserve, once more. Worthless creatures, mortals. Present company excluded, of course."

She didn't take offense. She was educated enough to understand human failing but compassionate enough to realize that most didn't know any better. "Why have you told me this?"

"So you will know the truth, Una. The Sidhe are what keeps this land, and you all, alive. If we leave, you die. If we retreat into the Oiche Ar Fad once again, you die. If mortals retake the Continent for themselves, they will multiply out of control, consume and destroy until nothing is left. The Sidhe are tied to this land. If we go, you go."

"I don't understand—"

"I've shared this truth to prepare you for the next." He dug his fingers into the iridescent earth beneath his hand. Black soil blossomed in his palm, the color of a beetle's back. "I am the heartbeat of the Otherworld, but even my strength is not limitless as you claim yours to be. If what you say— and what I can feel from you, that 'otherness' I can't explain— is true, you are perhaps more Sidhe than I."

A thousand thoughts and questions tangled in her head. She took a deep breath to clear them, chewing on her tongue. His words wove an invisible question around her kneeling frame, a shimmer of purpose that was alien and familiar as her skin.

Yes, it said, and she turned to catch a glimpse of a small dark girl darting through the trees beyond. Her thick braid caught the wind as she leaped and bounded through the bracken, giggling. Una's heart thudded at the vision.

Siora, she thought.

Yes, the wind repeated.

Una's eyes snapped back to Diarmid, but if he'd seen the girl, he hid it very well.

The trembling along her spine subsided. She closed her fist tight. "I don't know what this means or why it should happen to me, but I know what I feel."

"And what's that?"

I am the spine of the world.

In my blood, you are reborn.

In my heart, you rise.

"Strong," she answered without fear.

"Good," he said, standing. "Show me."

X

A MASSIVE BLACK BRUISE GATHERED in the sky to the north, bearing such wind that torrents of smoke and heat were blown into the frigid Boinne valley, extinguishing all but the most stubborn flames over the border. Lightning struck from snow-heavy clouds, the slow, cold grey haze at the mass' center. Thunder rolled over the hills, rattling every stone to its foundation, nearly striking men from their feet. The storm had appeared from nowhere— simultaneously darkening and lightening the sky within its strange, unearthly power. Sheets of thick, wet snow began to fall in heavy white torrents over Aes Sidhe until all that remained for the raging inferno that had raged for hours and stretched miles and miles to the far horizon sizzled out beneath a cloak of cool, clean precipitation.

Rosweal's defenders cheered from the walls, blackened by soot and caked with ash and blood. The storm spun south by southwest, choking the life from the blaze on both sides of the river, and coating semi-scorched rooftops and walls with snow.

In the cellars below *The Hart and Hare*, which Barb set aside for a makeshift hospital— Rian looked up from dressing yet another wound at the gleeful outbursts above. Rose struggled down the stairs with a fresh basket of linens, still wet and stained red, but would have to do.

She was smiling.

"What's that all about?" asked Rian blithely. She was impervious to alarm at this point. Almost fifty men were stacked head-to-toe on makeshift cots, filthy mattresses, and hastily assembled gurneys inside her close, musty little clinic. Still more men, perhaps a hundred give or take, waited in long queues upstairs and up and down the alley outside. Rian only had two hands and one mind to occupy with priorities. She'd been stitching, binding, severing, cauterizing, and sometimes euthanizing those who were beyond hope since the fires began last morning. Nearly two days of nonstop work with no time to rest or eat would eventually exact their toll if she didn't keep moving.

The man Rose came back down with new bandages for was going to lose his leg. There was no saving it. His calf had been partially severed; if he didn't bleed to death within the hour, he would undoubtedly sicken with sepsis and die anyway. There was only one cure Rian knew for such a wound, and it was likely to kill him anyway.

Another lad, no more than twelve, had been designated her assistant by Barb yesterday afternoon— a kitchen lad, by all accounts. Barb's girls called him Strong Tim, though Rian had seen twigs with better musculature. The boy had proved to be worth more than she'd given him credit for. He was serious, stoic, and seemed to own a constitution belonging to a grown man twice his size and experience. He'd already assisted in two amputations and had administered belladonna to those who couldn't be saved. Just then, Strong Tim raised his eyes to hers, expectant. It seemed he knew what was coming without asking. But Rian's attention was on Rose, who set her bundle down with a delighted squeal. "Isn't it wonderful, Rian? Them fires is out!"

Rain blinked. "Inside?"

"That's the best part! *All* the fires, mistress. Both sides o'the river."

Rose's cheeky, beatific grin made Rian scowl. "All? How?"

The Hart's favorite splayed her hands as if to say, 'who knows.' Her once lustrous dark curls were singed and coated with sticky grey ash. Her heart-shaped face was streaked and smudged with sweat and soot. Even wearing a leather smock that had once belonged to the town butcher and had been dipped in countless vats of blood and gore— Rian was easily the cleanest person in the room. "Not that ye'd hear it with all this dirt above our heads, but a loud, ugly, mad beast o'a squall just blew down from the north. Never seen anythin' like it neither. Fair fills the sky, it does."

Rian set one tool down and wiped her brow with a damp elbow. She had no idea what Rose was on about. "A storm? It's raining?"

"Snowing, silly! And already past me knees in places too! Look, my legs are right blue—"

Rian bent back over her patient, who'd thankfully passed out. To Tim, she nodded. "Go get Dabney. I'll need him to help me hold this one down." The boy darted off, but her voice caught him at the landing. "And tell him not to bother whingeing about it this time! I've enough to deal with as it is." While he disappeared, she dipped her finger in charcoal, drew a circle on the man's forehead with her index finger, checked to ensure his tourniquet was as tight as it could be, and then moved on to the next patient. Yet another lad barely twenty. In truth, she wasn't much older, but the fear in the young man's expression made her feel a thousand years his senior. She gently tugged him forward to inspect the seeping hole just beneath his shoulder bone. He yelped, but she ignored him. "Who pulled the arrow out?"

"My mate. Dunno if he did it right."

"He did fair enough, considering you're talking and not bleeding to death on that stack of crates." She prodded the muscles along his back. No tearing, she could spy. "Can you move it?"

"I... I think?"

"Good," Rian said, tearing two stained but clean strips out of the linen sheet Rose handed her and went to work winding it round and round his arm and shoulder.

He looked away, his doughy cheeks a bit grassy.

She finished, tugging his torn tunic back over the wound. "I expect they'll need you on the wall again. You wouldn't want to leave your mates up there pulling your weight, would you?"

He swallowed, knowing his next wound might not be so lucky. "No, mistress."

"Then off with you," she said, turning to the next patient without waiting for him to leave. Triage in wartime was not a pretty nor poetic profession. She didn't have the resources to be merciful, and for every wounded man she could send back up top, two more seemed to take his place. The following three patients served as an example. One had taken a morbid gash to his neck and shoulder and wouldn't last. She drew a black 'X' on his forehead. He was carried away to the rear of the cellar to die. The girls would talk to him and hold his hand long enough, but when he passed, they'd drag him upstairs and line him up with the others.

Rian refused to think about how many were building up out there.

The following patient died before she got to him, and the third just as she reached for him. This was the way it was. They dealt death without thought outside, but she was the one that had to pull it close and hold its black hands. She backed away from the dead man, pressing a shaking hand to her temple.

"Ye should lie down for a bit, Rian," urged Rose gently, shoving a cup of something warm but bland into her palm. "You'll fall face-first into one of these boys, and then where will they be?"

"I can't, Rose. You know that." Rian took a long, grateful sip only to realize the cup held more than a dollop of uishge. She was so tired that she couldn't even taste anything anymore. The sights and smells of her makeshift ward were too monotonous. "Tell me more about that storm, please."

She downed the rest of her cup and followed Rose to the other side of the room, where most of Robin Gramble's raiders lay propped against the far wall. Only a third of the sixty men that had volunteered for the honor had returned. Most were either hacked to death by Lord Bishop's knights as they fled or blown to bits in the explosion— which, thankfully, had dealt a disastrous blow to the Southers' foreword infantry, artillery, and cavalry. The Greenmakers, however, had been caught between the blast and its intended targets and paid dearly for the mistake. They'd been tasked to raid, set the charges, and vanish— but Bishop's men had been waiting for them. They couldn't escape fast enough, so most did not leave the Navan Gate alive.

… those that did…

She found Robin where she'd left him, with his back to the wall, legs stretched out before him. He cradled Gerrod's upper body against his shaking chest. The lad's legs were missing. Rian had applied tourniquets and managed to cauterize much of what remained, but nothing would save him. He'd lost far too much blood. His color and weakened breathing told all. When Robin finally turned, Rian could barely blink off the tears that burned her eyes. He nodded.

"Aye," he choked. "Figured as much." Robin himself had taken a fairly severe slash to his midsection, but he'd refused her every attempt to treat him.

"Oh no, no. Gerry, love," wept Rose, slipping to her knees beside him. She clasped the lad's fingers in hers and sobbed when he tried to give her one of his winks. His weak smile was for Rian, who sank beside them, filling his vision.

He opened his mouth to speak, his expression telling her everything he wished to say. She knew he would never have the chance. She smoothed his cheeks and gave him the best smile she could manage. "That's all right, Gerrod. I know, and I'm here."

This seemed to please him. He settled back against his foster father and stared at her as if he'd burn every curve of her face into his memory. She took one of his hands from Rose and lay beside him, pressing her lips against his cheek. "Tell him about the storm Rose."

As Rose began her tale, Rian whispered in Gerrod's good ear. "You are loved, Gerry. I'll never forget you."

He gave a last sigh and was gone before Rose spoke her first word, but Rian didn't stop her. She tucked herself against Gerrod's body and cried openly. Robin held them both the while.

"Ah, ye should see it, Gerry. The snows are so thick, ye can't catch a glimpse o'yer own nose ahead o'ye, and the fire's all blowed out. Can ye imagine? And what ye boys done— wiped half that bastard's army clean out of mercy, ye have." Her voice caught when Robin closed the lad's eyes. He'd been smiling. "Ye did good, Gerry. Yer ma'am, yer sisters, everyone... we're so proud o'ye."

With an unhealable tear in her soul, Rian pushed herself up to her feet, wiping her streaming eyes. Dabney was suddenly behind her, his arm steady. She didn't see his face but only had to hear his snuffling to know he understood what had happened here. She took a heaving breath, tucking lovely, bright-eyed, gorgeously good Gerrod Twomey deep within her heart. That is where he would live now, same as her parents.

She went back to work, moving dutifully from tragedy to another.

※

Later, though she couldn't be sure when exactly, Rian found Eva upstairs in the alleyway, watching the sky swirl with smoke and dwindling cinders. She leaned against the cold brick wall, smoking rolled witchroot. Without a word, Eva lit and handed Rian one of her own. She had never smoked a day in her life, but she'd try just about anything at this point.

"It'll give you a boost," Eva said, not looking at her.

Rian took it, attempted a small puff, and coughed. After a minute, her lungs warmed from the inside and her head cleared. She tried another.

Eva eyed her sidelong. "Better?"

"I guess so." She scrubbed her eyes with her free hand. "Why aren't you with Ben or Una?"

"I'm more useful here, for now. Your girls mean well, but they are hardly fighters."

Rian empathized. Neither was she. "That's not a good thing, is it?"

Eva didn't answer immediately, but after a beat, she said, "I'm not all-knowing. I can't see everything and certainly can't summon that part of my Spark at will, so you know."

"I gathered... but you know more than you're saying."

Eva gave a humorless laugh. "Too sharp by half, you are."

"So you keep telling me."

"I can't tell you anything you haven't already deduced was a possibility and prepared for."

"Great, thanks so much," sighed Rian. She stubbed the smelly roll of gold tobacco out in the snow. Witchroot was a costly, very odorous habit. Grown in Aes Sidhe by mysterious methods and only traded through the Dalriadan reaches, the golden leaf was scarce and hard to come by. Thus, it was the particularly nasty habit of very wealthy persons... and Barb Dormer, who had her sources. "That is a disgusting habit." She didn't bother to admit that it had made her feel better.

"And so delicious."

"Humph," said Rian.

Rose's voice drifted upstairs, and Rian let out a long breath. She smoothed her apron and flexed her aching fingers. "All right then."

Eva's arm caught her elbow as she prepared to sweep back downstairs, gently spinning her around. Rian couldn't see her face, it was so dark, but she could see the solemn cast to her amber eyes. She passed a small tincture of blue glass with a silver stopper, and Rian took a startled step backward. "That's—"

"You'll know when to use it."

Rian's eyes filled with tears. "How soon?"

Eva gave her fingers an encouraging squeeze. "All is not lost... but it will be a trial unlike any you have known."

"Eva, *when?*"

She looked at the sky again as if lost to things Rian couldn't see. "Be ready."

Nowhere to Run

n.e. 509
24 ban apesa
Rosweal

Kaer Yin met Fionn at the Western tunnel mouth, Tam Lin just behind him. Jan Fir, Niall, Mordu, and Shar trickled through the dank opening— bloodied but breathing. Kaer Yin did a cursory headcount as the Dannans came up into the snow-bright, ash-leaden evening air. He stopped at twenty and frowned. Twenty Sidhe left out of nearly double that number. His throat ran dry. They might be satisfied to have spent that many good men for the decimation they'd just handed the new King of Eire, but the cost was high, regardless. Kaer Yin could only pray Robin and his Greenmakers had fared better.

Fionn, leaning against Shar for support, shoved the taller man away. His chin jerked high at the sight of his crown prince. "We were successful, *Mo Flaith*," he declared proudly, despite the wheeze in his lungs. He looked like he'd been toiling at the bottom of a cauldron all day with his singed hair and blackened face, neck, and hands. Every man, woman, and child in Rosweal was positively caked with ash and soot, and not a single defender along the wall had come away from the battle without their share of burns, cuts, scrapes, or debilitating wounds.

However, these twenty returning Sidhe bore evidence of toil and slaughter that no others could match. Fionn's cloak dripped runnels of blood into the freshly fallen snow.

"*Danu*,' exclaimed Tam Lin, whose teeth and eyes were the only humanizing features in his obsidian face. "You look like Donn himself chewed you to bloody bits."

Tam Lin had been fighting fires first over the Ward Gate facing the Quarter with Mel Carra and several others for nearly thirteen hours. Thanks to their resolve and the backbreaking labor of Rosweal's citizens, he'd managed to keep the wall intact and protect the majority of the buildings inside. If it hadn't been for them, there might not have been anything left to defend.

As for Kaer Yin, he'd taken command of the Eastern Wall— as he would again tomorrow when the Southers came in force at the critically damaged Navan Gate. Whatever they had managed to exact from Damek today, he hoped it was enough to make the Southers move on. Failing that minor miracle, having deprived Bishop of so many men and supplies, they'd at least be dealing with a drastically reduced threat. It would be hours before they could sort out the numbers. Lack of sleep, exposure, casualties, and cold took their toll on the city.

They could not keep this up much longer.

"What happened?" he asked Fionn, nodding for Tam Lin to grab his arm before he toppled into the snow face-first. Fionn put up an admirable front, but in the end, Tam Lin's weight won out. To Shar, he said, "Take the others to *The Hart*. Rian's got a half-decent clinic running down in the cellars."

Tam Lin swore under his breath.

With exaggerated slowness, Shar saluted Kaer Yin with a bloodied arm. He was no longer Tam Lin's man, and being sworn to Una meant his next liege lord was Kaer Yin himself. Kaer Yin scowled at both of them. "Today, if you please. None of us has time for this grandstanding."

"*Ard Tiarne*." Shar dipped his head, gathered the wounded Sidhe, and led them away without another word.

Tam Lin watched him go, a hard tick in his jaw. "I hope someone has the sense to see to their own cuts and bruises so that girl can take a rest. She'll work herself blind if someone doesn't stop her."

"I know, but she's right; there's no one else."

Tam Lin looked like he had more to say but patted Fionn's shoulder instead. "You had a time of it, I reckon?"

"We came from the southwest," Fionn answered, spitting out a wad of reddened ash. "As planned, we took them completely unawares. At first, anyway."

"The siege weapons?" asked Tam Lin.

"Destroyed. All but one catapult set too far back in their lines."

Tam Lin clapped his hands together over a ghoulish, macabre grin. "Yes! You bloody beautiful, brilliant bastard. I'd kiss you if it wouldn't knock you over." Fionn's lip quirked at the praise, but his expression was far less enthusiastic.

Kaer Yin scratched his grimy chin. "How many supply trains?"

"Fifteen or more, *Mo Flaith*. But we ran out of powder halfway through and were forced to call our secondary unit from cover to get us out." He paused on a sigh. "We cut through their reserve infantry who awaited orders at the Taran approach. Our archers marched out of the trees to give cover. That was when Bishop and a large cavalry contingent returned from the vanguard."

"Damn it to the seven hells," grumbled Tam Lin. Like everyone, he hoped Bishop would have met his end in the first or second explosions at the Navan Gate, but Kaer Yin had known it wouldn't be so simple. Things rarely work out as one might wish. He'd been on the Eastern Wall and had watched Bishop survive each blast and ride for his rear. Kaer Yin was disappointed, but he couldn't say he was surprised.

"Diel, my lieutenant, directed his bowman to fire at their mounts. That bought us a little time, but that man—" he bit back a slur. "I believe he must have been born under Balor's star, the luck that creature has. It began snowing heavily before Diel's archers emerged to give cover. Maybe four or five minutes of near blinding snow— and Bishop dodged every arrow, driving his horse into a snowbank. His officers rallied around their lord and dragged him to cover under locked shields."

"I don't suppose his horse happened to roll over him in the process, maybe crush his legs or his blasted skull?" Tam Lin groused, annoyed that luck had not been a factor today.

Fionn shook his head. "Once they were out range, he got back up, urging his cavalry to give chase. That large, scarred fellow he keeps at his side gave me this personally." He pried his hand away from his right side, revealing a vicious wound that might have ended a mortal man. "I beg your pardon for not killing him on the spot, *Ard Tiarne*, but I will correct the error tomorrow… I vow it."

"No." Kaer Yin squinted at the whitewashed horizon, thinking about the next stage of his plan. They'd weakened Bishop today, sure, but he would regroup and refocus in the morning. They'd lost so many men in this attempt that Rosweal might not have enough defenders left to man the walls come another day like this. One day, maybe… two, definitely not. He needed another plan. "I'll need you handling the Navan Gate first thing tomorrow, Fionn."

His jade green eyes flashed. "I owe that bastard now, Kaer Yin. Those are my men out there in the snow."

"Yes, and there are many more of your men in *here*. I think I'll visit our Lord Souther myself this evening, and I can trust no one else to defend our people as you can, Fionn. Do you accept this responsibility?"

Fionn mulled that over in silence for a while. "You would raid his camp?"

"I would murder that blight in his bed if the Gods are kind."

"*Yes*," hissed Tam Lin with an eager grin. "By Herne, I volunteer."

Fionn nodded. He knew well what another twenty-four hours of siege would cost them. Fionn O'More was the greatest commander in the Ard Ri's legion for a reason. "I will do as you ask, *Ard Tiarne*."

"Thank you, My Lord. If we fail, we proceed to stage three, as planned."

"Understood." Fionn saluted.

"Jan Fir?" Kaer Yin craned his neck to acknowledge the Scotian regent. "Will you escort Lord O'More to mistress Rian and get yourself seen to while you're at it?"

Jan Fir sported a few nasty cuts that would take a while to heal, even for a Sidhe of his age and pedigree. Kaer Yin's brother-in-law offered

Fionn a shoulder but paused to give him a serious look. "Mordu and I go with you."

"My sister won't like it."

Jan smirked. "Who's going to tell her?"

"Not me; I like my fingers, thank you," muttered Tam Lin.

"Meet us here at dusk," Kaer Yin told him and crossed his arms while he and Fionn took their leave. "Let's get to it?"

Tam Lin followed him through the Southern yard, with its rows of burned-out ramshackles and free-standing walls that had once belonged to buildings that had been excavated for stones. Up the ladder to the wall, then another toward the south-facing rampart. The snow still fell in heavy, wet sheets, covering the valley with an increasingly grey coating. Charred trees in every direction, but their immediate east popped and cracked beneath its weight, releasing little puffs of steam. All around the walls, the devastation was plain. Men and horses lay in haphazard puddles of gore, now slick and sparkling with frost. Successive blasts had opened several pits along the eastern ridge, punctuated by corpses and splintered trees. The arrow blinds Barb had worked so hard to install between the city and the killing field were toppled or reduced to piles of smoldering ash. There was nothing between Damek's advance forces and Rosweal now, save uneven ground and ghosts.

"How many do you think we cost him today, Yin?"

Kaer Yin exhaled slowly. "Not enough. A thousand?"

"Mostly officers and heavy cavalry, though."

"Yes, and good for us, but if he keeps his head, we've already lost."

Tam Lin absorbed that with a stiff lip. "We have to take him tonight or evacuate the city tomorrow."

"Agreed."

His cousin sighed, leaning over the railing. "He'll take the gate by midmorning tomorrow at the latest and overrun the city by the afternoon."

"Yes."

"Unless we kill him first."

Kaer Yin narrowed his eyes at the blast pits. "Even if we don't."

"What do you mean?"

He reached into his ruined tunic for his bone-flask, which he passed to Tam Lin first, then took a long-deep pull, smacked his chapped lips, and slipped it back into his pocket. "I say we give him what he wants."

Tam Lin didn't need further explanation. They knew each other very well. "Thought that was the last resort?"

"Your Da isn't going to make it in time, Lin."

He considered that with a wince. "The headwoman is going to scratch your eyes out."

Kaer Yin made a face. "Someone else gets to tell her."

"Fuck, not me. I don't know why you surround yourself with so many harpies."

"Yes, you do," laughed Kaer Yin. "Go get some food and ale into you. I'll need you at your sharpest tonight, Prince O'Ruiadh."

"Who drinks ale anymore?" Tam Lin toasted him with his flask of rotgut uishge. He glanced at the storm above. "She did this, you think?"

"Yes. I have no idea how."

"Diarmid will fight for her."

Kaer Yin snorted. "I was worried, but now I'm not."

"Why's that?"

Kaer Yin pointed at the blinding center of the maelstrom. "Diarmid might have been able to do this alone, but I doubt it. She's something else... something he fears."

"Even more reason to be wary, Yin."

"I'll cross that river when it's time. For now, we have a red carpet to roll out."

Tam Lin's answering smirk was knife-slash against the ghoulish streaks crisscrossing his face. "Should we set our wagers now or later?"

Kaer Yin's expression burned cold. "If Donn loves me, I alone will bear the honor."

X

Uɴᴀ ᴀᴡᴏᴋᴇ ᴏɴ ᴛʜᴇ ʀɪᴠᴇʀʙᴀɴᴋ, lying in a warm bed of heather and clover. The clearing smelled of fresh snow, even if the air was warm and sweet as a summer's evening. Blinking up at the rosy half-light, she knew she was still in the *Oiche Ar Fad* but had no idea what had happened when Diarmid grasped her hands. Had they done it? Was Rosweal safe from the flames? Yawning, she sat up and looked around. There was no sign of him. Groggily, she rubbed at her eyes with the heel of her palms. She hadn't slept so well in ages! A languid, fulfilled sense of peace pervaded her thoughts. Slowly, lazily, she looked around for Diarmid, a pleasant smile on her face. "Diarmid?" she called out but heard no response but the breeze rustling through the leaves overhead and the lapping of water against the shore.

Una stopped, blinking away the cobwebs.

Where was she?

The copse beside the river was long gone. Instead, she stood beside a mist-shrouded lake surrounded by low hills, tall, elegant rowans, and birch trees. Now aware if unfazed by the change in scenery, she strolled along the water's edge, hoping she might find Diarmid somewhere nearby. Perhaps he, too, had fallen into a blissful repose? What was it they'd been doing?

She struggled to recall.

Birds chirped from their boughs, beautiful, jeweled plumage flashing colors she couldn't name. Delighted, she watched them launch into the violet-tinted gloaming, singing merry tunes she found herself humming. Before she realized it, she'd walked a fair distance. The sand behind her bore her meandering, rhythmless footsteps. Feeling a little drunk, she giggled.

How silly! She'd been turning herself round and round.

"Diarmid?" she laughed into the forest.

Where was he? Did he leave her to enjoy herself while he went to do whatever he had to do? What was it again?

She couldn't recall.

A silver and sable doe drank from the lake around the nearest bend. The water's mirror-like surface cast a haunting glow around her reflection, making Una gasp. Had she ever seen such a magnificent creature before? The doe's dappled white ear tilted toward her, but she did not rise, as if a woman in torn tunic and muddied trousers, with wild hair and a dazed look, was the least exciting thing around her.

Una had no idea how long she stood and stared at the graceful creature before it finally bounded away from the lake, but before she realized it, the darker evening slid in from the west— stretching long, cool shadows between the trees.

They reached for her like fingertips.

I have ssssuch ssssights to sssshow…

She started.

Suddenly, a frigid blast of wind blew over the lake, striking her full in the face. Everywhere the wind disturbed, heavy, blinding snow followed. Reams of blue ice raced over the lake toward her, and her hair blew back, dripping with frost. She threw up her arms to protect her eyes but staggered backward in the surge. The trees behind her groaned under the white assault, bending under the weight of winter's sudden wrath. Half-stumbling, half crawling, she dragged herself out of the wind to hide behind a copse of sturdy rowans. Breathing hard, she wiped at her eyes, her head clearing.

What in Siora's name are you doing here?

She cast her gaze around the forest, noting the swiftly darkening sky peeking through the tree boughs above. Whispers danced through the snow and ice, echoing from tree to tree. Menace as cold as starlight crept over the tiny, damp hairs at her nape. Full awareness of her situation dawned over the next few breaths. She was on the wrong side of the sun in the Oiche Ar Fad. Panic gripped her heart like a talon. Not even the blistering change in temperature could penetrate this veil of fear.

What do I do? What do I do?

The first pair of glowing yellow eyes appeared twenty paces ahead of her. Frantically, she clawed at her collar to locate the quartz stone around her neck. Finding nothing, she froze.

The *ogham* stone Diarmid had given her was gone.

A low, rumbling growl rattled the bone-white leaves opposite. Una had no time. She got up and ran through freezing bracken, bramble, and fern toward the east, where the sun still shone.

Something silent but swift followed.

X

"Yer bloody mad!" Barb shook her finger at Kaer Yin, spilling uishge over his boots. He grunted and shoved her hand away, but that didn't staunch her tirade. "Why'm I workin' so damned hard to defend the place if yer just gonna blow it to the hells anyway?"

They stood together on the western rampart facing the north wall. The snow still poured from the sky in a steady cadence, concealing much of the day's atrocities, save for the black husks of mighty trees from one horizon to the other. Thankfully, no such flame would stand such a chance again, as the valley was pregnant with damp and spin-cracking cold. Barb's heavy sealskin cloak was coated white, but her deep, fur-lined cowl did little to conceal her angry scowl. Kaer Yin, having taken the time to change into something warmer, wore a gray cloak and tunic of a similar fashion, only lighter and better suited to the sword strapped once more to his side. For a raid like this, he needed every blade available and thus was forced to eschew Nemain's back-mounting sheath. Instead, his lark handles protruded from a hidden fold behind his cowl, which would allow him to draw without uncovering his face.

Beneath this, a plain white cuirass fitted over a pale grey tunic and leggings, bound tightly together with wool and greaves of white leather. The vambraces at his shins and forearms were pure sylvan steel. Every Sidhe in his entourage would be dressed the same.

In the dark, they would appear as wraiths to the untrained eye—vapors in a snowdrift. "Barb," he said. "We could wait until they do it for us or take the initiative. I think I prefer the latter."

She sneered up at him, stomping down the rampart in a huff. "Feck's sake, Ben! We've lost more n'enough as it is, damn ye. Ye want more still?"

He crossed his arms. "I'm not asking, so you know."

She opened and closed her mouth like a fish.

He sniffed, ignoring her discomfiture. "Besides, you stand to lose yet more the longer we delay. What's left but boys too young to fight, women who can't fight, and old men who might die climbing the stairs? I mean, what choice do we have? Tomorrow will be worse."

"Yer Sidhe mates—"

"Have *died* defending you and yours. They will do so as long as I command them to, but their loss won't save you, and you know it."

She stopped, cursing. "We can hold out a few more days."

"To what end? He's got the numbers. He's going to win."

"Ye don't believe that."

"Knowing when to retreat is a commander's duty. I'm more concerned about saving as many of your lives as possible than Bishop claiming this territory temporarily. You know we'll never let him keep it. He knows that too."

Her jaw softened. She set a mittened hand on his elbow as a mother might do. "I've never heard ye give up like this, Ben. Rosweal's yer home too."

"Yes, and it can be rebuilt. The lives it houses cannot."

Sensing she had no other cards to play, she dug through her cloak to find her bone-handled pipe. Dabney struck a match for her. She took several silent puffs before she nodded at Kaer Yin. "Yer right."

Kaer Yin slapped a hand against his heart. "Why, Barb Dormer, did I hear that right?"

"Ach, stop. It's not the first time I've admitted ye had the right o'things."

Yes, it bloody well was, but he wouldn't press the point.

"Rosweal is done, and may it be his tomb."

She picked a stray speck of witchroot from her tongue and bobbed her head. "What do ye want me to do?"

"You know."

"*All* of it? Can't we just—"

"All of it, Barb. Every last barrel."

Grumbling to herself, she scanned the horizon and sucked at her pipe. Finally, as if accepting a loss she couldn't quantify, she wiped a tear away with her sleeve and squared her shoulders. "Get to it then." She turned to leave but paused at the top of the ladder. "I'd better have me own palace when this is all over, Ben, with a pond and fountain full o'the finest uishge."

He laughed; the sound bore more irony than mirth. "If we pull this off, I'll erect a statue to you right here and toast your deeds every Imbolg."

"Bloody right ye will."

X

WELL PAST MIDNIGHT, WHEN ALL the preparations in the Eastern End were finished, Kaer Yin, Robin, Tam Lin, Skinny Colm, Shar Lianor, Jan Fir, and about twelve other Dannans gathered at the Western tunnel mouth. Another twenty Sidhe bowmen approached from the alleyway behind. Kaer Yin nodded at Robin, who he'd been glad to learn had come through the raid earlier that morning with only a few scratches. He looked around. "Where's Gerry?" he asked, expecting to see the scrawny lad sharpening his knives. "This is just his sort of game."

Robin didn't smile back.

He glanced away, a tick in his jaw.

Kaer Yin's grin flickered. "Robin?"

Robin shook himself, tugging a half-hearted shrug out of his shoulders. "Restin', he is. I expect he's doin' better than we are now, freezin' our bollocks off out here."

A jolt of concern speared through Kaer Yin's middle. "Is he… is it serious?"

"Nah." Robin waved him off. "Don't worry. Mistress Rian gave him one o'her drams, and he drifted right off. He's sleepin' soundly now."

Kaer Yin let out a long breath, reassured. "Thank Danu for that. Are your men ready then?"

"Eager, ye might say," Robin growled.

"Excellent." Kaer Yin turned to Tam Lin, who passed around a bowl full of ash for the men to douse themselves. He'd scrubbed his face clean of soot and donned a clean grey tunic like Kaer Yin. They'd be tough to spot in the snow without anything dark to distinguish them. "All right, bows forward. We split up at the fork, where you'll head east. Stay out of sight no matter what happens to us— no exceptions!"

"*Ard Tiarne*," the archers chimed, saluting.

"Their officers aren't roughing it in the cold with the men. From Fionn's scouts, we know Bishop and his top brass have taken over a farmstead halfway between Rosweal and Vale, approximately two and a half miles from his front line. They'll be expecting a raid on their remaining supply trains and will have doubled the guards standing at ready."

Kaer Yin sent his silver gaze around to every ashen face.

"Bishop is in the house with his two top captains— O'Rearden and that bastard Ridley."

Robin bared his teeth at the name.

Kaer Yin shot him a pointed look. "Not yet, Robin. If he's the first out, he's yours. If he lingers to guard his Lord Marshal, you'll leave him. Understood?"

Robin spat. "Don't like it, but I hear ye."

"We're out for the barn, where the other officers spend a nice, warm night by the fire. They won't expect a raid on the brass, so we'll have the element of surprise— but not for long. We have minutes to get in and get out. Make them count."

Tam Lin stepped forward, sweeping a lark pommel around. "Here's the most important part. We're in, and we're out, no dallying. I'll personally hamstring any fool who thinks to make a hero of himself. Am I understood?"

A bevy of 'ayes' went round.

"Good, because I haven't had much fun in the past two days. Spoil it for me now at your peril."

The raiders snickered back.

"One last thing, and this is crucial," Kaer Yin added, noticing a familiar face materialize from the shadows ahead. "We're in as a unit and out as one. From the west to the east and back up the Navan High Road— make sure you're seen heading in that direction. We don't want Bishop to miss the opportunity to chase, do we?"

"Hells no!" Roared Robin with the others as they pounded their cuirasses in unison.

"We are ghosts—"

Thump.

"We are blades in the dark—"

Thump.

"We feel no pain, no cold, no fear—"

"*Is muid an ghaoth*[1]—"

Thump.

"*Rianta báis inár ndiaidh*[2]!"

As one, the raiders bellowed their enthusiasm, then followed Tam Lin into the ancient, stinking sewer mouth. Kaer Yin lingered, allowing Diarmid to emerge into the unnaturally bright night. He didn't look happy.

"Where's Una?"

Diarmid cursed, "She's not returned?"

Kaer Yin felt the blood drain from his throat. "What do you mean?"

Diarmid gathered himself and set a hand on Kaer Yin's shoulder. "I will find her, I vow it."

"What happened, Diarmid?" Kaer Yin lunged, dragging his uncle's head down to snarl in his ear. "Where did you leave her?"

"I didn't leave her anywhere. One moment she was there with me— such power, Yin— I have never felt." His expression went almost slack with shock. "I didn't call this storm. Somehow she tapped into my power and ripped it out of me like a thread she could unwind. I can't... in all my years..." his voice trailed off, awestruck and horrified.

---

[1] 'We are the wind.'
[2] 'Death trails in our wake.'

Kaer Yin wrapped his long fingers around Diarmid's throat, shoving him against the iron grate behind him. He didn't struggle. "What have you done with her, gods damn you?"

"As soon as the sky darkened and the clouds descended, she simply wasn't there beside me any longer. I don't know what magic could have managed such a thing." His jaw set. "I will find her, Kaer Yin."

Kaer Yin backed away from a sudden thought. "Una's in the *Oiche Ar Fad?* Alone?"

"That's what I'm trying to tell you. I don't think it matters if she's alone or not. The girl is… she's a Skysinger… I don't know how. Even *I* don't hold the power she doesn't realize she has."

Kaer Yin had no clue what Diarmid was on about. He only understood that the woman he loved was in the most dangerous place in all the realms, alone, and likely hunted for the mortal blood in her veins. She would die there, he knew. "I'm going. Catch up to Tam Lin and tell him to stay the course."

Diarmid caught his arm. "No! I'm telling you, she's strong there—impossibly so! Never mind the details. I doubt any harm *could* come to her. You don't understand Yin."

Kaer Yin shoved his arm away. "Your doubts are no comfort to me, Diarmid. If anything happens to her—"

"It won't. I swear it by Nuada's Star, I will find her."

Heart racing, Kaer Yin considered him for several breaths. There were too many lives depending upon his plans tonight for him to leave and too many emotions tugging him in the opposite direction.

"Go. I only came to you to rule out the possibility that Una would return alone. There is nowhere in my realm that I can't find her. I'll bring her back."

"Damn you, Diarmid," Kaer Yin's voice had gone dangerously low. "If you don't, I'll nail your head over the mouth of Bri Reis with my own two hands."

As much as it pained him, he didn't have time to worry about Una. His instinct was to let Robin and Tam Lin take the lead and dash off into the Otherworld to find her himself, but he couldn't, and he knew it. There were hundreds of lives, mostly women, children, and old people, depending on him tonight. If he faltered now— no matter how just the cause— many, if not all, could die tomorrow. He had to trust Diarmid to keep his word. More than that, he had to have faith in Una to save herself.

There was no other way.

He didn't even have the introspective luxury to ponder the meaning of Diarmid's cryptic claims about her.

A Skysinger? Una? That was impossible. No mortal ever born could boast of such. Although, if any Milesian woman were capable of it... she *would* be the exception. Kaer Yin must trust her. He *did* trust her. Una was the strongest woman he'd ever met. If anyone could do it, she could. Kaer Yin sent every prayer he could think of to Danu, in her wisdom, to make it so.

Tam Lin was the first to mark the determined white line Kaer Yin's teeth made as he emerged from the dank, narrow tunnel mouth into the frigid wastes of the western Greensward. "What is it? He steal your girl after all?"

"Worse. He lost her."

Tam Lin's eyes flared. "You can't be serious? In the—"

"Yes."

"Ah, Yin. I'm sorry." Tam Lin had the grace to own his careless words. He scratched at his ash-coated cheek. "The old man can spot a flea on a mare's arse from a thousand leagues in the Oiche Ar Fad. Try not to worry."

Kaer Yin felt Robin's hand clasp his shoulder. "Frankly, Ben, that woman scares the shite outta me. I say that with all the respect I have in my black heart. She'll be fine. Believe it."

He did. He *must*.

He cleared his throat. "Now then. Who's ready to pay these Souther cunts back for the past twenty-four hours?"

In the snowlit, pre-dawn darkness, several more pairs of white teeth sparked ghostly white in answer.

The Better Man

n.e. 509
25 ban apesa
Rosweal

In the wee hours of the morning, the farm was as still as a pond. The officers quartered in the oversized barn were quiet at last— worn out from a frenzied night of mourning and drink. Damek couldn't sleep, not that he slept much these days. He was marshaling the conquest of the North— a feat that required every ounce of energy, strategy, and endurance he could muster.

He'd lost over seven hundred men today.

Good men.

Solid, earnest Southers— *his* men.

For someone who rarely made such mistakes, he was highly disappointed in himself for the only one that mattered. He'd ignored his own advice and underestimated the Roswellians for the second bloody time. It had cost him, dear. Four catapults, three trebuchets, an entire supply train (that must now be replenished in winter, a feat about as likely as finding gold buried in the snow) consisting of nearly a dozen wagons full of food, tack and rigging, weapons, and necessary oddments. At least a hundred and fifty men who'd clambered over the wall would never return, and another three hundred blasted to bits in the explosion beneath the Eastern Wall. He lost fifty more on the Navan Road to raiders and a hundred or more in the raid on his supplies. Not to mention the two dozen warhorses he's sacrificed in his charge at the raiding party and the inconvenient hitch he'd acquired in his stride from his charger spilling into a frozen gulley beside the road. If it hadn't been for the deep, unnatural snow that had yet to cease squalling, he'd have broken his godsdamned neck. The loss of his second favorite horse, notwithstanding.

He had expected raids and guerilla attacks. This was Rosweal in the borderlands, after all, and entirely outside the typical Innish social collective. In Bethany and even to a degree in Tairngare, the usual martial tactics tended to apply. Surround a walled city of any considerable size with a moderate to swelling population. You'd either find cause for negotiation, engage in civil siege, or simply wait out the city's dwindling supplies. In Rosweal, the concept of honorable warfare was a foregone conclusion. He found it somewhat ironic that he'd managed to take Tairngare— the greatest and most populous city in Innisfail— with fewer losses than tiny, insignificant Rosweal had cost him in a single day. While his valet saw to his wounds, he poured over the area's maps for hours on end to puzzle out Rosweal's next surprise.

By the ninth bell, he'd thrown his cold meal against the far wall and sought out something living to vent his frustrations upon. The farmer's young daughter seemed as good a place as any to pour his malice into. The farmer himself hadn't been pleased to surrender his farm and his life, and now his dripping head graced a wooden pole at the gate, along with his fat wife and their three snot-nosed sons. His daughter, however, had round teats that would serve her well in her next profession, and Damek was filled with enough spite to break her in himself. He would be sorry for his actions later, but his misery needed a home. Why not the broken entrance to this girl's blooming womanhood? Why should the women be spared?

The servants were in the barn with his officers. After a day like today, his men deserved the distraction. The girl had stopped weeping a few hours before, but as he sat at the window, naked and smeared with her blood, her occasional whimpers irked him. He turned, flagon in hand, to spear her with a warning glare. "Shut your mouth."

She complied by cramming a fist between her teeth.

He hated the satisfaction it gave him.

You're every bit what she said you were.

He drank rather than see Una's brows cinch in disgust. If only that Dannan bastard had killed him today, this girl's family would still draw breath, and her virginity would be hers to bestow on some lucky fool one happy eve. So, he drank, turning his thoughts to strategy rather than carnivorous self-loathing.

The Sidhe posed the only real threat here. Even outnumbered, they were still a considerable force to be reckoned with. On the field, hand-to-hand, or from a distance unseen— the Dannans earned their martial reputation with every minute this conflict pressed on. That bastard earlier, for example. Damek ground his molars, feeling very stitch Hisk had sewn into his abdomen at the memory. The Dannan had short, silver blond hair and a smattering of gold chains in his right ear. That made him a lord or someone of import in Aes Sidhe.

That son of a bitch had almost cut his heart out. If Damek's honor guard hadn't been nearby, he'd have died face-down in the snow with so many of his officers.

His fingers tightened around his flagon, threatening to break the glass to shards. If he'd known how bloody taxing Rosweal would be, he'd have heeded O'Rearden's plea from the first and told Falan the Younger to fuck himself raw.

I lost five hundred men today.

For what?

For a woman who didn't want him. For an overlord he didn't want to serve. For himself... for pride?

You're here to surrender the crown you earned with your own sword to a father who couldn't have given a shite less if you died to bring it to him. You're here for nothing. You are committing treason against a benevolent high king for nothing.

Your men are dying for nothing.

Damek sneered at his reflection in the glass.

Some king you are.

He only had so much time left to linger in this backwater. His uncle spread his venom throughout the south, burning and murdering in his God's name. How long before the south fell entirely into Henry's greedy, vindictive hands? What then? It would be a pointless goal to rule a unified Eire that is far from unified. The longer he wasted at this border picking a fight with the Sidhe on his 'father's orders,' the greater the chances he would lose everything he'd earned on his own. Damek heard the girl whimper and knew he shouldn't even be here.

He should have listened to Martin.

A true King of Eire did not need the Sidhe to rule.

As if summoned by Damek's toxic thoughts, Martin shoved the door open so hard that it bounced from the wooden wall, rattling the windows. His grizzled features purpled with a barely restrained fury at the sight of the weeping girl in Damek's bed. Her black eye and bleeding nose might have borne Damek's blazing red hand. Martin sputtered, collected himself, and waved the girl toward him. "Come on now, sweeting. There's a bath and food for you in my quarters, and I swear to Reason no hand shall touch you there."

Terrified, she glanced at Damek, who shrugged on his dressing cloak as if she didn't exist. He didn't turn to Martin when the girl leaped from the bed and darted for the hall.

Martin slammed the door shut behind her with the heel of his boot. "Long night, My Lord?"

Damek pretended to examine the map on his desk, unable to meet Martin's accusatory stare. "What's it to you, Commander?"

"That girl's face was far fairer this afternoon, as I recall."

"You were all for this last season, so don't pretend you care about any of the women here."

"It was you who put a stop to it, remember? That asides, those girls volunteered and were *paid* for their time. None were beaten within an inch of their lives, either."

"That's a rather fine hair you're splitting."

"Is it?" Martin laughed. "There are two dead women in the barn this time, Damek. What was done to them was unspeakable. You encouraged your men to behave that way… and came up here to make a mess of your own."

"So?"

"What the hells do you mean, '*so*'? You should be ashamed of yourself!"

"Are you my mother?"

"I bloody well wonder if that's not what you need."

Damek's shoulders shook. He couldn't look up.

"Was it not bad enough to kill her entire family and leave them for the crows, but then shame and beat her for transgressions that aren't hers too?" Martin stalked over until he towered over Damek's bent head. He leaned forward on his knuckles so the judgment he wielded could not be misinterpreted. "Tell me, My *King*, have you and your cunt uncle somehow merged beneath the flesh? Because the boy I raised is not a base rapist and murderer, or have I been laboring under a misapprehension all this while?"

Damek snapped up, filling his face with every ounce of loathing he had. "You watch your tone, Commander. I am your liege lord and—"

"*Fuck your title*, you sniveling gobshite!" Martin roared. He dragged the map out of Damek's reach and shredded it. "I'm speaking to a lad I taught to sit a horse, eat like a gentleman, draw the bow, and tilt like a fine Souther knight. Is he in there under this entitled snit, or not?"

Damek turned away, pouring himself a tankard from the glass flagon that shook with shaking hands. He left it on the table and moved to the mantle. "Martin, I—"

"Again, I ask you, what would your lady think of this, hm? This girl you claim to love above gods and men. What would she say to you now if she saw what you've wrought here?"

Damek said nothing.

She hated him… and she was *right* to.

At this moment, he realized he was the villain of this sad tale. His motives had always been impure. His actions were high-handed and self-serving. His beliefs… everything, were irrelevant to his ego. Damek was every inch the monster Una knew him to be, Falan wanted him to be, that Patrick had tried to mold, and Martin feared he'd become. He was a patchwork of evils, woven together by lofty ambitions. "Maybe this is who I am, Martin."

Martin made a sound like a half-strangled bear. He swatted the flagon to the floor, where it shattered, leaving a bright red puddle on the pine floorboards. "I will not hear that! I've been with you from the start, young lord. I loved you, raised, and supported you from your first breath because I believed in my bones that you were best for the South— for Innisfail. Reason knows you have your flaws, lad, we all do, but rape and unjustified slaughter are *beneath you*." He drew himself up to his full height. "Until now, I've never doubted my loyalty and love of you was right. Tell me, will you do the same to Una when she's in your keeping at last?"

Damek choked. "No, I would never. I..."

"You what? You love her? Isn't that why you started this campaign in the first place? Why half a thousand men are rotting in the snow tonight. Because you were going to save her, save us all from tyrants and unworthy rulers. Isn't that what we're all bloody here to do?"

Damek's gaze flicked upward. He hadn't seen such a look of disgust and disappointment on Martin since that night those many years ago when Una had fled the comfort of her father's hall. That night, Damek had driven away the only thing he'd ever really wanted for himself by behaving much the same as he had tonight. Then, as now, the same emotion shone from his foster father's steady gaze.

Shame.

That was it.

Shame not for Damek, but *because* of him. That look spoke of a deep disgust caused by raising a creature of no worth to heights he could never have aspired to otherwise.

Mistake.

Grief.

Damek couldn't bear it. He shrank under that derision.

Martin was the only father he'd ever had.

"If you mean to conquer just for its sake, do what you will. I cannot gainsay you. You're a brilliant commander and a fine leader of men, but I will never serve you again. You lost me tonight, boy. You may accept this as my formal resignation."

Damek stumbled forward, pleading. "Martin, no. I'm sorry. I am a terrible man… I need you to make me better."

Martin blew a stream of air from his nose. "It is not our victories that make us men, Damek. Our worth is proven by how we handle defeat and loss, how we get on with things, and how we treat those who depend upon our mercy. That makes a man, Damek. A *king* would know better."

Damek felt like he'd been lanced straight through the heart.

You are no king. First Una, now Martin.

A man should be judged by the quality of those who spurn him. He struggled to find a word, anything that might make his adopted father look at him with less disappointment. The well of excuses from which he usually drew was bone dry. He had none. He couldn't breathe another lie into life. He just stood there, quivering like a leaf in a gale, staring at his own feet below the hem of his purple robe.

Martin mocked a salute. "Now, we shall finish this farce of your father's if for no reason other than that I swore you my sword for its execution. When it's over, whichever way, we are done, boy. Do you hear me?"

Damek could but nod. Hot tears stung the pits of his eyes and burned his throat like acid.

"Good. In that case, do you have any orders for me, Lord?"

After a while, Damek managed a weak response. "Have we doubled the watch on our supply trains?"

"We have," Martin replied dryly. "Though it's quiet as a tomb out there and cold enough to freeze the air in a man's lungs. I expect they're licking their wounds tonight, same as we are."

"Don't count on it. They'll raid tonight. It's what I would do in their place. They know I have more men than I can feed, and with our stalemate this afternoon— their only shot at getting out of this on one piece is to encourage desertion in our ranks."

"We'll be at them again at dawn, regardless. Southers don't care much for these Norther snows, but we're made of harder stuff than they expect."

Damek winced. None of them deserved such faith from this most excellent of men. "If the Crown Prince claims her, I might as well sign my death warrant."

"I'm aware, My Lord."

"Martin, I... I don't know what to do."

Martin heaved a heavy sigh. "Sleep on it. It'll come to you, as it always does."

"What if it doesn't?"

Martin visibly wrestled with the words he wanted to utter and those more prudent. In the end, he shrugged. "You lost the moment you marched here. Falan sent you to ruin yourself, and you, like the arrogant, headstrong fool you are— committed to it to save face. If the greatest warrior in the history of Innisfail doesn't kill you tomorrow or the next day, your rule will certainly finish here... and miserably, I might add."

Damek's chest bled all over again. "I know."

Martin chuckled. "If you know, why bother to ask? We're here to die at your word, My LordKing. I'm so happy to spend mine for so vaunted a cause as your wounded pride. Will that be all?"

The great chasm between them was hundreds of miles wide and deep as the blackest fathom. "If I could go back, Martin—"

"I don't care to hear. If there are no more orders, I'll be off to discipline your officers for behaving like their worthless king. I expect to hang four men tonight and will brook no refusals. Are we clear?"

He cut away, prying the door open with quaking fingers.

Just then, a chorus of screams rent the night outside.

His hand paused on the knob.

Damek rushed back to the window seeing nothing at first but swirling snow, until there, in the storm-bright darkness, he caught the glint of steel in from the treeline. Damek felt the blood drain from his face. He *had* said they'd raid tonight; he just hadn't imagined they'd penetrate so deeply into his rear lines nor come for the one commodity he couldn't replenish— his well-trained, fiercely loyal officers. "Gods damn those Dananan cunts!" he spat, rushing over to tug his discarded clothing on.

Martin was out the door well before him, and it wouldn't be until much later that Damek would realize he'd never thanked the old bear for raising him nor for the wisdom and justice of his council. The shame he felt at Martin's disapproval had always been the guiding star of his life. Martin's faith in him, his steady, stable nobility, was the only reason Damek had *any* redeemable characteristics to speak of. When this affair was handled to whatever end, Damek swore he'd see Martin rewarded for his unwavering loyalty and prayed he might still be worthy of it.

X

They were in the barn before a single sentry caught the slightest sound. There were roughly twenty men inside, slumbering in stalls heated by iron biers loaded with slow-burning peat logs. Those not afforded the privacy of a heated stall gathered together in the center aisle on cots piled high with furs around a hastily dug firepit that had burned to cinders. Rough accommodations, to be sure, but much better than the infantry forced to brave the elements outside. In places, the snow had piled so high that tents became igloos. Half of the farmhouse had been swallowed nearly to the chimney.

The time was much closer to dawn than Kaer Yin would have liked for the effort required to wade through such a thick coating of snow over the forest floor. Now that they had finally made their mark, he wasted no more. Miming a silent signal, the Sidhe moved through that barn like the shadow of death itself. The affair was over in moments.

Kaer Yin's party slinked past the sentry, who took his last piss at the end of Colm's blade. The first knight closest to the door he sent to Tech Duinn with a quick dagger jab to the clavicle, then held the lad's mouth shut while he choked to death on his own blood. The second startled awake in the next stall. Kaer Yin leaped over the short wall and onto the fellow's chest before he could stand up to alert his comrades.

That one, Kaer Yin, took through the eye.

Robin and Tam Lin wrestled and slashed their way forward outside the stalls in a gruesome ballet— step, pivot, cut, turn, slash. Jan Fir caught up with a large man who tumbled from his cot, still tangled in his furs. His lark came through the back of the fellow's throat before he could gather his voice to call an alarm.

Although they slew most everyone in that barn before they could get away, Kaer Yin had anticipated that they wouldn't get to everyone without a sound. Two men escaped their clutches and spilled out into the snow outside, screaming bloody murder. Shar made short work of both, but not before the men gathered in half-buried tents nearby, and indeed, the whole of the farm was roused to the danger. Kaer Yin finished off one man after another until a red-bearded captain in a stained tunic leaped to his feet with a sabre in one hand and a short-handled axe in the other. This one swiped at Kaer Yin with his axe, which Kaer Yin ducked without effort.

"Kinney, kill that blond fuck!" One of his comrades screamed as Tam Lin's lark lashed out, taking his head from his shoulders. To his credit, Kinney tried. It did him no good, but the effort was admirable.

Kaer Yin cut him in half with one stroke from Nemain's broad blade.

His top half blasted through one of the closed wooden shutters. The shouting outside increased in frequency and nearness.

Well, so much for our surprise.

"Men comin'," warned Colm, wiping his knives against his dirty wet trousers.

"How many?" Kaer Yin asked, drawing Nemain's point from another man's corpse.

Tam Lin dashed for the open door. "Shite. All of them, looks like."

Robin shuffled over. "What now?"

Kaer Yin answered by kicking the wooden slats out of the back wall and spilling into the night outside, his sword high. So many men poured out of the farmhouse and grounds toward their raised position; they might have been ants streaming from a hillock. "Kill anything that comes at you, and don't stop until we're over the far ridge."

The Sidhe coursed forward, dealing elegant death without a break in stride. Each comer was met with equal and swift ferocity, slipping into the snow, missing heads, limbs, or sporting holes and gashes from which there could be no recovery. As the Southers' numbers increased, so too did the dead. The Sidhe could not be stopped even in such a small number. Shar had grabbed a torch from a fallen sentry and busied himself with setting fire to anything that might catch— wagons stacked near the farmhouse, outbuildings, and even the smattering of tents gathered close to the barn. Colm had freed what few scrawny animals were left to die in the pen, thus bleating sheep and cattle charged ahead of the Sidhe, trampling many defenders well before they could greet the edge of the sylvan weapons headed their way.

The farmhouse door tore open, spilling light and soldiers from its interior. A large man Kaer Yin recalled seeing in Bethany at Bishop's side like a faithful shadow, emerged sporting a fairly wicked crossbow. "Sound the horns!" he bellowed, his voice cracking like thunder. He pointed his crossbow directly at Kaer Yin. "Let none leave alive."

The quarrel he fired whistled through the air and would have taken Kaer Yin through the throat if he had not moved away quickly enough. He lost several strands of silver hair in the process. Another whizzed by, forcing him to twist his body into knots to avoid being struck somewhere dear. Before he had time to move out of range, two men came at him from the sides. The snow was up to his thighs, impeding his ability to wiled Nemain with ease. He sheathed his longsword, drawing his larks from their holster behind his quiver. Some Dannans wore their larks high to use gravity as a natural aid in close combat by eliminating the time it took to attack from a draw.

Kaer Yin wore his upside-down, preferring to draw from the sides and strike low in the opponent's guard. Most swordsmen fought with a high guard, like Neithana but with far less finesse. The purpose is to halt one's opponent by using his inertia against himself. For Kaer Yin, who moved in a complex series of loops when engaged— the lark served best at the unguarded torso, ribs, the pit of the arm, the hip joint, and kidneys. Stringing his holster upside down saved him the precious time he would have lost on a downstroke.

The two soldiers went down just as fast as they had come on. Three more followed suit, one slightly faster and more skilled than his fellows. That one, Kaer Yin was forced to take seriously. The Corpsman's sabre sliced forward, rending a gash on Kaer Yin's bicep before he backed up and scored a second line at his shoulder. Kaer Yin gnashed his teeth and spun right, sweeping his left hand horizontally across the Corpsman's ribcage. He then pivoted, wobbling forward just a hair. Kaer Yin's knee connected with his forehead just as his right lark bit into his neck joint. As the dying soldier crumpled into the driving snow, Kaer Yin used his falling body as a platform to launch himself out of the drift and back in line with his comrades.

"Yin, behind you!" shouted Tam Lin from several lengths ahead.

Barely fast enough, he whirled, catching the big man's stroke from behind with both lark blades— shoving it back and away. He grunted with the effort. This Souther was made of stronger stuff than the others. Damek's man grinned and lunged forward with a dagger, inches from Kaer Yin's eyes. He jerked back, tipping the point away with his left blade and ducking beneath a second slash. The burly was good, *very* good for a man his size. Even in this sucking snow, he wielded a longsword as easily as his fellows used their lighter sabres. Despite the sword's weight, he made each stroke look as effortless as a reed in the wind.

Kaer Yin scrabbled backward, using his larks to maintain his footing. Before long, he realized he was sweating. Still, the grizzled old soldier grinned down at him from the high ground. Larks were no good against longswords. The blades were too thin, even if they were made of folded, refined steel that was much harder than the average Milesian make. The difference came down to fundamental physics. A heavy object propelled by a heavier force exerts more power— superior craftsmanship aside.

Cursing, Kaer Yin tucked his larks back into their sheaths and reached for Nemain again. He would have to maintain a high guard due to the snow, vastly decreasing his mobility and speed. The Souther knew it too. His smirking face complimented his height, which was close to if not higher than Kaer Yin's own. Having the high ground meant he didn't need to exert half as much energy to swing his bloody sword. "That's right, you pretty, prancing prick," he laughed, a grey-bearded bear with a crooked chin. "Let's see whose arm is stronger."

"Gods damn it, Yin," snapped Tam Lin from somewhere close. He must have circled back. More men poured from the farmhouse nearby. "You weren't supposed to stop."

Jan Fir and Shar came hurtling through any men who approached the two combatants on the hill, but Kaer Yin barely noticed. "*A fháil chun clúdach*[3]!" he barked while absorbing each of the larger man's sword strokes with molar-rattling impact. He tried to inch back toward the trees, which would strip the Souther of his height advantage. Displeased by Kaer Yin's seeming lack of interest, the Souther growled and redoubled his efforts. Kaer Yin saw dozens of men shuffling uphill from the farmstead below, many held torches or crossbows.

He was out of time.

Kaer Yin spun away as neatly as possible in the heavy, boot-sucking snow, switching Nemain's pommel to his left hand. The big man's eyes widened at the reveal. Many Milesians could never understand that to practice Neithana, one must be as effective with either hand. His right might have taken a beating warding off his blows, but he had another that was just as strong and somewhat rested. Moving his left foot forward, Kaer Yin whirled right, dodging a startled thrust. When he turned, he faced the Souther's broad back: Nemain's blade dripped gore from a point above his tailbone. Spitting blood, the Souther gripped Kaer Yin's arm as his sword dropped from his fingers. His eyes were surprised but almost amused. Kaer Yin didn't remove his arm as he slid Nemain from the Souther's body.

Though he shuddered against him, he gave a small smile. Someone screamed "Martin!" in the distance.

Despite the fatal blow, the Souther's hand snaked out and grasped Kaer Yin's by the back of the neck, smashing his hard forehead into Kaer Yin's nose. A thousand stars burst behind his eyes, and Kaer Yin stumbled, feeling sure he heard something crack. The big Souther chuckled, resting his girth on one fist while the other uselessly attempted

---

[3] 'Get to cover!'

to stall his guts from working free. His eventual death would be slow and painful if Kaer Yin left him this way. He was clearly a brave man and a capable soldier and deserved better.

The truth of his situation must have shown on Kaer Yin's face. He nodded. "An honor, *Ard Tiarne*."

Kaer Yin exhaled long and hard. "The honor is mine, Commander."

The Souther pulled himself up as far as he could, spread his arms, and shut his eyes. He was still smiling. Kaer Yin sent Nemain through the man's heart to the hilt. He doubled forward again as Kaer Yin withdrew, then slipped sideways into the snow. Men and arrows came charging uphill at him, but he spared the time to salute the old soldier as he deserved.

He had been a worthy foe.

X

Amidst a swirl of white and grey, Damek saw red. His piercing fury was a glowing stain in the night. Martin's grinning corpse lay cocooned in swiftly darkening snow. Half-burned trees tore at the sky in a deafening keen. Men screamed. Dark shapes struggled uphill with blazing torches. White-tipped arrows streamed from the shadows. His guards dragged him back from the arrows covering the raider's retreat. Several bolts hissed into the snow on either side. He couldn't see them and didn't care. The only thing he cared about lay in a blooming pool of white and red.

Martin was dead. His foster father, his body still steaming, lay curled up in a darkening snowbank. Dead. Martin was... *dead*.

Memories flashed before Damek's eyes: Martin tucking his fingers around a spoon, wrapping a cut with a thick white bandage. Martin laughing as Damek foundered in his first suit of armor, beaming down at him from the dais at Damek's wedding. Damek sucked in a breath, rooted to the spot by feet that could no longer obey him. He relived his whole life in the space of a few heartbeats, and for nearly every moment, Martin had been there. His dearest friend. *No*, he thought with deepening rage and pain—my *father*.

The only father he had ever needed.

Martin O'Rearden was dead.

"Milord," prodded Ridley, his hand finding Damek's right shoulder. "Should we pursue?"

He didn't look up. He couldn't. Not even when the unnatural snowfall ceased and the light from a weak, mottled sun peaked over the trees.

His men filed around him, waiting, unsure.

All Damek could see was Martin, staring blankly at nothing. The big, callused hands that held him atop his first saddle placed a wooden stave in his hand, drew his fingers back over his bowstring, dusted his kneecaps after a fall— those hands that seemed to carry him through every stage of his life, now clenched with rigor over still seeping wounds. It was *so* like Martin to die with a smile. He always did admire an opponent who knew his business. Damek had watched him fall from a useless distance, too far away to stop the Prince of Innisfail from cutting Martin's heart out right in front of him.

"Milord!" Ridley cried, face gone purple with emotion. There wasn't a dry eye among his men. Martin O'Rearden was a legend in his own time. Better men simply did not exist. Some of Martin's favorites had given chase without Damek's consent. "Do we pursue?" asked Ridley again.

Damek collected himself, hearing Martin's voice come out of his mouth. "Take your best trackers up that hill. Bring down anything you can catch, alive if possible. If not, I want to know how they renter that cesspit of a town… in detail."

Some of the last words Martin would ever speak burned in Damek's gut like red-hot coal.

Their worthless king.

"What if they've laid more traps, My King?" Ridley had lost dozens of men the day before. For a soldier of his ilk, it was a blow from which he'd be slow to recover.

"They haven't. The trap is inside the walls."

"How do you know?"

"This was an invitation to follow. They came here to make sure we do it sloppily, dash headlong at the Navan Gate." Damek knelt, allowing himself only the barest touch of Martin's cold hand.

"So, we're not going to attack?"

"Did I say that?"

"But the men? Without their captains, how will we direct the siege?"

Damek shrugged off his cloak and laid it gently over Martin's still form. "We're going to give them exactly what they want, Ridley. Only we will show them what a grave mistake they've just made— tossing kindling at a brushfire."

He trained his eyes north, watching a menacing fog settle over the hills. "I want every man we have ready to march in three hours. Every last one."

Ridley's face took on a murderous sheen. "It will be done, My King."

"And Ridley," Damek said over his shoulder as he signaled to have Martin's body lifted from the snow. He took Martin's sword and laid it over his chest. "Tell the men I will personally award a thousand fainne to the first hundred men over that wall and another ten thousand to the man that brings me that silver-haired cunt's heart on a platter."

Siora's Chosen

n.e. 509
ban apesa
oiche ar fad

Una ran around the lake as fast as her legs would carry her. Something large, with snapping teeth and a snarling maw, dogged her every step. She leaped over an overhanging tree limb up a slight rise just in time. The air whistled over her neck as the thing's claws swept past her head. She redoubled her efforts, dumping Spark into both legs at a rate she could never survive in her realm. A dip in the terrain ahead heralded an overgrown but mostly dry ravine that terminated at the lake's rim. With a cry, she ducked under the creature's next strike, rolling into the ditch by inches.

Una scrambled up the far embankment before the thing could turn— snapping tree boughs and rending great rivulets in the earth with its massive foreclaws. It keened in frustration, displaying rows of fetid, razor-sharp teeth.

"Siora!" she squeaked, finally catching a full glimpse of her hunter. This was the same creature Kaer Yin had slain at Rian's farmstead. *Ghast*, he'd called it. Una had no weapons, nothing to protect herself with, save the swiftness of her own two feet.

The ghast lunged for her, upending a few ancient trees on the way. Wasting nothing, she slid straight onto a game trail about ten paces abreast of the ravine and darted forward with all the speed she could summon. There was quite a bit more than usual, she couldn't fail to notice, and a good thing too. One swipe from the ghast's claws could cleave her in two. Regardless of how fast she was in the Otherworld, so was the ghast. She felt its breath on her skin, torpid and sour. It gained. From one breath to another, a stinging gash opened over her upper spine. She bit her lip against the pain.

If she stumbled or faltered now, she was dead.

Instead, she raced onward, branches and thorns tearing at her hair and clothing. She poured all the Spark she could safely manage into her core, feeling it burn like bottled starlight— and ran. She ran until the woods around her were blurred until the ghast howled in fury. She'd outpaced it, thank every one of her ancestors. Being chewed to bits by such a monster was not a death she craved. With inhuman amounts of Spark and a bit of luck, she rounded a bend atop the next hill, completely removing herself from the ghast's sight. Its grating, knife-sharp keening trilled not far behind, but she forced herself to stop and turn west into denser foliage. Her hands shot out to two enormous elms, standing side-by-side over a creek.

"*Braid*," she huffed, her Spark flooding from her fingertips like water from a spring. As swiftly as possible, she touched all of the trees in her immediate vicinity with the same command, then pulled deep at her Spark to summon speed all over again. The trees she'd touched knotted together behind her, roots tugging out of the earth and winding together like interwoven threads. She'd made a wall of wood nearly thirty feet high, which moved toward the ghast as it sniffed the ground after her. She didn't wait around to watch what happened.

Howling snarls and the sound of splitting wood rent the air. Her wall wouldn't last long.

She stopped again, chest heaving, and held her palms out. "*Catch*," she gasped. The air shimmered with sparks and cinders. She dug into something behind her belly button and pulled hard. "*Multiply*." The shimmers of heat divided and divided again. She held her breath. "*More*." Soon her cheeks started to sweat from the heat. She waited until the ghost burst through her impressive but useless wall of trees, its rows of shark-like teeth clicking with glee.

Through the eyes, through the mouth, she meant to say aloud, but the flames flared without her verbal command. They zipped into it like tiny, glittering missiles. The creature's shrill screams made her clap her hands over her ears. She would hardly be surprised to discover they were bleeding after such an unearthly trill. The ghost struggled onto its hind legs, clawing its eye socket out in desperation to stall her flames. When it opened its jaws to roar, she caught the glow of an internal fire raging down its throat. It choked and thrashed, sending up huge chunks of earth and bisected trees.

Still, it did not die.

Una had no idea she could actualize thoughts on this scale.

Brushing a stray lock of hair from one's eye was not the same as burning a Dor Sidhe beast from the inside without uttering a sound. If this was her new reality...

What else can I do?

She backed up further from the thrashing creature, reaching into that tingling inferno at her navel. It responded like an eager animal.

Break, she thought.

The ghost's bones snapped. Its jaw unhinged from its skull. It sank to the forest floor, dying. Its one good eye trained on her in total fear. *Fold*, she thought. As if in a cosmically powerful vacuum, its body twisted in on itself, bones and sinew crushed together by some unseen hand— like a fist crumpling parchment. The whine emitted as it died almost made her feel pity for it.

Obliterate, she thought next.

All of its parts compounded in upon themselves until the ball of mass suddenly winked out of existence with an ear-splitting pop.

When it was gone, Una sank to her knees. She stared at her hands as if they had been screwed onto her forearms by some mad god. What had she just done? She trembled. She *shouldn't* have been able to do anything like that... no matter where she was.

It was impossible. *Unthinkable.*

Una had no idea how long she sat there pondering what sort of monster *she* might be before that same little girl she'd spied before appeared among the trees ahead. She had dark braids, lovely nut-dark skin, and bright, amber eyes. She opened her mouth to call out to her, but there was something in the child's enigmatic expression that clapped her mouth shut— a warning.

She understood too late.

A faint giggle from behind her spun her around. A woman stepped from the night, wearing the white robes of a Siorai Prima beneath a simple grey cloak. Her short, black hair curled around slightly curved ears marked black at the lobes. *Fir Bolg*, Una's studies informed her, though she'd never met one aside from Damek before, and he was only half Bolg. The newcomer's eyes gleamed a brilliant violet in the Otherworld twilight. "Now that was something, I must admit," she laughed.

Una thought her voice sounded familiar though she couldn't place her. "Who are you?"

The woman merely smiled and stepped forward. Una could tell she was unwell. Beautiful she might have been once, her shorn hair revealed several patches of scalp that seemed to reject any further growth. There were deep bruises around the cavities of her eyes, and her cheeks bore skeletal hollows and faint, pinkish scars. She seemed naught but scar and bone, this strange Fir Bolg visitor.

"What happened to you?" Una asked without thinking.

A brief flash of fury tracked through the women's features, then faded. A wry smirk graced her too-thin lips. "I am *so* glad you accepted my invitation, Una Moura. I so rarely have the pleasure of meeting my prey face-to-face."

Una's hands were still splayed before her, crackling with an unending supply of cosmic wrath. Her brows drew close. "I know you. Your voice."

The woman curtsied. "Left my bell at home, I'm afraid."

Come and feast… all the warmth you require is just ahead, Una's memory sang. She lifted her chin.

"Thought I killed you."

"I'm very hard to kill, My Lady."

Una sniffed, cracking her knuckles. She got to her feet, which didn't help her advantage. She was at least a foot shorter than this skinny tower of a woman. No matter. She was stronger... and she had no doubt. "You wear the robes of a Prima, whoever you are, but you are not Siorai. I would know."

The woman pursed her tiny, malformed lips with a slight shrug. She moved into the light of the menacing moon. "Remember every Siorai in the Cloister, do you?"

"I... well..."

She snorted, "Of course, you wouldn't, sweet pet that you are. You and I moved in different circles, I'm afraid."

Una gasped. "*Aoife?*"

In her mind's eye, she recalled the tall form that stood beside Nema without a single exception; midnight curls, curves to make any woman mad with jealousy, and bottomless malice that saw many Siorai skittering away from her in fear. *This* was Aoife Sona? It couldn't be? "What happened to you?" she repeated.

"You and your thrice-cursed cousin happened to me, girl. You and Damek did this together." She held her arms out. "See your mighty works and despair."

Una felt a quick jab of pity but quickly swallowed it. "You murdered innocents on Samhain. You'll get no sympathy from me."

"Oh," chuckled Aoife. "I've murdered *many* more than that, Una dear. I could argue some were outside of my control, but there'd be no point in lying, would there? It's rare for people to love what they're good at, but I've been blessed that way."

Una glared back. "So, you interrupted Diarmid's power? How?"

"Irrelevant. Here we are now, and that's all that matters."

"Let me guess. This is about Damek."

"The same."

"Take him," Una scoffed. "He and I have nothing to do with one another."

"A bald lie, but that's neither here nor there. I owe him, you see. He took something from me. Now I'm taking something back."

"I have no quarrel with you."

Aoife slowly lifted her own hands. Dark buzzing energy trickled through her fingers. "Oh, Una, I don't care."

✕

Diarmid could move through the Otherworld more swiftly than any Sidhe alive. As the Dannan Skysinger who had assumed the Dagda's place in their tribe those many eons past: he'd developed the ability to mold time in the Otherworld to his will. Here, such flashy, depletive magic would cost him practically nothing. Time did not move in the *Oiche Ar Fad* as it did in Innisfail. It was less predictable, less structured. He would liken it to spilling water down the face of a large, cracked stone. The water would find its way down the edifice, seeking the swiftest path possible. Even if droplets separate from the main bulk, eventually, they must converge again at the bottom. Just as the water sought the lowest point possible, time also sought its eventual confluence. If one was not careful and clung to a fragment too long or strayed too far from the main course, one could lose the path and be forced to wander those fragments forever.

Diarmid had many thousands of years to ponder and perfect his use of time in the Otherworld. As a result, he could travel forward, back, and around as he saw fit— provided he didn't linger in any fragment too long and never attempted to dare such volatile magic in the corporeal realm. Time was only fluid in the Oiche Ar Fad, a domain just below, between, and besides living reality. Its environment, features, and landmarks were nearly identical, the dark twin of the realm above.

In Innisfail, time marched only forward without pause, but in the Otherworld, time was softer and more malleable. There was no rule he knew of, but often, a week or so here would comprise a month or more in Innisfail. Sometimes more, sometimes less. For Diarmid and only Diarmid, as far as he knew, this allowed Diarmid to travel the length and breadth of the Shadow Path at a clip nearly in pace with the progression of time in Innisfail. Searching high, low, in valleys, dells, and dales— he passed through the sky like an intransient vapor, constantly moving but indefinable as a whisp of cloud.

So, imagine Diarmid's profound surprise when he felt himself torn into a fragment, not of his own making or management. Ripped from the air, as a falcon dives for prey, he came down hard, crashing into a hillside with enough force to rattle large tracts of granite free. The resulting avalanche swept half of the mound away.

Disoriented, confused, and infuriated, he struggled upright. Careful not to lose footing in the loosened scree and snow, he looked around. The wind screamed around his ears, blowing his cloak back over the mark he'd made on the face. Frowning, he brushed dirt and dust from his sleeves, only to discover a trickle of blood running from one nostril. Immensely displeased, he stared at the stain on his fingers with rising fury.

Who would dare?

A faint impact behind him, followed by a familiar laugh, sent his pulse into the atmosphere. He turned. A craggy, unkempt Bolg with milky, light-deprived eyes and stringy black hair waved at him from the summit. "Son of Nuada! How lovely to see you again!" cried the ugly figure with genuine glee.

"Ruidraghe?" Diarmid made a face. "Who let you out?"

The Bolg Firesinger sneered back. "I prefer the solitude of my hall, but no help for it. I come when called."

"A stinking pit in the earth's bowels can hardly be called a 'hall' Ruidraghe, but that's beside the point. What are you trying to do— be careful. I'm not overfond of being interrupted."

"Nor of bleeding, I shouldn't wonder." Ruidraghe gave over to a rasping fit of laughter, clearly enjoying himself.

Diarmid didn't have time for this. "Get to it, old man. What do you want?"

"Your death, *Fiachra Dubh*. Failing that, I'll settle for marking up that lovely face. Maybe I'll scorch the skin from your bones or boil your eyes from their sockets? Who knows?"

That was Diarmid's cue to laugh. "Had some time to think things over, I see. But we've been here before, Ruidraghe, and you and I both know you can't beat me. I wonder who permitted you to try, hm? An attack upon me is an attack upon the Ard Ri, after all."

Ruidraghe made an obscene gesture with a gnarled right hand. "Fuck your *Ri*, you Danna twat. I couldn't spare a tinker's fart for your tribe's absurd hierarchy. I came for *you*."

"I suppose I'm flattered. Still, if you're brave enough to try now after all these years, you must have been granted permission by someone from Armagh. Your lord, perhaps?"

The hermit's toothless leer made Diarmid's lip curl. Of all the Brehons in Innisfail, and there weren't many to be sure, this Bolg dog hated him most. He wouldn't be here, acting with such definite confidence, if he hadn't been sent to do so by the Bolg Ri— Falan the Elder himself— and if this was true, the fire in Aes Sidhe had served another purpose than a siege against Rosweal. Una's absence might not have been by her design.

Suspicions tugging at Diarmid's subconscious for many days seemed to bear more weight than previously assumed.

"I'm not here to talk," Ruidraghe assured him. "Which do you choose? Skin or soft tissues? I rather like the idea of you going around eyeless, myself. What an absurd pantomime you'll make."

Diarmid shook his head, reaching into the sky for his power, feeling it whirl around him in eager, electrical readiness. Whatever Una had given him in Tech Duinn was a great deal more than mere replenishment of his own 'Spark,' as she would call it. This surge of strength felt like she'd pumped a hundred years of stored power into him with a single touch of her hand.

The girl was a prize like nothing in all nine realms.

"Well," he said. "You'll have to forgive me for making this quick, but I have business elsewhere. I wish you'd tell me which MacNemed I have to thank for our reunion… however brief it will be."

"Does it matter? Come on then, great *Fiachra Dubh*. Come and die."

With speed no mortal eye could track, Diarmid accepted his invitation with relish.

Bracing herself for impact, Una was tossed bodily against the trunk of a large oak. The tree seemed to groan beneath her weight, its multi-faceted leaves shivering in a bevy of sighs. All of the breath in her lungs rushed out of her at once. Galaxies swirled behind her eyes. "*Corrupt*," chanted her attacker, with a grin Una could *hear* in her voice.

Una cried out as the oak began to blacken beneath her, stinging any exposed skin like acid. She turned away, throwing out a hand to protect her face from the oncoming miasma from Aoife's raised fingers.

"*Suspend*!" Una exclaimed, throwing a hand out. The black wall of corruption froze mid-reach, like ink trapped in ice. Breathing hard, she got to her knees, each palm bleeding profusely. She turned back to the Bolg Prima. "*Return*."

The miasma expanded in a stinking cloud, shooting up over the treetops like a pillar of smoke, then rushed back into Aoife's startled face. She backed up with a grunt and closed a fist. "*Dissipate*," she said through gritted teeth, clearly exerting more Spark than she thought she must. The miasma blew away, scattered into the forest like fog before a gale. She clutched at her ribs, panting. "That was very good, Una. Quick thinking."

Una didn't care for her praise. She got to her feet, her skin healing with every breath.

Aoife, who shriveled where she stood, saw. "How are you doing this?"

"I'd tell you if I knew."

Aoife made a sound. "I'd be disappointed if it were easy to kill you, anyway."

"What have I ever done to you, Aoife? My grandmother was a corrupt ruler, and my family was heavy-handed in their reach for power— I can admit to and accept that— but what have I done to you, personally? Your mistress has tried to kill me at least three times that I know of, and you have tried and failed once already yourself. What's the point?"

"I told you," Aoife growled. "I owe Damek. It's nothing personal aside from the fact that you irritate me by breathing. A sad, spoiled little princess ever waiting to be used by the next hand that would hold her. Pathetic thing. Your lack of purpose offends me."

Una scowled back. "You steered me on this path from the very beginning, Aoife. You and Gan made sure I was at the docks that morning in Drogheda and that Rawly and his men would find me."

Aoife shrugged, leaning against a tree to catch her breath. "I'll admit it. I, like you, am a tool wielded by others." She laughed to herself. "What irritates me most about you is that you're too self-entitled to see the many opportunities you had to make your life mean something in the process. Me, I've never been more than my *seanmáthair's* slave. You could have been so much *more*. What a waste you are."

Una chafed under the derision in her violet gaze, more or less because her conscience had echoed the same sentiments many times. "I... know."

Aoife perked up, tucking a finger behind one black-bottomed ear. "What's that?"

"I can admit when I have been wrong, Aoife. Can you?"

"Oh, no one cares what I think of anything, little Princess. I'm *no one*. You were supposed to be *someone*. Not some simpering female cowering behind various male protectors. You are Siorai! You were meant to rule. Alone, and mighty as the sea." She waved a dismissive hand. "How pathetic you turned out to be."

Una failed to respond for several moments. When next she spoke, she measured her words with care. "You're truly Siorai, aren't you?"

"Of course I am. While I hated Nema more than anyone, Tairngare was a miracle. An idyllic society governed by rational, empathetic females. Men's baser urges were put to use in the places they served best but eliminated from rule. Tairngare never declared war for gain. Never starved, raped, or tortured their citizens. The people were largely educated, successful, and enamored of justice. Although my grandmother went mad and destroyed what she'd created, Tairngare had been her great vision all along. I shared that dream, I must admit, and am more disappointed than I can say at the overall outcome."

Una swallowed. Her fault, essentially. "What could I have done to stop Nema, Damek, or anyone, Aoife? Truly? Who am I but the product of people who want it all?"

"You could have taken up the mantel you were meant to, for one, instead of whingeing your way to escape like the vain, selfish child you are. How many women might you have saved, educated, or improved? How many evil men might you have punished? How many just and fair laws might you have implemented? Instead, you're off to marry a bloody prince." She snorted, slapping a fist against her chest in mock shock. "Color me impressed."

She had omitted many essential things from this diatribe, but she was right. Aoife's loathing of men and oversimplifying Innish politics aside, Una *was* meant for more than this. The feeling she'd had in Bethany when she'd discovered the slain girls in her father's keep swept over her once more. How many lives might she have improved if she had accepted the crown? How many women could she have lifted out of insignificance? How might she have righted the ills of Eire if she'd taken the role she was born to play?

Her heart squeezed to think of Kaer Yin, whom she loved without question. She would happily die for him... but was that selfish? When was a woman in such a position of power with the potential to uplift so many of her sex?

None was her answer.

Not since the Ancestor walked Innish shores.

She stood for a while, staring at her own feet, her cheeks inflamed.

"Struck a nerve, have I? Good."

Una drew herself up to her full height.

Enough, a voice called from somewhere deep. It was a voice she'd never heard before— and suddenly realized it was her own, assured, resigned, and confident. *I've had enough.* "Aoife," she said aloud. "I am sorry for your many misfortunes. Truly. Please, let's end this here. I don't want your life."

Aoife twisted her chin. "Oh? Feeling magnanimous, My Queen? I'm not."

Una met her eyes without a shred of mirth. She understood this creature, even if she did not know her well. Maybe they shared a misfortunate star? Each of their families meant to wield them to achieve more than their due. Aoife let it rot her from the inside.

Una would not.

Today is the day I choose.

"Thank you for teaching me this lesson. You are right. I must do more."

"Ugh. What gave you the idea that I wanted you to do anything? Just answering your questions as honestly as I may. I'll never let you leave here alive."

"Killing me won't change anything."

"It'll make me feel a teeny bit better. That's worthwhile, you ask me."

It was Una's turn to snort. "For Damek? Seriously?"

"No, no, my sweet," Aoife opened her hand, and that same dark energy burned above her palm. "*Because* of Damek, which is entirely different. This is an act of vengeance against him for depriving me of an honorable death. Your death will destroy him... and maybe finish Armagh's bid for the High King's throne at a stroke. The fact that it will also be a pleasure is my own business."

"Fine," said Una. She was done apologizing and done being a victim. Done pretending power didn't suit her like a second skin. The universe wanted her to choose... so she did.

I will choose for myself... as Siora did.

The small clearing filled with a deep current, making the hair on her arms and nape stand on end. Aoife scrubbed at her arms in confusion. Still, Una pulled power from nothing until the space between them felt like a balloon about to burst. "I'll give you what you want in my cousin's place."

Aoife hesitated, confused. "How are you doing this?"

Una had no reason to lie. "I am stronger here."

"That's not possible."

Una closed her eyes and raised her chin to the sky. The air rushed beneath her feet, lifting her high. She heard Aoife's gasp. When Una cast her gaze upon her opponent again, she looked down on her from ten feet above, held aloft by winds rife with limitless power. Aoife had no idea that Una held the King of Tech Duinn's power in thrall. She had no idea that Una's Spark was far from drained nor that it grew more potent by the moment. Aoife had led her to this place in hopes that the creature she'd summoned would have killed her, and if not, her Spark would be so depleted that she'd stand no chance.

Una smiled. "You look tired, Aoife. You sure you want to do this?"

"But, the cost… you should be drained. You should be…."

Una crooked a finger, and several trees ripped themselves from their roots. She would get the hang of this in no time. "Guess you were wrong, huh?"

She fired every missile Aoife's way at once.

Unbearable

n.e. 509
25 ban apesa
Rosweal

Kaer Yin emerged from the tunnel mouth last, sending Jan Fir ahead to his next task. He then continued in the other direction with Robin and Tam Lin, past the remnants of the south slum.

"*Ard Tiarne!*" called Aoedhan Mol, another of Fionn's lieutenants, from the southern parapet. "They're gathering in the Navan woods!"

"How far?"

"A mile, Highness. Maybe less." Aoedhan hid it well, but like all Sidhe, he loved a fight as well as the next man. Many who hadn't been on the raid seemed eager to meet the Southers face to face rather than hide behind the shoddy walls or be picked off on the ramparts. Kaer Yin might agree if not for the people who called Roweal home— people who depended on him and these men to save them. Kaer Yin hit the ladder to the southeastern rampart without slowing. Robin and Tam Lin followed, but Aoedhan was already there, having raced over from the other side. Everyone else returning through the tunnel dashed off to make final preparations below.

"They beat us here," said Tam Lin, at least having the grace not to smile. "You were right, Yin. They're gagging for it now."

"They still outnumber us. Let's not forget, more is yet *more*."

"Aye, a starving, angry, desperate lot they are too."

Kaer Yin sent him a long look over his bow shaft. "Tam Lin, you are closer to me than any brother." He clamped a hand over his shoulder so he couldn't miss the sincerity of his statement. "But you're insufferable. You know that?"

Tam Lin laughed, but Kaer Yin was already shouting orders down to the men moving into position along the wall. Robin wheezed a bit at the indifferent Sidhe all around him, he'd run the same distance they had, but none of them seemed to feel it half so much as he did. "Couldn't ye at least pretend to be as knackered as we poor mortals?" he grumbled, coming up beside Kaer Yin. "Anyway, the lads below said they're all set. How long did it take us to get back?"

"Too long," Tam Lin complained. "The bloody snow saw to that. Whatever Una did, worked too well, you ask me."

"Better than being on fire, I think," frowned Kaer Yin.

Tam Lin cleared his throat. "Anyway, what of the women and children?"

"All save Barb, Mistress Rian, that Siorai woman, and a few lookin' after the boys under *The Hart*— safe as they'll get for now," Robin answered.

Tam Lin shot Shar an unkind look as he'd taken up real estate near Kaer Yin's back instead of his own. "Can't you make her see sense?"

Shar didn't rise to the bait. He kept his eyes forward. "She knows her mind, *Mo Flaith*."

"Yes, but she risks much. That bloody girl—"

Kaer Yin's hand pressed into his chest, stopping his advance. "That bloody *brave* girl, I think you mean? And invaluable. She's doing what she must, like all of us. Respect her choice."

"I don't like it."

"I don't either, but I won't devalue her by forcing the issue, and neither will you."

Shar looked away, something moving in his jaw.

"She could die down there, Yin," argued Tam Lin softly.

"I know that; believe me, she knows it better than any of us." Kaer Yin let go of his cousin's lapels and faced the incoming threat.

"Now, they're going to come from every angle they can—no orders, nor direction. Bishop will give them their head— he must. Leaderless men are impossible to direct without captains." A ruthless sort of chuckle circled the returned raiders gathered around him. "They'll be mad dogs. Their only purpose is to get over or under this wall. When they do, their blood lust will make them sloppy. That's good news for us."

"*Ard Tiarne!*" everyone shouted but Tam Lin, whose thoughts were elsewhere.

"A sloppy soldier is a dead soldier." He snatched up an arrow from the pile beside his murder hole. He'd had them placed there before they'd gone on their raid. Hopefully, they had enough to make a convincing display. "When that gate comes down, I don't want to see any of you trying to be a hero. You move to Phase Two. Am I understood?" His command was relayed to every parapet along the wall, then down to the men below. "All right." He turned back to the killing field, bow ready. "Let's give these Southers what they came for. *Boghdóirí*[4], nock!"

"*An dara cór*[5]," Tam Lin shouted down to the yeomen on the ground. "Hold!"

They waited.

X

Ridley and his last remaining captains managed to assemble every available troop into something resembling an organized line. Every unit, minus the highly disciplined cavalry that Damek himself led, the archers that Earl Murphy and Sir Angus Simmons held in neat rows, and the remains of the Steel Corps and other heavy infantry that Ridley held in check at the front— were a teeming, screaming, chaotic mess. Nearly a thousand men, mostly infantry at the front, waved axes, sabres, clubs, and spears at the defenders lined up on the wall. It had only taken two hours to get them all here and less than two more to get them ordered, but here they were. Every man was ready to end their short-lived but brutal sojourn in the northern snows.

---

[4] 'Archers'
[5] Second corps.'

Damek had promised the first hundred over the wall a thousand fainne each. That few, if any, of those men would live to claim that boon wasn't the point. The din was all-encompassing.

"All is ready, My King," said Ridley, nodding to the catapult that was already loaded. Damek kicked his mount forward and waited until his remaining officers shouted the bulk of his forces to silence.

Wearing black from head to toe, the device on Damek's breastplate was Macha's golden bull, crowned by the Southernmost Star. Today, he wanted none to doubt who he was and what he sought to claim. When it was quiet enough, he lifted himself in his saddle, rising above his Bolg *garda*'s long shields. His aunt Grainne's paramour Leal was first among them. Eyes blacked out with kohl, hair tipped with ash— the Warhammers were a dark smudge against the landscape, save for the golden bull on each shield. He hoped Kaer Yin was watching.

You're not the only Crown Prince on the field today.

"Who wants to go home?" Damek asked. He waited for his question to be repeated around. There was a nervous murmur at the front. "I said, *who wants to go home?*"

The crowd howled in commingled rage and bloodlust.

Damek drew the longsword at his side; Martin's longsword. He had vowed to bury his father with it, dripping with Kaer Yin Adair's blood. "Which way is south, boys?" The answering roar shook the ground beneath his mount's hooves.

"Bethany is *that way!*" He pointed the longsword at the charred and battered hamlet. "A lordship to the man who brings me Kaer Yin Adair's head... and *ten thousand crowns* to the man who takes the most Dannan scalps!"

His men surged past him without ado, a sea of bellowing, red-faced bulls. They swarmed the wall from the southeast as one mob, dragging ladders, anchors, and ropes over their shoulders. Dozens fell before reaching the center of the killing field, but many more did not.

Damek rode back to Earl Murphy. "Loose." Hundreds of arrows launched into the sky, arched, and came down over the wall. Then another volley, and another. The defenders were too occupied with the horde scaling up the wall to do much about volleys sent from the ground at two-minute intervals. "Ridley!" Damek turned again to nod at his newly appointed Corps Commander. "I want that fucking Gate down now!"

Ridley saluted and marched down the line to the Navan Road, barking orders.

Simmons approached Damek from the left. "Permission for pitch?"

"Granted."

Simmons moved to the rear line of yeomen— longbows loaded with flaming shot. Many of their infantry would die— but Damek was beyond caring about the details. He expected to be within Rosweal's smoking corpse within the hour.

"Corps two, nock!" screeched Simmons in his high-pitched voice. The longbowmen dug their yew bow shafts into the earth at their feet and drew back, nearly pressing their backs into the dirt for heft. The shot gathered at every arrow point was heavy with iron and flaming pitch. Even from a distance, Damek could feel the heat on his face.

"Fire at will!'

Damek smirked at the glowing arc of fire as it sailed straight up into the sky, stopped at an angle, then plummeted over the wall like a bright red scythe. He didn't listen to the men die on either side nor witness several of his foot soldiers plummet to the snow with flaming bolts in their backs or chests. He kicked his horse toward the road, where his last two catapults were already hurling vast chunks of masonry, pitch, and fire at the buckled gate. After a dozen strikes, the gate groaned inwardly, a large crack splitting its face in two. Damek raised his sword high at the cavalry gathering behind him. The final load was piled into the catapult while the top half of the gate toppled inward. The last shot would do it. "Hold until the dust clears!" he shouted to his men.

Another well-aimed shot— a direct hit at the busted center of the gate. The resulting rumble was ear-splitting. The gate pitched backward into the city, taking half of the eastern wall with it.

Smiling, Damek's teeth filled with dust.

He kicked his charger forward, his faithful *garda* at either side.

X

Kaer Yin spun, using a lark with his left hand and Sinnair's silver-capped butt in his right. There was already a pile of dead Southers beneath his feet; even more had fallen over the parapet into the mud behind him. Still, they came. A mass of hacking, breaking, screeching beasts that barely held the frame of men. Thankfully, in his haste to get inside the walls, Damek's archers had done half the work for Rosweal's defenders. The Southern dead outnumbered the defender's arrows by a tidy sum. They littered the uneven ground of the killing field, strewn over ladders, tangled in piles along the battlements. The black fletching of every arrow that had speared one or more of these men was a testament to Bishop's lack of control. He craved only vengeance. By Herne, Kaer Yin would see that he got what he came for.

Kaer Yin ducked under another volley, using the corpse of a dead infantryman as a shield. Without time to recover, another opponent came howling at him from the right. He tossed the corpse directly at him and then turned to engage the next comer without waiting to watch the first tumble from the wall. He took the one combatant through the kidney and spun away to meet the next with Sinnair's shaft, cracking his skull like a gourd.

"Yin!" Tam Lin called over the steaming mass of wriggling, slashing, burning bodies. "Time!"

Kaer Yin stopped, kicking the man he'd slain down the ladder. He flung the blood from his lark before returning it to its sheath. "To the North Wall!" he bellowed, slinging Sinnair around his shoulder so he'd be free to nock and draw. He'd purposefully loaded triple the regular number of arrows into his quiver, saving them for this moment. While running, he took four men that stood in his path through the eyes and throats in less time than he'd spent on a single breath.

He raced over the bodies littering the rampart, dodging every hand or blade that reached out to stall him, to the crux of the mortally wounded eastern wall and the gaping hole where the gate had been— and aimed. Even from this height and distance, he could make out the men shouting orders to Damek's archers. He exhaled, loosing one shot and another, then drew again. One arrow struck the nearest Souther commander in the center of his forehead, sending his armored body backward into the mud *sans* his brains. The second was challenging to see because the yeomen commander was much further back in their line. Longbows were always placed in the rear because they had range and carried the burden of greater weight and bulk. That is, for Milesian archers. Dannan archers practiced firing longbows from trees, on horseback, and even in close quarters. His second shot found its target from a pace of nearly two hundred and fifty yards. The redhaired Souther's head split open like a melon, coating the men beside him with gore.

Kaer Yin hadn't realized Shar and Niall were right behind him until he heard one of them whistle. Grinning, he slung Sinnair over his shoulder to free his hands for the climb down. He took a moment's satisfaction to witness the terrified, awed stares of the Southers who'd made it up the wall. The shot would have been impossible for any mortal man, and indeed, for most Sidhe. The remaining commander below stared up at him white-faced. He was the only infantry captain Damek had left that wasn't currently riding into a trap with him. Kaer Yin spared the man a grin.

"Shall we, gentlemen?"

The defenders on the wall took up a cheer as he and his chosen men descended into the city, beginning phase two.

X

Ridley raced to catch up to Damek's mount through the hot smoke and dust that blew down on them from the collapsing gate. "Murphy and Kinney, My King," he huffed, out of breath and near purple with rage.

"What?" Damek shouted back. He could hardly hear a word.

"Our infantry commanders. Kinney and Murphy, they're both dead. I don't even know the fellow who's left, but he can't hold that many men in check on his own. Troops are deserting."

"*What?* How, for fuck's sake?"

Ridley pointed to a familiar silver head as it ascended the ladders to the northern stone wall. The way that figure moved, with such sure-footed grace, there could be no mistaking him for anyone else. Damek cursed under his breath. He knew what had happened before Ridley could finish getting the words out. "I've never seen anything like it. Took 'em both through their crowns from almost *three hundred yards*!" He shook his head, open-mouthed and pale. "Who would have believed such a thing was possible?"

"Who gives a shite?" Damek snarled back. "When this dust clears, I want *you* to show *them* why the whole bloody Continent fears *us*!"

Ridley's jaw clenched tight. "Aye, My King."

"It doesn't fucking matter what these cunts cook up or how the least among us might shirk their duty. The Steel Corps can dismantle this hovel on their own."

"Yes." Ridley's face colored with fury. "You're right."

"Now, get your men ready. Send word for our remaining archers to follow our cavalry inside. I'll assume command. After that, I want your men over that debris and your ass up that hill. Lead us inside, Captain."

Ridley saluted; murderous grin restored. The Steel Corps moved into position, sabres rattling against their steel breastplates in a deafening roar. Their two-foot-tall steel-coated shields slammed into the debris beneath their horses' hooves in a thunderous rhythm.

"Cavalry!" Damek bellowed, swiping Martin's sword forward. "Advance!"

⚔

INSIDE, AS EXPECTED, THE SIDHE had picked off or ridden down any soldier too foolish to avoid the narrow alleys and twisting lanes that crisscrossed a toppled neighborhood in the south end. Near the northeast, just before the massive hole in the wall where the gate once stood— Fionn Shiel O'More, the High King's Champion and the most accomplished cavalry commander Aes Sidhe had ever known, sat a giant, cloud white destrier at the center of the Navan High Road, in the heart of town. The Dannan cavalry held the high ground and the network of lanes that spider-webbed from that point outward. At the reinforced Southern Gate from the Taran approach, merely twenty Sidhe horsemen and archers had all but eliminated Damek's straggling infantry inside the walls. Those who were wise regrouped behind Damek's Corpsmen or fled back through the eastern wall. Now, the factions inside the city stared at each other from the east and center.

The Sidhe, it should be obvious, didn't appear the least bit alarmed by Damek's superior numbers. They were serene as house cats, smirking back at Damek's rattled Corpsmen as if it were a sweet summer's day at a fair.

Ridley called a curt command, and his flank marched forward over the debris, shields snapped together in neat rows to craft an impenetrable wall around his men; a mounted phalanx, rendering arrows and spears useless from shoulder to shin, and also protected their mounts' soft underbellies from harm. His unit advanced through a hail of arrows fired from atop the wall, each missile pinging from their steel-dipped shields. They made fantastic progress until they came within a hundred yards of Fionn's waiting equestrians.

The Southers halted. Ridley barked, "Break away!" and the shields separated. Foot soldiers raced up from the rear to stack their shields until the wall was twice as tall as the vanguard, and pikes were inserted at each joint. "Advance!" Ridley shouted from somewhere inside the armored knot of men and horses.

As he watched Ridley move up the road to Fionn's waiting *garda*, Damek considered the ramshackle rooftops laden with sharpshooters. He'd ordered his archers to the front before his cavalry, tucked neatly behind their wall of shields, and divided into two filing rows. For every arrow that scored one of his men's shields or somehow made it through a chink in their armor, four more were fired into the city in answer. It wasn't long before the defenders' arrows thinned to the merest trickle. Despite the genuine concern that he was doing exactly what he was expected to, Damek nodded for more of his archers to root out defensive positions along the alleyways ahead. He was likely sending men to their deaths, but he had to trust his men to get the job done. Meanwhile, Ridley's phalanx continued up the road. Fionn didn't move a muscle.

Damek didn't like it. He glanced around the rooftops, alert for the next surprise. Ridley's men neared Fionn's line, and Damek's wait was over.

The Dannan cavalry split ranks, dividing at the center. A screaming tangle of blue-faced warriors— over seventy strong— came crashing into and over Ridley's shields from the high ground. Shieldmen were knocked down or cut from their feet, banging into each other as they tried to maintain their footing. They bayed in alarm and reared up, dislodging several riders in the process.

It couldn't hold; the phalanx broke apart, forced back downhill from three sides. Foot soldiers were forced to abandon their shields and engage while the equestrians hacked down at men who harried them in teams, dragging heavily armored Corpsmen out of their saddles. In exactly ten minutes, the unit was mired in a common street brawl with a mob who had rendered their shields and horses useless. Behind this, Fionn called an order Damek couldn't hear but could guess its gist. "Gods damn it!" he hissed. "He's going to divide his forces and get behind us. Pull Ridley back!"

But Ridley and his flank were too far up the road to back down. Ridley's only chance now was to spread out and hope to penetrate deeper into the city while preventing Fionn's men from bottlenecking them in the streets. Ridley was on his own.

When O'More's horses backed off, turned flanks, and split into five directions, Damek cursed anew. "Six men abreast. Get down those lanes now!" he ordered, kicking his mount into a canter and steering sharply right with his Bolg *garda*. He headed for the North Wall, shields at the front. Whatever nasty presents Fionn intended for his men, Damek had no intention of being there to greet them. However, it seemed Fionn had anticipated this decision. He saw Fionn's riders keeping pace with them between neighboring lanes. About twenty lengths ahead, two of his riders darted east along the alley ahead. They were trying to hem him in! "After them! Break the Sidhe line!" Damek belted, and a handful of his men prepared to do just that when something he didn't expect came hurtling down his north-facing lane. A flaming barrel raced downhill from the stone wall. Thinking quickly, Damek jumped an abandoned pushcart and leaped into the next alley, but two of his honor guard were not so lucky. Men and horses went down, dragged over the cobbles toward the eastern dip in the main road.

Another and another barrel followed suit.

Damek watched in horror as the barrels careened into buildings at the base of the hill, exploding on impact. The main of his cavalry were caught in the open, unprepared. In the resulting explosions, a hundred men were knocked from their saddles, went down in a mess of broken limbs and steel, or were blasted apart wholesale. That quickly, his cavalry was fractured at its center. The vanguard he'd led to cut off Fionn's double envelopment was scattered or unhorsed. He kicked his mount into a second canter and crashed through a wooden doorway. Without stopping, he burst through a low-slung window, maintaining his seat by sheer will alone. He heard the fifth explosion downhill and the screams of men who hadn't had time to escape.

He heard a shout on his right and saw one of Fionn's knights galloping straight for him. Damek drew his sword and spurred his horse broadside. The Dannan didn't have a chance to turn, so he tried to rein in. His horse's hooves skidded over the snow-slick cobbles, causing a collision with Damek's larger mount.

This was why Bethonair cavalry decked their horses out in padded steel. His horse grunted but was otherwise unmoved by the impact.

The Dannan's eyes flew wide as his horse buckled beneath him and went down screaming. He was jolted upright, where Damek's vambraced arm shot out to drag him the rest of the way. He slit the Sidhe's throat, hefted him over the opposite side, and trampled the remnants. Turning north again, two blue-faced Roswellians slammed into his horse from below, splitting its unprotected guts onto the cobbles.

Damek tucked and rolled away as he went down and came back up with his sword drawn. He decapitated one villager with a single slash and spent maybe two minutes with the second, simply for lack of space to swing. The lanes were tight here, and his arms were long. The Greenmaker was slightly better with a sword than he'd hoped, but it wasn't enough to save his life. He split the man's skull in two, then kicked his wilting corpse into the next group that meant to rush up at him.

Four of Ridley's shieldmen made short work of the rest.

Everywhere Damek looked, his men were fighting and dying. Knowing he needed to regroup, he moved toward his brawling forces at the foot of the hill— but a flash of pale hair drew his attention like a bloody red hand to the base of the north wall. In the middle of a cross-alley, the unmistakable gleam of gold winked in the figure's ears as he danced left and right, cutting through foot soldiers, archers, and Ridley's surviving Corps like cheese. Damek killed the next few comers without blinking. His blood roared to flame in his chest. Suddenly the battle, the South, hells, even Una— faded from Damek's mind like dry leaves blown away in the wind. He could only see Martin's cold, grinning face staring at nothing.

Kaer Yin Adair saw Damek too. He held his arms wide, bloody blades dripping as if to say, 'Here I am.'

Far be it for Damek to keep him waiting.

With a cry he didn't know he was capable of making, Damek threw himself up the lane toward the only foe that mattered.

Belladonna

n.e. 509
25 ban apesa
Rosweal

Perhaps the wisest move Lord Bishop had made that morning before the gate came down was to send a ragtag of men around the wall to the west. On that trek, there would be nothing but scorched trees and deep gray snow rolling into a smog-laden horizon for miles and miles around. Rosweal's defenders, knowing the wall was strongest at that end, had left it primarily unguarded to prepare the city for Phase Three. The bulk of the defenders collected along the eastern wall and tracked north to give the Dannans cover. Robin himself spent most of these last furious hours prepping the quarter for the next challenge. A cold needle of dread tapped along his spine when the horns blew atop the western wall.

Most of the people in Rosweal huddled in cellars and sewers, waiting for the Greenmakers to get them out. So far, Robin wasn't anywhere near ready. Ben had held men in reserve for such a risk, but given the intensity of the fighting on the other side of the city, they were shorthanded. The horns called again. Robin looked at Colm and felt himself pale. They held a large cask of gunpowder between them destined to line Taverners' Lane. They had only just begun to deposit its contents when the first screams filled the air. "Oh feck," Colm said.

Robin blanched, "Knew that retreat was too bloody good to be true."

Colm dropped his end of the cask, which was bound for the lanes around Solomon Trant's brewery. "They're early."

"We don't have near enough fellas up there."

Colm sucked in a breath as a gang of fully armored marauders swung down the wall on ropes, making a beeline for the structures below. "Not infantry."

"No," Robin agreed, eyes narrowing. He lost count after watching at least forty men make it over and then dash into the streets. "Siora's tits!"

These bastards meant business. Armed to the bloody teeth, it was no mean feat to cross Barb's muddy moats, up a slick embankment with at least fifty pounds of added weight, then up and over a wall defended by men who were crack shots, despite arrows not being plentiful. The Southers were elite Corpsmen, Robin could tell at a glance, and there could be only one reason they would split from the main force.

"Vick! Get yer scrawny arse down to *The Hart* and get them folks to the river, *now*!"

"Now?" Vick parroted, wiping his filthy hair from his eyes with a sooty hand. "But we ain't finished—"

"I said now, Siora damn ye!" Robin purpled.

Vick must have recognized the horror in his boss' voice. He finally looked up at what he and Colm were ogling. "Oh shite. We can't get all o'em out in time. There's too many!"

Robin's hand snaked out, slapping Vick's ear into the cask he'd dropped. The lad cried out, a tear sliding over his grimy cheek. "If ye don't get there afore they do, everyone down there will die. Ye hear me?"

"I'll get there first. I swear it," Vick answered soberly.

"Ye'd better. Go!"

He let go and Vick, quick as an adder, zipped into the brewery on legs hastened by desperation. Robin could only pray he was fast as he claimed to be. His mother was down there with the rest of Rosweal's women and children.

The horns sounded for the third time, now from the North Wall.

Robin turned to Colm, who nodded back, knives drawn. The Greenmakers behind them followed suit. Robin hefted his own stolen sabre. "These lads came here for a brawl. Let's show 'em they came to the right town."

✗

Tam Lin raised his head at the third horn blast. He was back on the eastern rampart in the north corner, just shy of the debris gap. He and twenty Dannan bowmen, primarily his own Blood Eagles, lurked at crux to pick off Southers on both sides of the wall. Any of Bishop's cavalry that attempted to retreat through the gap never made it past the rubble. Their horses thundered away as their riders piled up at the gate, riddled with arrows. Fionn's mounted knights had done an excellent job of scattering Bishop's forces so far, and the remaining few had no idea what awaited them in the narrow lanes and alleys ahead. It had been Tam Lin's job to make sure Souther corpses blocked their sole means of escape while Fionn's men rode in seemingly every direction at once, either running down knots of straggling infantry, chasing the remnants of their cavalry, or throwing torches through the windows of buildings designated for Kaer Yin's Phase Three.

A fourth horn called, this time, closer.

Southers were in the Quarter.

"*Mo Flaithe!*" called Niall, tossing a bloodied figure over the rampart by his head. "That's the West Wall!"

Tam Lin was aware. He loosed three more arrows he didn't need to watch fall before drawing his lark to slay one opponent, then turned to open a gash in the throat of a second, who he then shoved off the wall. Covered in blood and every type of dirt imaginable, Tam Lin paused to look around. Nearly every one of his men was low on arrows and the fight though decidedly tipped in their favor now, was far from over. He looked west and saw the glint of steel clambering down the wall on ropes.

Where were the bloody Greenmakers?

There were people in the buildings below. No help for it. He muttered a foul oath in Ealig. "Niall! You have the wall. Jan Fir, with me!"

He barked orders on his long way around to the old stone battlements on the north side of town. Funny that Rosweal's ancient defenses were built to keep the Sidhe out, and now they were busy trying to help the modern citizens save the city. The irony, as always, was not lost on Tam Lin O'Ruiadh.

Despite several attempts to stall their progress, they made excellent time racing around the wall to the west. Kaer Yin's tangle of defenders occupied themselves with the barrels and casks of gunpowder and pitch they heaved over the wall into Bishop's men. Tam Lin didn't slow to help. Kaer Yin knew what he was doing.

As for Bishop and his men, he might have overestimated the wisdom of a full-frontal assault on such a small but lethally tight city like Rosweal. He and his cavalry were having all the fun Kaer Yin expected them to, thanks to Fionn O'More. Still, he *did* have more men, and they'd expected him to throw some at the Quarter eventually. Just, not so soon…. and certainly, not his best. Bishop was cannier than Tam Lin would like.

He threw Kaer Yin's strategy back in his face.

You took my best from me; Bishop seemed to be saying.

It appeared he was returning the favor.

What purpose did Kaer Yin have to defend this insignificant, unenlightened, and frankly unimportant collection of ramshackles at the rim of a wilderness but its people? The new 'King of Eire' might be after a crown and might even win it here today… but he intended to pay for it with innocent blood.

Pumping everything he had to spare into his legs, Tam Lin ran, shouting for all available men on the wall to follow him to *The Hart*— where most of Rosweal's people waited beneath the grandest, most obvious target in town.

⚔

On the street, Robin and his Greenmakers clashed with the first wave of Souther Corpsmen headed for a dense tumble of mostly intact buildings gathered near the northwest end of the city. These Southers were no madcap, lawless foot soldiers sent to choke the streets with fallen bodies, like so many pawns. These were professional soldiers. Greenmakers were hardly blushing girls, but they weren't decked out in thirty pounds of armor either. Speed would be their best chance. They came running at the Southers from the alleys and dropped down from the rooftops, hacking away with whatever devices they could get their hands on. Often, with the Souther sabres, lifted from the bodies of fallen men that littered the snowy lanes like scattered breadcrumbs.

Any hope that the invaders had worn themselves out hauling themselves over the wall in such heavy armor was a thin one. Robin directed his men to focus attacks on their heads, the back of the knee, and the unprotected spots under the arms. If their target didn't fall immediately, Robin warned his men to get away and come back for a second shot rather than attempt to cross swords with better-armed, better-trained men. Swiftly seeing Robin's strategy, the Greenmakers clustered together to watch each other's backs.

At least ten Corpsmen went down in the first blitz.

Unfortunately, the element of surprise couldn't last. The Southers rallied together in a lock-joint knot of sharp steel and practiced arms. Any Greenmaker who got too close wouldn't live long. Nonetheless, Robin was committed. He dashed through the center of a southbound lane, two streets west of *The Hart*, skidding down an icy slope on the cobbles toward a man brandishing two sabres.

The big Corpsmen hacked at anything that came too close; landing bone-crushing blows on either side of whoever was unlucky enough to sway into his orbit. Three of Robin's men went down before he slid to a halt at the Corpsmen's knees, jabbing his dagger deep into the Souther's booted foot. The Souther howled in pain, staggering off balance long enough for Robin to roll up to his knees and jerk a sabre point into the fellow's exposed underarm. With his heart and lungs critically damaged, the Souther tipped backward into the snow, coughing blood.

Robin relieved him of his sabres and passed them along to men who needed better fare. "Thank ye, sir," one said, then trudged down the lane toward the Ward Gate, where a handful of Greenmakers gathered to push the newcomers into the wall against Robin's orders. The Southers knew their business. Speed was only effective so long as everyone kept moving. "Siora damn ye, get outta there!" he spat, pulling as many men back up the lane with him as he could. Those he could not pry away died in moments. Traipsing over the fallen, the Southers moved uphill after Robin and his group as a unit. Robin paused a moment, thinking. The lanes would converge in Hilltop square about five blocks ahead. He didn't want to give them that much room.

"Into the narrows, lads!" They backtracked, intending to wedge these over-armed bastards into a space too tight to wriggle from, but another cadre of Corpsmen came jogging up the hill from the east. It seemed they had heard the horns and had their orders.

Robin saw Bishop's grizzled infantry commander— Ridley— he'd heard him called, emerge from the knot of newcomers. He was smattered with mud, and blood dripped from his beard and seeped from a cut above his swollen right eye, but he was otherwise live and hale. Their numbers were drastically reduced, but with these fresh reinforcements from the west, it wouldn't make a lick of difference to the Greenmakers.

"*Back*!" Robin raged at his men. "Get yer arses back to Wanderer's Alley, *now!*" He turned to run uphill toward the North Wall, reaching into his tunic to find the silver whistle he'd been hoping he wouldn't need all day.

X

Rian heard the horns before Barb did, her hands freezing over the half-smashed skull of a fourteen-year-old boy who'd been thrown from the east wall when the gate had come down. She watched the boy's pupils dilate with fear. A second and third blast echoed through the tap, then down the stairs to Rian's infirmary in the cellar. She stood up. That one was close.

Too close.

Barb waddled down the steps, her thinning face white as a pearl. She did not look well at all. Rian had a bad feeling that there was more to her weight loss than simple hunger. "Those are behind us," Barb said, clutching at her sagging bodice. She had lost nearly sixty pounds if Rian were any judge.

Barb Dormer was ill.

Rian cursed under her breath.

Why hadn't she seen it until now?

Barb cocked her head at her. "Did ye not hear?"

Rian opened her mouth, but the boy she'd been tending responded. "From the Ward Gate. Me Da said they wouldn't come from that direction."

Another horn trumpeted so near that it might have been over her head— and likely was— with men stationed on the roof. Everyone in the cellar had heard all manner of blasts, shouts, mumbles, and screams filtering into their hiding place, but none had been so close nor so late in the fighting. This could only mean that Lord Bishop had kept reserves for insurance. Of course, he would. Ben had said he might. That didn't make it any less a lethal blow. "Apparently," Rian sighed. "Your Da was wrong." The boy whimpered. Rian and Barb stared at each other over his head. "We have to get out of here!"

Barb moved faster than a woman her age should be expected to, Dabney's quiet bulk dogging her heels. "Get them up! Hurry!"

Frantically Rian moved from corner to corner, dragging those who could walk toward the cots and crates loaded with those who could not. "On your feet! If you're strong enough to walk, by Siora, I pray you're strong enough to carry! Show us the way, Barb." Rian got two people up beneath either of her arms, but she was hardly strong, and the going was tough.

"Be quick about it, Dabs!" Barb shoved Dabney at a grate on the floor. One-handed, the hulking figure hoisted the heavy iron grate out of the floor, revealing a foul-smelling passage downward. "Come on, come on. No! Not them that can't walk, girl."

"I'm not leaving them!" Rian snapped back.

Before Barb could argue, Vincent flew down the cellar stairs, two at a time. He was redder in the face than usual and wheezing. He must have run a long way. "Th-they're comin'! I dunno how many."

Rian leaped at him. "You! Good. Help me move these people—"

"Ye can't save everyone, Rian. They'll slow those who have a chance."

"I'm not bloody leaving them!" She fisted Vick's collar. "Help me."

Swallowing, he bent to take up the patients she had trouble balancing on her own. He wasn't much bigger or stronger than Rian, but between them, they managed to get about six people who could at least limp through the opening in the floor. Her new shadow, Strong Tim, held the ladder for them.

"Think you can hold it still while me and Vick pass some of the people who can't move down?" she asked him.

"Oh, fer feck's sake!" growled Barb in frustration, throwing her hands up. Dabs, ye grab that lot there, young Tim, help me with these here."

Between the five, they managed to move about twelve individuals from their sickbeds and hand them down to the walking wounded waiting in the passage. "Careful there, Dabs. That one there don't have much blood left in 'em, from the look o'things." Rian was busy dragging a man over by his shoulders, leaving a red stain in the dirt. Barb grabbed her wrist and spun her around. "That one's dead, girl."

"But he's still breathing! They all are."

They were all men sporting the ash 'X' she'd drawn on their foreheads. The 'critical' wing of her musty, highly unsanitary triage.

"No, they're bloody dead, girl. Ye said yerself if we move any o'em, they'll die. Well, *we* must move now— right bloody *now*— or *we'll* all die."

"But—" It was not in Rian's nature to abandon people that needed her.

Barb's hands came alongside her face, forcing her to look straight into her eyes. "Rian, yer a good girl, and I'm sore sorry I played a mean trick on ye once. Truly. Yer a brave, sweet soul, ye are, but listen to me now and listen well. Those poor devils in that corner may be spared just for posin' no threat and no profit, but ye, little lass— and all the other young things down that tunnel— will suffer a fate even an old professional like me has never even seen. Do ye hear me?"

Rian's eyes welled with tears, but she nodded.

"Good girl." Barb tugged her into an awkward embrace. "Now come away, quick! We still have two more cellars to empty before we can get outside the walls."

✕

It started snowing again as several dozen townsfolk gathered in a vacant building just shy of the stone North Gate— which was the official 'end of the line' for the Taran High Road. The North Wall had been constructed by actual stonemasons when Rosweal was incorporated after the Transition. It had been built to protect the docks from marauding river clans and, as always, dissuade attacks from Aes Sidhe just across the river. In the hundreds of years since, the North Gate had scarcely been used and hadn't been opened for as long as anyone could remember. No one was even sure if its mechanism— a complicated set of pulleys and weights—*could* be used anymore.

Rosweal's citizens took the long way around to get to the docks, which had been moved further west for its deeper channel. Since the gate was firmly shut, they had no choice but to escape below the wall. However, there were many buildings between them and the exit— at least four alleys and two broad cross lanes before the underground passage they sought. The sewer didn't connect the total distance from *The Hart* to the wall. It stopped two buildings closer, that portion having collapsed sometime in Barb's grandsire's youth. She'd been meaning to have it properly restored for years. Chamber pots dumped from upstairs windows were hardly a hygienic practice, after all, and Barb had always dreamed of better for her people.

Yet, the cost to refurbish a pre-Transition subterranean waterway was a mite rich for the hardscrabble outlaws and miscreants of Rosweal. Besides, Barb had spent nearly every copper she had to spare building their new and bloody useless wall, hadn't she? She frowned. The townsfolk emerged into the old goal, which served little purpose save as a storing house for nefarious goods or the odd Greenmaker who'd neglected to fork over his dues to the Guild. From a filthy, soot-streaked window, they had a decent view of the North Wall, where it connected with the charred timbers of the lower western. It wasn't snowing as hard as she hoped it would be. Against all that flat white, they'd stick out like a bleeding thumb. She grumbled something unintelligible.

"What?" asked Rian, from her elbow.

"I said, 'Siora's cunny.'" Barb turned to spit onto the dusty floor.

Rian looked for herself. There were hordes of men racing up and down alleys directly between them and their escape. Men fought hand to hand on the stone wall above. Men dashed along the western wall, or through the lanes, with weapons raised. Men slashed and hacked at each other from every conceivable direction. Too many men *everywhere*. They'd never make it. They couldn't even cross this street to the next without being seen. Barb watched the realization dawn on Rian's wan face and turned away to rub at her own eyes with her thumb and forefinger. "It appears we're stuck here," she said.

"Nonsense," argued a Dannan fighter that didn't bother to introduce himself. Rian had stitched a chunk of his scalp together, leaving a wicked line that snaked from the dome of his shorn pate to the edge of his eyebrow. His eyes, bloodshot and blackened, narrowed at the scene outside the glass. He, too, cursed at the sight.

"There now, ye see? Do I look like a silly girl to ye? If I say we're trapped, we're feckin' trapped."

The Sidhe officer blinked at her brass but backed off, appropriately chastened.

"We'll have to fight our way out," added Rian, her voice small.

Barb could practically see the cogs spinning in that fair head of hers. She snorted, "And what? Choke armored men to death with our bandages? Maybe club 'em to death with our crutches?"

Rian scowled over at her. "You have a better idea?"

"None. I need a bloody drink."

"We can't stay here and wait, Barb. They'll find that grate eventually, and even if they don't, you heard what Ben said, same as me."

That left a sour taste on Barb's tongue, sure. She had vehemently opposed this hair-brained scheme from the outset, and look! Now she didn't even have any uishge left to make it sting less! "Aye, I did. Them sewers aren't stable in the least. More cave in every year and with what His Arseness means to do— I doubt any will be there in the morning."

"So what are we supposed to do? We can't stay here."

"We could lead 'em off," said Strong Tim, visibly hoping no one would hear.

"What's that, boy?" Barb pressed.

He swallowed audibly. "We could split up. Half make a run for it, half stay behind to draw 'em into the narrows. We know our way 'round. They don't."

Barb fiddled with her chin while she considered the lad's comments. His arms were sticks dangling from ill-fitting shirt sleeves that swung from him like parliamentary robes. His brown, slightly hazel eyes were huge in their sunken sockets.

"No, Tim," Rian hissed and made to paw at him, but Barb threw out a hand.

"Let him be. It was yer idea to fight through— he just had a better one."

"He's just a boy!"

Barb nodded, her jaw tight. "Aye, and a good deal older than twenty more behind him.

Rian glanced around at the gathered citizens and wounded of Rosweal, who'd either been hiding in the tunnels or laid up in her infirmary and looked back down. She was quiet for a while. Her conversation with Eva began to make perfect, brutal sense. She couldn't help but wonder where Eva was now and what fate she saw for everyone else. She must have known this would happen and what Rian would decide. She finally shook her head. "Fine. But he's not going alone."

Barb reached out to grasp at her shoulder. "Oh, no, no, lass—"

Rian shrugged her hand off. "No, you were right. Rose knows what to do now if someone needs help. Don't you, Rose?"

Rose moved up the hall toward the window. "Rian, it should be me. Not you. You don't know—"

"No," Rian cut her off. "You're a comfort to those kids. They need you."

A bevy of protests sprang up at her decision, but she waved them all away.

"There's a lot of our men out there too— the Prince's men—" She pointed at the Dannan who'd spoken up. He wore the same device as the Prince of Connaught. "They know me. If they see me running around out there, I might have a chance to lead them back to help. I'm going. That's all there is to say."

"It would be my honor to escort you, Mistress," said the Sidhe, with a handsome bow.

"And me," added Violet, another girl who worked for Barb, one of her best.

"No," Barb said again, fighting tears she felt shamed to shed.

Violet patted her on the arm. "Got littles of my own in here. I wanna give 'em what chance I can. Me mam will look after 'em."

There was a murmur of outcry, but Violet shushed them all with a playful smirk. "Ye all know what a fast runner I am."

"And me," said Eva, who had been stone silent until now. She stepped forward, her robes a white smudge against the smoky interior.

Rian shook her head. "No. Rose will need you more than we do."

Eva's stare was unnerving. "Rian... you will need me."

Rian swallowed. The little phial she'd been given suddenly felt heavy in her pocket. "I'll be fine. Won't be alone." She gave her a weak smile.

Eva nodded. "May Siora walk with you."

When she walked away, there were tears in her eyes.

Rian pretended not to see them.

Three more lads, two older men, and a smattering of women stepped forward to volunteer. It took a while for the crowd to calm down. When it had, Tim moved to the window. "We should wait till it gets dark."

"We can't. If that whistle goes off—" she broke off. "We must get these people to safety while we have a choice." Rian smoothed her skirt and wiped her nose. She looked more ready to get on with it than afraid of what would probably happen to her.

"Well, logic says me and Dabs are the most expendable here," Barb laughed. "Besides, waitin' around with no uishge and my thumb in my arse is borin' me to tears. Think we'll be joinin' ye's, after all."

Rian's head snapped around. "You can't be serious?"

"I'm not lettin' ye go out there alone, girlie. Dabs neither. Would fair break his heart to leave ye. Wouldn't it?"

Dabney nodded, eyes misty. He didn't say much, but he had a heart; he did. Rian took his meaty hand in hers. "We'd better get going then."

Barb grabbed the girl's elbow, stopping her just shy of the exit. "I want ye to know, yer as fine a lady as yer friend, lass. Finer, ye ask me."

Rian sniffed, then patted Barb's thin fingers. "I appreciate what you're trying to say, but you don't understand her."

"We'll just have to agree to disagree there. Let's hope we run faster than I think we do."

X

ULTIMATELY, THEY DID NOT MAKE it through the following two alleys unscathed. They stuck together in one large group until they came to a stable overlooking the wider east-west cross lane, about twenty yards from the gaol. As the townsfolk snuck uphill toward the stable— a long line of sickly and wounded women and children— shouts sounded from the alley behind. Torches lit up the evening sky, and the sound of steel and stomping boots muffled by snow soon followed. Barb watched Rian pale.

The girl didn't have the first clue what her sacrifice would mean.

"All right folks, get yer arses to that gatehouse! Go, go, *go!*"

People raced by as Barb half dragged, half shoved Rian at the stable. "Fer fuck's sake!"

The nameless Sidhe in their company stepped between them and the incoming soldiers, drawing two thin shortswords from behind his empty quiver. He bowed to Rian and Barb, then jogged back toward the gaol, screeching like a hawk. Barb didn't wait to watch him clash with the Southers. Instead, she dragged Rian away as two more groups came howling at them from opposite directions.

"Run the other way!" Barb shrieked. Dabney kicked down a door on the far end of the darkened stable, and she, Rian, Violet, and young Tim threw themselves into that exit. Steel dogged their heels. Barb felt the air rush by her ear as a sabre swept past. They pushed and pulled each other through the narrow bottleneck in a tangle to get to the gatehouse ahead. They could see its dark maw, just there.

If only they could get there.

Rian ran as fast as her useless left leg would carry her. Twice she slipped in the snow, only to be hauled to her feet by Tim, who was much stronger than he looked. Laughing and whooping like dogs on a hunt, the Southers snapped at their heels, outnumbering them three to one.

A huge fellow snatched a hank of Rian's long hair. Crying out, she lost her footing again, but Violet launched herself at her attacker, gouging his eye with the cheese knife she kept in her bodice. The Souther howled and went down on his back, blood pouring through the fingers he crammed into the empty socket. His companions surged forward, but Tim ducked into an open doorway to the house next door, urging the others to follow, then slammed it shut behind them. Rian and Violet put all their combined weight into sliding a bureau against the wood, shoving it against the pounding door. The glass window blasted inward, and axes hacked at the soft, fire-damaged door.

"Go on!" Tim's voice broke as he gestured to the back of the house. The group burst through the burnt-out kitchen to the rear door, then again into the snow outside. "This way!" he cried, leading them through another alley. They could see the gatehouse now, ever closer, yet still so far. Barb had the intense satisfaction of watching several haggard shapes make it through that tiny black hole. At least the majority of their folks would make it. That was the point, wasn't it? That four Souther soldiers chased them inside; Barb would leave to Siora. She had her own problems at the moment.

At the end of the alley, their luck ran out.

Two fully-armored men ran at them from the street, weapons raised.

Without thinking, Violet ran straight for them, brandishing her tiny blade like a longsword and screaming at the top of her lungs. "Get out of here!" she hissed at Barb, who didn't have time to think as Dabney already had his hand on the back of her neck, shoving her through another door.

"No!" Rian sobbed, but Tim would not let her stop.

They made for the next exit, then the next, now facing south and further away from the gatehouse. Tim seemed to realize his mistake and tried to course-correct, tugging Rian along by the hand. One of Fionn's knights rode west down the neighboring cross lane, trampling men like so much rotted fruit. Another, then another, galloped by. Rian tried to call out to them, but they were moving too fast to hear her.

Tim turned to yank her through a nearby door by the wrist, but when he nudged the door open, Souther Corpsmen waited on the other side. They must have heard Violet's screams through the houses on either side. With a chuckle, the soldier rammed his sabre through Tim's throat to the hilt. Rian screamed as he fell. His murderer withdrew the blade, only to rear back and slam his mailed fist into the side of Rian's head.

Dabney roared and threw himself into the pair of onlookers, but two against one— when two are coated in expensive armor, and one was not— was hardly a fair contest. Barb could do nothing but stand in the shadows and watch. Time seemed irrelevant, and everything moved in slow motion. She drew her dagger, weighing her options. She might kill one of them, but they would surely kill her and rape the girl anyway.

Feck me, thought Barb.

What do I do?

While she debated which one to sacrifice both of their lives to kill, the soldier ripped the front of Rian's dress to the navel, exposing her small, pale breasts to the biting cold. She fell backward into the snow. He covered her with his body, fumbling with her hem and the stays at his crotch. Barb didn't have time to mull it over any longer. She lurched forward to slit the nearest man's throat. He caught her arm and threw her bodily into the wall.

Something cracked in her chest, making it nearly impossible to breathe. Dabney bayed like an enraged bear but took a sword slash to his side that would have split a smaller man in two. He staggered forward, huffing, while the men behind him gathered up his massive arms and pulled. The Souther who came for Barb didn't even bother to finish her off. He chuckled and turned back to the entertainment on the ground.

Barb heard glass break.

"What's this then?" asked the one atop her, lurching away.

Another who stood above them scratched his chin. "Whatever it is is, it smells like shite."

The first sniffed and spat. "Ugh! Fucking whore tried to poison me."

He pummeled the girl beneath him with a meaty fist. Barb could only whimper. Hot tears spilled over her cheekbone.

"Mouth's no good now."

"She drank some?"

"All, seems like."

"She get some on you?"

"No, but close enough."

The second said, "What a waste. That was a pretty enough lass."

The first shrugged, removing his sex from his trousers, working it back to rigidity. "Still warm, though."

"Warm is good," agreed the second. "Hurry up."

"Can you be poisoned if it gets on your cock?" asked a third.

"Why?"

"Knock out her teeth, and I'll show you." The soldier leered.

Barb gagged.

Siora, please… not this way.

Strong Tim's murderer jerked himself toward Rian. Barb heard him moan and wished for the sky to explode with Siora's vengeance. She must have squeezed her eyes shut, for several loud noises snapped them back open. Two tall figures leaped into the gaggle of soldiers from their rear. Jan Fir made concise work of the three Southers at the entrance while the Prince of Connaught snapped two necks on his way to Rian. The Souther made a sort of strangled whimper when Tam Lin's blade slid into his guts from the groin, and slowly, very slowly, up and up and up. Lip curled, Tam Lim kicked the Souther's split halves into the muck.

Freed, though dramatically slowed, Dabs made it to Barb's side as quickly as he could, scooping her up as he might an injured bird. She struggled to breathe. "Not me. Get her off the ground." But Tam Lin had already done so and was tucking her into his cloak.

"Please," croaked Barb. "Belladonna. She's had it all."

His violet eyes flashed her way. "How long?"

"Minutes."

He looked over at his companion. "We're in time then. Are you sure that's what it was?"

Barb couldn't bear to look at the lass's poor, bloodied fingers as they dangled from his now blood-stained white cloak. "I'm sorry, milord, but a woman in my line o'work never forgets that smell."

His gaze was steady. "That means we'd better hurry. Can you walk?"

"I'll carry her," gruffed Dabney.

"Good. Let's be gone before that whistle blows."

The Tenth Law

n.e. 509
banp apesa
oiche ar fad

Una took a hard blow to her side as the uprooted elm nicked her on its way past. Aoife grunted, and the massive bulk of wood smashed into a granite cliff face on the trail ahead. Una rolled away with a cry. One of her ribs was broken, and although she knew she could heal in minutes given the mysterious strength she'd discovered in the Oiche Ar Fad, she didn't have time to wait. Aoife was powerful. She seemed able to move objects four times her size without contact— something Una had never seen before or had even imagined possible. Soon as she got to her feet, Una was obliged to dodge a heavy rain of stones by jumping down a dry creek bed to avoid them. They pounded into the earth near her feet with a ground-shaking impact.

"Stop moving around so much, little Princess," Aoife huffed from the debris field she'd formed around herself. At least it *sounded* like she was finally tiring, though Una had to admit she'd seen little evidence of that so far. She was bleeding from about a dozen places, and the woods around them looked like a giant claw had cleaved through the forest from the heavens.

"Hold still, and I'll make it painless."

Una had no idea how Aoife was Manipulating using only her thoughts. She had done so only briefly herself and by accident. To do so on this scale was… was that another secret the Otherworld held for her? Could she do the same? As if in answer, she felt a warm vibration at her center. Her fingertips, skin, and even the roots of her hair tingled in response. She climbed out of the creek bed and faced Aoife from the opposite side.

Nema's pet's breathing told the tale of her fatigue— the oncoming spark drag that Una was waiting for— but the sheer confidence she bore, the power shimmering in the air around her, gave Una pause. Aoife might be accruing cost, but it wasn't happening fast enough. There was no telling how long she could maintain her Spark. Una was suddenly unsure that her strategy was working in the least. She had to stall as long as possible.

She dug her fingers into her screaming ribs, breath coming hard. "Surely that can't be all?"

Aoife cocked her head. "What was that?"

"Pissing on Damek isn't worth someone's life. Why are you doing this?"

She pursed her chapped lips. "Fun, I suppose. I won't lie and say I ever liked you much, sweet girl. Watching you haunt the halls of the Cloister, burying your prim nose in whatever tome you fancied while the rest of us worked ourselves to the bone to please our mistresses. That's one." She examined a torn nail. "Two, my cousin's infatuation with you aside, must you *always* be passed from man to man, dear? Do you not have a spine of your own?"

Una stood up a bit straighter at that. "I'm flattered by your concern."

Aoife made a rude sound. "Jealousy's a collection of feelings, you know. You were free when I was enslaved, cossetted while I punished, loved where I was reviled … and you waste all."

Una coughed. "I haven't had a moment's peace since that day at Drogheda. Don't pretend you could have done better in my position."

"Oh, but I would have. I'd have taken the crown ages ago if I were you." She shook her head. "Do you know what your uncle wreaks in the south? How people suffer under his resurgent faith? I would never have surrendered my agency or birthright for a *male*. I would have claimed the throne of Eire from my first bleed and crushed *anyone* who stood in my way."

"I don't crave power, Aoife, and pity those who do."

Aoife laughed; brows pinched together in mockery. "You're radiating it now, and you'd bother to lie to me?"

Una swallowed. Target struck. The heat boiling in her blood was better than any feeling she'd ever had. She *did* love it. The shame she felt at the thought didn't sting as much as it might once have. Aoife was right. Una had to admit that on some subconscious level, she had always craved this power... this, *everything*.

She could feel the river racing toward the lake, the wind in the trees, the spinning sun and moon above. If she crooked her finger now, might they bow to her whims?

Who was *she* now?

"These men are nothing to you, you realize. Only women are born with the Spark, Una, and only those of Macha's bloodline could ever dream of the power you and I share."

"What do you mean?"

"We're kin, obviously. However distant the relation. Who do you think founded the Moura bloodline?"

Una's heart skipped. "Liadan."

"The same. You might say Tairngare had always been her goal. She came from a time when no man could be a king if he were not consort to a powerful queen, and there were never queens as powerful as the Daughters of Emain Macha. Liadan dreamed of a return to the old ways. You wouldn't exist if not for her hand in your making."

Aoife spoke true. Una could feel it in her bones.

She doesn't hate you, her Spark whispered.

She wants to be you.

From nowhere, a flash of Aoife's life tracked across Una's vision, a lifetime of pain and servitude in an instant. The violence of it, the sadness, insecurity, and fear. It staggered her. She wobbled, dropping to one knee.

She wants you to kill her.

Una looked up at Aoife's confused face. "I'm sorry."

"For what?"

"All they've done to you."

The hiss of air between Aoife's teeth narrowed her eyes to slivers. "Keep your pity, little cousin. I'm here to murder you." Sliding off the slab of smoky granite she straddled, she moved back about five paces and shrugged off her cloak. The bones of her chest strained against the parchment of her skin, like a bird stripped of feathers. She took a deep breath and cracked her knuckles. "Right then. I'm curious which of us is the better breed."

Una said nothing.

She saw the beads of sweat gathering on Aoife's forehead.

She is tiring.

The granite slab Aoife had been perched upon moved a few inches.

Good, Una thought. Another demonstration of power would be her last. Aoife put a good face on it, but like any other Manipulator, she would wear out. That's what Una hoped for, anyway.

But not you said the other voice in her ear.

You're different.

She bit her tongue rather than retort.

Una knew she was stronger, could hear the wild, frantic pulse beneath the veneer of her reality, taste its charge on her tongue. As if the particles around her were a slumbering leviathan in the bedrock of her bones. Una was the mightier, but she'd come to this realization late. Aoife was more *skilled,* and the difference might prove fatal.

Throw the fucking rock, damn you.

As if she knew the direction of Una's thoughts, Aoife paused. "I'll have that crown, I think. When I've finished with you, our sweet cousin is next. His arrogance begs an answer. His father won't mind much, as Damek has ever been a means to end and nothing more."

"This Falan pretender? The High King will make short work of him."

"Pretender? Well, I shan't argue that. His sense of entitlement came directly from his beloved grandmama, as all things do. You can't imagine a more deluded, twisted individual. Still, he'll make a good ally on my way to High Queendom."

"You forget the Dannans. Midhir will never—"

"Love, you know next to nothing about Aes Sidhe. Just because you take one of their cocks to roost does not make you an authority on the Sidhe. Midhir is dying. Hasn't been seen in decades. Armagh has its spies, you know. Falan, for all of his scheming, does have good timing."

She's stalling now.

The beast inside Una shifted in its sleep.

Not yet, she told it. She worried that to unleash it would be like trying to hit a gnat with a sledgehammer. However, if Aoife didn't make her move soon, Una might implode.

"What's the matter, Aoife? Are you tired?"

She smirked back, and a four-inch gash opened on Una's cheek. "Hardly."

Una swiped at the blood with the back of her hand. "Then let's get to it. Kill me if you can."

Aoife threw out a hand, and Una was tossed backward into a tree trunk. The impact rattled her teeth and cracked her spine. White sparks glittered behind her eyes.

Almost there...

Una struggled to her knees. The rock shifted another few inches, and she heard Aoife grunt with the effort.

That's it.

"Goodbye, Princess," grinned Aoife one last time. With a wrenching, guttural cry, Aoife hurled the two-ton stone at Una with everything she had.

Even if Una attempted to dodge the mass, it was too wide and heavy to be avoided. It hurtled toward her, blotting out the sky overhead. She was unconcerned. The leviathan reared its head, claws unfurling.

Stop, she thought, and the stone froze in midair, hanging as if from an invisible chord. She felt its weight in her mind— heavy as half a city wall— but it might have been a pebble for all the difference it made to her overwhelming Spark. She discovered that she didn't even have to focus on the object to hold it in place. The slow, satisfying smirk she sent Aoife made the other woman pale by nine shades.

"How?" Aoife gasped, incredulous and visibly exhausted.

"Who cares?" laughed Una dryly and thought *Rebound*.

The stone flew backward so quickly that the ground rumbled for a full minute when it struck. Aoife had managed to use her Spark to scramble away, but Una saw her gulping air like a drowning man. A long red trickle of blood dribbled from her right nostril. Her eyes were black pits of fear. Fresh out of sympathy, Una chuckled and looked up at the trees around her. *Up*, she thought. At least fifteen massive trees groaned their way out of the earth, leaves shuddering as their roots snapped from their trunks. Into the air, they rose, held in place by Una's will alone. *Down*, Una thought, and they shot themselves at Aoife like a bevy of spears.

Aoife, the silent menace, the knife in the dark— covered her face and shrieked, "*Within!*" a heartbeat before Una's missiles landed. When the dust settled, Una saw the mound Aoife had erected to protect herself from the impact, but it hadn't been enough. Aoife clawed herself free from a half-excavated crater at the top, below a pile of lance-sized splinters. Bloodied and covered in dirt and splintered wood, she drew in a noisy, grasping breath. Her one remaining eye found Una standing a short distance away. "Wh-at a-re…" she tried to ask, but her jaw was smashed inward and twisted awkwardly to one side.

"I have no clue," answered Una, truthfully. "But I'll say this much; I'm not going to complain." She inhaled long and slow, allowing the current to sweep through every particle of her being. "Give my regards to the Sluagh, cousin. I think you'll find their embrace warmer than you deserve."

Open, she thought, and the dirt below Aoife dropped away, sucking her and all the tree trunks Una had torn from their roots into its gaping pit.

Fold.

Aoife of Armagh gave one last pitiful scream as the earth clapped over her head, sending a spray of splinters, blood, and other tissues into the air in a geyser of gore.

Una stood there for a moment in silence, cataloging what had transpired. She wasn't human any more than Aoife had ever been. Had circumstances differed, perhaps she might have been as polluted a creature, and their situations reversed. Fate, as ever, made japes of everyone.

In the darker reaches of the trees, several pairs of glittering eyes watched her fearfully. In her mind's eye, she knew their terrible shapes and felt nothing. They could not harm her now. Not here.

In the *Oiche Ar Fad*, she might be a god.

Not one to gloat, Una turned toward the Otherworld dawn.

The universe quaked in her steps.

✕

Diarmid could still hear Ruidraghe screaming into the wind behind him. Their skirmish, as expected, took all of five minutes. Whoever had sent him— and Diarmid felt confident he knew which MacNemed would dare— knew very well that a Firesinger, even one as powerful as Ruidraghe, didn't stand a chance against a Skysinger with the great Dagda's blood flowing through his veins. They didn't call Diarmid the Raven King for nothing. No, whoever had sent Ruidraghe had come for Una, not him, and hoped to stall him long enough to get at her. Diarmid hadn't wasted time with the Bolg Brehon, realizing immediately what was afoot. He'd left him on the mountaintop, partly fused to the rocks at the summit. Unfortunately for him, he'd be up there for ages, as long as it would take him to burn through the igneous particles that held the dark, carbon-infused rocks together. Being that igneous rock was harder than granite— it would take decades. That is unless another Skysinger with the ability to tamper with time and air particles happened by. That Diarmid was the only Sidhe Brehon born with this power made him very much doubt that possibility. He frowned at the thought.

Una was no Sidhe.

Yet…

The girl was something new. The sheer impossibility of what he suspected about her could only mean that for all his years and all the fairies he had met— some he'd even sired— none had been born with power approaching the Brehonic, not even a modest Earthsinger. For Una to possess the abilities of a Skysinger, she *should* have been born to a noble, ancient Sidhe lineage of immense power. But such was not so. Her parents and grandparents had been human. Though he did have to admit, whatever went on in the Cloister often produced women with uncanny abilities. He had always been impressed with them and their practical, scientific approach to magic. Regardless, some things should be beyond any mortal, no matter how gifted.

The fact that someone had gone to so much trouble to get to her told him that he was not the only one who knew how horribly powerful Una was. Even he could not summon magic in the Otherworld without incurring a cost. His tiff with Ruidraghe had slowed him, despite the added strength Una had given him so blithely as if she held a personal tap into the internal mechanism of the *Oiche Ar Fad* itself.

Hells, maybe she *did*.

How was the bloody question.

He could sense no Sidhe blood in her essence, and he could always tell. Faerie genes were hardly a boon to the host, even if one was born powerful or gifted. It would corrupt them, haunt them, and often dominate every aspect of their lives. In Mistress Rian's case, he believed the girl funneled the obsessive genetic predilection into her studies, which would explain why she excelled at them and what kept her from the madness that was so common among her kind. In others, like Damek Bishop, who bore no outward deformity, the madness took a darker and more insidious turn. He appeared sane, attractive, clever, even maybe brilliant— but inside, he carried that genetic imbalance in force: the obsession, inhuman ambition, and perversion. Megalomania had ever been a hallmark of the powerful and bored, but in Damek's case, his was exacerbated by his most ancient Sidhe bloodline. If he survived this conflict he had started to glorify himself, he would be afflicted by self-loathing and depression on a scale humans had no metric for. He would either slay himself or become something worse than he was already.

As for Una, he sensed no such thing from her. She was odd, indeed. A bit self-absorbed as most wealthy young women tended to be. Hotheaded at times and a bit authoritarian in her opinions of the world, she was also unfailingly kind, mentally strong, cautious, and ethical. He found that he rather liked her and was more than a little jealous of his errant nephew for his luck. Yet, through all this, she was still mortal. She couldn't be carrying a latent Sidhe gene, but what else could explain her gifts? These were unmistakably Sidhe-born powers.

He swore under his breath for the dozenth time that day. This was a puzzle he had no idea how to solve. It ate at him, now more than ever, and someone wanted her dead badly enough to risk the wrath of *Fiachra Dubh*.

Ahead of him, through the swirling fog he traveled through, he felt a sudden shiver of power that nearly stopped his heart. It was too strong... *too much* to be misconstrued. He had found her!

He stepped from his fragment and into a warzone. Not war as it was in Innisfail, with men rushing at each other with blades or other grisly weapons, but old war, the sort that harkened to the Innisfail before the Transition. What he was looking at now reminded him of the battlefields he'd walked over a thousand years ago. "*Herne*," he breathed, marveling at the utter devastation around him.

Whole trees, some a hundred feet high, had been ripped from their roots as if by a giant's hand and tossed about like so much kindling. He found a dead ghast not a mile from the lakeshore and beyond that, yet more horrors. Here, not just the trees had been uprooted. The ground had been blasted apart to expose gaping pits filled with shredded bracken and splinters. Shorn tree trunks jutted from each like stickpins from a sewing kit.

On top of the dust and the pervading scent of split lumber, the reek of death and blood greeted his nose. He covered his mouth as he approached one curiously constructed mound. A trail of blood and guts spilled from a hole in an unnatural hill just ahead as if a gory spring had burst from its middle. Already, piskies and other Lu Sidhe beasties gathered to lap at the feast. They scattered at his approach but wouldn't go far— this was Ban Sidhe blood, after all. *Old* Sidhe blood, at that.

Fir Bolg blood.

Interesting.

He backed away to appreciate the enormity of the scene fully. What Una had wrought here— for it was surely she who had done this— was a vulgar but Herculean display of power. He looked around, trying to glean any indication of where she had gone. Opalescent eyes gleamed at him by threes on the dark side of the clearing. *Goblins.* Drawn, no doubt, by the overpowering stench of rare, High Sidhe blood. He could hear the repellant creatures' jagged jaws clenching in excitement. They would surely dig up whoever had died in this hole and gorge themselves insensate. They waited a respectful distance away. No Dor Sidhe would dare cross *Fiachra Dubh*.

"You may as well come out," he said.

Shyly, three haggard, misshapen figures moved into the morning moonlight.

"Did you see who did this?"

The largest of the goblins, a fellow with teeth too large and sharp for his mouth, stepped forward, head bowed low. "Smelt her, not saw," it hesitated. "Not your kind, but for them who dwell under the lake."

"Not this one, the other… the victor."

The goblin shuddered. Goblins were famous liars and deceivers and could not help but prevaricate and embellish. It was in their nature. Though, not even the bravest of them would dare lie to the King of Tech Duinn… much. "This one smelt of Sionnovar, *Fiachra Dubh*. We would not try for her clan, be she not dead already."

Diarmid snorted. The first lie.

He raised a hand, and the creature fell to its knobby knees, gasping for breath.

"The next lie will be your last."

"This one be Sionnnovar's girl-child! We think to catch her, but the great lady appear, so we wait. Hope for the best." The other goblins snickered. "But the lady, she do… this." It gestured to the mound of gore. "We scared. She terrible, like you, milord."

The Great Lady, indeed.

"Which way did she go?"

The goblin pointed, its razor-sharp teeth grinding in fear and hunger. Diarmid stilled himself to feel the pull of her power once more.

Of course, this was in the opposite direction the lying little beast had indicated. He turned away, and the goblin screamed behind him as its intestines burst from its deceitful gut. Its fellows wasted no time launching themselves at their fallen brethren, then on to the mound full of the precious nectar that remained of Aoife Ap Sionnovar's mighty Fir Bolg blood.

X

UNA WALKED FOR SO LONG, her feet bled. The power she felt coursing through her might have kept her Spark unbelievably plentiful, but it did little to assuage the fatigue she felt in her bones. She had liberally applied Spark to every wound, causing all but the deepest to close. But as she did so, she realized there were *some* limits to this newfound ability, after all. Her Spark might be boundless, capable of performing any Manipulation she set her mind to with abandon, but the flesh had trouble holding and processing this impossible strength. She could feel the vitality of her human cells wither before this new external energy as if it were sapping her dry from the outside in. This was the opposite of the usual Spark drag and much worse. The more she expended, the more she invited this overwhelming force to shove her human cells aside or away altogether. She felt like she was evaporating, breaking apart in this vacuum; her cells altered and replaced. With every step, she grew stronger and weaker at the same time. The vessel of her body was no longer sufficient to contain her external presence.

Beside a lovely, trickling stream, she finally collapsed. Allowing herself to be bathed in the warm but weak sunlight in the day side of the forest, she shivered in the sweet-smelling grass. Strange, curious creatures flitted overhead. Her eyes drifted closed, and she slept. An unknowable span later, a humming over the thin trickle of water woke her. The little girl she thought she'd seen before smiled back at her. Her large, dark eyes were still and wide as a mirror. Had she been following her? Una felt a dash of fear. Things were never what they seemed in the *Oiche Ar Fad*.

Could she fight if she needed to in this state?

At this rate, your Spark might consume you, she warned herself.

"Poor child," the girl said, her voice at once high and endearing as a child's but earthly and robust as a woman grown. Una was in too much pain and feared to marvel at the sound. With nothing to do but watch her death approach, Una could only gurgle upward at her when the girl came to her side and laid a warm hand against her temple. "You must learn control, or your gifts will devour you."

Where her fingertips brushed the hair back from Una's forehead, she felt a steady calm spread inward, clearing her mind. The sensation radiated downward, uncoiling her muscles and soothing raw nerve endings. Tears of relief spilled from Una's eyes. Whatever the girl had done eased the pain and fatigue to such a degree that it felt like she'd doused a fire in her blood. If she ate her now, at least Una wouldn't die in knots.

But the child did not display any fangs nor appear interested in her mortal flesh.

Instead, she smiled down at Una and sang,

"I knew a place
Far Away
In a dell
Upon the lay...."

She stroked Una's hair.

"A maiden waits near
What does she there?
With the rain in her hair
We may only fear...."

Una thought she'd heard the song before but couldn't recall where. The song was a balm, warming the cold cockles of her heart. She wandered in the clouds above.

"Will she dance
Or will she sing
Who, oh who knows these things?"

It was a nursery rhyme. That was it.

Someone used to sing it to her when she was a bairn.

"He comes now, Una. All will be well. I will have his vow."

Una believed her but was too exhausted to ask how or why.

She sank into a lovely dream, with the girl's fingers combing through her curls.

X

Diarmid felt a strange presence he could not place, something ancient and nearly familiar. He braced for another surprise, but as he emerged from the fragment, he found a small girl staring up at him with huge, liquid black eyes. His brow furrowed. The girl seemed and smelled like nothing but another human. He could sense neither the undeniable magnetism of Sidhe blood in her nor the taint of the Lu Sidhe, who were native to the Otherworld. Yet, she was *not* human. If anything, he could feel the oppression of mind-boggling age— non-threatening but overpowering nonetheless.

Una lay just beyond her, beside a bubbling stream, sleeping peacefully.

The girl had woven flowers into a garland for Una's tangled, bloodied hair. Humming while she worked, her eyes never left Diarmid's face. "So, you've come for her now?"

Diarmid moved slowly into the pleasant wildflower scented dell. "Who are you?"

The tune she hummed sounded so familiar. She wove another ring of violets around Una's temple, unconcerned by his authoritative tone. "You know who I am, Diarmid, son of Crom Dagda— even if you think you do not."

He had no clue how to interpret that. "I assure you; I would remember."

"Perhaps it'll come to you when it must?"

He frowned. "It is ill manners indeed to insult a king, child."

She laughed. The sound raised the hairs all over his body. He suddenly felt very small, young, and out of sorts. Diarmid had never felt so… even while his father lived. He took the slightest step backward. "You are not in any position to make demands of me, boy."

In his mind's eye, he had a sudden impression of a shape, a behemoth afterimage that blotted out the sky, the earth below, and the stars beyond. Its mass obscured all. It snatched the air from his lungs and nearly stole the ground beneath his feet. He blinked, and the image dissipated. She was just a girl again, innocent and unafraid.

"*What* are you?" he gasped.

"More than you will ever be, Brehon, and I am disinclined to submit to your fumbling interrogations. Be still and hear me while I deign your presence."

Diarmid sputtered. He was King of Tech Duinn! Whatever this thing was, it had no right to insult him in his domain. He opened his mouth, but she cut him off.

"It is hardly your realm, Mac Crom," she sneered. "Though I sometimes find your people's arrogance amusing, I find it taxing just now."

"My father wrought this realm from his blood, carved my people's future from his bones. The *Oiche Ar Fad* is mine! I don't know what or who you are, but you will give her to me now or—"

"As I said, pure arrogance," she giggled. "But, I will let you take her for now."

Suddenly, she was behind him. Her eyes glowed amber, pupils mere slits against her irises, like some mythic beast of old. Her small hand shot out, clapping over his forearm with a strength that dried his throat. He could feel her power, the staggering, shocking, near cosmic *vastness* of her. He sank to his knees under her limitless gaze.

"Be warned, ambitious thing that you are. I give her to your ilk for a time only. You may not keep her. None of your line should dare to try. She is my child, my gift. Try to harness that at your peril."

"I… I don't understand."

She looked away as if seeing a horror above his head. "It comes. You cannot stop it; this time, all shall be consumed. The girl is the sole hope you have. She is the bridge, the gift I leave you. You will return her to me, in the end, or perish."

Diarmid's heart spun under the obliterating weight of her fingers. "What comes?"

"Death."

Just as swiftly as she'd touched him, she disappeared. The pressure that ground him into the earth vanished with her presence. His head cleared, and the blood pumped once more through his veins. He fell forward onto his hands, a most undignified position for a Sidhe king of his age and station. What *was* that thing? And what in the nine hells had she meant by 'death'? Of course, it was *his* realm! The implication that Crom Dagda hadn't created it was absurd. Diarmid had been there! He remembered every detail as if it had happened yesterday. Yet… He was a Brehon, the highest in the land. He could taste a mistruth, could smell one, as easily as breathing. He could discern no falsehoods from his strange visitor. She had told no lies. Whomever she was— *whatever* she was, every word she said rang true. Shaken to his core, Diarmid swallowed his confusion down deep. Now was not the time. He would ponder these strange events as soon as he returned his nephew to Aes Sidhe, and the latest Milesian threat to the Daoine Sidhe was laid to rest.

Gently, he lifted Una into his arms. She was such a small, slight woman for all her mystifying strength. How could anything so fragile, so mortal, carry what she did inside and not be broken apart?

He didn't know.

Perhaps as the creature vowed, he wasn't meant to? Troubled, he moved into the fragment, his thoughts torn between death and a pair of dragon-colored eyes.

Sacrifice

n.e. 509
25 ban apesa
Rosweal

Kaer Yin slashed through a Souther Steel Corps line toward the battlements' northwest corner. He leaped from the higher stone rampart to the lower, hastily assembled western wall, which bore the charcoal-tinted remnants of yesterday's catastrophic blaze. These Corpsmen were fresher and more skilled than the infantryman who littered the streets and ramparts in various stages of death. They hit back a lot harder too. Though far from beat, Kaer Yin had to admit that his arms weren't what they were at the start. He hadn't slept in days, and his legs burned, worn from pumping pure, unfiltered adrenaline for almost fifty straight hours. His hands felt like two heavy stones.

But the Southers didn't stop coming.

Left, right, over, under, and aside; he moved through men with every breath. He killed with a sword, fists, feet, fingers, and bow. Every way he turned, another combatant came at him, thus, another man's blood stained his skin, clothes, hair, and steel. Everyplace he stepped, a pile of misspent bodies sprang up, and there seemed no end to the mind-numbing monotony of battle.

One fellow ran straight at him, his gauntleted fist swinging forward to ram Kaer Yin's skull onto his sabre, but Kaer Yin spun away, jerking another Corpsman forward instead. The two men died in shock, having killed each other instead. Another he took through the eye. Yet another, through the skull below the jaw. On and on it went this gruesome symphony of death.

Below, in the cross-lane behind Wanderer's Alley, he saw what he had both been hoping and dreading to see ever since the horns blew over the Western Gate, what felt like many hours gone by. A limping, skulking line of Rosweal's citizens running as fast they could manage in knee-deep snow. They were pursued by many fully armored soldiers and some wild-eyed, undisciplined infantrymen who had managed to survive everything the defenders had thrown at them until now. Kaer Yin dodged a wildly thrown dagger and rolled back up with Nemain's heft, delivering a backhanded slash that severed the Souther's neck almost to the shoulder. He jumped over the next man on his way to the ladder, which was clogged with men fighting up and down its rungs. He didn't have the time to spar with them.

"Shar!" he called ahead to Una's new (and only) liegeman. Shar was elbow-deep in a Souther's ribcage. His head snapped up— a grisly sight indeed. "*Ullmhaigh clúdach a thabhairt!*[6]"

Shar nodded, then bellowed orders to the Sidhe beyond him. They stepped away from the wall in twos, every second and third bow on the rampart turning from hand-to-hand combat to aim at the rear of the fleeing citizens on the ground.

"*Tine ag toil!*[7]" Kaer Yin ordered, leaping onto the ladder from a distance of at least five feet, raining death on any Southers barring his way down its rungs. By the time his boots crunched into the snow, ten more men lay dead at its base. From ground level, the fighting was thinner and less intense, which was owed almost entirely to Fionn. The barrels had played their part by relieving Bishop of his Bolg *garda*, but Fionn and his brilliant cavalrymen had done the hard work. They'd ridden down scores of men faster than Kaer Yin could light pitch. Standing soldiers were no match for mounted knights, less so when clogged into narrow lanes and alleys only a few handspans wide. Everywhere Kaer Yin looked,

---

[6] 'Get ready to give cover!'
[7] "Fire at will!"

dead Southers lay trampled, cleaved, or smashed into the snow-ridden cobbles. He couldn't help but smile at that. Bishop had thrown in his last little surprise, costing them, but the number of upright defenders was beginning to outpace the pockets of fighting Southers.

They were winning!

He shoved that surge of relief way down deep.

They still had nearly two hundred fresh Corpsmen to deal with, and at least thirty of those were now chasing Rosweal's women and children toward their sole exit. He saw Robin racing toward those Corpsmen from the southeast with a small but lethal host of hardened Greenmakers at his back. The whistle he'd blown like mad swung at his neck and glinted in the fading light.

Time was almost up.

As he ran downhill to help cover the people's exit, Kaer Yin looked around for the figure he was sure he'd seen running toward him earlier. How long ago now? An hour, less?

So many groups fought in close quarters here that he could hardly distinguish any individuals among them.

Where are you, Damek?

He scanned the whole north end of town, from Taverner's Alley to the Hilltop Dells. *I don't want you to miss what happens next.*

Kaer Yin figured Una's cousin must have been caught in another skirmish or had already run back to the rear of his scattered force to regroup. Either that or he was dead... Herne willing. That angry, tortured look he'd given him went far beyond the calculated, level-headedness Kaer Yin had come to expect from the self-appointed 'King of Eire.' Even the filthy, murderous glare he'd shot him at parlay did not come close.

If Kaer Yin had to guess, that large, brave man he'd been forced to kill upon their escape from the farmstead sprang to mind. He hadn't wanted to kill him more than any man, but he'd seen the two of them together and understood him as Damek's right hand. Martin O'Rearden had been his name, Kaer Yin vaguely recalled from the parley. When they'd caught sight of each other earlier, the fury in Damek's eyes had burned with profound grief. But Kaer Yin didn't have much time to mull any of that over now.

He caught sight of Eva, huffing and clutching a screaming child under each arm, as she trudged uphill toward the gatehouse. At least fifty people in varying stages of health limped along after her. She saw him and nodded as if he were right on time. Rose sidled up behind her, trailing a gaggle of filthy children. "Ben!" He darted to them, catching Eva before she stumbled into the blackened snow. The children wriggled, red-faced and terrified. She had a wide gash over one leg, dying her once-white skirts a sopping, red-brown.

"What happened? Mel was up on the wall, last I saw."

He didn't like the look of that wound at all. If it went untreated—

Eva clutched at his hopelessly filthy tunic. "They're getting between us," she exclaimed, putting everything she had left into getting the kids up the slippery hill and through the cracked gate as fast as she could.

Soldiers harried those who followed their group from the sides, and a knot at the rear seemed to grow in number and ferocity, like wolves scenting prey. Kaer Yin shoved the women toward the gate, tossing his exquisite, priceless bow into the bushes beneath the shadow of the stone wall, along with his empty quiver.

Eva paused long enough to grip his arm hard. Her eyes were flat sheets of golden glass. "It isn't over. Remember."

"I don't understand."

Rose grasped her hand. "She's been this way for a while, but we wouldn't have made it this far without her. The things she made them soldiers do, Ben." She shivered. "Dunno who'm more afraid of, her, or yer Lady."

Eva's sightless eyes stared straight ahead at Kaer Yin, seeing things he couldn't see. Una had told him about this. They didn't have time to discuss her vision, but Una had said her prophecies were rarely wrong. He felt the blood drain from his face. "You need to go, now!"

Eva dug her nails into his arm. "It isn't *over*."

"Rose, take her and go!" With Nemain in his right hand, he drew a lark with his left. "Shar!" he roared upward. Many accurately aimed

Sidhe arrows answered, mowing down leering, redfaced soldiers like they'd simply been standing still, waiting to die. Another volley and another until Kaer Yin counted three dozen Roswellians making it safely through the gate. Robin neared from the far side, interrupting another pursuing force with gusto. Kaer Yin decided where he was most needed and ran downhill to give the Greenmakers a much-needed hand. He shoved more people at the gate on his way past them until he lost count.

Suddenly, Jan Fir's bloody face emerged from the cross at Wanderer's Alley with Barb and big Dabney wheezing behind him. She sobbed when she caught sight of him, and he couldn't help but notice that Dabney was carrying her clumsily in one shredded arm. He opened his mouth to ask what happened when he saw Tam Lin and what— *who* it was he carried— and the state she was in.

Kaer Yin's heart stopped altogether. "*No.* Is she—"

"Alive," replied his cousin. "But not for long if I don't get her out of here.

Kaer Yin's eyes burned with tears he could not shed. He reached out to touch her face. Her right cheek was swollen black and cold as ice. Her clothes were torn from what he could spy beneath Tam Lin's gore-stained cloak. "Was she—"

"Near enough. She drank something. I don't have long."

Men were spilling from the alleys and coalescing nearby.

"Barb?"

"Yeah, love?" she answered. Her voice was small.

"Still with me?"

She gave a hacking cough that said otherwise. "Always."

He patted Dabney's back and gave Rian's frozen fingers a squeeze, but his attention was on Tam Lin. "Get them over. Do what you must."

"I will."

"Jan Fir, Niall, with me. The rest of you follow Tam Lin out. We'll cover you."

He stepped in front of Tam Lin, putting all worry and sadness from his mind. There were still fifteen stragglers being harried uphill on the way out. He met Robin's eyes over the mass of Corpsmen racing up at him. He thought he caught Robin's nod.

Nearly time now.

Jan Fir growled, slinging blood from his larks. Kaer Yin knew he could count on him to help thin the Souther herd.

They went to work.

⚔

Making his fourth circuit around the inner walls, Fionn reined in at the remnants of the Eastern Gate. His first shield commander drew up beside him, spattered red from his forehead to his horse's pale forelegs. The underbellies of each beast were a grim sight from the carnage they had wreaked in their passage. There was not much left to do at that end of the city now, save tread over the corpses of fallen Southers or watch them flee through the rubble like beaten dogs. Fionn couldn't hold back an ear-splitting grin. They'd done their work well. His Wild Hunt were the finest horsemen in Innisfail, and let none forget it. He had never been prouder of his men than he was at that moment. For a force less than two hundred strong, to defeat an army over five times their number— with so little loss of life— was nothing short of a triumph.

He whispered prayers to Brida for watching over them.

"Shall I sound the horns, My Lord?" asked Diel, also beaming with pride.

"Aye, let us return to the Western Gate once more to drive the remaining rats into the nice warren we've made for them."

Fionn couldn't wait to see the look on Midhir's son's face. Indeed, the Prince of Innisfail was alive and hale. As much as he was hesitant to admit it, the man *was* a gifted commander, and in combat, well, he had yet to see his equal. Fionn would never tell him this, of course. He preferred the stony, tight-lipped respect they'd developed over the last few days. He doubted he would ever call the Ard Ri's heir a 'friend,' but in his heart, he realized he would be pleased to call him *'Tiarne.'*

He was still smiling when he and his four nearest turned about to ride back west through the alleyways. Diel blew his horn loudly and proudly for all to hear. The enemy was in retreat! Lord Bishop's cavalry had long since given up the ghost, and now, only the most determined, bloodthirsty infantry and stubborn Corpsmen were left in various pockets throughout the city. The alley narrowed, forcing Diel in front, his mount dancing gingerly over fallen bodies in the snow and slimly avoiding overhanging awnings, eaves, and shutters. A third blast— the horns on the North Wall then sounded in answer. It wouldn't be long now. Fionn and his knights crept down the twisting alleyway for their last circuit around the wall when something heavy struck Fionn full in the chest. He went flying backward several feet. Knocked clear of his horse, he landed flat on his back. If it hadn't been for the snow, the fall alone would have cracked his spine like an egg. His horse screamed— Winter, his name was— Fionn heard him go down with a last pitiful whinny. Fionn tried to get up, but he couldn't move. He felt something warm and wet under him but could see nothing but the snow falling through a crack in the twilight sky. He thought he heard Ciaran shout his name… but from far away, like the wind through a glen.

A dark smudge appeared above him, and he knew.

The shape reared back.

He closed his eyes before it came down.

✗

KAER YIN HEARD FIONN'S HORNS as he pried Nemain's edge from a Corpsman's skull. Robin was at his elbow, dealing death in every direction with a fallen Souther's sabre. Jan Fir stood at his back, guarding the iron grate that led into the gatehouse and the tunnel that wormed its way below the north wall. He had one hand tucked into his cuirass; his tunic dripped blood down his bare arm to the torn sleeve at his elbow. Still, even one-handed, Jan Fir Bres was no easy victim. He'd slain more than his fair share of Southers with only a single lark. There were only a few dozen enemies left in their immediate vicinity, and from their uphill vantage, perhaps four hundred Southers left to fight in the streets, much less on the walls. Their numbers were far better matched now!

With Fionn's horns, Kaer Yin knew the Southers had already begun to retreat. Bishop's cavalry was either dead or fled, and only foot soldiers and clusters of Corpsmen were left. The Dannans had outshot their archers hours ago, and those who remained were well outside the wall. All told, Damek's force had dropped to a mere tenth of its original number. Most seemed to have fled after so many of their infantry had been swallowed up in the streets, and the rest had either been cut down or had never bothered to clamber over the walls in the first place. It was nearly over now! There was only one move Kaer Yin had left to make... one surprise left in store for Bethany's thieving, pillaging, raping throng of overconfident thugs.

He rushed for the ladder again, about fifty paces from the gatehouse, and nodded to Jan Fir, who kicked the portal closed so hard it dented inward. Robin slid the iron lock in place, smashing the knob inward with the butt of his sabre. No chance anyone would get that door open in time to retrieve any of the people who'd fled that way. Both soon followed close at Kaer Yin's heels. "Right. Get into position," he barked over his shoulder, killing two Corpsmen who blocked their path to the ladder and their last stand. "Now, Robin!" he added, meeting another sword thrust crosswise, which sent the sabre's tip glancing from Nemain's wider blade. With his right hand, he reached down to hamstring his attacker, then drove his lark to the hilt through the man's screaming mouth.

Robin reached for the whistle around his neck but froze before he could set it to his lips. He stared straight ahead, showing teeth. Kaer Yin followed his gaze, seeing a familiar shorn head making its way up the wide cross lane toward them. The Corps Commander Ridley did not know Robin, who glared bloody murder at him over the smattering of bodies struggling between them. Ridley's eyes were all for Kaer Yin, who recognized him from the wall on sight. Robin yanked the whistle from his neck and threw it to Kaer Yin, who was forced to dodge a blow to catch it. "I want this one, Ben," Robin said, spitting a wad of blood from his mouth, then placing himself between them. "I'll be right behind ye."

Kaer Yin didn't bother to argue. Robin was the most dangerous Milesian he'd ever met. Still. He paused at the ladder. "Don't you dare die, damn you. You still owe me fifty fainne for porter and uishge!"

Robin spared him a look that said exactly where he could shove that remark.

Kaer Yin was already up to the rampart before he blew the whistle in earnest.

X

Damek heard the whistle just as he and ten of his remaining Corps made it back to the North Wall. That he'd all but lost this fight in Rosweal's twisting lanes was not lost on him or any of his men. It had been a long hour since he realized he'd been beaten. His cavalry broken, his archers dead or deserted, and at least a thousand infantry and yeomen lay dead within the clever trap that the Prince had made of Rosweal. Many of Damek's commanders outside the walls had blown the retreat already, despite his fervent orders to send in more men to deal with this rabble. Disloyal traitors, the lot. He had ordered no withdrawal. Would not. While he drew breath, he would not allow that grinning silver-haired cunt to see his backside.

Kaer Yin Adair might yet have won the day, but that didn't mean he'd live to crow about it. Damek would have his head if it were the last thing he ever did.

His Corpsmen seemed to share his sentiments. With grim, determined murder glowing in their eyes, they trekked to the wall with weapons stained red with blood. Some Southers might be soft-bellied cowards when faced with a serious challenge, but not Bethany's Steel Corps. They would march to their death before they'd turn tail and run. Damek still had the numbers, if not by much. If he could dismantle the Sidhe leadership by killing their commanders, his Corpsmen alone could yet tame this fracas. But this was less about winning at this point, less still about saving face.

Whatever happened, he had one goal in mind.

As they neared the North Wall, elbow to elbow, shield to shield, Damek scanned the smoky ramparts for his foe. The rage in his heart was a propeller, driving him forward. He couldn't look away now if he tried. His men gnashed their teeth in a similar vein. None seemed cowed by all the losses they'd taken this day.

Vengeance was all.

At last, his eyes found what he sought. A hundred paces down the stone rampart whirled the bright-haired Dannan he longed most to behold. The hatred in his mouth burned. "Draw them back!" he said with a calm he did not feel. "We march in unison."

He watched Kaer Yin move down the wall toward him and saw him blowing that absurd, irritating whistle. The retreat, Damek presumed with a tight smile.

About fucking time!

That still wouldn't save him.

"Single cover!" Damek ordered, drawing the stragglers back into their ranks and behind the protection of their long shields. They gathered another thirty soldiers west along the wall, with more queuing up every moment. Now a shielded phalanx, they cut down everything in their path on their way uphill. Damek barely blinked. He watched Kaer Yin swing his two-hander around him like a dancer twirling a ribbon and smiled. He would fucking have him now, by Reason. Nothing in the way that he couldn't trample or climb.

I've got you, you bastard.

I've got you.

Kaer Yin blew the whistle a third time, and defenders who'd been fighting for all they were worth suddenly backed away— abandoning each fight, some midstroke. Without ado, they tucked tail and ran for the western rampart in a tangle, heedless of any chase. Many died in the attempt; many did not. Not bogged down by heavy shields or armor, the Dannans were light enough to get up and down their ladders at a fair clip.

Damek's heart stilled in his chest. He glanced around, eyes darting between lanes, noting abandoned houses, darkened windows, and empty streets. No light save the stubborn smolder of trees miles distant. Where was O'More's cavalry? Had they pursued his fleeing infantry outside the walls? Everywhere he looked, Rosweal was deserted. Nothing was left alive in any lane, alley, or structure save his men. On a sharp breath, he glanced upward to witness a host of Sidhe archers line the western ramparts along the wall. A snap and hiss, and each arrow flared to life. The smell of pitch coated the air as two dozen arrows caught flame.

Damek's eyes bulged.

He threw out a hand as if that would help.

Fuck!

"Break ranks!" he bellowed. "Retreat, retreat!"

Too late.

The arrows whizzed overhead, bursting through open windows and overhanging gutter. Why hadn't he thought about the fucking windows?

"Gods damn you all! *Run!*" His shout drowned in the terrible pops he heard go off in the remaining neighborhood behind him. The second floors of several buildings burst into loud, spitting flames. Structures shuddered, and he backpedaled, throwing himself behind a wagon beneath the stone wall and covering his head with his hands. His men either followed suit or stood dumbfounded as half the buildings in Rosweal blasted apart from the inside out or top-down. The chorus of explosions buckled the street beneath their feet, sending them flying upward, tossed into a more extraordinary succession of blasts that ripped them to burning shreds in a matter of heartbeats. Stones catapulted into the snow-laden sky, at least twenty feet overhead, along with substantial wooden pylons, joists, and floorboards scattered to dangerous, flaming wreckage.

Damek howled in fury and pain as the wagon rolled over him, burying him beneath a mountain of piping hot debris.

Crown of Ashes

n.e. 509
25 ban apesa
Rosweal

Tam Lin waited for the explosions to quiet before deciding it was safe enough for his charges on the riverbank. He nodded to his Blood Eagles to climb back up the wall. There was still work to be done in the city, he knew very well. Not satisfied with a straightforward victory, The Tuatha De Dannan would crush this upstart king and all hope of another like him, here, this night. Kaer Yin was slow to anger despite his general air of perturbation but woe to any fool that thought him weak. This was the same man who had smashed every rebellion the Southers had mustered for nearly a thousand years.

Tam Lin hoped his cousin had the bastard's head in burlap by now. With a deep breath, he let go of Rian's hand to examine her wounds. She'd taken several blows to her face that bore broken bones, a seeping gash to her side, and the back of her head was swollen and black from where her would-be rapist had smashed her head into the cobbles. This was also work that needed doing, and since Diarmid had seemed to bugger off on holiday with Kaer Yin's girl, there was no one here with the blood to do it but him. Una's aunt was no use. She'd taken a spear to the thigh and was in grave danger of bleeding out before they made it across the river. The girl Rose was doing her best to treat her, but she hadn't moved save for the occasional moan. As for Rian, her external wounds were serious, but these weren't what was killing her. Barb had said she'd downed a bottle of poison. He'd waited to act in case she might live unaided, but she grew colder by the minute. He took a second breath and nodded.

No one else here with the blood.

Decision made, he knelt and scooped Rian up from the clammy riverbank. She weighed less than she had an hour ago if that were possible. He carried her to a small curragh moored nearby. Barb came at him like a furious gnat, for all that she could barely walk herself. "What are ye *doin*!" she spat, clawing at him. "Ye shouldn't move her. She's bleedin' inside her skull!"

He shoved Barb gently against Dabney, who hooked a meaty arm around her lest she collapse. "Get in the boat with as many kids as you can manage." Tam Lin's tone brooked no refusal. Dabney hefted Barb beside Rian before helping several frail women and children into the far end. Each stared up at the red and black stained prince with owlish eyes. He could guess what he looked like to them. Barb curled herself around Rian protectively. There weren't enough boats for everyone, meaning many healthy adults would have to risk the icy current or wait ashore for any Souther stragglers that may attempt to drag them off for sport or ransom. No help for that either, as no plan was perfect.

Sighing, he pushed the little boat into the water, just shy of the current. The river's chill seeped into his trousers above the knees, but he scarcely felt it.

You can't let her die.

If he allowed himself to feel anything right about then, the fact would singe his nerves with rage. Why should it be him? He was the least talented of his entire cursed bloodline. She deserved better.

Yet... he thought.

You're the only one here.

He stared at her like a broken bird he wasn't sure wouldn't be better off under a rock. Barb saw the expression on his face and frowned. "I don't like the look o' ye just now."

"I've never done this before."

"Forgive me. She's gonna die slow if the belladonna doesn't do her first," she choked back a sob. "You're right. Sweet lamb deserves a rest."

Whatever she'd just said sent hordes of flies buzzing in his ears. His thoughts clouded. This furious little thing had a twisted foot, an angry brow, wits as sharp as any blade, and a tongue to match. Infuriating. Loyal. Rude. True. Ugly. Lovely. Errant. Wise.

He realized then he wanted her to live.

More than that, though, he did not have the words.

Tam Lin O'Ruiadh did not speak such a language.

Kaer Yin, you bastard.

With a groan, he reached down and dug his fingers into the mud just below the waterline, whispering ancient odes he'd heard only once when they were spoken over his mother's sickbed. She'd taken an arrow wound on a raid into the midlands, and were it not for his uncle Midhir, she would have died then. In the end, she sailed away to Tir Na Nog with her sisters and away from his father forever.

The Dagda blessed our family with this burden, Midhir had said. *I use it now not for your mother, nor your father, but for you, my boy. May it teach you balance.* The Ard Ri had clapped him on the shoulder, looking deep into his eyes. *There is no life without sacrifice.*

Tam Lin withdrew the mud, smearing it between his palms. He drew his dagger along his wrist, letting the blood and soil mingle in his hands.

Barb drew Rian close as if to croon to her, but Tam Lin ignored her.

Over Rian's side, he packed the mixture, then the ballooning wound at the base of her skull, and the myriad cuts along her collarbone, face, and finally the ruin of her brow. These, he knew, were only the visible hurts. What lurked inside was far worse and final an agent than mere cuts and bruises. Gently he pried her lips open to drag a bit of the mixture over her teeth, satisfied that some had worked itself into her mouth. He closed his eyes, drawing the words inside himself, then imagined them flowing down his arm and into her heart, from his flesh to hers.

Blood is first, said the Midhir in his memory.

And Crom's is sacred.

When the last line had been uttered, Tam Lin didn't have to wait long.

His knees buckled, and he sagged against the boat, boots trailing sideways in the current. Dabney's massive hand caught him before his head could dip beneath the surface. A good thing, too, for Tam Lin would surely have drowned. He had *never* felt anything like this. The bones in his face creaked under new pressure. A bright flash of stars swirled in his vision as if his head had been cracked against a stone wall. He gasped for air as the rush of black belladonna sped through his blood toward his heart. Dabney held him aloft while he flapped around like a dying fish.

"What in the *hells* did ye just do?" Barb demanded, agog.

Tam Lin couldn't answer for several minutes because of his impending death, but then as suddenly as it accosted him, it lessened until it stopped, leaving aches and pain behind— if no immediate threat of doom. He breathed a bit easier and let himself dangle from the side of the boat for a few minutes, exhausted and feeling worse than he ever had… but better than he should. He wiped a trickle of fresh blood from his nose.

"What did you do?" Barb repeated.

Get up, he silently commanded himself. After a moment, he managed to push himself upright without vomiting. Gods, he felt like hammered shite. "What needed doing. Take care of her," he told Barb, turning away. He would ignore the pain. He had other business.

A cold, clammy hand snaked out of the boat to clutch at his fingers.

Rian's pale, bruised (but no longer broken) face stared up at him. "T-the cost!"

He smiled at her with genuine relief. "Was worth it. It'll take more than that to kill the mighty Prince of Connaught." He winked with an eye half swollen shut, then shook himself and shuffled onshore with renewed purpose.

"Wait!" she cried. "Where are you going in that state?"

"To watch my fool cousin's back, where else?"

With the north end of Rosweal in flames, all that was left for Kaer Yin and his archers to do was to pick off any stragglers that tried to climb the wall to escape the blaze. The Southers had come here dealing fire, and now they were trapped in a hell of their own design. Kaer Yin has always been a great fan of irony. Any Southers who made it through the gap in the Navan Gate hours before could count themselves lucky. Dannan archers made short work of any Corpsmen who managed to stumble out of the inferno unscathed, and at this stage, the act was mercy for most. Those who hadn't been blown apart in the recent explosion wandered the streets in such a state of deformity and shock that the arrows must have been a relief. None of the Sidhe were feeling very sympathetic to the Southers' plight after nearly three straight days of violence… but neither did they revel in misery. Screams did not make pleasant music.

The day was a red, unequivocal rout!

Every goad, every trap Rosweal's defenders had lain, had achieved the impossible— the obliteration of Damek Bishop's incredibly numerous vanguard. They had not only survived this vicious assault, but they had bloody well won! So much for Bishop's advanced artillery, superior weaponry, and numbers.

He'd suffered as ignominious a defeat as one could at the hands of a ragtag group of poachers and thieves led by a smattering of Sidhe warriors. They had done it! Nothing short of a miracle, considering Roswell had been outmanned nearly five to one. Kaer Yin was almost too relieved to bother killing any more Southers. As it was, only the very determined had the bollocks to climb the wall in search of vengeance, and the rest were either grievously wounded or fleeing for their lives. Besides, he was bloody tired. Nemain felt like a two-stone weight in his hands, and the air in his lungs tasted of blood and charcoal. He needed a nice warm place to lie down and sleep a week or more away. Frankly, he was beginning to feel a *wee* bit sorry for the Southers. They had been led to this backwater at the edge of their world by a lie—the promise of a great glory that was not to be— not today— not for them.

Not at Rosweal!

He turned, remembering that half the town was burning and most of the other half was already burnt black or in pieces. These were people's homes, their livelihoods, their very lives. He had to remind himself that a victory at such cost was not so cheap that it bore something as crude as levity. Even a well-earned moment of gloating glee had to be tempered by the lives lost to achieve it.

Jan Fir strode toward him through the haze. The look on his face mirrored Kaer Yin's sentiments. They'd been fighting back-to-back through most of the day, and Kaer Yin thanked Herne his brother-in-law had had the grace to come to Eire with Fionn. It was not every day that a King should bleed for a group of miscreant mortals, but bleed he had. His arms trailed a bit at his side, blackened and swollen. Still, he flashed white teeth at Kaer Yin, who returned the gesture. But alarm flickered in the depth of Jan Fir's green eyes, and he frowned. Kaer Yin's head swiveled around to see what he was looking at.

A booted foot connected with the back of his left leg, making a crunch. Kaer Yin cried out and threw himself forward into a rolling dive, just in time to narrowly miss the sword thrust that came from behind him. The air whistled in his ear as the blade swept past. Grimacing in pain, he watched as Damek emerged from the smoke beneath a light but a steady dusting of fresh, clean snow.

Damek was wounded— badly, clutching the dented, singed remains of his formerly shiny breastplate. His hands and one side of his face were pocked with severe burns, and his bare right arm that held his sabre wasn't much more than charred meat; what remained of his cloak dangled from his back in strips. Most of his hair had been singed off.

Kaer Yin had never been so glad to see someone in his life. "Good! I would hate for you to have missed any of this!" He held his hand out to the puttering flames below. The snow would again save Rosweal from further damage— as he'd hoped it would.

Damek made a rude sound. "It doesn't matter to me how many you killed today or yesterday, you Dannan cunt." His voice shook with a rage Kaer Yin knew all too well. With grief. He had been right. That big man *had* been the Lord of Clare's weak point.

And all that fury had cost him thousands of men and, likely, a crown.

"These men are replaceable," he went on. "As long as *you* die— as long as I can carry *your* head out of here tonight— I'll count this a worthwhile endeavor." He slid his right foot forward, leaving a black streak against the snow, a high guard. "I think I'll fuck *my bride* on a bed carved from your lovely bones. What do you say? Maybe we'll drink a toast out of your skull at her coronation?"

"I wonder if you can smell the shit as it spills from your mouth, boy?" Kaer Yin laughed.

Damek smiled back mirthlessly. "Did she tell you that she bore me a child, Your Highness?"

Kaer Yin stopped. His grin faltered.

"That's right. Our marriage was consummated, making it a legal arrangement in *whatever bloody court* you hope to contest it in. All of this," he waved his hand. "Is for naught. You jumped in the middle of a family squabble for a woman you could never hope to understand." He stared straight ahead, eyes dark as pitch. "Did she tell you my daughter was four years old when she died? Una doesn't know I know. Her name was Zeah. She had black hair, like me."

It took a while for Kaer Yin to find his voice. "Una is a free woman, Damek. You did not own her then and don't own her now. You had many chances to respect her and spat on all of them. *That* is the only law I know."

"Everything I've done has been for her, for Zeah… for all the children we may yet bring into this world. No Patricks to twist the law to suit his whims, no High King to flatter, no Aes Sidhe to lord over Eire's good, honest people. *We* were born to rule here, to found a new dynasty, to lead our people out of the bloody dark age your kind have built for them."

"You'd have me believe you betray her for her own good?"

"Giving her a crown is hardly a betrayal."

"Tell that to the women of Tairngare, all of whom your grandmother destroyed— with your help. You knew what you were doing when you allied with Armagh. How many of Una's people, her family, have died for your greed?"

Damek shifted where he stood, hesitating.

Kaer Yin continued, "I can see you struggle with the concept of selflessness, Damek. For someone who claims to have committed every sin for the benefit of someone else, that someone seems to have suffered most for each of them."

"I don't—"

"None of this is love. Using someone to gain power is not love. Hurting someone for hurting you is not love. Refusing to respect someone's decisions is not love. *Murdering thousands is not love.* You have done absolutely *nothing* for Una, save take from her, exploit her name, and destroy what she cares for. How can you honestly tell me you have aggrandized yourself… *for her*?"

Damek was silent for a moment, teetering between emotions Kaer Yin could not discern. After a few breaths, he finally laughed a dry sound. "You're just like *him*. You're using her too, same as he did, as her grandmother did, her aunts— everyone who has ever met her. Deny it. I dare you."

It was Kaer Yin's turn to stew in culpability for a spanse. While he chewed on his retort, one of Damek's Corpsmen ran up to Damek and placed a hand on his shoulder. He opened his mouth to shout something in his ear, but Damek shrugged his hand off, drew a dagger from his belt, and shoved it into the soldier's throat without a backward glance. As he withdrew the blade from his dumbfounded subordinate, he didn't watch him fall. His hateful glare was all for Kaer Yin.

"*Ard Tiarne*!" Jan Fir shouted, clutching his lark in his good hand.

Kaer Yin threw a hand out. "Don't interfere!"

"Well? Tell me a lie, son of Midhir. Tell me all of this," he wagged his dagger back and forth. "Didn't start with that little *geis* you earned yourself at Dumnain. Tell me that you never meant to use her to better *your* position. Tell me that you, the most famous butcher Eire has ever known— that you fight for her out of the kindness of your heart."

"What's between us is not your business."

"Fucking hypocrite. Now *that* is living up to my expectations of you." He snorted and adjusted his guard, expression hard. "Are you ready? Talking to you is boring the shite out of me."

Kaer Yin nodded, swinging Nemain up over his shoulder. "I thought you'd never ask." He shot forward so fast that he might have been an arrow.

X

Robin was exhausted. He had never gone so long, or so hard, without sleep. He'd never know how High Elves did this shite— making it look so bloody easy. Well, most of 'em, anyway. He fought off two burned Corpsmen trying to drag him and the Dannan he carried from the ladder. Thankfully, the two Southers were so wounded they didn't stand a chance, even one-handed. They'd come for the ladder as he had, looking to escape the smoke in the city below. His eyes and tongue stung something awful; even with the torn scrap of tunic he'd tied over his nose and mouth, he had trouble breathing without coughing. The Sidhe on his back— Shar, if Robin recalled correctly— was nearly beyond that now. He'd almost dropped him in the last tussle, and it took a few precious minutes of hacking and coughing to right him again.

He'd dragged the elf a good twenty yards along the wall already, and the big bastard wasn't getting any lighter. Shar had saved his life from the sneaky dagger thrust Ridley had tried to plunge into his guts by shooting the red-bearded fucker in the face from a dozen yards. Winded and disoriented by the smoke and chaos, Robin hadn't had a moment to salute him before watching a fleeing infantryman jab a short sabre through his back and out of his chest. Shar fell face-first from the wall and was half-burnt to a crisp by the time Robin made it over to drag him away. When Robin rolled him over, he'd smiled weakly, more in surprise and humor than anything else. He sputtered a few times, blood bubbling from his lips, then the sputtering stopped altogether. Shar still breathed, but barely. With all the flames, smoke, and roaming soldiery— Robin decided he would not leave a man who's saved his worthless life to die alone on a pyre. He hadn't known the fellow long, they'd barely spoken four words between them, but he was a Greenmaker too.

Greenmakers didn't leave men behind.

Robin might have made a different decision if he'd known how bloody heavy he'd be. Mercifully, by the time he got to the second from top rung, a hand came down to pull them up the rest of the way. This one was the other Dannan noble, the one Ben called Jan. Robin lay back, gasping against his makeshift facemask, while Jan Fir examined Shar.

"Is he—" Robin huffed.

There was such a sincere expression of mournfulness that Robin felt himself tearing up despite not knowing him long or well. They'd all lost people here today. All of them, even the Sidhe. Jan Fir slid his palm from his temple to his chest— several of his nearby companions did the same. He glanced over at Robin, green eyes tearful. "You carried him."

"He saved my life. Couldn't let him burn. Not like that."

Jan Fir nodded. "For this, we thank you." The respect Robin saw blooming in his eyes put him at a loss for words. Usually, Daoine Sidhe, like Jan Fir hunted Greenmakers for plying their trade. It was quite odd to feel how swiftly a perception could change. His included.

"Where's Ben then?" he asked, uncomfortable.

Jan Fir hefted Shar's body over his much taller, much wider shoulder, tugging his chin toward the bend in the wall. Ben was engaged in a serious swordfight, moving like water through a canyon. It took a minute with all the smoke, but Robin's eyes flared when he realized whom he fought. "*Siora*! That's bloody Lord Bishop, hisself. Somebody shoot that prick!"

"We can't," sighed Jan Fir. "*Mo Flaith* has ordered us to go. In any case, he is peerless."

Robin blew air over his lower lip. "Never played Porter with his Arseness then, I take it?"

Jan Fir gave him an odd look. "No. Why?"

"Because Ben always lays the best strategies," said Robin watching Kaer Yin with genuine concern. They were all dead tired, and he might put a good face on it, but the Prince of Innisfail was slowing. "But he never considers that his opponent is *always* trying to cheat."

✕

Damek came back at him— switching between Adrac and Neithana with smooth, practiced ease. He pressed forward, his footwork much like the inner workings of a clock: a step, one-second pause, rotate, then step. Every inch he moved, his sabre came down from his high guard, then around his body for a slice at Kaer Yin's midsection, then back up for another high thrust. It was predictable but methodical and difficult to counter without leaving his side or head exposed. With the slippery, snow-dusted battlement being both narrow and coated in scattered debris and ash, every back step Kaer Yin took to defend himself became more and more precarious. Not to mention, he was beyond exhausted. He might have been born with the immortal, seemingly boundless constitution of his forebears, but after nearly three days without sleep, two battles, two raids, and the endless killing he'd been forced to do— his bones felt like jelly beneath his skin. If he allowed this to go on too long, he might make a mistake that could cost him his life.

Damek also had to be tired, but he was fueled by desperation and hatred Kaer Yin had never seen glowing from a man's eyes so brightly before. The Lord of Clare knew very well that if he failed to kill the Crown Prince now, he would never get the chance again. He also must have realized that today's loss would sorely dent his reputation as a newly minted King of Eire, and the head of the Ard Ri's son would be a consolation any of his backers would respect. Perhaps even the zealot who had usurped his seat in Bethany.

Well, if he survived.

Kaer Yin Adair had never lost a duel.

On the advance, Damek switched to his left foot, sliding forward on the balls of his feet to resume his clockwork cadence. His purpose was clearly to hammer away at Kaer Yin's worn-down dominant arm. A clever stratagem, as every stroke reverberated through Kaer Yin's bones with excruciating regularity. He braced himself against the pain. Damek grunted with each thrust, putting everything he had into each jab.

Kaer Yin knew his right arm couldn't stave off this merciless rhythm much longer, so he flipped Nemain broadside, glancing Damek's sabre and breaking the concentrated pattern in his footwork. He staggered back a half-step, forced to block Kaer Yin's next stroke on vertiginous heels. Swinging Nemain over his opposite shoulder, Kaer Yin brought her back down in an elegant slash that terminated in a down-striking spin.

Damek caught himself and leaned against his sabre for support. "That's a fancy guard for an arm as weak as yours."

"Come try it and see."

Shrugging, Damek slid his right foot to the side, thinning the line of his body and taking a low guard. He would twist his blade crosswise as Nemain came down from above, then turn, taking advantage of his vulnerable side. Kaer Yin realized the danger in a flash. He didn't have the strength to play chess with Bishop.

He must end this now.

Kaer Yin slipped his left foot forward as if he would begin the terminus of his slashing guard. Damek, as expected, committed to moving in from his undefended side and under Nemain's descending stroke. But Kaer Yin slid back onto his right foot at the last moment, pushing himself out of the way and causing Damek's sabre to dash uselessly to the left. Kaer Yin flipped Nemain broadside, smacking his opponent's chest with the flat of the blade— drawing his exposed back onto Kaer Yin's lark. The thinner, more rigid blade slammed into Damek's kidney with ease. The Lord of Clare whimpered in pain, dropping his sabre. He clawed wildly at Kaer Yin, trying anything to dislodge him. Instead, Kaer Yin rolled his left soldier, slowly forcing him onto his knees while withdrawing his lark. As he stepped back, he swept Nemain across Damek's chest, biting through the gap in his breastplate, leaving a vast chasm that spilled dark blood.

Damek gasped a sick, wet sound.

His expression marked disbelief.

Kaer Yin resheathed his weapons, breathing hard.

"All hail the King of Eire," he sneered and turned his back.

He didn't wait to watch Bishop fall. It was only a matter of time now, and he didn't care to watch him die. Kaer Yin had people to look after, a woman to find, a city to rebuild, and a family to return to. He'd expended all the energy he intended to on Damek fucking Bishop.

As he walked west along the battlements, he nodded at his men helping each other down the ropes toward the river, their faces blurred in the haze. He was pleased to note how deserted the city felt just then, as everyone who hadn't died in the streets was long gone or leaving.

Flames still raged in the Greenmakers' Quarter along the western wall. Even *The Hart* was a torch against the night sky. He stood and watched it burn for a moment. The sight was soon eclipsed by a cloud of smoke and cinders that sent him backward, hacking.

Right, he thought. *Best get to it then.*

He made his way to the ropes his men had already descended, even though he could scarcely see his fingers four inches from his face. Now that the Quarter was finally in flames, the smoke had become a maelstrom. He clasped the top of a rope ladder and hauled himself nearly over the wall, save for his left leg, which he used for balance as he adjusted his scabbard to climb. Something sharp suddenly bit through his calf, pinning his leg in place. He cried out in surprise. Damek's blistered hands snatched out and wrenched him back over the stone rampart.

He struck Kaer Yin with fists, elbows, and skull— anything he could. Disoriented, Kaer Yin felt himself being dragged back toward the fire. Damek hit him full in the face with his forehead, filling his vision with white lights. He reached up in time to catch Damek's right fist as it plummeted toward his heart with a bloodied dagger point. The angle was not to Kaer Yin's advantage, and Damek laughed manically, spurting blood into Kaer Yin's eyes and mouth.

He gagged.

The dagger's tip plunged through his cuirass and into the skin above Kaer Yin's ribs, tearing a hiss from between his clenched teeth. Further still it came, inch by inch, until he felt it scrape across his breastbone, threatening the organs beneath.

"That's Ard Ri Mac Nemed to you, you Dannan Piece of shite." Damek laughed as Kaer Yin's weakened right hand began to give.

Kaer Yin wrestled as much as he could, but every motion brought the blade further into his flesh. He felt bone give way and knew it would tear through his heart at any moment. He was about to die at Damek fucking Bishop's hand.

Maybe he *was not* such an admirer of irony, after all.

A rush of hot air swept over his head from the west, and suddenly, Damek was knocked backward. A jagged gash split his face open from ear to nose. He screamed, scrambling away to regain footing, but Tam Lin launched himself forward, larks spinning through the air between them. One entered the hollow of his gut, and the other took his right hand off at the wrist. Damek had time for one last wide-eyed shriek before Tam Lin withdrew the lark and placed his foot over the wound—shoving him from the wall to the licking flames below.

"I bloody well warned you, didn't I?" Tam Lin asked as he fell, howling into the smoke rising from the street. Tam Lin spat, resheathed his larks, and turned back to his cousin, who was trying to stand up. He threw out a hand to help him. Kaer Yin sagged a bit against him. "Some men just don't know when to stay dead."

"Indeed," agreed Kaer Yin, as they limped to the ropes and escape.

The Dawn Tide

n.e. 509
26, ban apesa
Rosweal

For a few hours, the survivors watched the snow pile up over the walls from the safety of their boats or sheltered behind fully armored defenders gathered on the docks. Some blessedly brilliant individual had at least thought to stock the area with enough tents and tarpaulins to spread over the shabby, partially burnt-out rooftop over the main pier. Thankfully, they did not lack for dried-out timber to build fires; stone pits were thrown together on either side of the snow-dusted bank, around which dozens of people milled for warmth, simply happy to be alive.

Under the last tent, Rian's patients were laid out side by side for body warmth and shelter from the elements. Despite the harsh, barking command Tam Lin had tried to give her— she moved among them, tying bandages with torn tunics, petticoats, whatever she could get her hands on. Though Tam Lin had taken half her wounds upon himself, she was still fairly covered in bruises, minor cuts, and several scabbing scratches. Thankful or not, she ignored everything that came out of Tam Lin's mouth and treated him first, bearing a stony-eyed determination that snapped his mouth shut tight.

In the end, he had learned it was wiser to concede defeat.

When she'd finished wrapping him up like an invalid, she ordered him into the line of wounded waiting for broth along the wall. Grumbling, he sat next to Kaer Yin, who watched him sidelong.

"What?" he gruffed.

Kaer Yin pursed his lips. "Not a thing."

Tam Lin muttered something unintelligible.

"Glad to see she is feeling better."

"Her evil is strong," nodded Tam Lin.

"Hm," said Kaer Yin.

"Must be Dian Cecht's blessings."

"Interesting that you both bear the same marks."

Tam Lin shrugged.

"You going to tell me about it?"

"No."

Kaer Yin let the matter drop. He declined a lukewarm bowl of broth and a scrap of moldy bread from one of Tansy's girls (others needed it more, as far as he was concerned), then slapped his knee. "Right then. We have work to do anyway." The dead needed counting, and though Kaer Yin would rather not bear the terrible knowledge he was about to tally, the responsibility was his. Tam Lin's grim expression mirrored his own. He merely nodded once.

A job no one wanted was a leader's burden.

Kaer Yin had no idea how many familiar faces he would discover lying face up in the snow upriver, but he did know there were hundreds. Among them were Damek Bishop and a score of his officers. Kaer Yin had ordered that they be left for Una to choose their method of burial, less Bishop's armor and rings of state. These would be sent to Tairngare, Armagh, and Bethany, respectively, along with the Crown Prince's sentiments.

Innisfail has but one ruler.

He had many things to see to and many additional fires to put out across the Continent, but first, he must make it through the day. He and Tam Lin walked through the still-smoldering remains of a once healthy forest toward the one duty neither wished to see through. The dead had been stretched out by the townsfolk as honorably as they could be. More people were carried from the city every hour and lain out beside their fellows: friend and foe alike. Say what one would about the North; they understood dignity, even for those who did not deserve it. Kaer Yin spotted Damek and his men first, for their cobalt and scarlet cloaks. Damek's face had been covered with a scrap of his banner, his blackened arms folded over the gaping chest wound Kaer Yin had given him, his right hand missing.

Find peace in Tech Duinn, brother, Kaer Yin thought and steadied himself for the sea of forms ahead.

"Ben!" called a familiar voice from down the shore. "Is that ye 'neath all that blood and grime?" Robin hobbled up the causeway to stand beside him.

Kaer Yin clasped his forearm. "Glad to see your ugly face."

Robin threw his arms around his friend, slapping his wounded back hard. Neither had dry eyes. He cleared his throat as he broke away. "Well, I woke up on the bank a while back. My sweet woman nearly beat me half to death for glee."

"Is she all right?" Kaer Yin's expression clouded. She hadn't looked very good when last he saw her.

Robin waved his comment away. "Mistress Rian is the boss, Barb has learned. Got her laid up under a pile of furs taller'n me an' sippin' broth like a good lass. She'll be fine, I 'spect."

Tam Lin shook Robin's hand. "Pleased you aren't dead as you look, mortal."

"An' I'm happy to see ye Sidhe bastards bruise like the best o'us. Look like oversqueezed shite, highness, if ye don't mind me sayin' so."

"Not at all," laughed Tam Lin. "I'm hoping it makes me more dashing."

Kaer Yin rolled his eyes and pulled Robin away by his shoulder. "The Greenmakers?"

"Putting out what's left of the fires. Ye won't believe it, but *The Hart*'s still in one piece, if a bit charred. Stone foundations."

Kaer Yin smiled. "The luckiest woman in Innisfail."

"Ain't she just?" Robin jerked a flask out of his bloodied vest. "To Barb Dormer, more lives than a barnyard cat!"

He took a long pull and passed the flask.

Kaer Yin's eyes misted at the smell of raw *uishge* inside. "Oh, you bloody beautiful bastard." He tipped it back with a groan of pure pleasure. The fire it lit warmed him clear to his arse. He took a second sip and passed it to Tam Lin.

"A bed in my future," Tam Lin toasted, smacking his lips after a long gulp.

Robin reclaimed the vessel and glanced around to ensure no one saw him. All the uishge was meant to be at the bottom of the river in barrels, but Robin couldn't help but keep a stash. If Barb found out, she'd have his guts for lacings. "Any sign o'yer girl yet, Ben?"

Kaer Yin frowned. "Not as yet." He was trying not to think about it. The least he could be sure of was that she did not await him amongst the pile of defenders he was about to tour. He'd given orders to report any sightings of her or Diarmid. Una's aunt and uncle were both wounded but relatively in one piece. During their flight through the streets, Eva had taken a serious wound that Rian had spent the better part of ten hours stitching.

The Siorai Alta would live, though she would likely never walk again. Barb had already told him what happened in the cellar and what they had been forced to do to escape. If not for Eva, all of the children might not have arrived at the gatehouse in time.

Knowing what happened to Rian and Barb only streets away, told Kaer Yin everything he needed to know about the gravity of Eva's choice, for surely she had known what would happen to both groups. He sighed. He still had no idea if she'd been talking about Damek when she warned him it wasn't 'over.' He'd be sure to ask her next time she was conscious.

"Well, she'll turn up. No doubt there," said Robin, like a man who said far less than he needed to.

"What is it, Robin?"

"Well, I dunno if it's the time to… I dunno."

"Just say it, man," Tam Lin cut in. "What's one more tragedy?"

Robin shot him a sharp look but seeing the fatigue and resigned preparedness in his expression, he immediately softened. "No help for it then, milords. Follow me."

Kaer Yin didn't need to be told where they were headed. He was already aware that two clearings had been prepared. He tucked his head down and followed without bothering to glance up once.

※

THE GREENMAKERS HAD BEEN MOST respectful. Shar, Fionn, Mordu, and over a hundred and fifty of Aes Sidhe's finest were stretched out, side by side, below the blackened western wall. Their faces were uncovered one at a time for identification, then recovered gently by Robin's shaking fingers. "We know ye don't bury yer fallen as we do, and we wanted 'em to have the honors they damn well earned."

Choking, Tam Lin fell to his knees in the snow, weeping openly at Shar's feet. They had been friends for decades, no matter how the affections of one woman might have divided them. He wept like a child, blubbering apologies Shar would never hear. This was a regret Tam Lin would bear for the rest of his life, and it was painful to watch.

Kaer Yin swallowed hard, throat dry and cracking. "Thank you, Robin."

Jan Fir was already there, huddled a few paces away, whispering prayers over Fionn's nearly cleaved body while his fingers wound through Mordu's. They had been lovers all their lives, and it broke Kaer Yin's heart to see his wracking sobs. Eri would be devastated. They had made a family, despite their marriage of convenience, and Eri loved Mordu perhaps as much as she loved Kaer Yin.

After several minutes, Kaer Yin let out a long, haggard breath and turned around to wipe his burning eyes. "They sail to Bri Reis, where they'll feast with the Gods on their way to Tir Na Nog."

"*Bíodh sé amhlaidhsaid*," said Tam Lin, tracing the line from his forehead to his heart. He dug his palms into his eye sockets. "Does Rian know?"

"Not yet," answered Robin soberly. "Haven't had the heart to tell her, 'specially with all she's been through."

"Gods, Yin, how do I begin—" Tam Lin's voice broke.

"I'll do it. You must prepare his boat," Kaer Yin said firmly.

Tam Lin nodded.

Robin was shaking when next he spoke. "Not to dig the blade deeper, but we're burying our own now, Ben. The lads, well, it would mean the world to them if ye'd come say a few words."

Robin was perhaps more stoic than any man Kaer Yin knew, and to see his jaw trembling that way could only mean one thing. Barb was accounted for.

"Robin, where's Gerry?"

Robin covered his face with both hands, and Kaer Yin clutched his shoulder. "Follow me," he managed to say again.

✕

At dawn the following day, the sun shone over a white and black landscape that was startlingly beautiful, despite its many woes. When the boats had been hewn, and the Sidhe were laid out in their biers, when the townsfolk had finished patting earth over their loved ones' graves, Kaer Yin lined up with his fellows, facing the rising sun. He wore white from head to toe, as was the custom among the Tuatha De Dannan— as white was the color of death and rebirth. His hair had been braided by Tansy's children, Robin's new wards as the Lord of Navan.

Tansy, Violet, and even Gerry were all tucked beneath the forest floor, waiting for spring rains to bless their graves with the flowers each deserved.

"Great Bel," he said in the common tongue, so all might hear. "We give you these souls to carry with you that they might sup in the halls of your kin, forever and a day." The gathering repeated his words, saluting the rising sun with their heads bowed low.

Kaer Yin waded out to the curraghs held just shy of the gentle current between the city's scarred stone wall and the misty, blackened trees on the opposite bank. He waded among each, pushing their footings downriver as he passed. The last two were Shar and Fionn's. Both were decked out in every scrap of fine fabric the women could find. Their hair glittered with shining beads spread out around their seemingly sleeping faces. Fionn's hands had been wrapped around the hilt of his greatsword, while Shar Lianor's pale fingers clasped the bow his father had made for him the day Bov Dearg had chosen him to serve the Prince of Connaught. In repose, he seemed to be smiling.

"Only the glorious dead live forever."

Kaer Yin severed a lock of his hair and gifted it to his father's champion. A gift for Donn, who would know the price Fionn had paid to protect Crom's Clan. To Shar, he gave two of his daggers so that he might boast of his deeds in the Dagda's Hall. After pushing both boats into the current, he waded back to shore, where Tam Lin, Jan Fir, Robin, and a score of others waited with flaming arrows. Kaer Yin took Sinnair from a boy he did not recognize. The bow was blackened at the ends but was otherwise unharmed. He dipped his arrow into the bonfire and drew, waiting for the boats to huddle together at the nearest bend where it widened into a deep, churning pool, then onward toward the sun.

Rian's white skirt swirled in the shallows as she and the other women tossed flowers after their dead. He heard her sobbing, and it wrought fresh sadness—poor girl. To have found and lost love so swiftly was a terrible fate for a heart as worthy as hers. He felt for her, and worse, for the stolid suffering it gave Tam Lin to realize the truth of his feelings amidst so much grief.

Kaer Yin mourned for all three.

What else could he do?

Jan Fir's damaged right arm quivered against his bow, but he did not complain. Mordu's passage was his responsibility. Kaer Yin also mourned for his sister, whose heart would break anew.

As the sun crested the hills to the east, they let their arrows fly: once, twice, three times, until every bier roared to light, sailing into the rising sun and, eventually, the sea.

X

After the funeral, Kaer Yin walked through the western woods toward the graves of so many Milesians he'd come to care for, stopping finally at Gerrod's. He couldn't help but admire the odd twist of fate that had placed him here among those he swore to loathe all of his life— and in the end, had been willing to die for. Silently, he thanked his father again for the *geis* he'd been given. It had saved him, sure as the sun would set in the west. In his wisdom, the Ard Ri had blessed his son with compassion, humility, kindness, and the understanding of true courage. To be brave, one didn't need to be the finest warrior or hold the highest titles. Bravery was the willingness to lay one's life down for those *weaker* than oneself, to stand up for people the powerful deemed valueless.

That was what it truly meant to be brave.

After a thousand years in Innisfail, Kaer Yin had learned this last and hardest lesson. It took three decades among those he never had a thought for to drive the point home. He felt a surge of gratitude for his father's incredible mercy, tolerance, and patience. For the lives that he'd been honored to be a part of. For the sacrifices they had made for his decisions. For the purpose they had given him. He stared down at the large rock that served as Gerrod's headstone, the cairn marked by the dagger Robin had made for his fifteenth birthday. Its brass scabbard had been polished to a high sheen.

Kaer Yin felt Gerrod's loss acutely as if he'd been a brother… and perhaps he had been.

"Never again," he said, unsheathing his dagger and sweeping it across his palm before snapping the blade back into its sheath. He buried it beneath several of the smaller stones and closed his eyes. "Innisfail shall be one land, one people, and no more boys should die for the whims of rich men. I vow it as *Ard Tiarne* of the Tuatha De Dannan— your sacrifice shall not be in vain."

A stray tear wound its way down his cheek as he stood. "Farewell, my friend."

He was silent on his walk back to town, mulling over all the mistakes he had made in his attempt to shirk his destiny. No more. This land would not fall prey to power-hungry madmen as long as he drew Innish air into his lungs.

A twig snapped in the bracken, bringing his head up sharply. He set a hand on his pommel. There hadn't been any Bethonair stragglers in days, but that didn't mean they weren't out there, waiting for their chance to raid or attack unwitting villagers for coins or food. Scanning the wasteland for his unseen visitor, he waited. Then, Una stepped out of the barest beam of sunlight. The air shimmered with Otherworld power for a heartbeat. She didn't see him at first, wide eyes taking in the crippled Greensward with a gasp, her hands flying to her mouth.

He must have made some sound, and she turned, her face the most beautiful thing he'd ever seen. With a cry, she launched herself into his eager, open arms.

X

IN THE GLOAMING, FOG-SHROUDED, and bitterly cold evening air, several large gray flags bearing the white stag of House Adair snapped to and fro in the wind that chewed its way over the frigid Boinne. Overnight, the winter had returned with a vengeance, forcing the people of Rosweal back inside the city to reside in Sol Trant's undamaged brewery. It would house everyone inside its high stone walls and mostly intact roof until the Quarter could be rebuilt. Kaer Yin had no doubt the Greenmakers would set it to rights in no time. With the funds he, Una, and Tam Lin had given them— they could build two Rosweals with proper walls.

Kaer Yin admired the city from his saddle with a small smile. Maybe the Quarter would be the wealthiest district in the North when he returned?

Robin and Barb stood together on the wall, waving like lunatics. The former shouted something about *uishge* and a woman's fat thighs.

Kaer Yin laughed and turned toward the far shore, its omnipresent mists swirling just ahead. Tam Lin, Rian, and Jan Fir road ahead, breaching that smoky white curtain before him. As his mount neared the bank, the land beyond revealed itself in hints: a hill and a knot of dark trees. Una waited patiently behind him, knowing what this moment meant to him. Grinning, he closed his eyes and drew that mist into his lungs, his heart.

It had been so long, so *very, very* long.

At last, he was going home.

"For Herne's bloody sake, pull yourself together, you sentimental girl!" Tam Lin admonished from somewhere beyond the mists.

Laughing, Kaer Yin kicked his horse up over the bank, eager to race his cousin over the hills of Aes Sidhe.

–FIN–

The Waning Moon

n.e. 509
29, ban apesa
armagh

"*Mo Flaith?*" a polite voice issued from the interior hall behind him. Falan didn't turn, for only bad news would prompt intrusion. Instead, he set his card down and picked up his wineglass. "Speak," he sighed.

Sionnavar took a deep breath before he replied. He wasn't as brave or cunning as his father, but he was a useful servant, nonetheless. "I have news."

Falan swirled his glass, emotionless eyes forward. "He's dead, isn't he?"

"Yes, My Lord. My deepest apologies."

Falan didn't move a muscle. "How?"

"We cannot be sure, but Leal, your sister's champion, vows he died fighting Midhir's son."

"A good death, at least. Where is his body?"

He felt Sionnovar's flinch. "The Moura girl insisted he be taken to Tairngare for internment. Many of his men have sworn her loyalty, as it happens."

"As well they should if their sole alternative is that murderous boil in the south. Where was he, last we checked?"

"Ten Bells, *Mo Flaith*. Riding back to Bethany, as far as my sources can glean."

"A stunning victory."

"A slaughter."

Falan pursed his lips, staring into the flickering flames ahead. "Ther can be no victory without it."

"He murdered the town's nobles, the Libellan charter, the Mercher's Guild, everyone." Falan heard the anger in his voice. "His men razed the Sidhe Consulate to the ground and crucified its inhabitants. Their gruesome corpses decorate either side of the High Road a mile in either direction."

"How devout he is," Falan smirked into his cup. "How many men did he leave in the city?"

"Not enough. If we aim to reclaim it."

Falan laughed through his nose. "Not at all. Let Midhir's son deal with Henry FitzDonahugh. The longer they busy themselves with yet another Souther distraction, the closer we shall come to our true goal."

"Yes, *Mo Flaith*," answered Sionnovar, without hiding his displeasure.

Falan did turn then. "We aim higher than Bethany, do we not?"

"Yes." Sionnovar flushed and nervously looked away.

"I take it the Bretagn's ships are now in his possession as well?"

Sionnovar nodded.

"Excellent. Promised him his newborn daughter or some such?"

"Yes. Had the girl formally betrothed to him after the battle. Gaelin's son had many ships to lend to the effort, each bedecked with cannons. Blasted away half the Merchanta Quarter."

"Too bad Castor won't live long enough to claim his prize. Henry will use the boy to take Tairngare, then dispose of him in short order." He chuckled to himself. The cards he'd laid out in front of him bore ominous sigils. He set his glass down and reached out to reshuffle the deck. "In any case, we've lost the element of surprise. Midhir's son won't take kindly to our intervention."

"He will take that information to his father."

"Is that where he's headed now?"

"Should have arrived by now."

Falan's hands paused over his cards. A slow smile then broke over his face. "Well, I suppose that places all of our prey in one place."

Sionnovar shared his laugh, if without the same humor.

Falan was still smiling to himself when he set down the next card.

Death and the Waning Moon.

"Be seeing you, Kaer Yin," he whispered to himself. "Soon."

BONDS

n.e. 509
30, ban apesa
bethany

Castor, son of Gaelin, Lord of Bretagne: patricide, plotter, hostage, and meat for the Eirean grindstone: sat his mare without the slightest hint of the internal war raging within him. A single head among thousands in the Grand Duch FitzDonahugh's procession, Castor's shorn and scabbed scalp and faded silk doublet marked him out like a bloody thumb. Amidst so many men in full-black and blue armor, Castor looked every inch the hostage he was despite his efforts to pretend his breeding made the slightest difference. The men around him couldn't care less about his pedigree nor the vaunted heights he imagined he'd fallen from so recently.

In the lead, nearly a half mile ahead, sat Henry himself. Castor noted his position beneath Bethany's bright blue and scarlet pennants that snapped in the wind beneath Henry's flat black standard. As usual, Henry was decked out in glossy black gauntlet and greaves, hoping to further the legend of the famous Black Knight of Bethany.

From Castor's middling position down the line, he could barely make out the flash of white beside the old man. Lady Penwyth, even now, attempted to fatten her coffers from Henry's leavings. Since her daughter had displeased Henry by birthing him a worthless girl and then dashing off to a nunnery somewhere in Cymru, Penwyth was desperate to maintain the alliance with the soon-to-be King of Eire by offering him another virgin daughter to abuse. Unless the old bastard were a fool, he'd accept, as the Sidhe outnumbered him by the thousands and were undoubtedly going to take exception to every ill his family had visited upon Innisfail in the last months, sooner or later.

Castor should know. He was now betrothed to the worthless girl-child Henry had forced upon his fifteen-year-old child bride. Not that Castor had a choice, but was death not the alternative, he would have far preferred a bride whose father proposed better prospects than the ensuing genocide Henry had invited upon them all.

For the thousandth time that day alone, Castor made a face.

They were all going to die.

He and his countrymen included... unless...

If he could escape, he might make *different* allies. Better allies. Ones that did not get themselves killed tangling with the Sidhe.

But who?

He had hoped to ensnare Lady Penwyth at the previous evening's feast in Damek Bishop's former hall at Clare. Not one to forgo an opportunity to capitalize on another man's successes, Henry, of course, had taken the manse and town for himself. There wasn't much left of Ten Bells to amuse an army of this size, so Henry had proposed one last venture as a lark for his men. And what a lark it was. The Christianized Bethonair troops marched into Clare like locusts, consumed everything in their wake, and left nothing but the white stone manse overlooking the harbor amidst a barren wasteland.

It had been much the same in Ten Bells.

Once, when Castor had been young, his père had taken he and Vexos to Ten Bells for the festival at Imbolg. Until he'd seen that glittering city with his own eyes, he'd never imagined such beauty was possible. Every street and cobbled lane was scrubbed and gleaming. Charming houses of every color trekked downhill to the Bay, their polished roof tiles catching the sun. Stone bridges replete with fine glass streetlamps dotted every river crossing, and the smell of fresh bread and cinnamon-dusted scones wound through each lane. The apparel... *lá*... Castor had been so enraptured by the fashions on display in the city of Ten Bells that he'd been having his clothing imported ever since. It was a place of learning, commerce, and culture that had no equal.

Ten Bells had been the wealthiest, cleanest, most lovely place he'd ever set eyes on until Henry FitzDonahugh passed through. Now, it was a coal-black scar against a white hillside: a pyre spilling billowing trails of smoke and ashes over a cerulean and turquoise sea. Its once beautiful schools, libraries, and markets were toppled and plundered. Its lanes were choked with corpses or the human scarecrows left behind. Ten Bell's coffers were emptied: its wealth a memory. Its people were either enslaved, left to starve, or had been nailed to crosses for a mile in every direction. Castor had never heard of such atrocities as Henry committed at Ten Bells… all because he imagined he had been slighted.

The hate that burned in his heart for such a brutish, disgusting reprobate, Castor could scarcely qualify. He had hated his own family, it was true. Despite taboos, he hated men who sneered at him for loving whom he pleased. He hated oafs and braggarts of every size and stripe imaginable.

Still, he hated Henry FitzDonahugh more.

A great pity that the dashing Damek Bishop had met his end in the North, for indeed, he would have marched south next to shove Henry's aging arse onto the point of his own cross. Alas, it was not to be. Soon enough, they would all pay the forfeit when the Sidhe roused themselves for revenge.

He shook his head. So many plans wasted.

Bishop had not been a fool, whatever Castor had thought of him. Once, before he had been summarily disabused of the notion, he had hoped to cheat the handsome young lord and had paid a hefty price for this hubris. Having spent the better part of a year in a moldy cell in Malahide had taught Castor the error of his ways. He'd had many months to consider another more mutually beneficial course that might have propelled Castor where he'd always wanted to be: of consequence in Innisfail. Then, that star had fallen, slain by his mortal enemy in a northern backwater by the High King's reborn heir, taking Castor's hopes with him. He had nothing now but a name. A name Henry would use to press his claims into greater Francia on his quest for timber and gems to make war against the Sidhe. Bishop's own plan meted out with far less finesse and concern for human life. Thinking of his losses once more only made the blood rush straight to the top of Castor's head, kindling shame and rage.

Ahead of him about four paces, a soldier turned to give Castor a small, embarrassed smile. Daniel, his newest paramour. The fellow had his uses but had as yet been too cowardly to help Castor flee Henry's entourage. Castor returned the gesture if his heart held nothing but the blandest disdain. He needed someone, someone with the *power* to do something about Henry. These little distractions were amusing, but none would save his life.

Who? He asked himself for the thousandth time that day. *Who can help me?*

The wind did not answer.

Bethany loomed in the distance, and he was no closer to his goal.

But then, he saw something very interesting at the front.

Henry's mailed fist lashed out and clipped Lady Penwyth on the crown. With a shriek, she nearly toppled from her horse until one of her grooms managed to catch her reins and right her teetering form. With very little interest in her fate, Henry and his vanguard rode past her, shouting abuse. Penwyth got her mount under control but was forced to the side of the column, glaring after the Duch with a venom Castor could certainly empathize with.

Perhaps all was *not* lost?

Immediately, Castor began to cough and wheeze as dramatically as he could. Rather than halt the column to give him any aid, he was pushed to the far right edge of the line. Soon enough, he found himself apace with the powerful Kernish noblewoman Henry had so publicly scorned... and Castor had been seeking all this while. She covered the lower half of her face so as not to display the blood streaming down her chin, but it was obvious to absolutely everyone, Castor included.

Recognizing his one chance, Castor tore a shred from his now threadbare silk tunic and kicked his horse free of the column. His guards would follow, but that would only improve his chances. When he arrived at Lady Penwyth's side, he shoved his revulsion toward her down deep.

Remember, this woman barters her children for power.

He would not forget this, any more than she might ignore the well-circulated rumor that he'd had his father and brother killed to take the Bretagn throne.

Allies are born of necessity, he told himself.

Castor pulled his mare up short, reached out to the dumbfounded Lady Penwyth, and passed her the fabric as if it were the finest lace. He caught her eye moments before his guards caught up to him. "We have made many mistakes, you and I, but perhaps we might fix them together," he managed to eke out as he was dragged from his saddle and flogged for all to see.

A Light in the Dark

n.e. 509
30 ban apesa
aes sidhe

Una stared into the flames, a woman possessed by turbulent emotions. They were less than a day's march from Bri Leith, but she grew more tense as they drew near. Though the company she kept was jolly indeed to be returning home after so much blood and toil, she could not feel that same jubilation. She smiled when appropriate, answered when spoken to, and otherwise made light of the urgent mood that had taken hold of her once they crossed into Aes Sidhe. Kaer Yin, so absorbed in the terror and joy of meeting his father again after three decades apart, was unaware of the turmoil boiling within her. This wasn't his fault, as it was him she avoided most. He could hardly suspect that his love struggled with emotions she could scarcely quantify if she smiled and laughed rather than broach the topic with him.

Rian, awash with grief for Shar, Gerry, Tansy, and Violet, spent most of her time forcing a silent but brave face during the day and weeping in her bedroll at night. For the thousandth time, Una felt a pang for her many losses. That she hadn't been there when Rian needed her most kept her awake at night.

But come to think of it, *everything* kept her awake at night or tortured her waking hours each day. She saw it all, over and over in her mind:

Aoife's hand attempting to stall her doom from above, the ghast's teeth as they reached for her throat, swirling flames without end, and the cold, dark stars burning behind her eyes.

My child, a voice whispered in her memory.

She shivered.

In the distance, the Sidhe played a particularly dangerous game that had them howling in pain and laughter. Apparently, the Dannans found it incredibly entertaining to beat the hells out of anyone who couldn't split another's arrows. Braying like donkeys, they pummeled each other with such relish, one would think they were mad, drunk, or both.

Well, perhaps both were true.

As for Una, she'd developed a small tremor in her hands that she had no idea how to stall. She tucked them around herself, where no one would see.

No one, that is, but Diarmid.

He watched her from across the fire, eyes burning with curiosity, judgment, and greed.

She frowned back.

"What?"

He leaned toward the fire, his eyes glowing emerald. "When do you plan to tell him?"

"Tell him what?"

Diarmid shot her a half smile. "I can see it on your face, Una."

"What is that?"

"That you're going back."

A hundred curses, rants, and arguments raced through her mind at once, but she refrained from using any. After staring back at him for a long while, she answered, "Yes. I am."

"He believes you will be wed. Have you decided otherwise?"

"Must I choose?"

He sighed. "That's a complicated question, you realize. My nephew is hot-headed and may feel you're breaking your arrangement."

She rolled her eyes. "You know, you're fairly thick for a man who's lived a thousand-thousand lifetimes."

He ignored the insult. "Una, you've sworn your troth to a future king. It's unlikely he'll allow his wife to march off to war."

"Nonsense, Sidhe women do it all the time. I've read about Kaer Yin's sister, Eri."

"That's different—"

"Is it?" she snapped. "I think you'll find he's marrying a *queen*, not the other way around. If I consent to marriage, it'll be on my terms... *Eire*'s terms, Diarmid."

He observed her in silence for a moment. "You don't have the men to stake that claim."

"She does, actually," said Rian from the opposite side of the fire. Her hair spilled from her bedroll onto the wayhouse's stone floor; her eyes sunken into her too-thin face. "Before we left, many of Damek's men swore her fealty. Besides them, all of Rosweal and anyone who wishes to see Henry deposed will follow suit."

Una's heart clenched. "I'm sorry, Rian, I didn't mean to wake you."

"I don't sleep much now," she sniffed. "Anyway, why do you listen to him, Una? He's just stirring up trouble, as usual."

"Young lady," Diarmid said. "You are being rude."

She sat up and shrugged. "Doesn't make me wrong." She turned to Una. "But he has a point. When are you going to tell him?"

Una stole a glance at a familiar blond head through the trees. He was slightly shorter than his fellows, but at nearly 7 feet in height, that hardly mattered. He was laughing, one arm around Jan Fir, one grasping a flask full of uishge. She let out a long breath. "My aunt Eva said we must retake Tiarngare before autumn, or Henry will seize it for himself."

"So? Ben will help. Remember, he still has to deal with the Bolg who were raiding the Midlands dressed in Dannan colors. Ask him, Una."

"You're right, but, he's fought so hard to come home. It would be cruel to ask so much of him now."

"He won't let you go alone."

It was Una's turn to shrug. "It's autumn or nothing. I'll ask him soon, but I must go whether he does or not. Henry won't stop until the whole Continent is in flames."

"Una, he'll go."

She hoped so, truly.

But it wouldn't stop her, either way.

She recalled Aoife's admonishments in the Oiche Ar Fad. She would never forget them.

Queens do not answer to princes.

Even those one loves.

"No matter how much I wish it were otherwise, Eva is right; Tairngare comes first. I must go home."

Rian nodded. "I'm going too."

Una didn't bother to naysay her.

Rian was a woman grown and had experienced war as Una never had. She was the smartest, bravest woman she'd ever met. "Thank you, Lady Ardgillan."

"Well," interrupted Diarmid once more. "Though I am loathe to make promises I may not have the fortune to keep, you may depend on me to help where I can."

This time, Una *was* surprised. "Why would you?"

He pointed. "You carry the next prince of Innisfail beneath your heart. I can't in good conscience allow either of you to come to harm."

Rian's sharp gasp made Una's ears burn, but she did not turn. "How did you know?"

He made a face. "Don't you know who I am, child? I am *Fiachra Ri*."

"Eva told him," said Kaer Yin from behind them. Una jumped half a mile. "Or he eavesdropped when she told me. Probably, the latter."

"*Siora's tits*," Una squeaked. "Don't bloody *do* that!" Flushing, she shrank away from him. "When did she tell you?"

Kaer Yin pursed his lips in thought. "When was it? Well, it doesn't matter, does it?"

Rian went red as coal. "Well, *I* didn't bloody know! Why didn't either of you tell me?"

Una shot to her feet. "I wasn't ready for *any* of you to know… I mean, I…" She flushed purple.

"Too late, love," said Kaer Yin with a sloppy grin, folding her into his oversized arms. "Now, what's this about 'autumn.'"

Kaer Yin & Una Will Return

GLOSSARY

INNISH NAMES, PHRASES AND TERMS; IN ALPHABETICAL ORDER:

A

- *Aenghus Mac Og-* (Aynn-guss-mack-Oh-ge) Dannan god of the Western Sea, love and poetry. Comparable to the Greek god Dionysus.
- *Aes Sidhe-* (Ayess-Shee) "Land of the ever-living', or 'Land of the Sidhe'. Northernmost region of Innisfail, home of the Immortal High King, and his people. Comprised of two major tribes; the Tuatha De Dannan, in Bri Leith and the Fir Bolg in Armagh.
- *Agrea-* (Ah-gray-ah) The Agriculturists Guild in Tairngare, run directly by the House of Commons in Tairnganese Parliament.
- *Alta-* (All-tah) A priestess second in rank to the Doma, in the Cloister of the Eternal Flame, in Tairngare.
- *Amer Gin Gluingel-* (Ahmer-genn-glonn-gall) "Amer the White kneed". A son of Mil Espanga, bard, druid and magician. Helped his brother Eber Finn, conquer Innisfail, and defeat the Tuatha De Dannan.
- *Aoife-* (Eee-Fah) "Radiant one".
- *Ard Ri-* (Ardh- Ree) "Highest King".
- *Ard Tuaithe-* (Ardh-too-ah-hee) "Highest Landsman". A common way to address a Sidhe noble. "Tuaithe", simply means 'countryside'.
- *Ard Tiarne-* (Ardh-tee-arh-nah) "Highest Lord, or Prince". A title reserved for the Crown Prince of Innisfail.
- *Armagh-* (Arr-mah) Capital of the Kingdom of Ulster, and seat of the ancient Kings of the Fir Bolg. As the Fir Bolg's power has waned over the centuries, the Kingdom of Ulster is less than one-third its size in ancient times. Ruled by the Mac Nemed Clan (House of the Black Bull).

B

- *Badh-* (Bae-ve) Sidhe goddess of discord, disharmony and dread. Pestilence and famine are also her domain. One of three divine sisters. SEE MORRIGAN AND MACHA. Her herald is the crow.
- *Ban-* (Bahn) "White", "Light" or "Bright". As in "Ban Lug"— or the Month of Midsummer (formerly August).
- *Ban Sidhe-* (Bahn-shee) "White Spirit" or "Good Folk". A term reserved for the higher classification of Sidhe (or Immortal Ones). The Tuatha De Dannan and Fir Bolg, belong to this class, on whole. See *DAOINE SIDHE*, for nobility.
- *Bel-* (Ball) The Sidhe sun god. Considered a male figure, but otherwise one of the few non-personified deities in the Sidhe pantheon, save for Samn, his mate.
- *Beltane-* (Ball-tinna) A festival celebrated on the first of the Month "Ban-Bela" (Bahn-balla), formerly 'May'. A celebration for seeding crops, full spring, and fertility.
- *Bethany-* (Beth-ahn-nee) The Southernmost Kingdom in Innisfail, and second-most powerful city in Eire. Ruled by the Donahugh Clan, under their line of ancestral Duchs. Seat of Duch Patrick Donahugh, fervent enemy of Aes Sidhe. Sometimes called the 'Machine City', for their use of cannons and other siege devices in warfare.
- *Bodhran-* (Bode-ran) A circular frame drum made from animal hide and polished wood. The Sidhe carry bodhrans into battle.
- *Bov Mac Nuada Dearg-* (Bove- mack- new-ah-dah-derrck) King of Connaught, and former High King of the Tuatha De Dannan, in pre-Celtic times. Known as 'Bov the Red', for his famous temper, and rash behavior. Rules from his capital at Croghan. Brother to the High King, Midhir.
- *Breccan-* (Breck-ahn) "Freckled one".
- *Brehon-* (Breh-honn) "Teacher" or "Knowing One". Brehons are the highest ranking magic users in Innisfail. They are considered 'holy men', for the ability to commune with both spirits and nature itself. Their advice is sought by Sidhe leaders before any major commitment, such as war, marriage, treaties, or policy making. They are as feared as they are respected, for to incur a Brehon's wroth is to endure all manner of travesties. It is illegal to harm a Brehon, and they are immune to Common Law. A Brehon may gainsay even the High King, without fear of repercussion.
- *Bretagne-* (Breh-tan-ee) A peninsula jutting into the Southern sea, from the old kingdom of Francia. A major sea power in its own right, and one of the few remaining kingdoms free of Innish over-rule.
- *Brida-* (Bree-dah) The Sidhe goddess of the dawn. The Dagda named one of his own daughters for her, who died in ancient times. The horse, is her herald— speed and strength, are her creed.

- *Bri Leith-* (Bree-leyth) "Highest Realm", or "Foremost Hall". Capital of Aes Sidhe, and home of the High King, Midhir. Ruled by the Adair Clan (House of the White Stag).

- *Bru Na Boinne-* (Broo-nah-boyne) A valley of ancient hillforts at the Northern border of Eire, along the river Boyne (*Boinne*, in old Innish). The passage tombs of Newgrange, Dowth, and Knowth— gird the river from the North, in Aes Sidhe. The passage tombs are older even than the Sidhe, having been built many thousands of years before the Invasion Cycles of Innish history. The Sidhe call these first peoples 'Fomorian', or sometimes 'Stone People'; for the complex network of standing stones, passage tombs, dolmens, and hillforts they left behind. Considered the holiest site in Innisfail, by the Sidhe.

C

- *Clare-* (Clayre) A sea province along the South-Western Coast of Eire. Ruled by Lord Damek Bishop.

- *Connaught-* (Cuhn-aught) Westernmost kingdom in Aes Sidhe. Ruled by King Bov, 'The Red'.

- *Croghan-* (Crew-Hahn) Capital of the Kingdom of Connaught, and seat of Bov Dearg, and the Marshal of the West. Ruled by the Dearg Clan (The House of the Red Eagle).

- *Cu Chulainn-* (Cu-hoo-linn) An ancient Innish hero, and champion of a Milesian King of Eire.

- *Crom Dagda-* (Cruhm- dagh-dah) The 'good father'. First King of the Tuatha De Dannan, and also a Skysinger of unimaginable power. Sacrificed his own eye to save Nuada's life after the battle at Magh Tuiredh, against the formidable Fomorian King, Balor. And years later, sacrificed his own life to save his people from the onslaught of the Milesians, after Nuada's death. He is honored at Cromnasa, each midwinter. Opened a path into the Otherworld with his own sacrifice, which granted all Sidhe tribes everlasting life.

- *Cromnasa-* (Cruhm-nah-sa) "Festival of Crom" or "Crom's Feast". Celebration of the Dagda's sacrifice for the Immortality of the Sidhe. Midwinter festival, celebrated on the Longest Night of the year.

- *Cymru-* (Kim-ree) An ancient Kingdom at the Easternmost reaches of Innisfail, having once been called 'Wales', before The Transition. A mineral rich country, for its mountains and hills are filled with precious ores. In the West of the Kingdom, their major export is wine, which is grown largely in the South, toward the capital at Swansea. Cymru is a Tairnganese colony but pays homage and tithes to Aes Sidhe. Over the Cyrmian mountains in the far east of the Kingdom, lies a region known as the 'Wastes', for its inhospitable, uninhabitable, and arid landscape.

- *Cymrian-* (Kim-ree-ahn) One who dwells in Cymru.

D

- *Dagda-* SEE CROM DAGDA, under 'C'.
- *Danu-* (Day-new) The goddess of the earth, in pre-Innish Europe. The patron goddess of the Tuatha de Dannan, who claim to be descended from her and her mate Donn, the god of death.
- *Daoine Sidhe-* (Doone-Shee) A term reserved for the upper echelons of Ban Sidhe society. The nobles and royalty of Aes Sidhe.
- *Dearg-* (Derckk) "The Red".
- *Damek Bishop, Lord of Clare-* (Dahm-eck) Alis Donahugh's illegitimate son, fathered by an unknown Sidhe lord. Adopted by Duch Patrick Donahugh after his mother's death. An accomplished soldier and statesman. Commander of Bethany's armed forces.
- *Dian Cecht-* (Diahn-caysht) Sidhe ancestor god, son of the Dagda. Forged Nuada's Golden Hand, after the battle at Maigh Turiedh. The Sidhe consider him the father of healing.
- *Diarmid Mac Nuada Dubh-* (Derr-mett-mack-nu-ah-dah-duvv) King of Tech Duinn, and Lord of the *Oiche Ard Fad*. Called *Fiachra Ri*, by the Sidhe- or Raven King, in Eire. A Skysinger, like his father Crom Dagda; and Brehon of the Tuatha De Dannan. He is the only member of his house, as he rules a kingdom of the dead. All lesser Sidhe call him 'King', including the Lu Sidhe, and Dor Sidhe- which would unleash themselves upon mortal kind, did he not guard the gates of the Otherworld with a firm hand. Brother to Midhir, the High King. An ambitious, mercurial man, whose loyalty can never truly be counted upon. Also known as "Diarmid, The Black". Servant of Donn- the god of the dead; and Donn's daughter, Morrigan.
- *Doma-* The title of the High Priestess of the Cloister of the Eternal Flame, in Tairngare. The theocratic and secular ruler of Tairngare. Holds a seat on the High King's Council, and the highest-ranking official in Eire. Currently held by Drem Moura.
- *Donn-* "Dark One", the Sidhe god of the dead. Mate of Danu, goddess of the earth. Donn is the only god the Sidhe and Milesians shared before the Invasions. Donn, was also the name of one of Mil Espagna's seven sons. He died after cursing his brother Ir. Diarmid as a Skysinger and Brehon, is his servant.
- *Dor-* (Door) "Black" or "Darkest", see also 'dorchas'. As in "Dor Samna" (Door-Sa-wa), or the Month of Winter's Birth (formerly, October).
- *Dor Sidhe-* (Door-shee) "Darkest Spirits", or "Evil Folk". A term to describe the darker denizens of the Otherworld. Unnatural beasts and spirits that harm and hunt mortals for food or sport. They only exist within the Otherworld, or sometimes on the fringes of the border with Aes Sidhe- where the veil between worlds is thinnest. Often roam wild in Eire on Samhain, when the veil vanishes altogether, once a year. Goblins, selkies, pookas, trolls, ghasts, giants, and gnomes- all belong to this classification.

- *Drem Moura-* (Drehm-More-Ah) The High Priestess of Siora, the Ancestor; in the Cloister of the Eternal Flame at Tairngare. Head of the wealthiest and most influential family in Eire, and most powerful woman on the continent. Not well-loved by the common people, for her frequent attempts to crown members of her own family Queen of the Commons; in order to shore up absolute power for the Moura Clan. Mother of Arrin Moura, and grandmother to Una.
- *Donahugh-* (Donnah-hew) The ruling clan of Bethany, and the greater South of Innisfail.
- *Dubh-* (Duvv) "Black".
- *Duch-* (Duke) A lord second only to a king in rank— but far removed from a High King, who rules over all lesser kings and lords equally.
- *Dumnain-* A village in the lower Midlands of Eire, which was destroyed by the Crown Prince Kaer Yin Adair, during the war with Bethany in '84. The site of one of the bloodiest battles in Innish history, and the very place Duch Donahugh lost his right to a seat on the High King's Council, in exchange for his life. Due to this battle, the Kingdom of Bethany pays the highest tithes and taxes in Innisfail, in reparation for the horrors inflicted on the Eirean people for Bethany's warmongering. Also, the site where the High King's son was exiled from Aes Sidhe for war crimes, after the extreme measures he took to safeguard his own troops.

E

- *Eber Finn-* (Everr-Feen) A Milesian King, son of the King Mil Espagna. The first 'celtic' king of Innisfail.
- *Eire-* (Ay-err) The Milesian (mortal) region of Innisfail. It borders Aes Sidhe at the Boyne in the Midlands and ends at the Bretagn Straits in the far South. Straddles the Straits of Mannanan in the East. Cities like Tairngare and Ten Bells have colonies in Cymru and Kernow (formerly Wales, and Cornwall).
- *Emain Macha-* (Aavvinn-mash-ah) A holy hillfort, in the Kingdom of Ulster.
- *Eochaid Mac Nemed-* (Yoh-hee- mack- nehm-ehd) Ancient King of the Fir Bolg. Slain by Nuada, king of the Tuatha De Dannan for his throne and the right to rule in Innisfail. Married to his cousin Liadan, by their Fomorian Grandfather, Balor. Was a just ruler, and fearsome warrior.
- *Eri Mac Midhir Bres-* (Ayre-ee-mack-med-heer-bray) Daughter of Midhir and Etain, Princess of Innisfail, and Queen of Scotia. Married to Jan Fir Bres, King of Scotia; and Lord of Skye.
- *Eriu-* (Ayr-yoo) One of the Dagda's daughters, for which Eire was named. Died in ancient times.

F

- *Faerie-* (Fare-ee) "Doomed One", or "Touched by Doom". A racial slur for those of half-Sidhe blood. Also used to denigrate people born with deformities, mental disorders, or those whom suffer from depression or madness. It is believed that the blood of the Sidhe is a curse for mortal kind, and often leaves its progeny unnaturally lovely, but usually deficient in every other area. Faeries (whether real or slandered) are largely reviled in Eire.
- *Fainne-* (Feene) The literal gold standard, upon which all Innish currency is based. Also called "Crowns", or "Royals".
- *Falan-* (Fahl-ahn) The given name of two members of the Armagh royal family, Falan the Elder, and Falan the Younger, respectively. An ancient Bolgish name.
- *Fiachra Ri-* (Fee-ah-cruh-ree) "Raven King". Refers to Diarmid Mac Nuada Dubh, the King of *Tech Duinn*— or the Land of the Dead.
- *Fir Bolg-* (Feer-Bolck) A tribe of Sidhe warriors, descended from the ancient warrior Nemed. They fought with the Fomorians for several generations, and were expelled for a time to Southern Europe, where they were enslaved by the Greek tribes in Macedon. Forced to carry bags of stone up and down ladders into mines, before their escape back to Innisfail, they became known as the "Bag Men". Close cousins of the Tuatha De Dannan from their mutual ancestor, Nemed- but dark complected, where the Dannans are fair. Sometimes called, "dark elves" for this trait. Their last stronghold in Innisfail is the city of Armagh, ruled by the Mac Nemed Clan.
- *Fodla-* (Fole-ah) One of Crom Dagda's wives.
- *Fomorians-* (Fov-or-ee-ahns) Ancient people whom lived in Innisfail before the first invasions. Worshipped dark gods of earth and stone, harvest and reaping, until a Comet known as Lug of the Long Arm came sailing out of the west, bringing calamity, and famine. They began to build stone circles and passage tombs to mark the heavens after this, to honor their new god. Defeated by the Fir Bolg in ancient times. The Tuatha De Dannan revere them as wise ancestors and keep their holy places sacred. They also adopted several of the Fomorian gods, like Lug of the Long Arm, Bel the sun god, and Samn the moon goddess. Also known as the "Stone People".

G

- *Geis-* (Gay-ehss) "Unbreakable Vow". A curse, taboo, or restriction placed upon an individual of power, to restrict their actions. In a Dannan warrior's case, it is an obligation one cannot break, without great personal sacrifice.

H

- *Hamish-* (Hay-mesh) A soldier from Bethany.
- *Herne-* (Hurnn) The White Stag, or God of the Forest. The patron god of House Adair.

I

- *Imbolg-* (Em-bolk) A festival in high winter, to summon spring. Celebrated on the first day of the Month of Blinding White, "Dor Imba" (Formerly February).
- *Innisfail-* (Enn-ess-fay-ehl) "Land of Destiny". A small continent at the rim of the Northern Ice Flows, comprising much of what was once Ireland, Scotland, Wales, and Cornwall. Much of what was England has largely become tundra, or inhospitable wastes; due to catastrophic climate change, and trace human corruptions of the land. In many places, the soil is either frozen under two feet of ice, or simply too toxic from long-forgotten nuclear reactors that have leached radiation into the soil. Innisfail is the last bastion of relative habitable land in what was Europe. Parts of Northern France, Spain and Portugal, are similarly liveable- but not as biodiverse. This biodiversity and ecological prosperity are due in large part, to the Sidhe, whom have reclaimed dominance over the land.

J

- *Jan Fir Bres-* (Yahn-feer-bray) King of Scotia, and Lord of Skye. Descended from the Half-Fomorian king Bres, whom married one of the Dagda's daughters, and emigrated to Skye. Second cousin to the High King and married to his daughter Eri.

K

- *Kaer Yin Mac Midhir Adair-* (Kayer-eeann-mack-med-eehr-ah-dare) The *Ard Tuiathe* of the *Tuatha De Dannan*, and Crown Prince of Innisfail. Son of Midhir and Etain, he was the first Dannan to be born in Innisfail after The Transition. Grand Marshal of the Wild Hunt, and Commander of Aes Sidhe's standing armies. Slayed Kevin Donahugh in single combat, during the first Bethonair War, and ended the war of '84, at Dumnain with another victory over the Donahugh Clan. Prince of Eire, and Cymru. A cold, unfeeling character, who values martial might over all other virtues.

L

- *Libella-* Tairngare's elite class of nobles. To be a member of the Libella, and its House in Parliament, one must hold a Patent of Maternas, which must be traced back at least three generations, in the Cloister of the Eternal Flame. Also, refers to the House of Nobles in Parliament.
- *Libellum-* (Ly-bell-uhm) Founded by the Tairnganese aristocractic class. The Educator's Guild in Tairngare, also a collection of schools, in which all Tairnganese citizens (even those whom live in the Colonies) may study free, although to earn a degree in any field, one must pass a series of aptitude tests before and after each school

term, to assure the student is devoted to his or her craft. The schooling might be free, but each school requires a sizeable donation from the family to ensure employment afterward. Most students who are not from Aristocratic families, often take secondary education in the Agrea for agriculture, or buy into the Merchanta to apprentice for a trade. The Libellum educates all children not accepted in the Cloister, until the age of 16, when the more expensive secondary education begins. Usually specializing in Law, Engineering, Rhetoric, or Medicine.

- *Liadan Mac Nemed* (formerly, Mac Balor) (Lee-ah-dann-mack-neh-mehd) Queen of the Fir Bolg in ancient times, and Dowager Queen of Armagh, after The Transition.
- *Lir* (Leer) A Sidhe ancestor god. His children were changed into swans by his second wife and were forced to languish in these forms for hundreds of years.
- *Lug-* (Lew) Lug of the Long Arm, was a Fomorian sky deity that the Dannans appropriated when they conquered Innisfail in ancient times. He is represented as a traveling god, who comes only once every eighty years or so— sometimes bringing fortune, and others, calamity. The Sidhe pray to him for luck and guidance. Often considered the God of Law, and Chance.
- *Lugnasa-* (Lew-nah-sah) Festival of the sky god Lug; to curry Lug's blessings upon the Harvest, and to guard the living from the coming starving season. Lugnasa is the time of year in which the Sidhe's major policies, treaties or major martial and agricultural matters are decided. Trials are held during Lugnasa, children are named, and funerals are held. Property may change hands or be gifted at Lugnasa. Celebrated at the start of Ban Lug, or 'The Month of The Bright Sky' (formerly, August 1).
- *Lu Sidhe-* (Lew-shee) Less powerful, wise, or long-lived denizens of the Otherworld. Some share blood with the Ban Sidhe, but many are simply spirits or other mischievous creatures who assume a human-like shape. Often, faeries and other half-bloods are classified as Lu Sidhe. Such as: Slyphs, satyrs, Pixies, Niskies, Dryads, Nymphs and Brownies.

M

- *Mac-* (Mack) "Son of", or "Daughter of".
- *Macha-* (Mah-sha) Sidhe goddess of strategy, ambition, and courage. She is associated with sovereignty. One of three divine sisters. See also: Badh and Morrigan. Her herald is the eagle.
- *Maeve-* (Mae-ve) Sidhe goddess of wisdom, magic, and mystery. Her herald is the Owl. SEE BABH, the goddess of discord, strife, and pestilence.
- *Magh Tuiredh-* (Moy-teer-ah) Site of two ancient battles, the first of which was waged on the Fir Bolg by the Tuatha De Dannan. The Dannans took control of Innisfail at the end but granted the Fir Bolg their own corner of the land to rule— Ulster. The second battle was fought between the resurgent Fomorians, where Nuada of the Golden Arm was killed.

- *Manipulation-* A form of magic studied by the *Siorai* acolytes of the Cloister of the Eternal Flame, in Tairngare. Using one's own body energy (or Spark*)*, one can force particles to join or separate, and even build unnatural chains which change an objects trajectory, composition, or shape.
- *Mannanan Mac Lir-* Sidhe god of the Eastern Sea. Son of the god Lir.
- *Merchanta-* (Merr-cant-ah) The Merchant's Guild of Tairngare, run directly by the House of Commons in Parliament.
- *Midhir Mac Nuada-* (Mehd-eer-mack-nu-ah-dah) *Ard Ri* of the Tuatha De Dannan, and High King of Innisfail. Brought his people out of the Otherworld at the end of the Third Age of Man- also known as The Transition. Conquered the surviving mortals and brought them firmly under unified Sidhe overrule. A kind and compassionate ruler, if distracted and detached.
- *Mil Espagna-* An ancient 'celtic' king, hailing from the Iberian plateau. Forced to search for a new home when climate, war, and famine struck his people; they came to Innisfail— a lush, green, fertile land— in such numbers and with far superior weapons than anything the Sidhe could muster. His victories forced the Sidhe into the Otherworld and began the long period of Gallic rule. To the present, all Sidhe refer to mortal men and women as 'Milesians'
- *Morrigan-* (More-ah-gahn) Sidhe goddess of war, bloodlust, fury and pride. One of three divine sisters. (Equivalent to the Greek Fates). Her herald is the raven.

N

- *Navan-* (Nah-vahn) A small town on the river Boyne, at the border with Aes Sidhe.
- *Nemain-* (Neh-mayne) Sidhe goddess of the waterways and springs. It was said that her beauty drove men to madness for desire of her, but her kiss was poison and tortuous death. Kaer Yin's longsword is named for her. Her sister Niamh is the goddess of purity and love.
- *Nemed-* King of the first Innish invaders, in ancient times. Mortal grandson of the earth goddess Danu, and her mate, Donn— the god of death. Their daughter Brida took a mortal lover, from the tribe of Abraham. An accomplished sailor and adventurer, Nemed led his sea-faring tribe around the Mediterranean before a storm swept them out into the ocean, to Innisfail. Nemed fought the Fomorians for almost thirty years, before his death. His people divided and fled in separate directions. One half went South and were enslaved in Macedon; the Fir Bolg. The others took their ships far into the north and west, battling gods and monsters, until they returned with 300 ships, to oust their cousins from Innisfail- The Tuatha De Dannan.
- *Niall-* (Nay-all) A Dannan warrior, in Tam Lin's retinue.
- *Niamh-* (Neh-ve) Sidhe goddess of purity and love. Dwells in the waterways and springs, with her corrupted sister, Nemain.
- *Norther-* One whom dwells in Northern Eire.
- *Nova-* An initiate of the Cloister of the Eternal Flame, in Tairngare.

O

- *Oiche Ar Fad-* (Eesha-arh-fah) The Otherworld. A realm that exists just below the mortal. The Sidhe retreated to this realm for thousands of years, until the Milesians nearly purged themselves from the world. Only the Sidhe may come and go from this realm unmolested. To humankind, it holds mainly horror, forgetfulness, or death.

P

- *Porter-* A game of cards and two-sided dice.
- *Prima-* (Preema) A tertiate acolyte of the Cloister of the Eternal Flame, in Tairngare.

R

- *Ri-* (Ree) A king, or high lord.
- *Ruiadh-* (Roo-ah) "Red".

S

- *Samn-* (Sow) Sidhe goddess of the moon. Bel, god of the sun, is her mate.
- *Samhain-* (Sow-ahn) Festival of the moon, and the onset of winter. Celebrated (or mourned, considering perspective) at the end of the Month of Oncoming Night or Winter, or "Dor Samna". Samhain is the passage of life into death, and of autumn to winter. It is the one night of the year, in which the dead and all manner of Otherworld creatures may wander free of its borders— to trouble, torment, or comfort the living.
- *Scota-* (Skoh-tah) "Fierce One". The Queen of the Milesians in ancient times. Wife of Mil Espagna. Died fighting on the beach during the first Milesian invasion. Her son Amer Gin, who led his own men across the sea of Mannanan, named the land east of Skye after her (formerly Scotland).
- *Secunda-* (Seh-koon-dah) An intermediate in the Cloister of the Eternal Flame, in Tairngare.
- *Shannon-* The longest, widest river in Innisfail.
- *Sidhe-* (Shee) "Ever-Living", Describes the Immortals who dwell or dwealt in the Otherworld. Some are powerful and human-like, the Ban Sidhe; and some merely aspire to take human form— or never wish to.
- *Siora-* Patron goddess of Tairngare, also known as the 'Ancestor'. A goddess of unity, knowledge, and feminine power.

- *Siorai-* Acolytes of the Cloister of the Eternal Flame. Considered witches, by most of the peoples of Innisfail.
- *Souther-* One who dwells in Southern Eire.
- *Spark-* The life-force, or energy within one's body, that can be harnessed to manipulate the actions and properties of an object's compositional particles.

T

- *Tara-* (Tare-ah) A midling-sized town in Eire, south of the Boyne. In ancient times, it was a hillfort, fortress and castle— belonging to the High Kings of old Eire. Site of the *Lia Fail*, or "Stone of Destiny", before which all Kings of Eire were crowned. Now, it is a hub of the Merchanta— or Merchant's Guild, in Tainrgare.
- *Tairngare-* (Tare-ehn-gare) A matriarchal city in the Northeast of Eire, at the mouth of the Boyne (formerly Drogheda). A city run by a religious order of women, and a Parliament elected from noble families and commoners. Founded by a woman named Siora, a former prostitute who had magical abilities she shared only with the women who swore their supreme loyalty to the nameless earth goddess she claimed to have been born of. She vanished after the women took over the city. They call her the 'Ancestor'.
- *Tech Duinn-* (Teck-Doon) "House of Donn", or "Realm of Donn". The god of death in pre-Innish Europe, also the mate of Danu, goddess of the earth. His realm is the land of the dead, and all whom share his blood (Such as the Tuath De Dannan, Fir Bolg, and Milesians alike), must come to his realm after death. In the Otherworld, Diarmid is the king of Tech Duinn, and Donn's servant. All whom are given the god of death's name, are said to be cursed, or bring misfortune to their families. Such as the son of Mil, whom was angered by his brother Ir's rowing abilities, and cursed him, causing the oar to snap and both boys to die. The realm of Tech Duinn is a peaceful but solemn one within the otherworld, and only once a year on Samhain, are the dead given reprieve to wander outside its confines.
- *Tir Na Nog-* (Teer-nah-noge) "Land of the Undying Ones". The realm of the Sidhe gods. Only great heroes or those with divine blood, may enter when they die. All else must go to Tech Duinn
- *Tir Falias-* A Sidhe city in the Otherworld.
- *Transition-* SEE TUATHA DE DANNAN.
- *Tuatha De Dannan (or Tuatha De Danaan, or De Danann)-* (Too-ah-ha-day-dahn-ahn) "Children of Danu". A half-divine tribe of warriors descended from the demi-god and adventurer Nemed. Unlike their Fir Bolg cousins, the Tuatha De fled Innisfail in ships, toward the north and west. They traveled from Isle to Isle, fighting monsters, hostile tribes, and brushing elbows with the gods. When they returned to Innisfail in ancient times, they defeated the Fir Bolg for supremacy over the land; then defeated the Fomorians, the old Fir Bolg enemy. They ruled in peace for many seasons, until they were defeated by the crafty Milesians from the Iberian Peninsula. Their greatest Brehon, Crom Dagda, sacrificed his life to the god of death— Donn, to give all those

whom shared the Dagda's blood immortality, and a piece of the Otherworld to rule. They remained there for thousands of years, vowing to return when the rule of Mil's spawn failed. In N.E. 1, when the Milesians were fast becoming extinct, the Dannans came back to reconquer what was stolen from them in ancient times. This is known as the 'Transition'.

U

- *Uishge-* (Whisk-ey) "Water of Life". An ancient, amber colored spirit.
- *Ulster-* (Ull-Sterr) Kingdom in the north of Aes Sidhe, its capital is Armagh. Ruled by the remaining Fir Bolg nobility, the Mac Nemed Clan. Has been one of the chief Innish kingdoms since ancient times.
- *Una Moura Donahugh-* (Ooh-nah-more-ah-donnah-hew) "Bright One". Prima of the Cloister of the Eternal Flame. Reigning Domina of House Moura, and proposed Queen of the Commons, in Parliament. Studying to ascend to Alta Prima, and being groomed to succeed Drem as Doma. Daughter of Arrin Moura and Patrick Donahugh.

V

- *Vanna Nema-* (Vah-nah-Nee-mah) Alta Prima, Mistress of the House of Commons in Parliament, and second-in-command to the Doma.

Dramatis Personae

eire-

Tairngare

- *Drem Moura*- Doma, high priestess of the Cloister of the Eternal Flame. Highest ranking noble in Tairngare. Represents all of Eire in the High King's Council.
- *Vanna Nema*- Alta Prima, Mistress of the House of Commons in Parliament, and second-in-command to the Doma.
- *Arrin Moura*- (Deceased) Former Alta Prima of the Cloister of the Eternal Flame. Former Queen of the Commons, appointed by the Doma, her mother. Taken from a market by Duch Patrick and made Duchess of Bethany, against her will. Committed suicide in *N.E. 487*, when her daughter was but two years old.
- *Una Moura Donahugh*- Prima of the Cloister of the Eternal Flame. Reigning Domina of House Moura, and proposed Queen of the Commons, in Parliament. Studying to ascend to Alta Prima, and being groomed to succeed Drem as Doma. Daughter of Arrin Moura and Patrick Donahugh.
- *Aoife Sona*- Prima of the Cloister of the Eternal Flame. Servant of Vanna Nema. Rumored to hold Fir Bolg blood.
- *Eva Alvra*- Member of the Libella, and Domina of House Alvra. Servant of the Doma, and former Prima of the Cloister of the Eternal Flame.
- *Pors Yma*- High ranking member of the Libella. A staunch opponent of the House of Commons.
- *Mel Carra*- Member of the Mercher's Guild, and highest-ranking member of the House of Commons. Ardent supporter of Vanna Nema.
- *Fawa Gan*- Steward, to Vanna Nema

Bethany

- *Duch Patrick Donahugh*- Ruler of the South. Ardent opponent of the High King in Aes Sidhe. Instigator of two wars, which cost him many men and most of his fortune— as well as his seat on the High King's Council. Chafes under Sidhe rule, and plots to take the throne for himself. Kidnapped Una's mother from a market in broad daylight and forced her into a loveless marriage of convenience. Una's father; he means to conquer all of Eire, and rule in her name.

- *AlisDonahugh*- (Deceased) Kidnapped by an unknown Sidhe lord in *N.E. 474*, returned home several months later, heavy with child and mad. After the child was born, she threw herself from the north parapet. Some say, her death prompted the battle at Dumnain, ten years later.
- *Henry Fitz Donahugh*- Patrick's illegitimate half-brother. Attempted to overthrow Patrick after his failure at Dumnain. Banished to the wastes of Cmyru, for nearly twenty years. A fervent Kneeler.
- *Damek Bishop, Lord of Clare*- Alis' illegitimate son, fathered by an unknown Sidhe lord. Adopted by Patrick after his mother's death. Accomplished soldier and statesman. Views himself as Patrick's rightful heir, and plots to conquer the whole of Eire to force his uncle to legitimize his claim to the throne. Commander of Bethany's armed forces.
- *Martin O'Reardan*- Lord Marshal at Arms, of Bethany. Damek's self-appointed right-hand man, and protector. Damek reveres him as a father figure and close confidant.
- *Wallace Cunningham*- Major of Bethany's Steel Corps (formerly, Captain, (Heavy Cavalry). An accomplished tracker, and talented swordsman.
- *Killian*- A lieutenant
- *Hamish*- A corporal
- *Douglas*- A sergeant
- *Dawes*- A corporal
- *Blane*- A ranger

Rosweal

- *Barb Dormer*- Madam of the tavern and pleasure house, *The Hart and Hare*. A former Nova in the Cloister of the Eternal Flame. Mistress of the Greenmakers' Guild. Aims to be the Town Headwoman, and dreams of modernizing their backwater town.
- *Robin Gramble*- A poacher, and town crime boss. Master of the Greenmakers' Guild, answers only to Barb, his undeclared mistress. Well-respected by his men, and greatly feared by his enemies.
- *Ben Maeden*- A drifter, and sometime poacher. Mysterious origins, and curious loyalties. Fond of drink, dicing, and women.
- *Matt Gilcannon*- A bootlegger, distiller of illegal spirits, and whoremaster. Owner of the *Black Corset*. A bordello of ill-repute. Fond of using the sons of his whores to do his dirty work. Desirous of destroying the Greenmakers' monopoly on trade, and opening new revenue streams outside of the North.
- *Solomon Trant*- A brewer and tavernkeeper, in the Greenmakers' Quarter. Member of the Greenmakers' Guild.

- *Samuel Trant-* A butcher, tanner and crime underboss. Brother to Solomon Trant, but not a member of the Greenmakers' Guild.
- *Gerrod Twomey-* A competent woodsman, and member of the Greenmakers' Guild, despite his youth and optimism.
- *Colm-* Tavernkeeper at the *Hart and Hare*, member of the Greenmakers' Guild. Barb's right-hand man.
- *Seamus-* A tracker and woodsman. A member of the Greenmakers' Guild.
- *Dabney-* Barb's dimwitted bodyguard.
- *Dean-* A bouncer at the *Hart and Hare*, and sometime hired thug.
- *Paul-* A hired thug, sometime member of the Greenmakers' Guild.
- *Rose-* A prostitute at the *Hart and Hare*, from a disgraced Tairnganese noble family. Soft-spoken and loyal.
- *Violet-* A prostitute from the Midlands.
- *Tansy-* A prostitute.
- *Vick-* One of Matt Gilcannon's street toughs.

Ferndale

- *Arthur Guinness-* (Deceased) Physician. Once a triage doctor for the Tairnganese forces in the war of '84.
- *Aednat Guinness-* (Deceased) His wife. Sidhe half-blood.
- *Rian Guinness-* Took over her father's practice after his death. Reviled by all whom seek her out for her faerie blood. Methodical, practical and intelligent- if not overly friendly.

aes sidhe-

Bri Leith

(House of the White Stag)

- *Nuada of the Golden Arm, Nuada Mac Crom-* (Deceased) Ancient ancestor of the House Adair (White Stag). Son of the Dagda, and King of the *Tuatha De Dannan*. Defeated the armies of Balor the One-Eyed, King of the Fomorians. Defeated the Fir Bolg King, Eochaid Mac Nemed in single combat for the title of *Ard Ri*. Slain by Eber Finn, son of Mil Espagna- a mortal man.
- *Crom Dagda-* The 'good father'. First King of the *Tuatha De Dannan*, and also a Skysinger of unimaginable power. Sacrificed his own eye to save Nuada's life after

the battle at Magh Tuiredh, against the formidable Fomorian King, Balor. Years later, sacrificed his own life to save his people from the onslaught of the Milesians, after Nuada's death. He is honored at Cromnasa, each midwinter.

- *Midhir Mac Crom-* Ard Ri of the *Tuatha De Dannan*, and High King of Innisfail. Brought his people out of the Otherworld at the end of the Third Age of Man- also known as The Transition. Conquered the surviving mortals, then brought them firmly under unified Sidhe overrule. A kind and compassionate ruler, if distracted and detached.
- *Etain-* (Deceased) Midhir's Queen. Died in childbirth, or some say, retreated to *Tir Na Nog* on the other side of *Tech Duinn;* to await her beloved in peace. Long believed to be the daughter of the sun god Bel, and Danu, the earth goddess. Midhir's winning of her hand, is its own tale.
- *Kaer Yin Mac Midhir Adair-* The Ard Tiarne of the *Tuatha De Dannan*, and Crown Prince of Innisfail. Son of Midhir and Etain, he was the first Dannan to be born in Innisfail after The Transition. Grand Marshal of the Wild Hunt, and Commander of Aes Sidhe's standing armies. Killed Kevin Donahugh in single combat, during the first Bethonair War, in (408), and ended the war of '84, at Dumnain with another victory over the Donahugh Clan. Prince of Eire, and Cymru. A cold, unfeeling character, who values martial might over all other virtues.
- *Eri Mac Midhir Bres-* Daughter of Midhir and Etain, Princess of Innisfail, and Queen of Scotia. Married to Jan Fir Bres, King of Scotia; and Lord of Skye.
- *Fionn-* Lord Protector of Aes Sidhe, and Midhir's sworn Sword.
- *Ysirdra-* High Priestess of Danu, and trusted advisor to the High King.

CROGHAN

(House of the Red Eagle)

- *Bov Mac Crom Dearg-* Son of Nuada of the Golden Arm, and King of Connaught. Called Bov 'The Red', by his people, for his fiery hair and disposition. Some call him the 'Red Boar of Connaught', behind his back- for his stubborn pride, short temper, and devotion to the hunt. A peerless warrior in battle, but too hotheaded to make much of a commander. Brother of Midhir, the High King.
- *Grainne Mac Eochaid-* Bov's Queen. A Former Fir Bolg Princess, daughter of Eochaid Mac Nemed, and his wife, Liadan Mac Nemed- also, his first cousin. She was married into the *Tuatha De Dannan* as part of a peace treaty with Armagh, after Nuada slew Ecohaid, and took his throne. She and Bov have a stormy relationship.
- *Tam Lin Mac Bov Dearg-* Prince of Connaught, and Marshal of the West. Son of Bov and Grainne, making him the only living Dannan prince who is also half Fir-Bolg. Beloved nephew of the *Ard Ri,* Midhi— and Commander of Croghan's Blood Eagles; an elite fighting force, second only to Bri Leith's Wild Hunt (*An Fiach Fian)*. Favorite cousin and trusted friend of Kaer Yin Adair.

- *Shar Lianor-* Tam Lin's First Lieutenant, and right-hand man.
- *Niall-* A Blood Eagle
- *Oisin-* A Blood Eagle

Tech Duinn

(House of the Raven)

- *Diarmid Mac Crom Adair-* King of Tech Duinn, and Lord of the *Oiche Ard Fad*. Called *Fiachra Ri*, by the Sidhe- or Raven King, in Eire. A Skysinger, like his grandfather Crom Dagda; and a Brehon of the Tuatha De Dannan. He is the only member of his house, as he rules a kingdom of the dead. All lesser Sidhe call him 'King', including the Lu Sidhe, and Dor Sidhe- which would unleash themselves upon mortal kind, did he not guard the gates of the Otherworld with a firm hand. Brother to Midhir, the High King. An ambitious, mercurial man, whose loyalty can never truly be counted upon.

Armagh

(House of the Black Bull)

- *Eochaid Mac Nemed-* (Deceased) Ancient King of the Fir Bolg. Slain by Nuada, king of the *Tuatha De Dannan* for his throne, and the right to rule in Innisfail. Married to his cousin Liadan, by their Fomorian Grandfather, Balor. Was a just ruler, and fearsome warrior.
- *Liadan Mac Nemed-* Queen of the Fir Bolg in ancient times, and Dowager Queen of Armagh, after The Transition.
- *Falan (the elder) Mac Eochaid-* King of the Fir Bolg, and lord of the ancient city of Armagh. A notorious philanderer and by all accounts, a terribly irresponsible ruler. Often wanders the *raths* of his Sworn Shields, to seduce their wives and avail themselves of their forced hospitality.
- *Falan (the younger) Mac Nemed-* (Deceased) Prince of Armagh, and former Marshal of the North. Despised his father so much, he took his grandfather's surname. Believed to have been the mightiest warrior in Armagh, and the greatest swordsmen in Innisfail— until he was defeated by Kaer Yin Adair at a tourney, years before his death. Slain at Dumnain, by a nameless Milesian soldier from Bethany.
- *Grainne Mac Nemed-* Princess of Armagh, and daughter of Falan the Elder and his third wife, Taliu. Half-sister to Falan the Younger, and an astute pupil of the Dowager Queen. Named for her aunt Grainne, whom married Bove Dearg in ancient times.

Author's Note

2022
Sunny Florida

This series was the culmination of 24 years of hard work, self-doubt, disbelief, giddy anticipation, relationship strife, stolid determination, depression, sidetracks, renewed hope, disappointment, stubbornness, imposter syndrome, begrudging self-respect, supportive peers, toxic peers, success, failure, and love.

In 24 years, Kaer Yin and I have stormed many castles, lost many battles, and found that inner peace we thought would forever lay just beyond our grasp. We weathered every negative thought and comment, each self-fulfilling prophecy, and every 'yeah, but what do you *really* do' question.

Kaer Yin and I have been together a long, long time. You might say we grew up together. Thank you for joining us on this journey.

We'll be back.

L.M. Riviere
www.lmriviere.com
Social: @LMRiviereAuthor

About the Text

This series leans heavily on Irish Gaelic. As a student of the language, I have done my level best to include the appropriate usage of every term and phrase, from syntax to punctuation. That said, I am not entirely fluent, and there are bound to be mistakes in the text.

Additionally, most of the terms I use were derived from the most archaic forms, as the characters and place names are meant to reflect a time period and etymology that precedes written alphabet by at least a thousand years. In that order, there are bound to be minor variations in spelling and pronunciation. Some terms I changed to suit myself and the rolling language I hear in my head when my characters speak... and I daresay, that is my prerogative in a fantasy novel.

For example, there a few obvious 'me-isms', like the use of '*Tuatha Dé Dannan*', which is historically spelled '*Danaan*', or '*Danann*'. I elected to place a hard focus on the interior 'n' to aid its pronunciation for non-Gaelic speakers.

If there are any mistakes or unbearable abuses of the language that distract from the text, please keep in mind that this story exists in a (semi) fictional continent a thousand years from now. A few liberties were taken.